'What would you get if you crossed *Big Little Lies* with 90s teen flick *The Craft* and threw in a splash of *Peyton Place* and a dash of *The Crucible*? The answer is something like this addictive novel' *Independent*

'*The Crucible* meets *Desperate Housewives* in this deft and gripping supernatural thriller' *Daily Mail*

'Thrilling . . . a compelling tale of small-town rivalries, mob vengeance and magic' *Guardian*

'Oh my god, what a fabulous book! *Big Little Lies* with witches. This one is going in my forever pile because I know I'm going to read it again. Trust me, this is properly addictive!' Emma Kavanagh, bestselling author of *The Missing Hours*

'*Sanctuary is Big Little Lies* meets *The Craft* and I can not put it down' Sarah Hughes, *Guardian* journalist

'V.V. James has created an interesting version of America here – and it'll get you thinking. In 2019, would we suffer a witch to live or not?' *SFX*

V.V. James is the author (as Vic James) of the contemporary fantasy trilogy *Gilded Cage*, *Tarnished City*, and *Bright Ruin*. *Gilded Cage* is a 2018 World Book night pick and a Radio 2 Book Club selection. V.V. worked as an investigative producer for Channel 4 News and now directs documentaries for BBC1 and BBC2.

EVERY TOWN HAS ITS SECRETS.

SANCTUARY

IS BUILT ON THEM.

V. V. JAMES

This paperback first published in Great Britain in 2020 by Gollancz

First published in Great Britain in 2019 by Gollancz
an imprint of The Orion Publishing Group Ltd
Carmelite House, 50 Victoria Embankment
London EC4Y 0DZ

An Hachette UK Company

1 3 5 7 9 10 8 6 4 2

Copyright © V.V. James 2019

A CIP catalogue record for this book is
available from the British Library.

ISBN (Mass Market Paperback) 978 1 473 22574 9
ISBN (eBook) 978 1 473 22575 6

Typeset by Input Data Services Ltd, Somerset
Printed in Great Britain by Clays Ltd, Elcograf S.p.A.

MIX
Paper from
responsible sources
FSC® C104740

www.gollancz.co.uk

To John – friendship is the truest magic

Principal Characters

The coven
Sarah Fenn, witch
Abigail Whitman
Bridget Perelli-Lee
Julia Garcia

The kids
Harper Fenn
Daniel Whitman, quarterback of the Sanctuary Spartans
Isobel Perelli-Martineau
Beatriz Garcia

The partners
Michael Whitman, Yale medical professor
Cheryl Lee, Sanctuary High principal
Pierre Martineau, Bridget's ex and dad of Isobel
Alberto Garcia

The cops
Detective Maggie Knight, out-of-town state investigator
Chief Tad Bolt
Sergeant Chester Greenstreet
Lieutenant Remy Lamarr, Connecticut State Police
Rowan Andrews, independent magical investigator

Thou shalt not suffer a witch to live.

Exodus 22:18, King James Bible, 1611

1

Harper

Our moms were drinking champagne when Daniel died. Sipping on bubbles as Beatriz screamed outside the burning party house and I was loaded into an ambulance.

Just before the first fire truck roared past where they sat, the four of them raised a toast, Mom told me. They lifted their glasses and drank to our futures. They congratulated themselves that despite us kids having our 'differences' – and the four of them having 'differences', too – we'd come through everything. The bad days were behind us, and our friendships and theirs were stronger than ever.

Lies, lies, lies. And they all knew it.

2

Sarah

'Here's to our kids finally becoming adults,' Bridget says. 'Well, your three, anyway. Here's to Harper, Beatriz and Daniel. A few weeks to graduation, then a long summer and bright futures ahead of them.'

Our hostess pushes aside her plate and leans forward to refill our glasses.

I say 'refill'. Bridget only poured the champagne a few minutes ago, so the rest of us have barely made a start. Her own glass is already empty, though. As are the three wine bottles that stand amid the remains of our dinner party.

Dear Bridge does like a drink. And tomorrow, she'll complain that the hangover potion I brew her isn't strong enough. But then, I'm a witch, not a miracle worker.

Well, except that one time.

That time the four of us sat round this very table on a warm spring night, as the salt breeze blew in off Long Island Sound. An evening a lot like tonight.

'Our kids,' I say, raising my glass so I can take a swig and ward off unwelcome memories. 'Julia, congratulations on Bea getting into the political science pre-law program. And Abigail, for Dan's football scholarship. You've both got stars in the making.'

Abigail radiates maternal pride. She lights up at the mere mention of her son's name. Always has.

'And to you, Sarah,' chimes in Julia. 'For Harper . . .'

She trails off, flustered. There's no scholarship or degree course waiting for my daughter this fall. Harper hasn't applied. After all, witches' children don't usually go to college. They begin apprenticeships. Harper doesn't have one of those lined up either, for reasons of which my friends are perfectly well aware.

Abigail, a veteran of awkward moments at the endless Yale faculty parties and sports socials she attends with her menfolk, leans in smoothly.

'Sarah, congratulations on all the opportunities ahead for Harper,' she purrs.

'Exactly what I wanted to say.' Julia seizes the lifeline she's been thrown. 'Exciting times for all our kids.'

'Well, *they're* out partying,' says Bridget, brandishing the bottle. 'So why aren't we?'

She pours yet again, so eagerly that the champagne foams over our fingers. We all laugh, and lick our sticky hands, and smile at each other.

I'm proud of these women – these friends of mine. It hasn't always been easy. I've kept secrets in order to keep the peace. I've done rather more than that. But we've held it together and stayed united despite *temporary differences*. Despite the break-ups and makeups among our kids.

A shadow falls across the light streaming through the French doors. It's Cheryl, hovering like she always does when the four of us gather at her house. Cheryl may be Bridget's wife, but when she sees us, she doesn't see a coven meeting to practice. Only a group of women to which she feels she should be admitted.

Cheryl's convinced she's not welcome because she's religious.

3

That's partly true – God and witchcraft seldom mix. But the main reason is that she wasn't there that night.

'How was supper?' she asks, coming to stand behind Bridget. 'It smelled delicious.'

'You never tried my seafood risotto?' Bridget swivels and takes her wife's hand, her butt nearly slipping off the chair. 'I put some on the counter for you, honey.'

'It's far too late to be eating. It's past eleven, you know.'

Whatever Bridge says in response is lost in the swoop and howl of a fire truck racing by. Then another. Then an ambulance. Flashes of blue briefly light up the side of the house as the vehicles tear down Shore Road.

Cheryl tuts. 'They'll wake Izzy.'

She fusses over Bridget's daughter as much as Bridge does. Izzy's not at the party tonight, supposedly because she's ill and went to bed early. I suspect the truth is simpler – either she wasn't invited or she didn't feel welcome.

Izzy keeps her head down. She struggled when her parents separated. And once the town found out that her mom's new partner was a *woman*? Well, we may be close to Yale, but Sanctuary's not as liberal as it likes to imagine. That the woman in question was the school principal was the kiss of death for Izzy's chances of fitting in at Sanctuary High.

Harper used to come home covered in bruises from getting into fights sticking up for her. It nearly split up Bridget and Cheryl, because Cheryl knew that if she came down too hard on the kids responsible, it'd only make things worse. Eventually – and with some 'help' from me – the bullies got bored and moved on to the next target. Izzy still feels safest inside her shell, though.

Cheryl lingers, her hands fretfully picking up and putting down the objects that lie among our plates and dishes: a bundle of twigs wrapped in red wool, a candle, silver wire twisted into

4

shapes that aren't quite abstract, aren't quite human. Bridget watches her unhappily, and across the table Abigail leans forward, all faculty-wife charm.

'You must be so busy with the end of semester, Cheryl. All us parents are so grateful for everything you do. I saw what looked like a stack of paperwork on your kitchen table . . .'

Julia smiles at Abigail's transparency, but it's got all of us out of an awkward moment, one time or another.

A phone shrills inside the house. Cheryl gathers the empty wine bottles with a martyred expression and goes to answer.

'Probably a student prank call,' says Bridget, with a roll of her eyes. 'We have to change the number every damn month. Or maybe junkies have tried to break into the school labs again. Goodness knows what they think is stored in there. It's not like the kids get extra credit for cooking meth.'

I snort into my glass.

'Fuck, no,' says a loud voice inside. Unbelievably, it's Cheryl. 'Are you certain? Yes, I can do that. *Fuck.*'

Cheryl blushes when she says 'shoot'. What is this? Has someone burned down the school? Is that where the fire engines were going? Bridget stands unsteadily, to go to her wife.

She's saved from the more difficult task of walking, because Cheryl rushes in. I thought she was pissed off, but it's worse than that. She's utterly distraught, and at the sight of her something tightens in my chest.

'There's been an accident,' she says. 'A fire. At the party.'

The party?

Julia, Abigail and I all duck under the table to grab our phones from our purses. We always put them away when the four of us meet. I thumb the screen and it lights up with messages from Harper. One after another. Too many to read, too fast to follow.

Call me Mom, says one.

Something awfuls happened

Beside me, Julia lets out a low moan as she scans her phone. Abigail has hers in a death grip. There are no notifications on its screen.

I swipe to Harper's next message.

They're taking me to the hospital but don't worry im ok

None of u are answering!!!! Told cops ur all together at izzys. Theyre gonna call now

And finally: *It's Dan*

My throat closes up as I read what follows, but Cheryl's already saying it. Speaking the words I wouldn't be able to force out. Words that I never, ever imagined I'd hear a second time in my life.

'It's Daniel.' Cheryl is looking anywhere but at the four of us. 'He's dead. Oh, I'm so sorry, Abigail. He's dead.'

3
Maggie

Kids. A party. Underage boozing. A tragedy.

Sadly, I see it more regularly than my gym class sees me.

Usually, it involves a car. A decade of mom and pop's payments into a college fund, years of nailing a GPA, sporting achievements, carefully crafted do-goodery – all crunching into a tree at 120 on an unlit stretch of highway.

Sanctuary has everything that story requires. I'd forgotten how swanky this town is. As I turn down yet another hushed suburban street, I sweep the trash on the seat beside me into the passenger footwell so no one will spot it. Sanctuary's the sort of place that's good at making you feel not good enough.

The houses are set so far back from the road you can hardly see them for trees. The yards are so wide you won't hear your neighbor's gardener on the ride-on mower. Pulled up in every driveway is a showroom's worth of vehicles: one for each family member, and a sports car for the weekend.

I'm Hartford born and bred, and when I was assigned down here for my first rotation, fresh out of Connecticut Police Academy, it felt like I'd moved abroad. People talk different, look different – even the air is different. Saltier. Fresher. More expensive.

I open my window to let it in as I turn down Shore Road. The afternoon sun spangles the ocean and bounces off the sand, and my eyes narrow against the glare. A track leads off to the sports club that I remember is a favorite teen hangout. The kids here don't know how lucky they are.

Except now tragedy has found its way among them. I glance at the file on the seat beside me. An automatic referral to us at state level on account of the age of the deceased. Flags for potential other felonies and misdemeanors include arson, drugs and underage drinking.

'You did some time in Sanctuary, right?' my boss had said, barely looking up as he tossed the file across his desk. 'Fire at a house party. One kid dead. Others injured, though nothing too serious. Wrap it up neat with a bow on top, and we'll see you back here in a week.'

The air through the window has changed. All soot and smoke now, instead of salt. And there in front of me is the house, Sailaway Villa. It's a fire-gutted shell, roof gone but the facade curiously intact, as if the blaze started in the middle and had burned itself out by the time it reached the walls.

A uniformed deputy is refastening a perimeter of fluttering incident tape while a colleague watches. All around is a churn of mud, where emergency vehicles went to and fro and fire trucks hosed the place down. My shoes sink into it as I get out of the car.

The spectating cop hurries across, waving his arms, until I flip my badge.

'You're the detective?' he says skeptically.

Maybe this asshole has never seen a black lady detective before? Though he's missing out on some great TV shows if that's so.

'Detective Knight?' calls his companion, tying off the tape and coming over. 'Chief had me prepare this for you. All the kids that were here.'

He hands me a list of partygoers and I wince at how long it is.

'Pretty much the entire senior class of Sanctuary High,' Helpful Cop explains. 'Plus girls from the private school outside town and football boys from across the county. From that mix it looks like Dan put the word out – he was a star athlete and a popular guy.'

No kidding. Dan was the All-Connecticut Mr Congeniality, by the look of it. I recall the photo clipped to the top of the brief: a thick swoosh of blond hair, and a smile that not even retainers could improve. A boy radiant with youth. Somewhere in Sanctuary is a mom whose heart will be absolutely shattered – though as I know too well, moms' hearts break over the mean and ugly ones, too.

Something tickles my cheek and falls onto the list. I brush it away, leaving a greasy black streak across the paper. It's soot. Long feathery curls of it drift through the air like someone blasted a whole flock of crows out of the sky.

Sailaway Villa was fancy, before it got carbonized. My brief says it was a vacation rental and empty when the party happened. Maybe someone blew the wiring with over-amped sound gear. Or kids got careless lighting spliffs off a kitchen stove. Perhaps it was just a phone charging with a frayed cable.

At any rate: fire first. Then a stampede to get out. And a boy falls and breaks his neck. A boy whose corpse will no doubt be found to contain epic quantities of alcohol.

So: impaired judgment due to substance abuse. Accidental death. Case closed. Maybe the parents can bring a civil suit against the property company, but it'd be a grubby business and they'd be better off quietly grieving.

I look at the list. The deceased's name is at the top. *Daniel Whitman*.

When I saw that in my brief, it sounded familiar. But there are plenty of Whitmans in Connecticut, all claiming to be related to the poet. Maybe some of them even are. I checked on his parents, and apparently Daniel's dad is a semi-famous Yale professor who's got a few rare diseases named after him.

Second on the list is a name that definitely stirs a memory. *Jacob Bolt*.

'Hey,' I ask Helpful Cop. 'Bolt. When I was posted in this district six years ago, Tad Bolt was the chief. Any relation?'

'He's still the chief. And yeah, Jake is his youngest son. He's got four.'

I try to remember what Chief Bolt was like. *Big* is the first word that comes to mind. *Popular* is the second. *Pink* is the third. I got plenty of call-outs here, but none that progressed. I always suspected that Sanctuary dealt with its lawbreakers through cautions and hefty donations to the Police Benevolent Fund. Less paperwork, nothing on your record, and everyone's still friends afterwards.

'I put Jacob up top,' says Helpful Cop, ''cos he's the best friend – *was* the best friend – of the deceased. And this is Daniel's girlfriend. Or ex-girlfriend. I'm not entirely clear . . .'

He's pointing to the third name, *Harper Fenn*, and that snags me too. It's startling how much I remember. I was in this district for twelve months, six years ago, and it feels like I know half the town. What must it be like living here?

Harper Fenn has to be the daughter of Sanctuary's witch. I wonder if Sarah Fenn's kooky shop is still on the square? I remember her because girls were always going in asking for love potions, or boob-boosting charms, or study-aid spells. Fenn was lax about it, and I'd have to keep warning her that witchery is an age-restricted product, like booze and cigarettes. She'd sigh and promise to do ID checks, then make me revolting herbal tea. Nice lady, if ineffectual, as most Main Street witches tend to be.

'If it isn't little Maggie Knight.'

A blow between my shoulder blades nearly knocks me flat. There's heartiness, and then there's assault. For a law-enforcement officer, Chief Bolt has got a shaky grasp on where the line is.

'Chief Bolt, good to see you, sir.'

One meaty paw holds me at arm's length for inspection. Though I now outrank him, I still cringe under his appraisal, as if I forgot to polish my Girl Scout badge. His eyes are a bright, hard blue, like his momma picked them out specially at a haberdashery button bin.

'Guess they promoted you from doing the coffee runs, eh, Mags? Sanctuary's glad to have you back. Here's how it's gonna be. Our community is *hurting*. Daniel was a good kid, a real good kid. Law-abiding, too. Can't tell you how many times he was over at our place, him and Jakey hanging out in the den. I'm proud my son had such an upright young man as his friend.'

I picture Daniel and 'Jakey' in the den, enjoying the time-honored recreations of all eighteen-year-old boys: playing gory video games, getting stoned and groping their girlfriends.

'There's gonna be questions asked, Mags. But here's the deal. That house was due repairs. Easy to see how the fire started. Easy as anything to see how those kids panicked. You coulda been sober as a judge and still had a terrible fall. Daniel was just damn unlucky. He's something of a local hero. First-rate quarterback. Used to coach the little ones. No need to besmirch a boy's reputation once he's dead. Nor go dragging other folks into it.'

The hand squeezes my shoulder again, for emphasis. Tad's warning me off. Protecting his own son as much as the reputation of the late Daniel Whitman. I instantly revise my assessment of what the boys got up to in their leisure time: perhaps Schedule 1 drugs, and rather more than just groping their girlfriends.

What will toxicology find was in Daniel's bloodstream when he died?

Yet the chief's right, isn't he? Whatever Whitman drank or smoked or snorted, it's not much of a crime. This was all a crappy, pointless accident that's ended some poor jock's life and probably traumatized the town's teen population. And the boss wants me back next week.

'Looks straightforward to me,' I tell him. 'I'll go through the kids' statements and get this settled quickly.'

4

Abigail

When the phone goes, I barely have the strength to reach from under the bedclothes toward it. Why should I? Half of Sanctuary has already called with its condolences, and the other half has filled my kitchen with casseroles, cakes and crocks of soup. They mean well, but I don't want to speak to anyone, or eat anything, ever again.

I just want to sleep. Because every time I wake up, for a few perfect seconds I think I'm waking from a bad dream and Daniel is still alive. The horror soon hits – faster every time – when I realize that, no, it's my life that is the nightmare. But how I crave those precious moments of confusion.

The phone drones on as my hand fumbles in my sleeve. I'm wearing the same things I wore to dinner two days ago – clothes I put on when Daniel was still alive. Things he touched when he hugged me as I set off for Bridget's. Some part of me imagines they still smell of him, though I know they won't smell of anything now except my own stale sweat.

I free my hand and reach toward the phone on the nightstand, knocking over the photograph there. Daniel's smiling image clatters to the floor and I start weeping uncontrollably.

Too weak to pick it up, I shrink back beneath the covers,

stuffing the edge of the comforter in my mouth so I don't have to hear my own sobs.

Autopilot got me through yesterday. Michael and I went straight from Bridget's to the hospital, but there was never any hope. My boy was dead before they even put him in an ambulance. Michael identified him. They advised me not to look. Then we went home.

I reapplied my lipstick, spritzed my perfume and sat on the couch through the night and the next morning receiving visitors. I nodded and squeezed hands offered in sympathy. Told people they were *so kind* and that their condolences meant *so much*. And all the time I wanted to do nothing except rock back and forth where I sat and howl at them to *go away, go away, go away*.

And now they have. Even Michael's gone to Yale – urgent faculty business. And while I raged and demanded he stay, I'm strangely glad, because now it's just me and Daniel. Me and my *thoughts* of Daniel. And that's how I want it to be, for ever and ever.

Except this phone won't stop ringing. I lift the receiver, intending just to drop it back down and terminate the call, but habit makes me press it to my ear and say, in my best faculty-wife tones, *Whitman household, Abigail speaking*.

And I find myself listening to the polite, formal voice down the line that says it's got *just one thing* they'd like *to check*, if *that's okay*.

The next thing I know, someone is tugging the phone out of my hand.

'Let go, Abigail. *Abi!*'

It's Bridget, by my bedside. She pulls the receiver from my grip. I fight her for it. I don't want to let it go. I want to beat my head with it until I bludgeon myself unconscious. That would make the pain stop, because I know that nothing else will. Nothing *ever* will make it stop.

Someone is shouting: *shut up, shut up, how dare you, shut up!*
It's me.

Bridget is speaking into the phone: *I'm sorry, it's really not a good time* . . . Then she pauses and looks at the receiver quizzically, before replacing it.

'There's no one there,' she says. 'Abigail, what was that? Are you okay?'

My baby. My poor, poor baby.

I lash out at the phone and it hits the wall. The act is satisfying. A release. I reach for what stands alongside it – one of Daniel's football trophies, polished and heavy. Fury has made me strong, and I slam it into my nightstand, hoping the glass tabletop will shatter, but it doesn't. I pound it again, harder.

If I can't break something, *I'll* break.

So I do. I drop the trophy, curl into myself under the comforter and cry until I come apart.

Bridget is trying to get my attention, anchoring me to this world in which my son is dead and someone is calling me up to spew lies and filth about him.

'Abi, what's going on?'

I try to resist, but Bridget is strong. She rolls me over toward her – and recoils at what she sees. She's never seen me like this. Or not for years.

'Leave me alone,' I plead. The adrenaline of a moment ago has gone, leaving me floppy and exhausted in its wake.

'You need food, a shower. Just the basics. Come on.'

She sets steam hissing in the bathroom. Pulls me up, helps me undress, even reaches into the shower cubicle and shampoos my hair like I'm a child. Like I used to do with Dan when he was little. I lean against the glass partition, too exhausted to cry.

Bridge has laid out clothes for me to wear, and it's such a maternal gesture that I feel myself buckle. I used to leave Dan's laundry folded on his bed. Lay out his uniform on game days.

'I'll be downstairs,' she says. 'Sarah made that zucchini salad you like so much. Get dressed and come join me.'

And she's right. It helps to feel clean. To paint my face back on. To style my hair. To become Abigail Whitman again. I put on my soft clothes like they're the hardest armor. Because I've remembered that phone call. That careful voice, mouthing lies as matter-of-factly as if it was scheduling a grocery delivery. Me shouting. Even after I could hear they'd hung up at the other end, still shouting, unable to stop.

Daniel's gone, but he still needs me.

Bridget doesn't ask until I've finished eating and have pushed the dish away. There's a tag from Sarah tied to it, lettered in her looping handwriting: *Love you and am here for you if there's anything I can do, S xo.* My fingers play with it as I tell Bridget what the voice on the phone told me. It's hard to get the words out.

'It was a reporter, I didn't catch where from, with all these awful questions. Did Dan ever take drugs? Did he drink? Were there drugs and booze at the party? And then . . . Stupid things. Sleazy things.' I have to stop and pull myself together. 'Some bullshit about a sex tape at the party.'

The minute it's out of my mouth, I regret having mentioned it, but then if the media knows, doubtless half the town already does. I'm sure Cheryl will scrape up every bit of gossip circulating at the school and relay it to Bridget over dinner. Give it a couple of hours and my friend will know more than I do.

'Sex tape?'

Bridget looks baffled. She can be such an innocent, like her daft daughter. For the first time ever, she must be thrilled that Izzy is a social reject who wasn't invited to what the local TV station is calling 'the party of every parent's nightmares'.

'Apparently several kids have told the cops something was

being projected on the wall. Not random porn – Daniel and a girl.'

'A girl? Him and Harper?'

'Who knows. It's just rubbish some kids have said. Kids who were *drunk* and in a building filled with *smoke*, for God's sake.'

'That sounds . . .'

Bridget doesn't have the words. I'm not sure there *are* words for something like this. And suddenly I'm not sad – I'm furious.

'The journalist said she was just "following the investigation". *What* investigation? Tad Bolt stood with me as Michael ID'd our son's body in the morgue and promised to make sure the state detective would put together a quick, clean report, then leave us in peace. But now someone's digging around for dirt. Isn't it enough that he's gone? My baby's gone . . .'

And I'm off again. Tears. Snot. Shakes. The full works. Is this my life now? Ricocheting from grief to wrath and back again. No place to rest. Just being struck again and again from all sides.

Bridget places a hand on my back and looks around my empty house.

'Where *is* Michael?'

'Faculty meeting. He'll be back tonight. Sticking to his schedule will help him cope.'

Or that's what he told me. And I screamed that our only child was dead and his faculty meeting could go to hell, but he went anyway.

Maybe it *will* help him. I should try not to resent that he can escape into his work. But it's a relief I don't have, seeing as I left my practice when we married.

That's when it hits me – *really* hits me – just how much I've lost. A husband I see only at weekends. A career I walked away from. Daniel has always made up for all that.

Now I have nothing. Nothing at all.

And some investigator is going to drag my son through the mud before he's even laid in the earth.

I won't stand for it.

I look around for my purse and car keys.

'Abi? I'm not letting you drive,' Bridget says.

'Well you're not stopping me.'

'Fine. Give me the keys. Where to?'

As I slide them to her along the counter, I see again that note of Sarah's. *If there's anything I can do . . .*

A crazy idea comes into my head. Instead of going to the cops, I could go to my friend the witch.

But that's madness.

'The police station, of course. I've got questions.'

5
Maggie

I came by the hospital yesterday to speak to Harper Fenn and some of the other kids who were brought in, but guess what? Smoke inhalation and scorching to her trachea means she's under strict instructions not to talk for at least thirty-six hours. And minimally thereafter. If she's anything like my cousin's two teens, maybe we can text our interview.

The witness reports claim she 'lost her chill' in the middle of the party. She was seen shouting and screaming. No one can tell me why, but you wouldn't have to be top of the class at training academy to suspect it's linked to this 'sex tape' several partygoers have mentioned.

Of course, they all claim to have not seen it properly. But they all use the same words: *sex tape*. Not *porno*. It doesn't sound like someone just streamed a dirty website for a laugh. A 'sex tape' is people you *know*.

And I know what the rumors are saying. That it's a tape of Daniel himself. Presumably a jock teammate put it up for a laugh. Maybe it's Harper in the film with him. Maybe it's another girl.

Either way, it's guaranteed to cause a fight between them. She storms off. He tries to go after her but is too drunk, trips — and falls.

'Ma'am?' The receptionist has repeated herself.

'I'm sorry. You said *discharged*?'

'Yup, she was released . . . oh, just a few minutes ago?' The receptionist frowns at her screen. 'It registers on our system as soon as the attending physician sends the authorization, but the patient will usually take time to change back into their clothes, visit the restroom, that sort of thing. If you're quick, you might find her.'

A few wrong turns later, I'm up on the observation unit. Harper wasn't the only one brought here from the party, and open doors and large windows make the rooms feel as bustling as a school. Two teens are chatting across their beds, to the annoyance of the elderly lady clicking knitting needles passive-aggressively opposite them. Another girl, her arm thickly bandaged and her neck gleaming with burn salve, lies in the drooling sleep of the sedated.

One bed is curtained off. I address its stiff blue folds.

'Excuse me, Harper Fenn?'

'Don't come in,' rasps a voice. The curtain quivers, as if she's just grabbed it from the inside.

'I won't.'

I step back, not wanting to make a scene. Already, some of the more alert patients are looking over, curious. A tip to would-be perpetrators: never commit a crime in a hospital ward, retirement home or classroom. The chronically bored make the most observant witnesses.

'I'll wait in the corridor,' I say. Where's Harper's mom? Surely the girl isn't making her own way home?

A short while later, Harper Fenn walks out. I take a good look. She's slender and coltishly tall, wearing ripped black jeans and a jacket that her mom must have brought in yesterday. Dark hair in a messy braid, and strikingly pale eyes. A piercing in her nose, and one she's refastening in her lip.

More rock chick than cheerleader. But I can see why she'd appeal to a boy like Daniel Whitman, with his Ivy League dad and *Real Housewives* mom.

'Harper? I'm Detective Knight, conducting a routine investigation into what happened at the party. I'd like a few words. Could I buy you a coffee downstairs?'

The girl looks at me. There's something uncertain in her eyes. Did she see her boyfriend die? Watch him push through the partygoers after their argument, then stumble and fall? Will she start crying and be unable to get out any words at all?

A beat passes before Harper points to her throat. 'No hot drinks,' she croaks.

'A cold one, then? Or maybe a deliciously room-temperature Coke?'

That doesn't raise a smile.

'I can't talk,' she says, and makes to move around me.

'Just a few questions, please. Did you see Daniel Whitman fall?'

'No. I was nowhere near him.'

'Where were you?'

'On the stairs. He went off the landing.'

That's what I've been told, and it tallies with where his body was found, allowing for disturbance as the partygoers fled the house. It's not *what* Harper's said that makes me pause, though, but how she said it. *He went off the landing.* It seems cold to use so few words, and such plain ones.

But what am I thinking? She's in shock. I've seen it plenty of times before – although I push down the memory of the last girl I interviewed in a hospital, who was all too desperate to talk before her time ran out.

'Had he been drinking? Were there drugs at the party?'

I expect a girlfriend's loyal denial, but again she surprises me.

'It was the first big party of the summer. What do you think?'

'Had you and Daniel had an argument that night?'

'I wasn't happy with him.'

'Witnesses say you were shouting.'

'Yes.'

'At him? What about?'

'Not at *him*.'

'At who?'

But she doesn't say, just massages her throat with her hands. A nurse frowns and moves toward us.

'Harper, do you have any reason to think Dan's fall wasn't accidental?'

'Not accidental?' And the noise she makes sounds weirdly like a laugh. Scratchy and raw. 'Dan Whitman would hardly kill himself over a nasty little slut like me.'

The words are shocking. No less so her clear, pale gaze as she says them.

With the merest nod, Harper Fenn walks away.

6

Maggie

Asshole Cop is on the front desk when I get back to the station. 'Got something for ya,' he says. 'And it's juicy.'

He thumbs toward the back room, where Tad Bolt, plainly not expecting to play host for long, has allocated me a desk and computer that look like they were fished out of a dumpster. Or maybe from the bottom of a canal.

I didn't see Bolt all yesterday. He's been with his son, who is taking Dan's death hard. Jake Bolt wasn't able to speak to me yesterday either. I want to get to him soon.

His daddy won't like the questions I'll ask. I remember the chief's not-so-subtle warning off anything that might draw scandal. And I understand, I really do. Two parents are grieving a child. Kids are grieving a classmate. A town is grieving a local star. Why prolong the pain with an unnecessary investigation?

But no investigation is unnecessary. The death of an eighteen-year-old should never go without an explanation, because it shouldn't happen.

So far, the Whitman death is looking straightforward. Just two things are giving me pause. One is the fire. Typically, a death and a fire is a homicide-and-concealment strategy, but it usually happens far from an audience. Charred bodies are found in abandoned cars, disused storage units. You'd have to be either delusional or a bona fide criminal mastermind to kill a boy in the middle of a crowded party, then burn the place down to cover your tracks.

The obvious explanation is that something exploded – a faulty appliance or a firework – and ignited the fire. Hopefully forensics will have answers soon.

The other wild card in this case is the alleged sex tape. I'll hazard a guess the desk sergeant's 'something juicy' refers to that and not new data from forensics.

Grainy footage is playing on my computer screen. Over the shoulder of a second officer, who is studying it with real dedication, I see a teenage girl dancing, holding aloft a can of Dr Pepper. She's wearing tiny shorts and a crop top and is shaking her sizeable booty at the camera.

'Yea-ah,' says the cop.

Maybe he isn't perving over my evidence. Maybe he's so dedicated he's assisting my investigation on his lunch break. Maybe my name isn't Maggie Knight.

'Looks gripping,' I say. 'Party footage, right? How'd we get it?'

He springs up, scowling.

'One of the girls questioned yesterday emailed it in. She thought it might be helpful.'

Good for you, mystery party girl. Even if you do have lousy taste in soda. I restart the clip from the beginning.

It's dark and crowded, so the phone camera isn't catching much. I keep watching, expecting any minute to see something shocking – Daniel Whitman falling or the flare of a fire igniting. But nothing happens. The song changes, the girl stops dancing and the camera wipes down toward the floor before the recording cuts off. Nothing has caught my eye.

I watch it through again, trying to position what I'm seeing using a floor plan, the rental agency pics of the villa and our own photos of the charred ruin. We're in a room adjoining the central atrium, where Daniel Whitman fell.

I replay it a third time, wondering what I'm missing. Maybe there's nothing and the girl who sent it is simply the conscientious type. We should trawl the public social media profiles of everyone who was there. Go through all pics and put out an appeal for people to voluntarily send us clips – because a high bar is needed to requisition phone footage, and I have nothing like grounds for that yet.

Then I see it. A strip of bright light plays around in the top of shot some forty seconds in. The resolution is poor on this monitor, but it's a moving image projected on the wall of the atrium behind the dancing girl.

I freeze and magnify it, and see pale skin against dark bedcovers. Unmistakably the curve of a female leg.

'You're the officer in charge?'

A tiny blond woman has burst through the door like a pastel tornado. The desk sergeant is right behind and makes a grab for her arm. She lashes out, and under other circumstances, it'd be comical – a chihuahua turned attack dog. But I recognize this woman as Abigail Whitman, the dead boy's mother. She gets a free pass on the bad-behavior front.

'Mrs Whitman? I'm so sorry for your loss.'

She stares around, her chin high and gaze formidable.

'My son's dead and you're here trying to prove, what, that it's somehow his fault? That he was drunk or high? Everything that journalist was asking about is just lies. It was an *accident*.'

A journalist?

'No one's trying to "prove" anything. This is a routine investigation. Right now, an accident appears most likely. But my job is to consider all possibilities.'

'*All possibilities?* You're saying maybe someone killed him?'

The loitering officer raises his eyebrows. Then turns on his heel with a *gonna-tell-the-chief* spring in his step. Asshole.

What's more important is that the woman standing in front of me just lost her son. You can never spare the parents pain in these cases, but you can damn well make sure you don't add to it. Abigail Whitman looks almost as put together as in the family photos I've seen, where she always has one hand on her boy or an arm around his waist. But there's a gleam in her eye that I recognize. It's wild, raging sorrow, barely held in check.

'No. I'm definitely not saying that anyone killed your son. What I'm saying is that when a young person dies, it's a tragedy, and people – the parents especially – deserve a full explanation.'

'My husband is a medical professor at Yale. We'll go through every toxicology report, anything you come up with to try to smear him. If your test-tube jockeys have made the *slightest* error, we will sue you for defamation.'

'There'll be no smearing, Mrs Whitman. I have a simple job to do, which is to get to the bottom of what happened. I hope it'll bring you closure.'

Mrs Whitman quivers. Bereavement does this, especially the sudden, violent kind that falls on you without warning and rips half your heart away. One minute, rage; the next, helplessness and despair. Abigail Whitman has a long, hard path ahead. She'll walk it for the rest of her life.

But she's not walking it alone. I don't know where her husband is, but the friend who came with her gently presses her down into a seat.

'You heard her, Abi. It's routine. They just need to rule out foul play.' The friend turns to me. 'You *are* ruling out foul play, aren't you?'

'I can't say anything prematurely, Ms . . .?'

'*Mrs*,' she corrects me. 'Bridget Perelli-Lee. My wife is Cheryl Lee, the high school principal. You can imagine she's got a lot of upset kids on her hands.'

'I certainly can imagine. Now, Mrs Whitman, I'm doing everything I can to resolve this, and I'll keep you and your husband informed of any developments.'

'You will, will you? I suppose that's why I got a call asking about some pornographic video of my son being shown at the party.'

'This call – you said it was a journalist?'

I need to know if anyone else is asking around, talking to witnesses. That can lead to evidence contamination – especially in small communities like this. It can also build up the notion that something was a crime when it was nothing of the sort.

But while I'm worrying about a nosy reporter, Abigail Whitman's gaze has slid past me to my computer. To the screen that's exactly as it was when I sprang up after she came storming in here.

The screen that's displaying the phone footage.

Fury kindles in her again. Was the fire in the party house as sudden and blazing?

'That's from that night, isn't it? They were right – you *are* digging. You bitch! Leave him alone!'

She flies at me, fingers clawing at my face. But she's already crumpling, the rage burned up in the instant it flared. Just grief now, insubstantial as a curling flake of soot. She collapses against my chest.

'My boy's dead,' she whispers. 'Dead.'

I wonder how many times she'll have to say that to herself before she believes it.

'May I?' asks Bridget Perelli-Lee, indicating the screen. 'It's just . . .'

I nod. The image isn't identifiable, or sexually explicit. Perelli-Lee bends to peer at it. She points to a cluster of marks that I'd assumed were dead pixels in the ancient screen. Now that she's drawn my attention, I see that it's on the girl's bare skin.

'There — that? Looks like a butterfly? That's one of Harper's. Izzy's obsessed with them. Copies them in her journal and begs me to let her get one done too. As if.'

So the tape *is* Dan and Harper. That explains her anger at the party. No girl would want an intimate video of herself played before all her classmates. And I wonder, again, at our society's double standards, when it's a mark of prowess for a boy to be filmed screwing a girl but a badge of shame for her.

Then I remember Harper's bitter words as she walked away from me in the hospital. *A nasty little slut like me.*

What if the boy on the tape isn't Dan?

7

Sarah

The sign in my shop window is turned to 'CLOSED', but I have work to do.

Hopefully I can fetch Harper home from hospital this afternoon. She'll need what I'm brewing. And Abigail will need it, too. My daughter and my poor friend have lost the boy who meant more to them than anything.

This is what my art is for. Modern society reckons it's found better ways than witchcraft of easing our paths through life: drugs for sorrow, apps for love. Insurance for sickness and lotteries for wealth. Across America, witches' booths are disappearing from Main Street.

But there's no more certain remedy for soul-soreness, no better balm for a broken heart, than the one I can brew up in my workroom.

Time heals all things. But when there isn't time, witchcraft will do.

I lift three tinted glass jars from the shelves, before picking a few ingredients fresh in the yard. That done, I take my time selecting the best chart for my purpose. The one I settle on is old and fragile, so I slip it carefully from the shallow drawer of my plan chest and carry it to the oak ritual table that belonged to my grandmother. I unroll the felt topper and place little brass weights on each corner of the chart to keep it flat.

As I lose myself in preparation, I feel my neck and shoulders unknot, my spirit relax for the first time since that terrible night at Bridget's. I measure valerian root into the weighing scales, then flatten it with the side of my silver knife. Aira twines around my ankles, mewing. She knows that I'm at work.

The rhythms of it are ancient. The Veteris Opus, they called it in renaissance times: the Old Work. And folk have never stopped hungering for witch rites. Barely were they done persecuting us when the Revolutionary War put us back in business. Generals needed cannonballs to fly straight, soldiers were desperate for lucky amulets, and sweethearts begged charms for faithfulness. The Civil War was just the same. Vietnam too, my gramma told me. War is good business for witches.

Heartbreak is, too.

As I chop and grind and chant, I pour my love for Harper and Abigail into the work.

I'm blending a draft of tranquility with a heartsease tincture – a standard preparation. But I'll add tea rose and sweet pea: the first for remembrance, the second for departure and farewell. I want them both to cherish their memories of Daniel but also to move past this awful loss. Which requires one final ingredient.

I pull up the key that hangs always around my neck. The top half of my filing cabinet is for client records, kept as carefully as any doctor or psychiatrist – we're bound by the same data-protection laws these days. The bottom half is my archive. It's ordered alphabetically, too, and inside each named hanging folder is a small vacuum-packed bag.

Their contents are always freely given. They have to be, for the magic to take properly. We witches knew about consent culture long before it hit sex-ed classrooms. But no one ever asks what happens to the . . . *leftovers*.

Everyone I've ever worked magic for is in here.

The folder marked 'WHITMAN, Daniel' holds two bags. They both contain hair: two shades of blond, one darker and coarser than the other. The older, fairer one I should have thrown away a long time ago. I rub its contents, which are silky fine inside the airtight plastic. I'll burn it when they bury Daniel.

But not today. I replace that bag and carry the other to my worktop. I harvested its contents last season, when Dan had a tendon injury and was impatient to get back on the field. Impatient enough to come to me, as well as the team physio and the sports-med specialist his dad's insurance covered.

I cut the pack with silver scissors and slide out seven hairs onto my worktop. The chart tells me I've a little longer to wait before adding them.

My fingertips tingle as they trace the chart's nested, interlocking circles, triangles, pentagrams and hexagrams. Its spirals, scrawled symbols and alphanumeric subdivisions. These marks are where the magic happens. These diagrams are witchcraft made visible.

They may look arcane, but, in truth, they're simply maps. Maps with many turns and branches. Magic is the art of choosing the best path to where you wish to be. And, as with life, where you end up is the result of the choices you've made.

When Harper was little, she'd sit in here drawing and coloring while I worked. Every now and then she'd lift her dark head and solemnly ask what I was doing. But I could tell she didn't quite grasp my explanations. Until one day I took the pen she was drawing with, always such clever drawings, and said: 'The ingredients and objects are your ink. The charts and symbols are your paper. And magic is the drawing you make.'

I'll never forget how wide she smiled.

Harper couldn't wait to be a witch. And I couldn't wait to teach her, just like my grandmother taught me. Each gesture and incantation that corresponds to a symbol or letter. Wisps of Aramaic, Egyptian, and languages so old they've vanished from the earth. Intricate finger signs that I had to practice over and over. If I made an error, Gramma whacked me on the thigh with a ruler – not the palm or knuckles, as I needed my hands in working order. Gramma was more than my grandmother. She was my mother in the craft. Every witch needs one. The paths we make are dangerous to tread alone.

'You'll be teaching her one day,' Gramma told me after Harper was born, as we both doted on her clear, guileless eyes and pudgy baby limbs. My grandmother never lived to see Harper's thirteenth birthday and to learn that her great-granddaughter was no witch.

A rattling at the yard door pulls me from my memories. The first thing I do is check the brew's progress. I've not missed a step, but the hourglass tells me it'll soon be time to add the hairs.

My visitor must be Bridget. She's the only one with keys and a token to let her through the protective wards. She'll be bringing an update on Abigail. The three of us have arranged a visiting rota: Bridget this morning, Julia this afternoon, and me tonight once I've finished my work and fetched Harper home from the hospital.

Bridge will just have to wait until this step is done.

To my annoyance, the door rattles again, then flies open. I turn, ready to give my friend an earful – but it's not Bridget, Harper looks as surprised to see me as I am to see her.

'Jesus, Mom. Brewing?'

Her voice is raspy, like she's been gargling with hot coals. Did they let her just walk out of that hospital?

I reach to hug her, but she evades with a graceful swerve. She does this more and more, and though I know it's just a teenage thing, it still hurts.

'Almost there,' I tell her. 'A tiny bit longer. Are you okay?'

I point to the chair my clients take during consultations. Half the town has sat there at one time or another. But Harper ignores me. She prowls over to the ritual table and stares at the chart.

It doesn't hold her attention for long, though. Her childhood fascination with witchcraft just disappeared one day. I don't remember exactly when, but it was before her thirteenth birthday. When, on that day, I performed the Rite of Determination and discovered she was giftless, it nearly destroyed me. I was terrified it would destroy her, too.

But she coped. She seemed almost relieved. And looking back, I understood that withdrawing of interest in my work was because she already sensed her own lack of gift. She was training herself to stop loving something she couldn't have. Of course, we've all done that, but it breaks my heart that my little girl had to learn it so young.

'What the fuck is this?'

She's seen the baggie containing Daniel's sample.

'Language, Harper.'

'What're you doing with the hair of a boy who died two days ago? Whose death the *cops* are investigating. Do you have any idea how suspicious that looks? One of them turned up at the hospital earlier to talk to me.'

A cop questioning Harper? We'll need to talk about that. But she has to calm down first. Her voice is rising and a doctor warned that shouting and strain could leave her with permanent damage. I could probably fix it, but I'd rather she didn't hurt herself in the first place. My fingers shape a low-level sign of pacification I usually reserve for bite-happy dogs and ornery parking attendants, but she notices.

'Don't *do* that shit on me, Mom.'

'Harper, please. The potion's nothing sinister. I just . . . It's for you.'

'For me?' She peers into the iron pot. 'Ugh, it stinks.'

The smell of sorrow. Even people who know nothing of magic can detect the essence of a potion. Those for love, joy or happiness are honey-sweet. Brews for sorrow, sadness and despair both smell and taste bitter. Those for anger or revenge are almost undrinkably foul.

'It's to help you and Abigail. It's comforting. Just a plain old tranquility draft with a side order of heartsease.'

The last grain has slid through the hourglass, and I reach for the seven strands I counted out. I drop them in, one by one, my fingers sketching a different shape in the air after each falls. The symbol at this point on the chart is ancient Greek. The words I chant are fragments of a song of farewell – someone standing on the banks of the river of the underworld, watching as their loved one is rowed away.

My heart aches as I do it. I'm saying goodbye to Daniel, too. He's been a part of my life since before he was born, when Abigail and I met at antenatal class. He and Harper grew up side by side, with Izzy toddling around after them, just a year younger. He had sleepovers at my house. Ate breakfast at my kitchen counter. Just two days ago, we were toasting his bright future. And now he's gone.

It's done. My hands drop to my sides and I feel empty. Like an athlete, my body is my work, and a brew as complex as this leaves me drained. It's why we witches have covens – non-magical assistants who share their energies with us.

Harper's been watching. But it's not the eager look from her childhood. It's something I can't place. Don't want to place. Something almost like contempt. I see this in her sometimes and it cuts me deep. As if, in teaching herself not to love magic, she came to despise it.

A faint mist rises off the brew. The evaporating bitterness drifts between us.

34

'It needs to cool. It'll help you make your peace with what happened to Daniel, so you can start to get over him.'

'*Get over him?* Jesus. I wish you'd brew me an elixir of oblivion or something so I can forget he ever existed.'

I stare at my daughter, shocked at the violence of her grief. She needs this potion more than I could have imagined.

'It'll be ready tonight,' I tell her.

'Well, I won't be here tonight. I'm getting out of this place for a couple days, away from it all. I just came to tell you.'

'Out of Sanctuary? What? Wait . . .'

I reach for her, to tell her that running away from her pain won't fix it. But she evades me again. The yard door bangs shut behind her, and I'm alone.

8

Maggie

Some cop skills you don't learn in police academy – you learn them in high school. And one is that when a girl won't talk to you, maybe her best friend will. According to the partygoers' statements, the best friend in this case is one Beatriz Garcia, aka 'Queen Bea'.

'Can I help you?'

The Garcia house is an all-glass affair by that fifties architecture school that screwed real-estate prices for normal folks round here. Bea opens the front door with the air of a sorority president eyeing uninvited guests on social night. She's in an oversize monogrammed sweater and her makeup is immaculate, though it can't fully conceal the puffiness around her eyes. A lollipop sticks out the corner of her mouth, a phone is in her hand, and . . . is that a criminology textbook under her arm?

'Preparing for my visit?' I point to the book. *It's a joke!* But Beatriz remains stony-faced. I was trying to put her at ease. She's lost a classmate and childhood friend, and now has a cop on her doorstep. But maybe Bea doesn't do humor. Or maybe it just wasn't that funny.

'Required reading. I start at Cawden in the fall – political science and pre-law. Please wait there.'

She pivots on her heel and yells, 'Mom!' The walls and floors are polished concrete, and her voice reverberates.

'It's you I've come to see, actually. I'm the detective looking into Daniel Whitman's death.'

Her eyes lift sideways, as if she's too unimpressed even to do the full roll.

'Of course. But I'd like to have my mom with me, *if* you don't mind. I'm pretty shaky from what happened and don't want to say something that could get anyone in trouble.'

When Beatriz says 'anyone', the word my cop brain hears is 'me'. But it's a reasonable request. And she's going to be studying law. I once saw a kid in hysterics over a parking fine because he thought it'd destroy his prospects of a legal career.

Julia Garcia joins her daughter. She's dressed as though she followed Abigail Whitman round the Saks apparel department saying: 'Do you have that in black?' each time her friend bought something. She lifts her glasses and inspects me.

'Officer.'

Without the glasses, her face is . . . familiar? I had a similar sensation when Abigail Whitman and her pal Bridget showed up and figured it was because I'd seen photos of the Whitman family. But I've seen no pictures of this woman.

'Officer?'

'I'm sorry, Mrs Garcia. I just had the strangest feeling I'd seen you somewhere before.'

'Well, I gather Tad Bolt told Abigail that you'd been posted here some years back. Sanctuary's such a small place, I'm sure our paths would have crossed plenty of times at . . .'

She bats away the thought, as unable as I am to think of a single place she and I would have had in common. Her accent is West Coast, flattened by years out east.

'May I come in?'

'We'd love to help, Officer, but can you keep this short? You

37

can imagine what a shock this has been for all of us. Dan was the first friend Bea made in fifth grade, when we moved here from San Diego, and I'm close to his mom, Abigail. In fact, I'm due to go check on her soon – we don't want her left alone for long.'

I give a noncommittal nod. This will be as short or as long as it has to be.

As Julia fixes us fragrant Japanese tea, I make small talk with Beatriz. It seems that while her architect dad and technical illustrator mom are 'creative' types (that gets air quotes), Beatriz wants to *make a difference* – at a top corporate law firm. Half my brain listens, and the other half studies the house's jaw-dropping interior.

This living room is glass-walled, and it doesn't look over a back yard so much as a full-on birch forest. Photos and artworks cover the walls, including two soppy marital portraits of Julia and her husband, prominently displayed. As my gaze slides over them, another piece catches my eye. I excuse myself to go to the restroom and take a closer look as I pass.

It's a witch's chart.

'Exquisite, isn't it?'

Julia is right behind me with the tray.

'It looks like a . . .'

'A spell chart? Yes. It isn't one, of course.'

'No?'

'No. You could say it's "inspired by". Sarah Fenn is a dear friend. You obviously know that our daughters are, or have been, close. As an artist, I find Sarah's charts fascinating and beautiful, and she let me copy some. I have others around the house. Only a witch can make a chart that possesses magical properties, though.'

I'm dying to ask more, but she's said only one thing that's relevant to my inquiry.

'*Have been* close? Have Beatriz and Harper fallen out?'

Her smile is tight. 'You know what teenagers are like, Detective. Dramas from one week to the next. And for that pair, sad to say, it was always going to happen. Harper's a bright girl, but . . . different aspirations. Bea's always taken her studies very seriously. She's got her heart set on Harvard Law for postgrad.'

Julia's face glows with pride as she looks over at her daughter. The textbook is open in the girl's lap and she's studying it, seemingly oblivious to our conversation, though something tells me she's listening in. The lollipop rolls in her mouth as she turns the pages, the phone gripped in her other hand. Beatriz Garcia is already multitasking like a CEO.

So, things have cooled off between her and Harper? It must be recent, if the school network still pegs them as best friends. But is that remotely relevant to Dan's death?

I give them the pitch: *routine investigation, interested in any untoward events at the party, et cetera*. Beatriz watches me over the rim of a tea bowl doubtless crafted by a hundred-year-old Kyoto artisan.

'I spoke to a cop already,' she says, when I'm done. 'Do I really have to go through it all again? Only it's hard to talk about, and we've got final exams, and—'

'The local officers took short statements from a number of partygoers, yes. But your friendships with Daniel and his girlfriend Harper go back years. All your moms are close, too, right? So I'm hoping you might be able to—'

'It's Jake you should be asking. He's Dan's bestie. Likes to stick close.' Bea's tone is neutral, but her lip curls.

'Jacob Bolt? So was he with Dan at the party? You saw them?'

'I guess he was. I didn't see much of either of them.'

'No?'

'It was a good party. Lots of people to hang out with.'

'Two things happened: Daniel's fall and the fire. Is there anything you can tell me about either of those?'

'I'm sorry, Officer, but not really. I was downstairs getting myself a soda when it happened. I was downstairs most of the night, actually. It wasn't as noisy.'

She's maintaining her poise, this smart girl, but something flickers in her eyes as though she wants to close them.

As if she wants to unsee something.

What is she not telling me?

My radio crackles. Of all the bad timing. I apologize and turn down the volume, but the radio is insistent, and amid the repetition of my name I hear the word 'urgent'. I excuse myself and step outside to respond.

'This had better be good.'

'Trust me, you want to hear this.'

I recognize the voice of Asshole Cop, but there's something off about his tone. He sounds agitated. Maybe even . . . *scared*?

'Chief has a witness at the station to see you. Says Dan Whitman was murdered at the party and he's got proof who did it.'

Lordy. My underage-drinking-accidental-death case just escalated.

'A weirdo, or someone to take seriously?'

And when the desk sergeant replies, I understand why he sounds so fearful.

'Definitely not a weirdo. It's Jake Bolt. The chief's son.'

9

Maggie

Tad Bolt collars me as soon as I step back into the station. I haven't seen him since he greeted me at the burned-out shell of Sailaway Villa. After that, he went home to be with his son.

And it turns out his son had news for him.

News that changes everything.

'Homicide?' I say. 'In the middle of a crowded party. There would have been dozens of witnesses, so how come no one else has mentioned this? You told me yourself you thought it was an accident. A fire, a panic, a fall. Easy-peasy. So what's changed?'

'What's changed is that Jacob has recovered sufficiently from his trauma to tell me the truth about what happened.'

'But *murder*? That's a huge allegation. What if the point is that he *hasn't* recovered, and this is his trauma talking?'

We're shut in the chief's office, just the two of us. Bolt's huge frame fills half the space, and the eyes in his fleshy face are sharp and bright. He could be – he *is* – intimidating. But I'm not the rookie who does coffee runs any more. I'm the state detective on this case and I stand my ground.

'Even an outsider like me can see how this death has hit Sanctuary hard. And, as Dan's best friend, your son must be really suffering. But have you talked to him about what an allegation like this would mean?'

'We've done nothing but talk for the last twenty-four hours. I had to make sure he understood what the consequences would be for him. What it'd mean for Dan's mom and dad. For the whole town. And when I took a break from talking to him, Mary-Anne was praying with him. Jakey feels this is his duty. And he's got proof.'

Proof?

That'd certainly make Jacob's allegation more than the grief-stricken fantasy of a bereaved boy. But still I struggle to get my head round it. An accident is what this looks like. I've entertained the possibility of suicide.

'But murder?' I say aloud.

Bolt nods grimly. 'I told Jakey he had to be absolutely certain. So he showed me, and as a lawman I couldn't be arguing with him once I'd seen the evidence.'

10

POLICE TRANSCRIPT: JACOB BOLT
Interviewing officer: DETECTIVE KNIGHT, MARGARET
Attending: BOLT, THADDEUS (father)

DET. KNIGHT: Beginning interview of Jacob Paul
  Bolt. Attending in a parental capacity is
  Thaddeus Bolt, the interviewee's father.
  Interviewee has come forward voluntarily to
  provide testimony. Jacob, please can you confirm
  that's all correct.
BOLT: That's correct, ma'am.
DET. KNIGHT: Thank you, Jacob. So, you're here on
  account of what you witnessed at the party three
  nights ago, at which Daniel Whitman died. Can
  you tell me what you saw?
BOLT: She killed him. I saw that bitch kill him.
DET. KNIGHT: Who are you referring to, Jacob?
BOLT: Harper. Harper-fucking-Fenn.
PARENT: Jacob ...
DET. KNIGHT: And you saw this?
BOLT: I was right next to her when she did it.
DET. KNIGHT: So you were with Daniel ...

BOLT: Not Daniel. Harper.

DET. KNIGHT: Harper. Okay. So where were you both?

BOLT: At the bottom of the stairs.

DET. KNIGHT: And Daniel was ...?

BOLT: On the landing.

DET. KNIGHT: The landing is where Daniel fell
  from. But if you and Harper were at the bottom
  of the stairs, then how ...

BOLT: Witchcraft. She killed him with witchcraft.

[The footage described can be accessed in the
  digital evidence database.]

DET. KNIGHT: What I'm seeing here is mobile phone
  footage that you say you shot at the party. You
  consent to it being examined by our analysts?

BOLT: I do.

DET. KNIGHT: Thank you, Jacob. So, we are close
  up on Harper Fenn. You look to be no more than a
  foot away. Correct?

BOLT: Correct.

DET. KNIGHT: And why did you start filming Harper
  at this moment?

BOLT: Because she'd just seen it. I thought her
  reaction might be worth getting.

DET. KNIGHT: And 'it' is?

BOLT: Some filthy tape. Her and Dan at another
  party a few weeks ago. Look, you'll see a bit in
  a minute.

DET. KNIGHT: The image isn't very clear, but
  you've turned your phone on to a wall projection
  that appears to show a boy and a girl engaged in
  sexual intercourse.

BOLT: Yeah.

DET. KNIGHT: And we're back on Harper again. She's

speaking, but it's inaudible. She appears to be
pointing at the projection.

BOLT: Yeah, she was furious.

DET. KNIGHT: About the projection?

BOLT: Keep watching. It's coming. You'll see
her ...

DET. KNIGHT: Harper's still shouting.
Gesticulating. Both hands raised now. She's
looking around, like she's searching for someone
or something, then she's back staring at the
projection. She's sort of ... wringing her
hands? And now ... ah!

BOLT: That's him. Jesus.

DET. KNIGHT: Now people are screaming. The angle
of the phone camera has shifted and we're seeing
Daniel Whitman on the ground in the centre of
the atrium, apparently having fallen over the
bannister at the top of the stairs. The screen
has darkened. Harper has moved further away from
you, and there's smoke. I presume this is your
voice we're hearing now?

BOLT: Yeah. I ...

DET. KNIGHT: You're calling his name. 'Dan. Dan.'
Correct?

BOLT: Yeah. Christ. Sorry, can we stop a moment?

DET. KNIGHT: And the recording ends.

BOLT: I went to help him.

DET. KNIGHT: Daniel Whitman?

BOLT: He was dead, man. He was already dead. That
fucking bitch. [Inaudible. Cries.]

PARENT: We'll stop there. My son needs a break.
Gonna take him home. An evidence technician
already made you a copy of that footage.

45

DET. KNIGHT: I'll need the device for exa—

PARENT: My son's lost his best friend. He and the other guys are getting each other through this. No way in hell are you taking his phone. Come on, buddy, let's go. And Mags?

DET. KNIGHT: Yes?

PARENT: Jakey just gave you everything you need. Don't go screwing it up.

[Interview concludes.]

11

Abigail

Julia's been and gone. She told me the cop had visited, asking questions. More digging.

Then Sarah stopped by. She brought me something, bless her, as she always does when one of us is suffering. The label reads 'Heartsease'. *It'll help*, she said, as she watched me take a first dose before she left.

Nothing will help.

But I do feel clearer. Calmer. I was a wreck when Bridget found me this morning. I've held things together all day, thanks to my friends' company. But now I'm alone, the memories of Daniel that were such a comfort before are crowding too closely round me, hungry and fierce. Only Sarah's brew is keeping them at bay.

Should I call Michael? Try again to tell him that I need him more than his faculty does? But Michael's work is everything to him. And I've only myself to blame for that.

No husband. No son.

My hands shake and I reach for the potion bottle, then lean back on the couch as gentle comfort washes through me. Sarah has bottled up her love. The tightness in my chest loosens, and my breath comes deep and even. *Heartsease*.

The next I know, I'm startled awake by banging at the door.

'Sorry to intrude, Abigail,' Tad Bolt says.

He's standing there with Jake. The boy's lank hair and dark-circled eyes tell me he's in a pit of his own. Emotion surges in me, despite Sarah's calming brew, and I've no name for it. Do I take Jacob in my arms as we sob over our shared loss? Do I spit on him for walking out of that burning house alive, without my son?

I can't deal with this. I begin to shut the door, but Tad jams in his foot.

'Jacob's just given a statement to the police. We thought you and Michael should be the first to know.'

So it's that. What tale has Jake tattled? I thought he loved Dan. I freeze, indecisive, before letting them in. Better to hear it and know.

But none of what Jake says makes sense.

'*Harper*? They were *dating*.'

'Not for a few weeks now. He dumped her after she acted like a complete ho. A recording of it somehow got played on the wall at the party. Harper was furious. She's been mad for ages, but that was the final straw. She must have thought Dan put it up . . . I dunno. She was *scary*.'

Jake pulls up his T-shirt to wipe his snotty lip. I look away, before the sight of him sends me tumbling back down into darkness again. I need to stay alert and make sense of this. I've heard about the sex video – the one the journalist asked about, and the cop is digging for. So it was real. And . . . Harper killed Dan because of it?

My friend's daughter *killed my son*?

I wasn't happy when Dan started dating Harper. She's attractive, but hardly daughter-in-law material. No witch folk are. It's in their nature to be a little . . . loose. Sarah always says witches are born with more love to give than most people. I never made an issue of it, though. High-school romances always run their course, and Dan wasn't short of more suitable admirers – Beatriz never made any secret of how much she liked him.

Bea would have been a better match. Harper is strange and free-spirited, always disappearing at weekends. I know that used to drive Dan mad, because she'd never watch his games and cheer him on as a girlfriend should, and they'd fight about it.

But for things to get so bad between them that she'd *kill* him? It's unthinkable.

'You mean they had a fight and it was an accident? She . . . slapped him? Or pushed him? And he fell.'

Jake shakes his head. His father nudges him.

'Tell her, son. She deserves to know.'

'It was deliberate,' Jake says. 'She killed him with witchcraft.'

I exhale and sit back. Because Jacob has got it wrong.

'You know that's not possible.' There's strangely little relief in saying it, and I realize how much I wanted an explanation for what happened to my boy. But I don't want *this* explanation. 'Harper doesn't have the gift.'

It's the overwhelming sadness of Sarah's life. No mom ever feels like she truly deserves her kids. We all imagine we fail them in a hundred different ways. Julia worries whether she did the right thing uprooting her family from California. Bridget frets about how much of Isobel's shyness is due to her split from Izzy's dad. I know my mistake and have wondered ever since what I might have chosen if Alberto hadn't made the decision for me.

But Sarah never had a choice, and we've all told her so. It was just bad luck. Sarah's own mom didn't have the gift. It's not uncommon for it to skip a generation. And it skipped Harper.

Jake pulls a phone out of his pocket. 'Got to warn you,' he says, thickly. 'You see where Dan . . .'

I don't think I'm ready for that. Not without some help. I

reach for the bottle of heartsease again, and swig. The chief eyes me curiously.

'That a brew? One of Sarah's?'

'She brought it round this evening.'

'I see. And it helps?'

'It does. Takes me out of myself a bit. Keeps me calm.'

Bolt frowns. 'Calm, huh? Well, I'm not gonna get ahead of myself here, Abigail. But when you've seen this, you might ask if there's a reason Sarah Fenn would like you calm and out of yourself.'

Is he serious?

Jacob hits 'play'. Harper fills the screen, but I pay no attention. I want to see only one thing: my son. And then I do. I see his body on the floor as kids scream, as smoke billows and partygoers run for safety, leaving him behind. Did Jake run too?

'You saw it?' says the chief. 'What she did with her hands? I know you're part of Sarah's coven – you recognize that witch stuff, right?'

'I didn't see. I just . . . Please, show me again.'

I wipe my eyes, and this time I do pay attention.

And I see it. Harper's hands in the air. I've seen Sarah making witch signs often enough when we meet, the three of us friends lending her our energies as she channels her gift.

It's . . . *magic*. Despite everything Sarah's told us, Harper is doing magic.

The girl gestures. Then my son is dead on the floor.

I shake my head. It's too much to take in.

Sarah has lied to me – to all of us – for all these years. She's kept her daughter's gift a secret.

As I lean toward Jake, I catch a scent of the body spray he's wearing – it's the same one Dan used. I flinch, feeling sick, but touch his phone screen and hit 'play'. Then again. And again. I want this seared into my memory.

My son dumped his cheating girlfriend, and she *killed* him for it.

And the woman I thought was one of my dearest friends . . . who has touched my life in so many ways and helped smooth it into the shape I wanted – or thought I wanted. She knew her daughter was capable of this and told no one.

Sarah. How could you?

I pick up the brew bottle and hurl it. It smashes against the white wall and something thick and bittersweet drips down. My breathing comes fast and harsh, and my heart is racing.

How can it be at ease knowing Daniel was murdered?

12

Maggie

Sunset and streaks of cloud are candy-striping the sky as Long Island Sound slides into view on the satnav.

Not far ahead is the millionaire's mile of Shore Road, where the ruin of Sailaway Villa stands. But before it is a cluster of more modest dwellings. Those once inhabited by fishermen, boatyard workers and perhaps a smuggler or two. Their price tag isn't so modest these days, though, thanks to their historic wooden shingles and cream-painted trim.

In one of them, I'm hoping for answers.

There's so much I need to know, but top of my list is whether Harper Fenn is a witch and the reality of her relationship with Daniel.

The satnav bossily announces my destination, and I pull over. It's a cute house. Dried starfish are propped in the small windowpanes. A Day-Glo pink ship's buoy hangs from a tree in the front yard, for kids to swing on. The enameled mailbox is decorated with birds and flowers, the family name lettered in flowing italic: *Perelli-Lee*. That's new.

That's new. Which is when I realize I've been here before, during my previous posting to Sanctuary.

I look at the house, waiting for a memory to prompt me. There wasn't a picket fence back then. And there couldn't have been that sports car parked in the drive. It looks almost brand new, and extremely expensive. But nothing clear emerges.

I rap on the door. The kid who answers startles at the sight of a cop – or maybe it's just at another brown face like hers. You don't see too many of us in Sanctuary.

'Can I help you?' Isobel Perelli asks, with the hint of a stammer.

She's a sweet little thing. She's got thick glasses and is wearing shapeless sleepwear, but she's got her mom's heart-shaped face and I find that I remember her dad, a good-looking dude who attracted minor traffic violations at twice the rate of the white folks in town. Izzy looks somehow childlike. It's hard to imagine she's only a year younger than Harper, Jake, Beatriz and the rest.

'I'm here to see your stepmom, Principal Lee. Is she in?'

'I'll take it from here, Izzy,' says a voice. 'Why don't you go back to bed? I didn't know you were downstairs.'

The kid looks relieved. 'I was just getting a glass of water, Cheryl.'

Her stepmom comes into view. Cheryl Lee is cradling a cat that's got a plastic veterinary collar round its neck. She gives a long-suffering sigh as she puts the creature down, but the concern in her eyes looks genuine as she pulls the girl to her and presses the back of a hand to her forehead.

'Okay, honey. It's good to see you up and about, but don't overdo it. Your mom's been baking cookies again; go and get one. But only one, you hear?'

The girl nods dutifully and trots off toward the kitchen.

'She's still poorly?' I ask.

'It's been a few weeks. Mono. Flares up from time to time at school – we've got three kids off with it at the moment. You know they call it the kissing disease? Well, poor Izzy got it without ever kissing anyone.'

53

Cheryl leads me to a cozy family room, unceremoniously scooping two more animals off a blanket-covered couch and offering me a seat.

'Sorry about the cats everywhere. I don't know how Bridget ever thought she wasn't a lesbian. Between us we've got enough for a coven.'

She gives a wry grimace, whether at the cats or the witchcraft, I can't tell.

'Your wife isn't here?'

'She's visiting Sarah to talk about Abigail. We're all really concerned, and it doesn't help that Michael Whitman for some reason thought this was a great time to go back to campus. Anyway, you said on the phone that you want to know about some of my students? I have ground rules. You're chatting to Cheryl Perelli-Lee, Sanctuary resident and stepmom, about kids I know, not interviewing Principal Lee about her students. Is that clear?'

I nod. Jeez, she's firm. She'll have me confessing to supergluing the class bully's locker next.

'Very well. As you can imagine, I have a school full of traumatized kids, and I spent my weekend trying to find the best bereavement counselors available for drop-in sessions. The sooner we have clarity on what happened, the better for my students. So ask away.'

And I do. Her responses are thoughtful and it's plain that beneath her brisk exterior Cheryl Lee is a principal who really cares about her charges.

I start off with Jake. Given that he's offered himself up as the star witness, I need to know how credible he is. How trustworthy. According to Cheryl, he's a steady sort of boy. Well behaved – unsurprisingly, given that his pop's the chief – though exaggeratedly courteous to girls in a way that wins him more scorn than approval. Academically average, she says, and as such, likely destined to follow his father into law enforcement.

'Not that I'm implying . . .' Cheryl catches herself.

'Of course not,' I say. 'How close was he to Daniel Whitman?'

'That would depend on whether you ask Jake, or anyone else.'

'Meaning?'

The principal sighs. 'Jake isn't sporty, isn't especially popular, not considered good-looking. You get the idea. Daniel was all of those things. It was as if Jake hoped that by being *with* him, he might become more *like* him. You can imagine what the school at large thought of that.'

I wince. 'Dan didn't mind?'

'Not at all. If anything, he encouraged it. Maybe he found it amusing. Maybe it was simply more evidence of his own superiority.'

'And what about Harper?'

'A complicated young woman. Bright, but doesn't apply herself,' Cheryl says, echoing what I've heard from Julia Garcia. 'Speaking for myself, I believe her life is blighted by her failure to take after her mother.'

'You mean her lack of magical ability?'

Cheryl nods.

'And she definitely doesn't . . .?'

'I have no PMP notification on file for Harper.'

Federal law requires that all persons of magical potential – i.e., witches – register as such by the age of eighteen. I already checked the state database for Harper Fenn. She wasn't on it, but it turns out she's the baby of her academic cohort and only turns eighteen over the summer.

Cheryl nods when I remind her of this.

'Eighteen is the legal requirement, but given that ability manifests by age thirteen – they have this ritual that confirms it – it's best practice to notify early of PMP status in certain settings, like healthcare and education. Can you imagine what it's like managing these girls in a school environment, Detective? Two sisters with the craft passed through my previous school in New Jersey. I assure you, they made no secret of it. They traded potions for cash during recess, tried to charm boys. You name it. I lost count of the detentions and confiscations. At one point the mother threatened the school with a discrimination suit.'

She lifts her eyes as if imploring the heavens. On the wall opposite us hangs a piece of devotional artwork – a dark-eyed Jesus teaching little children – alongside what must be Cheryl and Bridget's wedding portrait, both of them beaming while Isobel smiles awkwardly and holds a bunch of flowers.

'What else can you tell me about Harper? Has her behavior changed at all recently?'

Cheryl shifts uncertainly, weighing up how much to divulge.

'It's my belief Harper began self-harming about eighteen months ago. I don't *know*. I've not seen any injuries and neither have other school staff members. But she started covering up. You've seen those long-sleeved tops she wears under her T-shirts? Two semesters ago she claimed religious exemption from clothing regulations and started wearing them beneath her sports uniform.'

'*Religious* exemption?'

'Like Muslim girls wearing sport hijabs, or Sikh boys and their turbans. Which struck me as odd, because I never thought witchcraft was big on rules.'

That rings alarm bells. I've worked more than a few domestic violence cases. When women start covering up, it's often because they have controlling partners who don't want other men looking at them. Or because they've got bruises to hide.

'Mrs Lee, when did Harper and Daniel Whitman start dating?'

Cheryl shakes her head. 'I see what you're thinking, Detective, but they didn't get together until last semester. Now if you'll excuse me, I should go check that Izzy made it back to bed. Let me show you out.'

13

Abigail

I blink awake under the watchful gaze of Tom Elwy of the Philadelphia Eagles. A giant poster of the quarterback is pinned beside Dan's bed. We used to fight over it all the time. I said it spoiled the look of the room. I can't believe I ever gave Dan a cross word over something so trivial.

Before the Bolts left last night, Tad asked if I wanted his wife to come over and sit with me, but I refused. I didn't want handholding and prayers. I wanted to be alone with my son.

So I came upstairs to this room. It's next door to the one I started sleeping in when Dan was younger, after I told Michael that his snoring kept me awake. What my husband doesn't know is that he doesn't snore – and that I used my room even when he was away, so I could fall asleep to the sound of Dan laughing down the phone to one of his friends, or the muffled noises of a computer game or movie he was enjoying.

But last night I slept *here*, in Dan's bed. My clothes are in a heap on the floor, jumbled up with his clothes. I'm under his coverlet, just as I used to be when he was little and having night terrors.

Only now the terrors are mine. Every time I close my eyes, I see that final image from the video Jake showed me. Daniel, face down on the floor, as all around him kids shove past to get out of the burning house.

My beautiful, precious, brilliant son.

Perhaps – my *murdered* son.

I push back the covers.

If it were possible, I wouldn't get up ever again. Wouldn't wash and dress and go out into a world that holds nothing for me, because it no longer contains Daniel.

But Dan still needs me. Because his death wasn't an accident – he was killed by Harper Fenn. At least that's what the video shows.

I can still hardly believe it. I don't *want* to believe it.

I use Dan's en suite. His shower products. I can't stomach the thought of food but robotically make myself a coffee. I smashed Sarah's potion bottle last night and my sleep was just as broken, so I need something to sharpen me up. Then I snatch my car keys.

'Abigail. My God, are you okay? Come in.'

Sarah is shocked to see me. She draws me over her threshold and I duck, as all visitors must, beneath the bundle of wire-tied twigs that dangles above the door.

Inside, the house is the same as it's always been. I love this quaint little place. Tipped-down louvered shutters cast everything in a half-light. The rooms are full of clutter and it's impossible to tell the junk from the witch bits, the houseplants from the potion ingredients.

Witches adore that sort of ambiguity. Is their necklace just jewelry, or an artifact? Is the cat a pet, or a familiar? It's always charmed me. But now I think: is Sarah's daughter one more thing whose true nature isn't what it has always appeared?

'I was just making a pot of tea,' Sarah says, steering me into the kitchen. 'Would you like some? Maybe valerian . . .?'

Valerian's a sedative.

'I'm not here for tea, Sarah. I'm here because of what your daughter did.'

'Harper? What do you mean?'

'Harper killed Dan,' I say. 'The police have a witness. There's evidence.'

Sarah recoils as if I hit her. From the darkness comes a sharp mew, and Aira shoots into the kitchen. The cat butts against Sarah's ankles and she picks it up, burying her face in its fur. Anyone can see the communion between them: witch and familiar. An unbreakable bond.

I had a bond like that with my child. I still remember the smell of Daniel's skin as a newborn.

'Impossible,' Sarah says. 'You know how our beliefs reject violence against any living creature. And Dan was more than half a foot taller than her, and twice her size. And at a *party*, in front of dozens of people?'

'Witchcraft,' I say.

'No. You know that's not possible.'

'It is. There was a witness.'

'Who?'

I purse my lips.

'So no one you can name? Some kid who was drunk or delusional on weed? Abi, tell me who they are and I'll go shake sense into them. They should be ashamed of themselves, causing you more distress when—'

'Sarah, *could it be true*?'

My vehemence startles her, and our eyes meet. Sarah has been my friend for all these years. The woman I've trusted with my hopes and hurts. Has she lied to me – to all of us?

'It's *not* true. I'll show you.'

She leads me upstairs. A warped skylight casts a thin golden sheen onto walls whose every inch is covered: family

60

photographs, an old map of Long Island Sound, pale water-colors, botanical sketches, wooden masks, painted ceramic tiles. Swathes of faded fabric wrap around the banisters like wedding bunting. As we reach the landing, my cheek tickles and I brush aside scarlet ribbons dangling from a woven willow circlet.

The second door on the left has a calligraphed plaque bearing Harper's name. I freeze as Sarah halts beside it. Am I going to come face to face with my son's murderer? My heartbeat takes off frantically, and I remember Sarah's false comfort in a bottle. *Heartsease.*

Tad Bolt suggested that Sarah gave it to me deliberately, to dope me up. Would she? Does Sarah *know* what her daughter did?

The woman I thought was my friend is knocking on the door, calling her daughter's name. There's no response.

'You see?' she says, throwing the door open.

Her voice is fierce, almost accusatory. As if she's trying to prove something to herself as much as to me.

Harper's room is the opposite of the rest of the house. Its bare walls are finished in soft chalk paint, and white gauze is layered over the window, twisting in the breeze. There's a queen-size bed – I screw up my eyes, trying not to think about whether Harper ever shared it with Dan. Michael was very strict about that sort of thing not happening under our roof.

The shelves are half filled with books, half skincare products – the sort you buy at Sephora, not her mom's potions – and girly bits: a hairbrush, eyeliner pencils, ear studs and chunky silver rings. The desk is tidy, with a computer, a tub of pens and not much else. Strings of fairy lights are wound around the bookcase and bedstead. My eyes drink in everything, searching for clues. Is there something here that whispers: *I belong to a witch. I belong to a murderer?*

'Nothing,' Sarah says. 'You see? Nothing at all. No artifacts. No spell books.'

She yanks the closet doors so hard they bang against the wall. The contents of the clothes rail are as black as the room is white. Sarah is pulling open drawers in a frenzy, snatching up a handful of Harper's thongs and padded bras like they're some kind of proof.

'Just clothes. Normal girl stuff.'

She slumps onto the bed, the energy gone out of her, and wipes her face. When she looks up at me, she's crying.

'Don't you think I'd *know*, Abi? My own daughter. It was all I ever wanted for her.'

'How can you be sure?'

'Because of the rite – the Rite of Determination.'

'It must have been wrong.'

I look down at Sarah hunched on the edge of the mattress. Normally the sight of my friend so distraught would cut me to the quick, but I've no tears now for anyone but my son and myself.

Sarah's shaking her head.

'It's never wrong.'

14

Sarah

It's Abigail's grief speaking. It *has* to be. She can't believe this far-fetched story of police and evidence and witchcraft.

I'm the only witch in Sanctuary. Abigail knows that. Tad Bolt knows that. *Everyone* knows that. And they know that it's the sadness of my heart.

So I tell her everything about Harper's Determination. I was in bits afterwards, and my friends were the only thing that got me through, Bridget and Julia and Abigail. But I never told them the whole story. It would have felt like a violation of Harper's privacy – after all, she was the one who asked that no one be there.

In witch families, the rite is a big celebration. Think Christian confirmation, Jewish bat mitzvah, sweet sixteen and prom all rolled into one. The family's witch friends and non-gifted coven members will come from across the country to share their love and blessings.

My own Determination was one of the happiest days of my life. It was held a few weeks after my thirteenth birthday in a field my gramma owned, not far from her and Ompa's house. A creek ran through it, and there was a hazel coppice – a fertile place for magic.

Gramma had hung lanterns from the trees and set up a

63

long table laden with my favorite foods: sweet potato pie, mac'n'cheese and apple cake. There was champagne for the adults and dandelion wine for us kids. We danced and ran riot, then at moonrise Gramma made my Determination.

I remember how it felt when she'd finished her incantations and suddenly I could *see* it. We all could. My magic bright within me. For a few shining moments you're like a human firefly. It lights you up from the inside and sparkles off you like fairy dust. It soon fades, but you never forget what you carry inside.

Gramma always told me that a witch's purpose was to keep showing that light in everything we do.

When Harper was little, I'd daydream about her Determination. That field is still in our family; I go there to harvest ingredients. I didn't expect my mom to come up from Florida – I remember her at my party, sitting by herself and rebuffing all congratulations. People told me later she was drunk and vicious. But my aunts, uncles and cousins wouldn't miss it for anything. Nor my gramma's coven members who're still alive. Plus my own coven – Bridget, Julia and Abigail, with their children and partners. Harper would prattle about it too: *when I'm Determined* . . . she'd say. And I'd laugh and tell her she was born determined.

But the closer it got, the less she talked about it. I couldn't understand it at first. I wondered if she'd seen what happened that time . . . whether it had frightened her and she was scared of the power she'd have. I tried talking to her about it, to draw out if she'd seen or suspected anything, but she only withdrew further.

When I started party planning, she begged me not to. *Just us*, she'd say. *I don't want anyone there*. I couldn't understand it – was certain she'd change her mind. But her thirteenth birthday got closer and closer, and she was still adamant.

I never suspected the real reason for her reluctance.

It was almost five years ago now. A warm September night, two months after Harper's thirteenth birthday. I'd given in to her wish — no party. No witnesses. But I'd packed a picnic of all her favorite things. I was sure it was just nerves, the understandable anxiety of any child reaching the first significant milestone in their life. Once it was over, she'd be ecstatic. But we never ate a bite of anything I'd prepared.

Harper made me look away as she changed into the white ritual robe. Then, barefoot and grave, she lay down on the grass. I remember her eyes as I worked, wide and solemn.

I dug a trench around her and filled it with water scooped from the brook in a silver bowl. I set beeswax candles in a larger ring and lit them. Opened my wrist with my knife for enough blood to drip in a still-wider circle on the grass. Walked around all three rings, clockwise and widdershins, as I spoke the words of the rite. Harper lay there, girdled by water and fire, blood and breath. Her eyes watched me to the end.

Nothing happened.

I thought the sob was hers, but it was mine.

On my knees, I begged her forgiveness. I'd performed the rite wrong. Made a mistake. I'd do it again. It was all just a horrible misunderstanding. Of course she was a witch. Of *course* she was.

Harper put her skinny arms round me.

'You did it perfectly, Mom,' she said. 'But it's okay. It's okay.'

And my little girl comforted me as I cried.

'So you see,' I tell Abigail, as she stands over me in Harper's bedroom — the bedroom of a normal teenager — 'if it *was* witchcraft, it can't have been my daughter. I understand that you want some explanation or reason. But it wasn't Harper.'

I can see from her face that she wants to believe me. But if there's police and a witness involved, I'll need more than that.

I'll have to prove my daughter's innocence. Any way I can.

15

Maggie

The little Thai takeout just off Main Street has stayed open during my half-decade away from Sanctuary, and my taste buds are telling me their stupendous pad thai hasn't changed one bit.

Maybe I'm trying to trick myself back in time, to see if I can jolt my memories of why so many names and faces in this case seem familiar. Or maybe I'm just a sucker for good fried noodles.

I'm hunched over the piece-of-shit computer in the office, accessing my old case log. You'd think I could just CTL+F search the Perelli-Lee address and up it would come, but no such luck. I can't decide if the state law enforcement database was created by a person who hated computers, or who hated cops, or who loved overtime bonuses.

My fork is forlornly scraping the bottom of the takeout carton when I finally find it. My eyes can't take any more squinting at the grainy screen, so I hit 'print' so I can read it later in my rental apartment.

I'm just figuring out how to enter my authorization ID into the printer, and wondering if a fist on the keypad wouldn't work just as well, when there's a nervous cough behind me.

It's my new assistant.

The chief called me into his office this morning and we

discussed how his son coming forward as a witness affected my inquiries. I told him we'd best continue to keep Jake's statement under wraps, so as not to compromise the investigation. Tad bridled at first, seeing it as me questioning his son's testimony. (I didn't point out that questioning testimony is, uh, *what cops do*.)

But I convinced him that it was in everyone's interests. With a school full of traumatized students, I can't have a teen girl put at risk by an unproven allegation. And as for Jake . . . well, I reminded the chief of that proverb: *Even good witches make bad enemies*. His blue eyes bugged, and he gave me some bluster about Sarah Fenn being *a decent woman*. He got my point, though. Accusing a witch of murder could be considered a little risky.

So to speed the investigation along – in other words, to prove his son right – he's given me an assistant. Thankfully it's neither Asshole Cop nor Overly Eager Evidence Reviewing Cop. It's Helpful Cop, aka one Sergeant Chester Greenstreet.

Chester's so pale he's practically luminous, with a shock of light copper hair, freckles and invisible golden eyelashes that make him look permanently startled. But as I turn to wave him in, it strikes me that he's startled for real. I asked him to go through the lab results that came back from forensics on the party house and chase up toxicology for findings from the boy's cadaver. What he's got in his hand right now, though, is a big-ass law book.

'Can I have a quick word, sir – I mean, ma'am? In private?'

I hear a wolf whistle from Asshole on the duty desk as I motion Chester to close the door.

He lays the book on the table and you can practically see the puff of dust rising from it.

'I only got my badge last year and, well, I was so keen I actually read this thing. Cover to cover.'

It's the *Sentencing Guidelines of the State of Connecticut*. We all took classes on its contents during training, but it's stuff for the legals – the judges and attorneys – not us uniforms. My sergeant has marked a page with a coffee napkin.

'I'm glad you have faith in our investigation, Chester, but whatever Jake Bolt says, I'm far from certain yet that there even *is* a crime, let alone a verdict and a sentence.'

'Well, we're going to have to be certain,' he says. 'Very, *very* certain. Because there's a lot at stake.' He winces. 'No pun intended.'

His finger is pointing to a paragraph titled *Exemption to Repeal of Capital Felony*.

Which is all wrong, because there *are* no exemptions. Connecticut abolished the death penalty in 2012. Prior to that, our state had executed only one prisoner in about four decades. And just a few years ago, the state drew a double underline beneath its decision when it commuted the capital sentence even for the eleven perps on death row. Connecticut's got no stomach for execution.

There's only one paragraph because there's only one exemption: *Homicide by Unnatural Means*. I read it. Then read it again.

'That's saying what I think it's saying?' I ask Chester.

'Uh-huh. I did some research. The colony of Connecticut got its royal charter in 1662. Between then and the Revolutionary War, we executed dozens of people for crimes committed by witchcraft. The colony's leaders considered magic such a threat to the *moral and spiritual well-being of the people of Connecticut* – that's a quote; I've got nothing against witches myself,' he adds, hastily. 'Such a threat that when we joined the Union in 1788 and became the fifth state, we were granted *exemption in perpetuity* from future amendments or repeals relating to capital felonious witchcraft.'

I hiss through my teeth. This is no dead letter. It's an unrepealable, current requirement of Connecticut state law.

If what Jake Bolt alleges is true – or if a jury decides it is – then Harper Fenn will die for it.

16

INCIDENT ATTENDANCE LOG: BLACK HILL COUNTY,
SANCTUARY DIVISION
CALL RECEIVED: 10:32 p.m., 8 August
ATTENDING OFFICER: Sgt KNIGHT, Margaret
INCIDENT #: 14-1009

Notification received via call to central reporting line at 10:32 p.m. from female identifying herself as a neighbor of Pierre MARTINEAU and Bridget PERELLI of 258 Shore Approach. Disturbance reported – a female screaming. Also 'commotion'.

Caller stated this was unusual, as MARTINEAU and PERELLI are 'good folks' and 'usually quiet', although 'mixed up in witch stuff'. Caller then launched into diatribe about 'coven activity' and how neighbors had complained to PERELLI that it might affect property values.

Call handler (Sgt GRAYSON) brought caller back to specifics. Caller said it was 'probably nothing' but the screaming had been 'something awful' and she had felt it should be reported. Caller was thanked and told an officer would pay a visit.

Checks revealed no records held for PERELLI. Five traffic violations but no other offenses for MARTINEAU.

Sgt KNIGHT was dispatched. Arrived at house 10:57 p.m.

Attending officer found that a dinner party had been in progress on the property's patio. Present were Pierre MARTINEAU, Bridget PERELLI, Michael and Abigail WHITMAN, Sarah FENN and Julia GARCIA. Additionally, the house contained four minors, all children of the above-named adults.

One minor, Daniel WHITMAN (12), was lying on the couch downstairs, his mother with him.

Sgt KNIGHT was informed that the boy had taken a tumble down the stairs. On hearing the noise, the adults had found him unconscious and his mother had screamed. However, the boy had quickly come round and showed no apparent injury.

Boy was conscious and speaking. Stated: 'I went to get us cookies, but it was dark and I missed the stair.'

When the attending officer recommended that the child be checked over by a medical professional, Michael WHITMAN stated that he was a medical professional, being a professor on the faculty of Yale School of Medicine, and that he was satisfied that his son was 'a little shocked but unharmed'. 'We're all more upset than he is,' said WHITMAN.

A check was made of the other children (aged between 11 and 12) upstairs, who appeared agitated but settled. All children confirmed they were okay.

Officer recommended that minor Daniel WHITMAN be monitored through the night and that a second opinion be sought in the morning if he showed any ill effects.

NO FURTHER ACTION

17

Sarah

I couldn't read Abigail's face after I told her she was wrong. Told her there was no way Harper could have hurt Daniel by witchcraft – and no reason, surely, for her to hurt Daniel at all. I don't know if what she said about a witness going to the police is true, but it's shaken me to the core. Because even though the allegation is false, there's one awful problem about proving it.

Which means I can't let my daughter go another day without speaking to me. So when I've pulled myself together, I smear an enchantment around Harper's bedroom door.

It's not long after sunrise, and I'm dozing in my grandmother's rocking chair in the kitchen, taking a break from some insomniac late-night ingredient prep, when my spell activates and every clock, bell and chime in the house rings at once.

Harper bursts in, furious. When did my girl get so *angry*?

'What the fuck, Mom? You hexed my door?'

'We need to talk. I never ask where you go, but you've missed two days of school, and a lot more besides.'

'Not likely. There's nothing to miss in this place.'

And I know she means school, and parking-lot gossip, and coffee-shop hangouts – all the usual routines of teen life. But that *nothing to miss* cuts deeper than my blood-offering blade.

'Harper, I'm serious. Sit down.'

Sullenly, she drops onto a kitchen chair, drawing her feet up to the edge of the seat. She rests her chin on her knees and watches me.

'What?'

How do you tell your child that she's been accused of murder? How do you tell your daughter, bereft of the gift, that she's been accused of doing it by witchcraft? How to explain that a woman who has known her since she was born believes her capable of it?

I have to try. Without scaring her, I have to tell her the truth. Speaking feels more difficult than any spell.

'I had a visit from Abigail. She told me that someone has gone to the police and testified that you were responsible for Daniel's death.'

Harper goes rigid. That sullen gaze turns shocked and disbelieving.

'At the party?'

'It's ridiculous, of course. But it's going to mean that detective will be back with more questions.'

'That's impossible. I was nowhere near Dan when he fell. I was on the stairs and he was on the landing.'

And here's the hardest part. The subject that it felt like betrayal even to discuss with Abigail: my daughter's lack of the gift. I reproach my friend (if she still *is* my friend) for forcing me to reopen this wound.

'The witness says you did it by witchcraft.'

'By witchcraft?' Harper repeats. Then I'm amazed to hear her laugh. 'Well, in that case, there's nothing to worry about.'

'I'm afraid it's not that simple, darling.'

I can hardly bear to tell her. While the United States legal system is perfectly happy to indict crimes *performed* by magic, it doesn't permit evidence *obtained* by magic. Thank Alexander Hamilton and his *Federalist Papers* cronies. They got it written

73

in as an amendment: *None shall be convicted or acquitted upon evidence derived by means unnaturall*. The logic was that witches would cover up for each other – that they'd *always* say that magic wasn't used – or that they'd try to shift blame by accusing the innocent. In short, that witches were fundamentally untrustworthy.

What that means is that Harper's failed Rite of Determination can't be used to prove to a court that she lacks the gift. And guess what? Science has no way of telling either. There's no finger-prick test. Our blood doesn't glow. Our DNA doesn't have a third spiral, or our gene sequence an extra letter. Medicine draws a big fat blank when it comes to identifying us.

Essentially, once someone says they've seen you use magic, proving that you're *not* a witch is as impossible now as it was back when they ducked you in the village pond and the only proof of innocence was drowning.

I sense Harper coiling tight as I explain all this as gently as I can, and find myself almost afraid of the outburst that's surely coming.

'Who said it?' she demands. 'Who's the witness?'

'I've no idea. Abigail wouldn't tell me.'

'Jake. I bet it was that loser Jake Bolt.'

My blood runs cold. Because of course if it *was* Jake Bolt, the chief's son, then I imagine his word will carry more weight in a court of law than that of your average teen. Not to mention that Tad isn't likely to have officers working overtime to prove his son a liar.

I've always got on just fine with Tad Bolt. He's not one of those lawmen who see witches as low-hanging fruit when the team is a few results short of its targets. The fact that he's consulted me occasionally about his 'stubborn little problem' might be part of it.

But if his son is on the record as Harper's accuser, my little girl is in a whole world of trouble.

How the hell am I going to fix this?

18

Abigail

Julia and Bridget arrive at the same time. As I open the door, I wonder if they've been conferring on my doorstep about my summons.

We hug, and they examine me anxiously. Have I been sleeping? Have I been eating? They're relieved to see me washed and dressed. After all, they've often heard me repeat that simple truth I learned when studying for the psychiatry career I gave up: that maintaining the appearance of something can help bring about the reality of it.

In this case, that by *appearing* to cope, I'll *be* coping. Except that's not quite correct. There's only one thing keeping me going, and it's not a shower and a full face of makeup. It's ensuring Daniel's death is answered for.

I take them through to the conservatory. Michael is back from campus but has shut himself in his study to work on a paper. Despite my pleas, he's barely put an arm around me in comfort. If I'd thought what's happened would change him at all, I was wrong.

'Not like Sarah to be the last to arrive,' says Bridget.

'She's not coming.'

I pour the iced tea and tell them everything. Tad and Jake's visit. Jake's video of Harper using magic to kill my son. Sarah's flat denial when I confronted her. Her insistence that her daughter doesn't have magic.

When I finish, I'm aware of my two friends looking at me with the condescending sympathy of parents comforting a toddler who's insisting that there really *are* monsters under the bed.

'You know we're here for you, Abigail,' Julia says gently.

'And you're doing so well,' Bridget adds. 'Keep taking it one day at a time.'

They don't believe me.

'You're not listening,' I say. 'There's evidence that Sarah's daughter *killed my son*.'

'We heard you, but you can't ask us to take sides in this.' Julia darts a glance at Bridget to check she's okay with that 'we', and Bridge nods. 'Not on the word of a schoolboy.'

'Not *any* schoolboy. Jake. The chief's son.'

'Jake,' says Bridget, 'worshipped Daniel, fixated on Harper, and is probably half out of his mind with grief right now.'

'But what's on his phone *proves* it,' I hiss.

'Harper waving her hands and looking angry?' says Julia. 'I don't see how that proves anything.'

'Though they'd recently split up, right?' Bridget says, and I wonder if she's reconsidering. 'Some big scene in the school cafeteria.'

'Right. Bea told me Dan ended it, and very publicly,' Julia agrees. 'But that's hardly a motive. I cried for a week when my first serious boyfriend dumped me, but I certainly didn't murder him.'

'Abi.' Bridget lays a hand on my arm. 'Harper isn't even a witch. We all know that. She would have had to declare it.'

'We *don't* know that. We've been *told* it. You know Sarah's not as bothered about rules as she pretends. And she's got the secrets of half the town locked away in that filing cabinet. I bet she's done things for each of us here that no one else knows about . . .'

I look at the pair of them in turn. Julia shifts uneasily in her seat.

Upstairs, Michael's chair rolls on the floorboards of his study. I remember the day I went to Sarah, at my wits' end that this intelligent, promising man I'd married was stalling in his career. He had tenure, but hadn't advanced. I remember asking her — begging her — if she couldn't somehow make a difference.

How carefully she prepared. How many of Michael's possessions I had to gather and bodily tokens I had to harvest. A snip of hair, under the guise of tidying him up. A prick of blood that I told him I wanted to send off for 'ancestry analysis', and which earned me a lecture on how such tests are nonsense. The oils I had to dab on him in his sleep; the potions to slip into his drinks. The ritual Sarah and I performed in the study, drawing lines of power around his desk.

And then the results. The incredible results. How Michael's latent ambition and charisma broke out and achieved the results of which I had always known he was capable. The prestige research grants. The keynote invitations. The professorship.

I never told Julia or Bridget about it. But that's okay, because I'd wager they've asked Sarah for similar things over the years.

And so what if that meant Michael spending ever more time on campus, in the lab, or away at conferences? So what if, over the years, his confidence turned to arrogance? I had my little coping mechanisms. And I had Daniel. I gave my son the perfect home I'd always dreamed of. It was worth it, all of it, for him.

And now . . .

Now Julia is looking at me with pity — and isn't *that* ridiculous, when her husband was one of my coping mechanisms.

Her husband, who swore he loved me and would leave Julia. Except in the end, it was *me* Alberto walked away from without a backward glance.

'I'm not taking sides without evidence I can see for myself, Abigail. I'm sorry. I know this is hellishly hard on you. I can't imagine . . .' Julia shudders. 'But this isn't how you fix it. You're distraught. Jake's distraught. My daughter's in pieces. Bridget was telling me Izzy's having nightmares. This needs to be wrapped up, not dragged out, or it's going to affect all our kids.'

'Well it's certainly affected my kid,' I say. 'He's lying in a freezer with half his face burned off.'

'Christ, Abi!' Bridget yelps.

Julia gets up to leave. Have I shocked her? I'm not sorry. I'm not going to sit meekly in a corner looking sad, while everyone tiptoes around mouthing useless sympathy. Daniel's gone, but he still needs me. I'll fight for him with or without my friends' support.

'Come on, Bridget,' Julia says.

It's funny Bridget likes cats so much, because she's such a pack animal, a follower. When the pack splits, which way will Bridget go?

'Sarah can help you through this,' she says to me. 'Don't turn on her. Turn *to* her. There's nothing she wouldn't do for us – you of all people know that.'

She stands to join Julia. She tries to pull me up for a hug, but I'm suddenly too dizzy to rise. Words and images are blending in my head, and they're coming together to form something I hardly dare look at.

Sarah's not bothered about rules.

He's lying in a freezer.

There's nothing she wouldn't do for us – you of all people know that.

79

What if I put Bridget's words to the test?

And when Sarah refuses – because of *course* she'll refuse – I have the perfect way to change her mind.

19

Sarah

With Harper in danger from Jake's false allegation, I have to do *something*.

So I'm driving along Shore Road toward the ruins of Sailaway Villa. I need to confirm for myself that magic wasn't used that night.

My word on it wouldn't count in court, both because of the rules on evidence and because I'm the mother of the accused. But once I'm certain, I'll go for help to the Moot, our national magical association, if these lies about Harper's involvement are taken any further.

The Moot has been around for more than a century. It has spent decades campaigning against the shitty way the law treats us. There's a whole bunch of charges for even attempting certain acts by witchcraft – from seducing a minor to raising the dead. And for regular crime, sentences get an automatic uplift if magic is used. If robbing a store gets you two years, and robbing one violently with a gun gets you five, robbing one using magic gets you ten.

The Moot picks its battles. But a teenage girl charged with murder by witchcraft, when not a scrap of magic was used, will be something they can't ignore. The Moot is a respected body. One of its senior members is married to a California state senator. (Of course, we magicals can't run for public office ourselves, as we supposedly might bewitch people into voting for us.)

If I can persuade the Moot to inspect the villa and confirm that no magic was used there, how could any court refuse to acknowledge that?

More of the villa than I expected is still standing. The giveaway of what happened here is the blown windows. Each one is blackened with soot round the edges, like evil itself crawled out of every hole it could find.

Hazard tape crisscrosses the doorway, and ten meters out the cops have driven metal stakes into the ground and set up a flimsy cordon that flaps in the breeze. I duck beneath it.

One of my best friend's children died here – a boy I've known since he was born. And not for the first time, I cry for Daniel Whitman. I remember that his first word was 'more', and that he had a phase in which he'd eat only orange food. I was there when he cried because his first bicycle was red, not blue. I remember when I caught him sneaking quarters from my purse, age ten, even though Abigail and Michael gave him an allowance.

I remember that night at Bridget's house.

Dan was a complex boy. As he got older and excelled at football, he became full of himself. I wondered if that was because Abigail adored him, and maybe because Michael was a distant father, and if so, whether either of those things was my fault.

I remember my surprise when Harper told me she was dating him.

My horror as I read Harper's frantic texts from the party.

What *happened* at this villa that night?

I'd worried about leaving footprints, but the thick ash on the floor has been churned by dozens of feet – partygoers, forensics and police. If it held any secrets, they're long since lost.

Or lost to the naked eye, at least.

I reach into my Whole Foods tote and pull out a long hazel switch. It's forked, and I take one slender prong in each hand.

I've had my sticks since I was twelve years old. My grandmother drove me into the countryside one full-moon night, when I was on a sleepover. (My mom always knew those times were when we did witch stuff, but she never asked for details.) Gramma rubbed my hands with mistletoe juice, tied a red thread round each wrist and laid her silver sickle in my palm. Then she led me uphill to a coppice and explained what I was looking for.

It took me about an hour to select the sticks I now hold. Gramma coached me through the words and gestures as I set the blade to the wood. Once I'd made the cut, I sliced my thumb and sealed the tiny stump with blood. That's how magic works. It's an exchange. *Something given for something gotten* was how Gramma always put it.

Inside the villa, I hitch the bag on my shoulder and hold the sticks out before me, murmuring the relevant incantations. For hazel divining, I generally use early Celtic. This magic was refined in misty islands, ragged with rocks and betrayal.

The wood vibrates gently in my hand, and despite everything I can't help but smile, because the overwhelming sensation I'm getting here in the entrance is *horniness*. Excitement and anticipation. I can imagine the kids piling in, the girls' confidence boosted by makeup and carefully chosen outfits; the boys' by energy drinks and sheer bravado. I remember what eighteen felt like, and it was potent as any drug.

An emotional tide from the partygoers washes through me as I go deeper into the house. Beneath the hormones I feel the tug of darker currents: anxiety, insecurity, jealousy and longing.

I lower my rod as I move into the central hallway, taking it in first with just my eyes. The fire was fiercest in here, and I'll be no use to Harper if I break a leg falling through floorboards. Opposite are the stairs. The round head of the newel post at the bottom is charred like some fetish doll burned to curse its human likeness. The middle part of the stairs is gone, then the bannister resumes. It curves up past a high, wide wall, its once-white expanse streaked with gray and black like some abstract canvas for which Julia would pay a fortune.

At the top is the landing from which Daniel fell. The balustrade is still intact. Well above waist height for me, it'd be lower on a tall boy like Daniel. It's not hard to imagine him tripping, or staggering drunkenly, and momentum and his own centre of gravity conspiring to pull him over.

My eyes trace the path of his brief descent. There. The middle of the open atrium is where he would have landed. If he'd gone over head first it would have been an almost clinical snap of the neck.

It's all too familiar.

A dark idea grips me, but I force it down and go back to playing cop.

I picture the panic as Dan fell. Did the kids rush to help him, or stand back in horror? Was he still alive after he fell? Could he have been saved?

Could *I* have saved him, if I'd been here?

But there was also the fire. It must have flared up fast. An accident, or a prank gone wrong. I can see kids stampeding toward the door. Dragging in deep breaths of the fresh air outside, fingers hitting 911 on their phones, telling themselves the first responders would deal with both the fire and their injured friend.

No wonder poor Abigail is half mad with her loss. And maybe what's eating Harper is guilt, if she got the hell out of there with everyone else and left Daniel behind. I need to tell her there's no shame in that. Self-preservation is our most fundamental instinct – only parenthood overrides it.

That's all my brain can figure out of what might have happened here. Will my craft tell the same story?

I try to steady my hands as I lift my sticks again, bracing myself for what I know is coming. I'll be tuning in to it all: those kids' panic and fear, their horror and grief.

And I screw my eyes shut as it hits. It's too much emotion, from too many people. Too intense. It rips through me like claws.

Which is when the second thing hits me, and I gasp and fall to my knees. The sticks fall from my trembling fingers. I gag and spit acid bile into the ash so I don't choke.

Magic.

Powerful, brutal magic.

Enough to burn a house and break a boy.

And I realize what I've somehow never known until now: I'm not the only witch in Sanctuary.

20
Maggie

'Uh, boss?'

It's Chester. I've been reading over my old attendance log from six years ago, trying to work out if the fact that it shares a cast with my current investigation means anything or is pure coincidence, when my assistant sticks his head round my door.

'Phone call. Beryl Varley at the *Sentinel*. She's their news editor – a sensible sort.'

'Got it.'

As the phone connects, I'm braced for a question about whether it's true that we have a murder-by-witchcraft allegation, because in a place like Sanctuary, word about Jake's testimony is bound to get out sooner rather than later. Time for a trusty old 'We cannot comment.'

But when she comes on the line, it appears that Beryl Varley isn't that sort of operator. I guess this *is* a local paper, not *The Washington Post*. Varley lives alongside the people she writes about.

'Our intern just brought something to my attention,' she says. 'Relating to the Whitman tragedy. I figured you'd want to know.'

'Much appreciated, Ms Varley.'

'It's ugly. But . . .' she laughs uncertainly, 'you're a cop. You'll have seen much worse. Only, why do girls these days let these pictures be taken? They must know they'll end up all over the internet. I'll send you the link. It's a . . . a whatchamacallit? A screenshot. I'll send you the screenshot, Officer, 'cos apparently these things often get deleted real quick.'

'That's very kind, ma'am.' I've barely spelled out my email address before she's off again.

'And on the tribute page in Daniel's memory, too. It's just disgusting. What must his poor mother think? You've got to wonder if these youngsters aren't totally out of control.'

Beryl Varley's views are from another era, but I bet they make for popular opinion pieces — it's always easier to blame young people than to help them. I'm picturing a cardigan-clad old dear, maybe a graduate from one of the less distinguished women's colleges, when she slips in a question so easily I've almost answered before I realize what she's done.

'I take it Harper Fenn isn't a person of interest in Daniel Whitman's death, Officer?'

'I'm sorry, Ms Varley, but I won't be making any comment at this stage. You know how it is. Thank you so much for reaching out.'

I hang up to forestall any more unwelcome questions, the receiver suddenly slippery in my palm. Which is when it dawns on me for the first time what a colossal media shitstorm this case is going to be if Jake Bolt persists in his story and his father backs him.

No one's been executed for unnatural homicide in this country for years. That's probably because the last high-profile trial went down as one of the biggest scandals in legal history. It was a cautionary tale in a wrongful-conviction seminar back at police academy, and it's the sort of story that stays with you.

Somewhere in Pennsylvania in the 1950s, two rich folks were found dead in their bed. There was no sign of foul play, so their only son inherited. Then a couple years later some girl went to the cops and said the son had bragged that he'd killed his parents and gotten away with it. Turned out he'd made the same boast to a few other women, too. But just as the son seemed bound for the electric chair, he pointed the finger at his parents' maid, a Polish girl named Agnes Nowak.

Agnes was a witch, he said. She'd been in love with him and believed his parents prevented their marriage – and so had killed them with a curse. Bit by damning bit, evidence against her was unearthed. Spell-work trinkets knotted into one of his father's handkerchiefs and sprayed with his mother's perfume. And crucially, a backstreet midwife who swore the girl had asked for an abortion because her lover refused to marry her, even though she'd killed his parents to clear the way for them.

Nowak admitted to being a witch and to being in love with the son, who had indeed gotten her pregnant, though she'd lost the baby. But she denied any part in his parents' deaths. In court, the son had lawyers and a parade of witnesses. So it was Agnes that went to the electric chair. And there the case might have ended if the abortionist hadn't confessed on her deathbed that she had been paid and her testimony scripted.

A campaign saw Agnes pardoned, thirty years too late. Is Sanctuary ready to be the centre of another scandalous trial of a teenage girl?

The 'new mail' alert jangles on my screen.

Here goes.

The image loads slowly on this crappy computer, gradually sharpening from fuzzy lo-res, and this drawn-out reveal somehow makes the whole thing worse, even more obscene.

The first distinguishable thing is a young man's jeans-clad rear. The pants are settled low and gaping on the buttocks in a way that suggests they're unbuttoned at the front. A slender girl's leg dangles outside his thigh.

The next section of the picture makes it unmistakable what's going on. Mercifully, you can't see too much of the girl's body, but there's a jut of hipbone and a gleam of thigh. Her jeans and a panty string are bunched below her pushed-apart knees. He's not even touching her, except where their bodies are joined.

The girl's upper body is clothed − mostly. She's wearing a long-sleeved T-shirt, the bottom pulled up exposing one breast. Her skin looks sickly pale in the dim light of the bedroom, and coiling tattoos are blurrily visible on her abdomen.

I know who these two must be, and the final portion of the photo confirms it. That's Harper, her head thrown back on the bedcover, mouth open and eyes closed. The boy's back is to the camera, but he has a quarterback's broad shoulders and a sport jersey, and his haircut is an ultra-short, almost military style familiar from pictures of Daniel Whitman.

The screenshot ends with the post displayed above the picture. It's short and to the point.

Harper Fenn is a slut and a liar.

And worse.

The poster hasn't minced his words with the choice of username, either: *SanctuaryslutXposer* − and heck am I tired of only ever seeing that word applied to the girl in these sorts of situations.

I sit back and exhale. I'm looking at a screen grab from the sex tape that got projected at the party. No wonder Harper went ballistic, just like Jake described. What an absolutely gross violation of privacy.

Another thought occurs to me as I study the picture. How was this filmed? The angle means the camera can't be in Dan's hand. But did he set up his phone somewhere to record − or was someone else in the room with them? From this still image, I can't tell.

What about whoever made this ugly post? *SanctuaryslutX-poser* doesn't come right out and call Harper a murderer, just *a slut and a liar*. But that *and worse* plainly hints at more. Do they know about Jake Bolt's accusation?

Could the poster be Jake himself?

'Forwarding you an email, Chester,' I tell my assistant. 'It's got a website link and image attachment. Make sure the computer guys archive that asap. Flag it as explicit with an under-eighteen warning – "need-to-see" only. I've a few calls to make.'

This photo is in the hands of a journalist – one who is either sufficiently well informed or just plain astute enough to be asking questions about whether Harper Fenn is a suspect in Daniel's death. With Chief Bolt having a conflict of interests, I should loop in my boss back at the state level.

I have to follow protocol, to make sure my ass is covered. But there's rather more than my reputation at stake. There's a teen girl accused of witchcraft, facing a barbaric penalty. The clock ticks counting down till this story breaks just got louder and louder. And when it goes, it's gonna go big.

21

Abigail

I've knocked at Sarah's door twice, but no response. Her car is gone.

That's fine. I'll wait however long it takes.

Bridget's words run through my head, and I'm aware that I'm tapping the steering wheel as I say them to myself, over and over, like it's a promise. Like it's a spell.

There's nothing she wouldn't do for us.

Sheer curiosity drew me to Sarah when we first met in antenatal class. Our paths would never have crossed otherwise. You don't meet witches at the golf club or the spa, or accidentally get seated next to one at a dinner party. I'd always thought only gullible people used their services. I remember when Sarah laughed and told me she thought the same about therapists – she knew by then that I'd trained to be one.

That was when we hit it off. That, plus the fact that we were both attending classes alone. Sarah didn't have a partner on the scene, while Michael was sitting at home staring at his unfinished research papers, terrified about how we were going to raise a child on a barely tenured salary.

There's nothing she wouldn't do for us.

I saw the witch paraphernalia at Sarah's house when I went over for baby play dates. Bridget was Sarah's only non-magical assistant at that time, and I was eager to try it myself, lending her my energies as she crafted a simple enchantment.

I'll never forget the thrill when her magic touched me and drew from me the first time. It was a little like breastfeeding. To let someone else draw strength from you, but to want to keep on giving, however much they take.

I was tired after that first time. And the bigger magics I've helped with since can be exhausting. But you still want to give. Once a spell starts, it's almost as if you're hypnotized. The witch is the only one who can break that flow of energy and step away.

'You're dangerous people,' I told Sarah.

I'd meant it as a joke, but she took it deadly seriously. Started talking about how the foundational principle of magic was consent. How witches all stuck scrupulously to the law.

Well, that last bit isn't quite true, is it, Sarah?

There's nothing she wouldn't do for us.

It was our children that first brought us together. So it seems only right – almost destined – that the fate of our children is intertwined like this now.

There's nothing *I* wouldn't do for *you*, my darling Daniel.

From where I'm parked, in front of the house, I see movement at a window. Sarah has arrived home and gone in the back way.

I have to knock several times, and it's only once she's pulled back a curtain and seen that it's me that she opens the door. She looks pale and sweaty.

I'm half afraid she won't let me in, after our last encounter, but I've an excuse ready.

'I've run out of the potion. I need some more.'

'So you *were* taking it?' She looks relieved. 'I was worried – I thought . . . Come in.'

She leads me to the kitchen, chattering as if she's afraid of what I'll say if I have a chance to speak. As if I might name another witness who saw her daughter kill my son.

I say nothing, just let her bustle about. She's finding my silence unnerving. Whatever part of me feels a pang at what I'm doing to this woman, my friend, is buried beneath my rage at what her daughter did to my son – and my determination that she'll set it all right.

There's nothing she wouldn't do for us. For me. For Dan. But most especially for Harper. I'm betting that to save her daughter, Sarah Fenn will do *anything*.

She finally turns to me.

'Have you heard anything more about the investigation? Jake's evidence?'

'I daresay it's with the appropriate authorities.'

I wanted to intimidate Sarah, but something I've said satisfies her. It takes me a moment to realize that I didn't correct her mention of Jake. She's not as distracted as I thought.

Too late now. In fact, it might even help that she knows it's Jake. He's devoted to Daniel too. Sarah will understand that he'll support me all the way. And so will his dad, the chief.

'I'm not here for your potion. I'm not drinking it – I know why you want to keep me calm and tranquil. I'm here because I want Daniel back.'

Sarah ignores my barb. Her expression is kind.

'I don't do seances, Abi. Channelings. It's illegal, and you know I don't think those messages are real – from the deceased, I mean.'

'I'm not talking about a seance. I said *I want him back*.'

The silence stretches out between us.

'That's not possible. It can't be done.'

'You did it once before – or nearly.'

'*Nearly*.' The word comes out like a sob. 'Abi, I'm so sorry. I can't. Believe me, you're not the first to ask. If it was . . . calling him back at the threshold . . . I don't know. I would try – for you. But he's been dead for days. He's in the *morgue*.'

'Michael could get him out. We'd say we're transferring his body to the faculty hospital at Yale.'

Sarah is shaking her head wildly. She's acting as if I've led her to the edge of a cliff and have ordered her to jump.

'His body's all *burned*. There's nothing I can do. I wish . . .'

'You'll have to do better than *wish*, Sarah. Otherwise your daughter will go on trial. Jake wants Dan back too. When you do it, I'll get him to withdraw his statement.'

'Abigail, how could you explain away a boy *raised from the dead*?'

'I wouldn't explain. I'd just go. Move away and take Dan with me. We'd manage.'

Sarah shrinks a little further away from me. So I lean in and grip her wrist, hard.

'My son's life for your daughter's innocence. Isn't that exactly what your Old Work says: *something given for something gotten*. Let me know when you're ready.'

22

Maggie

I need to own this case before it owns me.

So far I have:

– one dead boy, and a preliminary autopsy result that tells me he died of a broken neck

– one accuser, who claims that the boy's fatal fall was due to magic

– one accused, the deceased's ex-girlfriend, who may have been after revenge for being dumped

– one item of footage appearing to show her using magic, although she's not commonly believed to be a witch

– one publicly posted photograph showing the deceased and the accused engaged in sexual activity. If non-consensual, that could provide a more substantial motive, but it's impossible to tell from the picture alone.

And now Chester's just added to the list. He's chased up the toxicology report on the corpse.

'No drugs whatsoever,' he says. 'Barely any alcohol. Which makes sense, 'cos Whitman was an athlete, going to college on a scholarship. He wouldn't risk that.'

'So much for the it-was-a-drunken-stumble hypothesis.'

'Yup.'

We both sit there. *What am I not seeing?*

'It all comes back to Jake Bolt's claim that Harper was using magic,' I say. 'We need to stand that up or knock it down.'

'Get someone to look at the video?'

'Maybe. There are other ways, too. Witches can detect strong emotion residue on objects and in places – think murder weapons and crime scenes. And they can also tell whether magic was used.'

'*Evidence derived by unnatural means is inad—*' Chester begins, but I hold up a hand to stop him.

'Yeah, yeah. You can't use it *in court*. But you can use it for clues and nudges in your investigation, as long as you then stand those up independently with police work.'

He's still looking skeptical. So it's time to share a story I keep close to my heart. I can't let myself think of it too often.

'Colleague of mine had an abduction case. He located a vehicle that fitted witness descriptions, but forensics couldn't find any traces in the car. He trusted his gut, though, so he drafted in a witch. She identified recent fear and trauma in that vehicle. It kept my colleague going, even when the car owner had a solid-gold alibi. And he got there in the end, the old-fashioned way. That witch's work gave him the confidence he needed to persist.'

I don't tell Chester that the colleague was my partner, and that one of those who said the car was a dead-end lead was me.

I don't tell Chester that though we caught the perp, we were too late to save his victim. We found Jenny Downes still chained where he'd confined her, emaciated and dehydrated. With our investigation dragging on, her abductor had spooked and simply stopped visiting. Jenny was so weak she suffered heart failure and passed away in hospital a few hours later, though not before identifying a photo of the man who took her. I couldn't look her in the eye as she thanked us, before she died with her family at her side.

She was fifteen years old.

I'll never put anyone else at risk by being rigid about how policing should be done.

'I'm thinking an independent magical investigator is what we need to move forward,' I tell him. 'Search online for a reputable one. Make sure they're based as far away from Connecticut as possible – we can't have anyone who might know the Fenns. I'll need permission to engage them, though. I'll go get that in person.'

Meaning: I've no desire to have Chester, still less the Sanctuary rank and file, and definitely not Chief Bolt, hear me getting bawled out by my boss.

Lieutenant Remy Lamarr is one helluva bawler.

23
Maggie

It's less than ninety minutes to Middletown along the I-95, and the drive does me good.

It's the first time I've left Sanctuary since I got assigned, and I feel free out on the open highway, instead of among the winding streets of the historic quarter where Sarah Fenn lives, or the endless suburbs where even the sunlight is tastefully filtered through trimmed trees.

HQ is a low smoky-glass building, stretching out in two wings like a pair of arms just waiting to wrap you in the loving embrace of the law. You can hear Remy from down the hall. I sometimes wonder if he F-bombs his children's bedtime stories, or yells pillow talk with his husband. But the thing about Lieutenant Remy Lamarr is that even while he shouts in your face, he has your back.

I knock, and with a final barked command Remy slams down the phone and waves me in. He sits in his usual freakishly upright posture as he listens to my account. I'm trying to lead him toward what I want – permission to use a magical investigator – while letting him think the idea was all his. His eyes gleam, and I wonder if I've succeeded or if he's seen right through me.

'So lemme get this right, Mags. You've got a kid dead and a house burned. And instead of this being what to anyone in their right mind it would appear *obvious* it is – a frat party gone wrong – you have half-assed allegations of homicide-by-witchcraft flying around. Presumably on fucking broomsticks.'

I cringe. Broomstick jokes have been ruled *offensive and discriminatory language* when applied to witches – an easy way to an automatic misconduct mark for any serving officer. But Remy sails on, unfazed.

'And the cherry on top of this multi-tiered, candy-covered shit cake is that said homicide-by-witchcraft triggers some ancient rule from back when sackcloth was a fashion statement that the perpetrator be put to death. And your alleged perp is . . . a seventeen-year-old schoolgirl? What a fucking shambles.'

'That about covers it, sir.'

'So, what do you propose to do, Detective Knight? Want me to toss it to the Feds? Let them fuck it up – or deal with the fallout from executing a child. They *wouldn't* execute her, of course. There's no way in hell the governor would stand for it. But even the possibility is gonna stink.'

Remy's words send a chill down my spine. Hearing him say it somehow makes an unthinkable scenario seem horribly possible. Harper Fenn, with her haunted eyes, on death row for however long it takes lawyers to wrangle over her fate? And despite Remy's confidence, I see no guarantee of clemency.

'I'm no lawyer, sir, but the way it's written, I don't think the governor would have the power to overturn it. It'd have to go all the way up.'

Our governor here in Connecticut may be a card-carrying liberal, but right now the White House and the Senate are conservative. They've got an electorate to answer to, and red states look less kindly on witchcraft than blue states. The Supreme Court isn't exactly witch-friendly these days, either.

'The girl's not registered?'

'She's not quite eighteen, but no. The school and local hospital don't have a PMP notification, and her mother, who's the local witch, swears she doesn't have ability.'

'So it won't be witchcraft, then.'

'The accuser is the town chief's son.'

'What's wrong with these yokels?' Remy steeples his fingers, scowling at the signet ring on his left hand. 'Sure, witchcraft's *great* at finding lost cats and curing earache. But the rest is superstition, a placebo that our ancestors clung to in this country to help them build a life here.'

I don't say anything. Like all cops, Remy is fiercely devoted to the things we can see and touch and prove. He thinks his million-mile-an-hour brain can solve everything. Mostly it can – he's set to make commissioner by the time he's forty.

But sometimes even a brain like his isn't enough. It wasn't on the Jenny Downes case. I know Remy was as broken up as I was by our failure to reach Jenny in time. I've laid emphasis on the party villa as the place where any alleged crime – or magic – happened and am hoping he'll make the connection himself.

He does.

'How about getting a magical investigator to rule out the presence of witchcraft? That frees you to figure out what actually happened. You said the boy was clean? A fault with the property, then. Something gave way, he fell. Insurance company can take the hit of a civil suit by the parents. We all know that grief wants answers, but sometimes life just serves up shit for giggles.

'And if the witness and his pop the chief kick off about you not taking their claim seriously, I'll back you up. A kid throwing around wild allegations of witchcraft? He's upset. It's only natural. Just shows how much he cares, right? A *super-nice* kid, not a *wacko* kid. Everyone comes out of this shit pile smelling like roses. Am I clear?'

'Crystal clear, Remy.'

'Good girl, Mags. See you back here soon. I'm missing our donut dates.'

I grin. Remy's in the gym at six every morning, and I don't think he's so much as looked at a bad carb in his life.

I've got the permission I needed. And I've got Remy's support. I'll have this straightened out soon.

24

Abigail

It's been a week.

A year. An eternity. Every day feels endless and unendurable since Dan's accident.

His team has a match tonight – the 'handover', when all the outgoing, college-bound players face off against the upcoming talent that'll be replacing them.

Do I want it to be its usual riotous fun, to distract me? Seeing Dan's beloved friends – Freddie and the rest – will surely lift my spirits.

Or do I want an evening of grief and mourning, to know the boys are all equally devastated? Can I measure out their love for Dan in their sorrow now he's gone?

Coach greets me and Michael before the match and keeps us talking. I'm convinced we'll miss the kickoff, until he checks his watch and leads us to our seats – and then I understand. As we enter, the crowd in the stadium rises to its feet. Down on the field, the band strikes up the Spartans' fight song. Only no one's singing. They're all silent. The boys lined up on the field have their hands over their hearts.

My breath catches. The huge digital scoreboard is showing a photo of Dan. It's his team portrait, his grilled helmet tucked under his arm. The strapline at the bottom displays his name alongside the Spartans' insignia. There are figures below it, but they're not, as usual, his performance stats.

They are his birthday and the date a week ago. The day he died.

I stifle a sob and Michael's arm comes round me. He pulls me tight. Too tight. He's trying to stop me doing something stupid, like bursting into hysterics. Or tearing my shoes off and hurling them at the scoreboard, because I don't want to see those dates there. I want to see Dan's passing yards, his touchdowns and completions.

The boys take their positions. I can't bear to look at the former student they've drafted in to take Dan's place on the senior team. With a final flourish of the drum, the game begins.

Michael is at my side. His eyes track the players, but I'm not sure he's taking much in. He was never a field-side father. He'd be at home or in the lab, working. Does he regret that now? I study his face for any clue, but it's been years since I could tell what he was thinking.

Without Dan on the field, the game holds no interest for me either, and I'm glad when it's over.

As the two teams mingle for the post-game handshake, I hear Dan's name over the loudspeakers. I recognize the voice: Freddie McConaughey, the Spartans' best wide receiver and Dan's closest friend, after Jacob.

'. . . and his parents are with us tonight. Mrs Whitman, Professor Whitman, I speak for the whole team when I say that Dan's loss has left a massive, *massive* hole not just in our offensive line, but in our hearts and our lives.'

The whole stadium has gone quiet and the floodlights have dimmed. There's just a spotlight on Freddie, microphone in his big ball-catching hands. On either side of him, the Spartans have lined up, helmets off and heads bowed. The coaching team and the refs have their caps in their hands.

Coach takes the microphone and describes Daniel's talent. How he knew from the first season he saw him play that he had amazing potential.

'He'll always be part of this team,' he says. '*Spartana semper.*'

He holds out the mic and the stadium crowd roars it back at him: '*Spartana semper!*' *Always a Spartan.*

Now each of the Spartans is taking turns to say a sentence or two. What they learned from Daniel. How much they liked and admired him. A few tell funny stories and the stadium reverberates with affectionate laughter. These boys are as devoted to Dan's memory as they were to him in life.

Which is when the thought comes to me — could I *use* that devotion?

'Please stand, everyone,' Freddie says, reclaiming the mic. 'We were silent before the game, but now let's sing this so loud that Dan can hear us up there.'

A girl steps forward, one of the team's cheerleaders, and lifts her voice in a soaring soprano rendition of the team fight song. Everyone around me rises to their feet. Somewhere close by, a girl is sobbing and smiling. Men's voices are hoarse.

Photos of Dan flash on the scoreboard. Laughing with his teammates. Reaching for the ball. Concentrating as he lines up a throw. Beaming as he shakes hands with the scout who matched him with his college team.

'Dan the Man!' Freddie bellows. 'We love you!'

He leads the stadium in three rousing cheers that make the stands shake. The boys jog off the field and their energy thrums through me too.

It feels like anything is possible. Anything at all. I just have to make it so.

I slip from my seat and go find Freddie. There's useful work he and his teammates could do.

25
Sarah

I think all witches, unconsciously, are waiting for the day something like this happens. It's a when-not-if situation that magical parents have to prepare their kids for.

I have protections on the house, of course. But they're not strong – they can't be, given how cheek-by-jowl properties are in this old part of town. Our house fronts onto the sidewalk, which means I can't put wards *around* it. The charmed bundles that hang above the doorways and windows ensure that someone needs me to open up for them to enter.

But we're not permitted to do much more than that. Unlike guns, 'defensive' use of magic isn't recognized in law. Witchcraft is considered offensive in all circumstances: even in self-protection if assaulted, even under stand-your-ground if attacked at home.

This was no assault. There was no violence in the things they used: eggs, flour and paint. But there's menace in it. Contempt and threat.

I felt sick when I first saw it. They came to our home in the middle of the night and did this. Thank the goddess Harper wasn't here.

I'd actually been woken in the early hours by male voices whooping from the street. But in Sanctuary, as in many places, the 'historic' district also means the tourist district. There are hotels and bars down this way. Things do get a little rowdy. So I turned over and willed myself back to sleep.

I saw it the minute I came downstairs, though. My first thought was that it was blood, dripping down the windows, and I called the cops. A patrol car dropped off that nice Greenstreet boy. His grandma is an occasional client.

He's a calming presence as I swing between outrage and fear at what this might mean. We're both surveying the damage when a second car pulls up – the detective on Daniel's case.

'Any idea who did this to you?' she asks. 'And any idea why?'

'The fact that it's you here and not a routine patrol shows that we both know *why*. But as for the *who* . . .'

She nods. What kind of person is she, this cop? She went to the hospital to intercept Harper, rather than speaking to my girl at home when I could be present. Why would she do that?

She will have heard Jake Bolt's accusations. Does she believe him – the son of her law enforcement colleague? Does she find him a credible witness?

How does she feel about magic?

I can't read Detective Maggie Knight's face as she studies the mess of my house. Then she frowns.

'What's the significance of that, there?'

Mostly the paint has been splashed on. But there's one bit plainly done by spray can – a slanted downward slash, then an even more skewed vertical, like a toppling 'V'.

Chester Greenstreet is watching Knight as she mimes the movement: down, then up. Down, then up. As she does so, I recognize what mark she's making – or starting to.

She's got it, too. And that tells me this cop is *good*. I don't know whether to be relieved or even more anxious. Will she use her skill to prove my daughter's innocence, or to build a false case against her?

'It's the first two strokes of a pentagram,' she says. 'But then they stopped. Interrupted maybe, which could mean someone saw them. Or they stopped themselves because they realized the consequences.'

'Ma'am?'

'It would be a hate crime, Chester. Marking out witches because of their identity. If it wasn't an interruption, then they didn't finish it because one of them was smart enough to know that.'

'*One of them*? How do you know it was more than one person?'

Knight points out the various substances adorning my house. 'Paint. Flour. Eggs. You ever tried running with all of those in your arms, or a grocery bag? I wouldn't recommend it. And you'd want to get it all done quickly before you're spotted. *Bam-bam-bam*. Many hands make light work.'

She turns to me. 'I need photographs and a sample of that paint. Sergeant Greenstreet here will get that done right away – there's an evidence kit in my car, Chester. Then you can get this cleaned off. Is there someone who can help?'

'Pierre,' I say immediately. 'He's a friend. A home renovator, does decorating, that sort of thing . . .'

'Good. Give him a call.'

My fingers shake as I dial Pierre's number. He's often busy on a job. But I needn't have worried. He picks up promptly. I explain things as matter-of-factly as I can, and he promises to be right over. Only when I end the call do I burst into tears.

What *is* this tawdry threat? Why did someone do this, and why now? It can only be because they believe the allegations against Harper – that pentagram tells me as much.

The detective plainly thinks so too, because she asks where my daughter is, saying she wants to speak to her again.

'Harper's out, Detective. She goes running early most mornings, and after that her comings and goings are a mystery.

Teenagers are like cats – you just have to trust they'll find their way home.'

She nods, plainly surprised that I don't know Harper's every movement or have her under lock and key. But that's not our way of childrearing, whether the child is magical or not. My daughter is a free spirit.

I avoid the stares of my neighbors as the detective gives her sergeant instructions, and none of them have the nerve to ask what happened. It's a relief to see Pierre's van round the corner.

He's outraged at what he sees.

'Jesus, Sarah!' He turns to the detective. 'I hope you plan on finding the creep that did this?'

Maggie Knight is staring at him. I mean, plenty of people stare at Pierre. He's a good-looking guy, his physique kept strong by the work he does and shown off in the T-shirts and jeans he wears to do it. But she's staring like she *recognizes* him.

'Mr Martineau,' she says, holding out a hand for him to shake.

I hadn't mentioned his surname, but then I notice it's written on the side of his van. Stay calm, Sarah. Don't get paranoid.

'I met your daughter a few days ago,' the cop's saying. 'Isobel, right?'

'Izzy?' And Pierre's face breaks into the smile he can't suppress when his daughter is mentioned. 'My little muppet is still fighting off mono. How was she?'

'She was well enough to answer the door to an officer of the law. She's a sweet girl.'

The cop is smiling back. Maybe she was only staring for the same reason all the women do, after all. Jeez, Pierre is such a charmer. I feel better just having him here.

I hope the cop will leave us to it, but as Pierre gets to work unloading a ladder and a tub of paint solvent from the back of his van, Detective Knight turns to me.

'I really need to speak to Harper, Ms Fenn. Would you mind

if I stepped inside to wait for her to come back? I'd appreciate a chat with you, in any event.'

And well-trained witch that I am, I know better than to refuse a police officer.

26

Maggie

It's Harper I want, but in the meantime I've a million and one things to ask her mom. So where to begin?

The question I *won't* be asking is the nagging one that Martineau's appearance has pushed uppermost in my mind. Why, in just the few days I've been back in Sanctuary, I have assembled a full cast from that night six years ago: Abigail Whitman, Bridget Perelli-Lee, Julia Garcia – and now Sarah Fenn and Pierre Martineau. The only kid I saw that night was Daniel Whitman, but my report told me the others were there, too: Harper, Isobel and Beatriz.

Coincidence?

Maybe not. But also not my priority right now.

I've never been in such close proximity to a witch. I've never used the services of one, and there weren't any PMP kids at my school. As Fenn fetches us both a glass of water, I study her face and the way she moves, as if they might give me clues as to the abilities of her and her kind.

She's tall, slender-waisted and broad-hipped, feet wide apart as if they're drawing strength up from the earth like tree roots. Her thick hair is dark chestnut, touched with henna to conceal threading gray.

I imagine generations of women like her: gathering herbs in

the Scottish Highlands, chopping and grinding on stone blocks, scooping rainwater in silver bowls. I picture one woman, who maybe looked a lot like Sarah, rolling her precious charts in oiled goatskin and packing them into a chest. Shepherding her children day after day toward the coast and a ship bound for a new country.

Standing there, strained though she is from the events of this morning, Sarah Fenn possesses an inner stillness that feels a lot like power.

'At this early stage I'm not making public any details of my inquiry,' I say. 'But Sanctuary's a small town. Would I be right in thinking that you're aware your daughter's name has been mentioned?'

I watch her closely. What will her face tell me that her words will not? Very little, as it turns out.

'Yes, I'm aware that Jake Bolt has accused Harper of killing Daniel by witchcraft.'

'I'm going to need to interview your daughter, Ms Fenn. Formally. If I miss her here, can you make sure she attends the station?'

'Of course.'

'She won't be under caution, but she can have you or a lawyer present.'

'I'm sure you're aware that Moot research has shown how, for witch suspects, the presence of a lawyer creates the presumption of guilt in the minds of law enforcement personnel,' Fenn says, a touch sharply.

'I assure you that's not—'

'My daughter's innocent, Detective. I understand she's accused of killing Daniel by witchcraft. She couldn't have done it *that* way, because Harper has no ability. And she couldn't have done it any *other* way, given that she was on the other side of the room from him.'

111

'Okay, that's clear. And you're *certain* your daughter lacks ability? I thought that was unusual? That the gift is inherited?'

'There's a reason it's called a "gift". You accept what you're given. My grandmother was a very capable witch, my mother is giftless; I have ability, my daughter does not. It can be tough, but it's better that way. Imagine if you could selectively breed for magic, like for strong hearts and lungs in racehorses. If two powerful witches produced even more powerful children, and so on, I think we know who'd be running the world right now.'

I did know that there are rare male witches — it made the news when the previous leader of the Moot became the first man in the post for more than a century. But two powerful witches having superpowered witch kiddies? I'd never thought of that, and the notion is chilling.

Then I remember Fenn's jibe about *presumption of guilt*, and check myself. I steer the conversation on.

'Your daughter was dating Daniel Whitman at the time of his death. How long had they been together? Did it seem like a happy relationship?'

Fenn is vague on the details. I get the impression that witch parenting is a hands-off, find-your-own-way sort of thing. But the time frame she gives matches what Cheryl Lee told me. Then my attention is caught.

'Of course their relationship caused friction with Bea.'

'Beatriz Garcia?'

'Yes, she'd been infatuated with Dan for ages. She even asked me once if I could help her draw his attention. So when Dan and Harper got together, it caused a rift between the girls. We had a few mom summits, trying to figure it out, before we decided we had to leave them to it. Then Bea started dating Freddie McConaughey, so it all worked out in the end.'

'Forgive me, Ms Fenn, but were Harper and Daniel intimate?'

'I believe so. My community has an open-minded attitude

toward the body's desires, Officer. Boys of that age tend to want sex, and I never got any sense that Harper didn't feel the same.'

'Did she seem happy with him?'

'What's the relevance of these questions?' Fenn asks. 'Trying to establish a motive? Look, I don't know details of what went on between them, but if every teen girl who has a falling-out with her boyfriend murdered him for it, then America would be depopulated in a generation.'

She smiles. A weak one, but it's there. If she's still capable of smiling, then she can't know about the death penalty, so I end our conversation before it feels like I'm misleading her by not mentioning it. Scribbling down my phone number, I reiterate that I need to talk to Harper.

Outside, Pierre Martineau has finished cleaning the house front and is loading his van. He looks up as I walk past.

'Do I recognize you, Detective?'

Oh.

Maybe I'll get some answers about that long-ago night after all.

27

Maggie

'As it happens,' I tell Martineau, 'I was posted in Sanctuary a while back. Maybe our paths crossed . . .?'

'Sure I woulda remembered if they did.' He breaks out a broad grin and I see there's a gap between his upper teeth. 'Looks like your colleague took your wheels to get back to the station. Do you need a ride into town?'

I'd told Chester I'd walk. The 'kitchenette' in my rental is a kettle and a microwave, and I'm getting too fond of takeout for my waistline's good. Besides, fresh air and the outdoors help me think.

But Martineau is the final name from that call-out log. He could be the piece that makes all the others fit.

Plus, there's that gappy smile. My ex had a smile like that. And the ex before him.

'That's very kind,' I say, and clamber in.

Martineau offers to take me by the 'scenic route' so I can refresh my memories. It's a good opportunity to sit back and let him talk and forget that I'm a cop.

'It's no trouble,' he says, his wrists resting on the steering wheel. 'I'm Sanctuary born and bred and proud of this place. All this area is The Cobb, the historic part of town — we've some of the oldest buildings in the state. That's why Sarah lives here. Witches dig their history.'

There's a rattle as our wheels roll over cobbles and things jounce in the back of the van. The roads and alleys are narrow and crooked. You can tell you're in a street plan dating from before asphalt and traffic lights, or any vehicles save horse and cart.

'Li'l clock there marks what used to be the town square. And see that, looks like a crumbly bit of sidewalk? That's one edge of the old salt-evaporating pan.'

He points to a low line of stones laid on edge. Next to it is an information board titled: *Black Hill becomes Sanctuary*. I crane my neck as we drive past and make out an old engraving that's been reproduced, showing a hunched dark figure fleeing before an angry mob.

'Black Hill?' I ask. 'It wasn't always Sanctuary, then?'

'Nope. Got its name from expelling the witches. While Salem was cutting up two hundred miles thataway' – he stabs a finger eastward – 'here they whipped the women out of town, and strung up their familiars from trees if they took too long going. Then the abandoned houses were burned and the ashes salted. Needed so much salt, that evaporating pan got made specially for the job.

'When they were through, Black Hill's elders claimed it was the colonies' first settlement to eradicate witches, so they renamed this place "Sanctuary".'

I shudder. Why on earth would Sarah Fenn want to live here, amid all these reminders of what was done to her kind? No wonder she's the only witch in town.

Or at least the only registered witch.

The Cobb may have been the original settlement, but it's peripheral in Sanctuary today. From the look of its twee cafés and boutiques, with names like Crafty Lizzie and At the Black Cat,

I imagine it's visited mostly by tourists. I spot one speakeasy calling itself a 'potions bar'.

Soon, though, we reach one of the channels of the Accontic River, which shatters Sanctuary into fragments like a broken plate. We roll over a low iron bridge out of The Cobb, the bowl of a football stadium to our right, and suddenly we're amid Subways and CVS pharmacies just like any other town. The streets become lines and angles. Main Street is around here, and I ask Martineau to turn down it – I want to check that Fenn's shop hasn't been targeted like her house.

I know this central street. We pass what's surely the only struggling Starbucks in the entire United States. Sanctuary's kids prefer a vegan café in the trendy area of the precinct. Martineau points out a statue of the town elder who renamed Black Hill. It's covered in seagull shit and someone's stuck an orange safety cone on his head, like a witch's hat – or maybe a dunce's cap. I figure Fenn would approve either way.

Just beyond the statue is the witch's little booth. Martineau pulls in to the curb.

'Everything's in order there,' he says, happily. 'I built that place for Sarah. Always like to see it looking tidy.'

The shop's neat exterior, blinds down, is sandwiched between a swanky optician's and one of Bridget Perelli's grooming salons – *Perelli's Pet Pampering!* proclaims the candy-pink awning.

It's a good moment for my question.

'I think I've figured out why I seemed familiar to you,' I say. 'Back when you and Bridget Perelli were together, I think I was called to your house once. Some kind of false alarm. Did I crash a dinner party?'

The mood in the van's cab changes instantly.

'That was you?' says Martineau, turning to me. His face has closed up with suspicion.

Damn. Not the reaction I was hoping for.

'Did you know from the minute you got in my van? You did, didn't you? That's why you accepted the ride in the first place.' He sounds angry now. 'You know what? The police station's only a few blocks from here and the weather's nice, so . . .'

He reaches across me and opens the van door.

Jeez. Poorly played, Mags.

'You make sure your white-coat boys do their job, 'cos I don't want to be cleaning any more crap off my friend's house, you hear?'

He releases my seat belt with a clunk as loud as gunshot.

'Thanks for the ride,' I say, feebly. And climb out wondering what the hell that was all about.

28

Abigail

'Thank you for graciously letting us into your lovely home, Mrs Whitman,' coos Beryl Varley. 'And for offering us this interview at such a painful time. I'm so sorry for your loss.'

The *Sentinel*'s news editor huffs her way over the threshold. She pauses in the hallway, mopping her brow and staring around greedily.

I can hardly bear to have her in my house. I suspect hers was the voice on the telephone asking about the party, that unspeakable first morning. But today I have a use for her.

Sarah hasn't spoken to me since I went to her house and demanded that she bring Dan back. I need to make her understand what's at stake. Freddie and the team made the first move, with their hit on her house. Today is my next step.

Varley's eyes fall on the family portrait I commissioned to mark Dan's sixteenth birthday. That was the year he got as tall as his father. Michael's pride wouldn't want to see himself eternally dwarfed by his younger, handsomer son, so it was the ideal moment to have it painted.

The artist got Daniel just right. His is the best likeness of the three of us. Several times I've stood here, torn between never stopping looking at it and shredding it with a knife for being a lifeless copy of a boy who was so full of life.

As for me, I've become one with my oil-and-canvas image. Each morning, I dress in her clothes and paint her smiling face onto my grieving one.

'How handsome,' says Varley. 'No wonder he was so loved. I wasn't at the stadium tribute, but our sports editor told me it was incredible. Maybe when our photographer comes by later . . . perhaps you, posed by the portrait?'

'Of course. Now do come through. I've refreshments for us, and someone else I'd like you to meet.'

'Someone else?'

Varley's beady eyes shine with curiosity as I lead her to the living room. As expected, she near bit off my hand at the prospect of an exclusive interview with me – nothing shifts copies like human-interest stories. But I have something bigger than she can dream of lined up for her today.

'Good afternoon, ma'am,' says Jake, rising to his feet.

'Jacob Bolt,' I say. 'The chief's son and Daniel's very dear friend.'

'It's good of you to keep Mrs Whitman company this afternoon, Jacob.'

'He'll be doing more than that, Ms Varley. But please, sit down and let me pour for you. Iced tea? Lemonade? And a little something to nibble?'

Varley makes short work of a cupcake, then rummages in a grubby book bag for her recorder. She starts with questions about Dan – what sort of boy he was. His activities and achievements. I could talk all day, of course, and at one point find myself noisily crying. But I hold it together.

'And Dan volunteered as a coach at the Sport on the Shore club, is that right? The junior girls' soccer team?'

I sniff. 'He was devoted to the team. Loved building their confidence. He was so disappointed when his own athletics commitments meant he wasn't able to continue.'

'Such community spirit.' Varley pouts with approval and reaches for another cupcake. 'There must be so many who feel Daniel's loss deeply. This tragic accident—'

'If I may, Ms Varley, I'd like to bring Jacob in here. I think you know that Sanctuary police department has an investigation into the *apparent* accident that cost my son his life.'

Varley catches my insinuation.

'*Apparent*, Mrs Whitman? Does that mean you believe that . . .?'

'That Dan's death wasn't an accident,' says Jake.

He's said it. The relief is overwhelming. I've been desperately hoping that he won't bottle out of what I asked. *This* is what I got Beryl Varley here to listen to.

And Varley is so rapt she even forgets about the cakes, as Jake lays it all out – the crime of Harper Fenn.

There's only one way for Sarah to save her daughter now.

29

FROM THE *SANCTUARY SENTINEL*

Front page

WAS SPORT STAR'S DEATH FOUL PLAY?

By Beryl Varley, News Editor

As Sanctuary still mourns the tragic death of Daniel Whitman,
who perished last week, shocking new claims have emerged
about how – and why – he died.

The *Sanctuary Sentinel* has spoken exclusively to an eyewitness and close friend of the deceased and his family. Their
version of events looks set to rock our community and turn the
police investigation upside down.

They allege:

– that Whitman's death was the result of an intentional
act

– that the fire that destroyed Sailaway Villa, endangering
the other partygoers and potentially preventing live-saving
emergency assistance from reaching Whitman, was started
deliberately

– that witchcraft was used in both cases

According to the witness, the alleged perpetrator was a former intimate of Whitman's, 'with a grudge': 'I was standing on the stairwell when [they] did it. Right next to [them]. [They] were absolutely furious. Raging. Any kid at school can tell you why.'

The eyewitness, who comes from a leading Sanctuary family, says that both he and the alleged perpetrator were some distance from Whitman when he died. Cause of death is currently believed to be a fatal injury sustained in a fall from the upper landing of the villa's stairwell.

'That's how I know it had to be witchcraft. [They] looked right at Dan, made magical gestures with [their] hands, and that instant he fell.'

The events were caught on cell phone footage, which has now been passed to the police.

Sanctuary's only known witch is Sarah Fenn, whose booth has been a Main Street fixture for more than twenty years. Fenn is a fully licensed magical practitioner and lifelong resident of Sanctuary. Her daughter, Harper Fenn, is believed to have formerly been romantically involved with Daniel Whitman.

When contacted by the *Sentinel* about whether anyone close to Sarah Fenn was a person of interest, the lead investigating officer, Detective Maggie Knight of the Connecticut State Police, responded that she was unable to comment at this stage.

No charges have yet been brought.

Inside

News
Page 2 A mother's grief: exclusive interview with Abigail Whitman
Opinion
Page 12 Is 'look-at-me' culture warping our kids?

123

30

Maggie

'With all due respect, Chief: what the fuck?'

I throw the newspaper down on Tad Bolt's desk, trying to keep my voice even.

'Your son, the prime witness in accusing Harper Fenn – no, actually, the *only* witness thus far accusing Harper Fenn – whose testimony we agreed shouldn't be disclosed so as not to compromise the investigation, has given a front-page interview to the local press?'

Bolt pulls the paper toward him. Can it be possible that he's not seen it either? Chester brought me this, hands shaking, after doing a coffee run. Apparently a stack of freebie copies is dropped off at the police station at the end of the delivery, once sales outlets have got theirs.

I watch a flush of red creep up from the snug collar of Bolt's uniform, until his cheeks are scarlet with it. What is it: embarrassment? Anger? He can't have known. Will he back me on this?

He finishes the article. Scans the interview with Abigail Whitman that follows it. Flips back to the front page. Reads again.

Then those large pink paws turn the paper around and slide it back toward me across his desk.

'I guess he got tired of waiting for you to actually do something, Detective. I can't say I blame him. You've got a witness and hard evidence. What's taking so long?'

So that's how it's to be.

I have to think fast. Do I, an outsider, need the town chief on my side for this investigation? Or is he too close to it all? Is there too much conflict of interest? Because the look in Bolt's blue eyes is shrewd and truculent.

Does he seriously want me to push his son's allegations to their logical conclusion?

'Tad, if your son is correct, then you have a teen girl, a life-long resident of this town, whose mom you surely know' – does Bolt's gaze flicker at that? – 'guilty of murder by witchcraft. Or to give it its proper name, *homicide by unnatural means*. And d'you know something about that particular crime in Connecticut? Thanks to an ancient, unrepealed amendment, it brings the death penalty. Harper Fenn would be executed.'

Bolt is silent a moment. Have those words landed? Does he realize that he is the one who can stop this? That, even now, it's still not too late?

But his words put paid to any such hope.

'Are you saying you're not acting on this case 'cos you've no stomach for our country's justice? Don't you call yourself a lawman – woman, *whatever* – Detective Knight? Isn't that your *job*, to uphold the law?'

'Of course it is. And I will. But on the one hand I've the word of your traumatized son and a shaky video, and on the other hand I have no record, held by any authority, that says Harper Fenn is a witch. I'd appreciate it if you can tell Jacob that this sort of thing isn't helping.'

Not the crushing retort I'd hoped to deliver, goddammit. I snatch up the newspaper and go find Chester. I've had enough of this bullshit. We need that magical investigator here right now.

31
Abigail

'Drop it?' I cry at my husband. 'This is your son's *life* you're talking about!'

Michael stoops and catches me by the wrists. He squeezes them together in one large hand – the template of Dan's clever, ball-throwing hands – and it hurts.

'Abigail, you are not behaving rationally. You need to leave this to the police or you'll make a laughing stock of us both.'

'I don't care what people think. I'm not going to give up fighting for Daniel.'

'Have some *dignity*,' my husband says. 'Every single good thing in your life is off my back, and this is how you respect me – by sharing our business with this rag. How do you think it reflects on me?'

He has no idea how wrong he is. Every good thing Michael has, *he* owes to *me*. His professorship. This house that it bought for us. The Vermont ski chalet, the European and Caribbean vacations. All *my* doing, because I went to Sarah.

I bite back the words. I can never say them – not while I want this marriage to last. Not while I want Daniel to have a family to come back to. Dan reveres his dad – brags about how he's a Yale professor. He never bragged about his housewife mom, but

I never cared. His father's success was one more gift I gave my boy.

'Even now he's gone, you're still putting Daniel before me. He's *dead*, Abigail. *Let. Him. Go.*'

And something in me snaps.

'Is there anything more contemptible than a man jealous of his own son? How about a man jealous of his *dead* son and taking it out on his grieving wife?'

Instantly, Michael's bent over me, his finger stabbing the air barely an inch from my eye. I flinch, hating myself for doing so.

'You do *not* speak to me like that. Not now. Not ever.'

As he withdraws, I lift my chin. My head is level with his chest, so I have to look up into those eyes that only recently acquired wire-rimmed spectacles for reading. At that thick hair that even at fifty shows no sign of receding, though it's turning silver at the temples. The very image of an eminent professor.

He'll have his work to outlive him. His contributions to science. Those dazzling filovirus studies that may one day bring him even greater recognition – 'the Swedish lottery', he and his friends call it, when they joke about being awarded a Nobel Prize. Except when I look at Michael, I know it's no joke for him.

I've only ever had my son.

There's a rap at the front door. Michael grabs my arm and shakes me out like a coat that's hung unworn in a cupboard too long.

'Pull yourself together before you answer,' he says. 'I'm going upstairs. I have a paper to finish.'

And the look he gives me as he goes is so full of contempt that I wonder for a moment if a tiny bit of him is glad that Daniel is dead, because it hurts me so much.

32

Abigail

It's Jake Bolt at the door. With him is his pops, the chief.

Tad peers at me and I wonder how bad I look. Usually, if anyone sees me after I've had a row with Michael, I have to make up some excuse – like arranging flowers that set off my allergies. But not now. There's nothing more unnecessary than a woman whose son just died needing to explain why she looks a mess.

Tad steps forward and folds me in a bear hug. 'Let's get you inside,' he says.

'No, wait. Michael's working. I don't want him disturbed.'

I want to be away from my husband's anger. And I've had enough of being shut up with only my grief for company. Dan was never an indoors boy. He was outside every moment he got. Training. Coaching. Spending every summer on the beach and coming home with his skin golden and warm from the sun.

So we get in Tad's patrol car and he drives us to the water. I look away as we pass Bridget's. I don't want to remember that night, barely a week ago, when I was still happy. Can I ever be happy again? That all depends on Sarah.

I know she can do this. I *know* it.

When Tad pulls into the parking lot at High Pine Point, I

cringe. The other road that leads here is from Anaconna, where the Garcias live. This is one of the spots where Alberto and I used to meet.

I hadn't been loved like that before – so passionately and intensely. I thought about Berto so much I could barely function. I'd forget to drop off Michael's clothes at the dry cleaners – or forget to collect them. I'd even sit during Dan's games not watching my son, but refreshing my messages every five minutes in hope of a new one.

I confided in Sarah that I'd fallen for another man. That if it weren't for Dan, I would leave Michael. But I could never tell her that it was Julia's husband, because even Sarah's sympathy would have stopped there. After Alberto cut off contact, there were days I thought I'd burst from holding the pain inside. It felt like a bereavement – or so I thought. Now I know what real loss is.

But being in this place makes Alberto's absence ache all the same. I thought he saw *me*. Not Professor Whitman's wife, or Daniel's mom. Just Abi Anderson, the one-time high-school volleyball captain from the Upper East Side, who dreamed of being a shrink at Mount Sinai. Who loved summer cookouts at her family's Connecticut beach house and could never resist a second helping of s'mores.

What would that girl make of the woman I've become?

How could her heart not break for me?

I'm grateful when Tad starts talking as we head down the trail that's popular with dog walkers. The scent of the pine trees rises up, sharp and cleansing.

'Here's the thing, Abigail – and I've already had this conversation with Jakey here, but I figured the three of us needed to talk it through. Witchcraft? Turns out there's some Connecticut law that's never been repealed that says the punishment for witchcraft is death.'

'Death?' I wonder if I've heard him correctly. 'Connecticut doesn't have the death penalty.'

'Yup. Except for witchcraft we do. The Founding Fathers wrote it into the Constitution – us and Massachusetts, on account of what happened here and in Salem back in the day.'

'That's insane.'

It is. There's no other word for it. I look at Jake. Has he processed what this means? That on his say-so and his evidence, a girl he's known all his life might go to her death? Jake has looked as fragile as I feel this past week, and he doesn't have my hot coal of hope glowing secretly inside to keep himself going – that Sarah's magic might restore Dan to us.

But as I look at him now, there's something burning inside him all the same. Anger fierce enough to destroy Harper Fenn for what she's done. And for a moment, the intensity of it shames me. Shouldn't I feel the same?

As a mother who's lost a child, could I condemn another mother and another child to the same fate? Could I do that and still be human? Shouldn't we end this now?

I hunch over. It's cold here in the forest, in the shade, without a jacket.

If Harper killed Daniel by witchcraft – and she did, she *did*, a voice inside me persists – then she'll die too. No juvenile facility. She'll be executed.

But it would never come to that. Connecticut is one of the bluest of blue states. Our governor would ban guns if she could – probably jails, too. She'd never let an execution happen on her watch. The sentence would be commuted.

Harper wouldn't die.

But the *threat* of it? No mother would risk that. You'd do anything to turn away that danger from your child.

And I realize that I'm not scared of this death penalty. In fact, it's *perfect*.

Since the interview, I've left Sarah voicemails asking if she's ready to bring Dan back. To 'do what we discussed', as I put it – nothing that would make me sound deranged if she played the messages to anyone else.

But Sarah has been silent.

I *know* she can do it, and I'd thought the mere accusation against Harper would make her comply. But so far, it's not been enough.

I've been raking my memory for any compromising details that I know. All those times she bent the rules or broke the law because her kind heart sometimes gets the better of her. I've considered threatening her with revealing those, if she won't help.

But this? A death penalty? It's perfect.

Maybe I'm already too late, though.

'Why are you telling me this, Tad? Do you want me and Jake to drop this because of some law that's not been used for centuries and *never will be*? You know the governor wouldn't allow an execution.'

'Exactly!' Jake blurts out.

And his pop nods, grimly.

'I wanted to make sure you knew all the facts. And if you and Jakey want to drop this, I'll support you. But if you want to carry it all the way, well, I'm right behind you. It's your call.'

They're both looking at me: father and son. Burly, buzz-cut Tad, and slim Jake, his mousy hair already flyaway fine. I always found Jake's devotion to Dan a trifle ridiculous, even pitiable. How readily he accepted life in my son's shadow, just to be near him.

But after all, that makes two of us.

'I don't want Harper Fenn dead,' I tell Tad and his son. 'But that won't happen. We all know it. I want her brought to account for what she did.'

'Understood, Abigail.' Tad actually touches the brim of his hat.

'Here's what we do next,' I say.

33

EMAIL SENT TO BERYL VARLEY, NEWS EDITOR, *SANCTU-ARY SENTINEL*

From: jakepaulbolt@gmail.com
To: bvarley@sanctuarysentinel.com
Date: May 22, 20:54
Subject: Whitman murder investigation – EVIDENCE of witchcraft

Hi Ms Varley,

You did a great job with the article.

I told you I had proof of what I said about witchcraft. I wasn't sure I should be sharing it with you, seeing as the police have a copy as evidence. But the state detective supposed to be leading the investigation has had it for a week now and hasn't done a thing with it.

So here are two stills from footage filmed by me at the villa party. They prove that Harper Fenn used magic to kill Daniel Whitman.

Maybe the detective's afraid of the scandal of a witchcraft trial. But I reckon the real scandal would be for how Dan died to be covered up.

You and the folks at the *Sentinel* know how much Dan meant to Sanctuary. Please help us get justice for him.

Sincerely,

Jacob Bolt

Attachments: HFwitchcraft1.jpg, HFwitchcraft2.jpg

34

Maggie

'I'd rather not have any more front-page interventions from the local hacks,' I tell Chester. 'So let's get this done. First, we clear up the issue of witchcraft. Assuming that's a "no", we move on to a much simpler question: murder or accident? So who have you got for me?'

We're holed up out back in Starbucks. Sanctuary loves its independent coffee shops, so this gloomy space with sticky tables is the quietest place in town.

Chester lifts his head from the whipped-cream peak of his iced mocha caramel abomination. He carefully wipes his top lip before pulling out his notebook and leafing back a few pages.

'Here we go,' he says. 'Quite a few outfits across the internet, most of them look pretty sketchy. I did come across this one, though . . . They've got some awesome degree from UC Davis – double major in magical ethnography and criminology. Their biography says they've been a state liaison for the Moot. And most importantly, a track record of advising police inquiries, with loads of references. Name of Rowan Andrews.'

He slides his phone across the table to show me the website.

Rowan Andrews is . . . *striking*. Skin the warm, bright tones of a penny, a strong jawline, with hair that's shaved on one side and falls in choppy layers down the other. Her hazel eyes are flecked with brilliant amber.

'Where's she based?'

'Oregon. And *they*. That's their pronoun.'

Chester has taken the phone back and is staring at Rowan's photo.

'Let's move on it,' I tell him. 'Due diligence. Put in a call to the Moot. You'll need to disclose that you're police, looking for an independent magical assessment of an incident scene, but don't share further details or where you're calling from. Ditto when you're speaking to Rowan themself, until you know for certain we can use them.'

'Speaking to them?' His voice squeaks with alarm and he colors up.

'*Yes*, Chester. Ask in what states they have connections among the magical community – if they say Connecticut, we'll need to look again. Make sure they'll sign a non-disclosure agreement, and that they're available right away. If everything checks out, we'll get them on the first plane.'

Chester is practically quivering at the prospect. He's entering a brave new world of policing beyond arresting shoplifters and cautioning public drunks.

In the meantime, I need to go back to the Fenns. I'm long overdue answers from both mother and daughter.

35

Sarah

That article as good as named my daughter as a murderer.

The first thing I did was try to reach Harper. She didn't answer the first time I called, or the tenth, or all the times in between. So finally I texted: *Stupid story in the* Sentinel. *Stay where you are. I'm going to do some investigating of my own. I'll never let anyone hurt you. Love you so much. Mom xoxo*

As much as I need desperately to see my child and hold her and tell her it'll all be okay, I don't want Harper here in Sanctuary where she might be harassed and intimidated. I don't want her here where the detective can scoop her up for an interview that'll frame her on the word of Jake Bolt. I want her away from Abigail and her grief-crazed accusations.

That cop, Detective Knight, seemed sympathetic. But if this is the direction her investigation is heading, I can't rely on her.

I need to find out how Dan died. That magic I sensed at the villa – whose was it, and did it kill him? When I know, I can go to the police and clear Harper of suspicion.

My booth hasn't suffered the same fate as the house. It's still neatly closed up, the blinds drawn. I slip down the alley that runs alongside Bridge's grooming salon and unlatch the yard gate. Aira darts off among the blooms as I check the rain barrel.

Chemically treated water from a tap is useless for brewing and even worse for my purpose today, divining.

The back door of my workroom is triple-secured, as is the door that leads to it from the consulting room at the front. I unfasten the padlock. Key in the security code. Trace a sigil on the door frame.

The wards here are like those on my house – as powerful as the law permits. Smash the padlock, crack the keypad and you'll find an open doorway. But unless I've lifted the ward or you have a token (and the only people with one of those are Harper and Bridget), you'll be hit powerfully at the mere thought of stepping through. I got Pierre to test it for me, which ended with the poor guy on his knees on the threshold, crying and puking and unable to go any further.

Today, I'll lock myself in. Some magic is too fragile to withstand disturbance.

Some magic is too dangerous to interrupt.

Today's ritual is all about seeing, so I don't switch on the electric lights inside. Instead, I find and trim four oil lamps. They're survivors from a time when Sanctuary's women set them anxiously on windowsills to light a sailor's way home from sea.

I hope they'll light my way to some answers.

The chart I've decided upon is at the bottom of the fourth drawer. I can't remember the last time I took it out, because I'm not permitted to use it for consultations with clients – another legal restriction, but for once, one that I wholeheartedly agree with. All magical practice is slippery, shifting, potentially treacherous. But divination more than most.

I let my thoughts settle as I make my preparations. Fear and anxiety, like silt, take time to sink to the bottom of my mind, leaving everything clear and still.

From the garden I gather white carnations, and from the locked greenhouse, bittersweet – one of the nightshades. Its

138

purple five-petaled stars lie in my hand. I'll pluck out and grind the fleshy yellow stamens. These two blooms are truth-tellers.

From the lowest shelf in my workroom I take two brown glass jars: one of dried cedar bark, the other of mugwort oil. Humble mugwort is one of our oldest aids – it's there in the Nine Herbs Charm and elsewhere in the *Lacnunga*. Chinese poems have praised it for more than two thousand years. I set the jars on my workbench, then fill one of my silver dippers from the barrel outside.

My scrying bowl I keep wrapped in linen. It's flawless obsidian and reassuringly heavy in my hands. At the sink I first rinse it with rainwater, then wipe it all over with mugwort oil. Finally, I place a handful of cedar bark in the burner and pass the bowl through the smoke.

It's a triple purification. To some, this appears a fiddly business. The occasional skeptic will accuse me of staging ritual work to inflate my fees. But it's no more than any other skilled practitioner does: the athlete who stretches, the surgeon who scrubs and gloves.

The final instrument to prepare is myself. This requires a tincture of salvia. Here in Connecticut, *Salvia divinorum* became a Schedule I substance in 2012. Licensed witches have exemption to cultivate and prepare it, but only for personal consumption. The salvia is in the same greenhouse where I grow the nightshades and a dozen more toxic or narcotic plants besides. I secure the lock once I've cut what I need with silver scissors.

Salvia's effects are short-lived, so I make sure everything else is ready before I down the infusion. I trim the lamp wicks. Soon I'll be seeing with the inward eye. I call Aira inside, then close and secure the door. It's time to begin.

A witch will only turn to divination in desperation.

I'm desperate.

36
Sarah

Throughout history, practitioners have tried to refine divination techniques. The ritual has countless forms, using objects ranging from bones and tea leaves to clouds and animal guts. Yet divination always requires a question, posed by the witch, and expects an answer, yielded by the ritual.

Often, though, no answer comes.

Despite centuries of magical scholarship, no one knows why. Was the question framed incorrectly, or the witch's mind insufficiently focused? One theory holds that there's *always* an answer; we're simply incapable of understanding it.

I need an answer today, for Harper's sake. So I've considered the question carefully.

'How did Daniel die?' demands a response that's too complex.

'Was Daniel's death an accident?' would be useful, but only if the answer is 'yes'. If it's 'no', then it brings me no closer to what I need to know.

So I've hit on what I hope is the right one.

In the dim light, I trace my chosen path through the chart. Words. Gestures. Wiping the bowl again. Filling it with rainwater. Dabbling my fingers in as I consecrate it to the true sight. Letting fall a single drop of oil, which spreads in a shimmering film across the surface, to cleanse perception so that it shows me no lies.

I drink the salvia preparation. The effect is almost immediate. The world inverts. All that is real is contained in this bowl. All that is illusory shimmers around me in the lamplight.

I feel the brush of Aira's fur at my ankles, and hear her mew. Familiars are our anchors to the real world, their animal natures closely connected to the earth. They keep us attached to all that is known – all that is *familiar*. More than once, it has been Aira's gentle presence that has guided me back to myself.

The final steps of the chart, those I've chosen for this divinatory journey, are ready in my head, at my fingertips and on my tongue. I speak words. Shape sigils.

And finally I look into my bottomless bowl and ask the question: *Who killed Daniel Whitman at Sailaway Villa?*

I look.

And I look.

And no answer comes.

My eyes dart around. The answer may be heard, or felt, or seen.

But I hear nothing, and feel nothing, and see only my own reflection, shimmering and distorted.

Then Aira screams as my obsidian bowl shatters, and its blank black depths are the last thing I see as I crumple.

37

Maggie

I'm nearly at Fenn's booth when the place explodes. At least that's what it sounds like.

I break into a sprint. The front door is locked and shuttered, so I run round back, and in the side alley I collide with Bridget Perelli.

She's hurtled out the yard of her grooming salon next door. Behind her is a bedlam of barks, howls and whines.

'What the hell?' Perelli bellows. She starts thumping on the gate that must lead into the yard of the witch's booth. 'Sarah, are you in there?'

Something crunches beneath my boots. Shattered glass. I check in both directions, but it's undisturbed by footprints.

Perelli is rattling the door handle, still calling for her friend. No reply, so she digs into her pocket and pulls out a bunch of keys, flipping through them.

'We've each got a key to the other's place,' she explains, fitting it to the lock. 'It means we can keep an eye out. My salon's got lots of gear that's easily swiped, and obviously there's plenty in Sarah's booth that someone might want. I guess Sarah's not in, as she keeps this unlocked when she is. But Pierre told me what happened to her house. Those fuckers.'

The gate opens and we both take in the scene.

The two windows on either side have blown out. The property's back door is still fastened but hangs oddly within its frame. There's a garden that looks mostly undisturbed, but here and there blooms have been severed, stalks mangled. A greenhouse in the corner is intact.

Through one of the gaping window frames I can see flickering flames. A fire started by an arsonist? But no, they're small. Regular. Candles or lamps. So Sarah Fenn must be inside, even though the gate was shut.

Why lock herself in?

Perelli is peering frantically through the other window, trying to get a view between the iron security bars.

'Sarah? Sarah?' she calls. Then, 'No, don't!'

That's for me. She throws out an arm as I reach for the loose back door, but I'm already reeling back. Something just twisted my guts in a powerful spasm, and bile is rising up my throat.

'Security ward,' Perelli explains. 'A deterrent. Wait, let me.'

I'm doubled over, coughing, and spit onto the ground. Perelli's pulled out her keys again and is fingering what I thought was the fob. I can see now that it's a small shining disk engraved with twisting witch marks. She wraps her fingers round it and steps up to the door, gingerly pulling at it with her other hand.

With a shriek, a long-haired tabby shoots out. Fenn's familiar. The creature dives into the alley.

'Sarah? Jesus.'

Perelli is inside, now. I see her crouch down by the workbench. Then, with a grunt, she's back, dragging Fenn beneath the arms. The witch is dazed, her head lolling. But there's no sign of an explosion. No soot or smoke.

'Check her over,' Perelli tells me, lowering Fenn to the ground. 'There are some broken lamps in there. They could start a fire.'

She heads back inside, and I'm vaguely aware of her moving

143

around the workroom. Then Fenn moans and my training kicks in. I perform the standard ABC first-responder checks, but her airways and breathing are unobstructed and she's returning to groggy consciousness.

I ask if she's hurt, and if so, where. But she murmurs 'no', and when I reach for my radio to summon an ambulance, she lays a hand weakly on mine.

'Not necessary.'

'What happened?'

'Brew gone wrong, yeah?' says Perelli. She's standing in the doorway, and it occurs to me she's been inside for some time. 'You okay, Sarah?'

The witch nods as I help her sit upright. The cat slinks back into the yard and jumps into Fenn's arms. The creature's presence rallies its mistress.

'What happened?' I ask again.

'Just brewing,' Perelli repeats, as Fenn says what sounds like 'Divining.'

'It's okay, Bridge,' the witch tells her friend. 'It's not illegal, not when it's just for me. I was scrying.'

'Scrying? Like, trying to see things? What things?'

'What do you think, Detective?' Her tone is harsher than before. As if she's wary of me. 'Who committed the murder my daughter is accused of.'

'And?'

'Nothing. I saw nothing.'

'But what caused . . .' I gesture to the glass, the loose door and battered flowers, the still plainly freaked-out cat, its tail flicking.

'I must have made an error in the ritual. Divining isn't something I trust much or perform often. But in this case, I thought it worth attempting.'

An error? I don't know enough about witchcraft to judge

how likely that is, or whether it would produce this sort of damage.

'Do you need help getting home?' I ask.

'Thank you, but I'll need to make sure my premises are secure. It's not just my things I'm worried about. I keep full client records and I'm obliged to ensure they're safe. Bridge, could you call . . .?'

'Pierre?' says her friend. 'Sure thing.'

As Bridget calls her ex and explains the situation, Fenn gets to her feet and takes cautious steps.

'You see,' she says. 'All in working order. How come you were so close by, Detective Knight?'

'I wanted to speak to you about that newspaper article. To let you know that it was in no way approved by me, and to say that if you and Harper feel unsafe at any time, you should contact the station and assistance will come immediately.'

'Thank you. We'll do that.'

'So Harper is back in town, is she?'

Fenn's face closes up. The cat in her arms opens its jaws, baring small, sharp teeth.

'My daughter is her own person, Detective. I'm sure she'll be back when she feels it's safe. But I'd remind you that she's seventeen years old, and in the past couple weeks she's been injured in a fire in which her boyfriend died, has been accused of his murder and of being an unregistered witch, and her home has been attacked. You can't blame her for preferring to be somewhere else right now.'

It's true. It's all true.

'Pierre's on his way,' says Bridget. 'Let's get you sat down inside, Sarah. Nice meeting you, Detective.'

She extends a hand for me to shake. It's a clear dismissal. Then she leads her friend into the wrecked workroom, leaving me on the wrong side of a door I can't enter.

145

I phone Chester.

'Have you made those calls?' I ask. 'In fact, is Rowan Andrews on a plane *right now*?'

'They check out,' he tells me. 'We had a good talk and they're available to come immediately. The Moot gave excellent references. Was just gonna give you a call when I got distracted.'

'Distracted? Eye on the ball, Chester. Book them a flight. You know this is our priority.'

'I know,' he says unhappily. 'It's just . . . I was driving back to the station and, well, the road goes past the *Sentinel* offices.'

'If you stopped to give Varley a talking-to about jeopardizing our investigation, then I take it all back. Excellent policing, Sergeant Greenstreet.'

'It's not that. They have a display case outside where they put up their front page each week. Special editions, too . . .'

'Special editions?'

'You'd better go see,' he tells me, "cos it's being distributed right now as a one-page free sheet to all the usual outlets. And it's really, really bad.'

Shit. What is Varley playing at? I need to see this. And I know the sad Starbucks regularly carries the *Sentinel*.

Except once I get there and see what Varley's done, I find I've lost my appetite.

And also, I reckon, my job.

38

SANCTUARY SENTINEL – SPECIAL EDITION

CHIEF ALLEGES COVER-UP IN 'WITCHCRAFT MURDER' SHOCKING NEW EVIDENCE 'IS PROOF' ACCUSED MAY FACE DEATH PENALTY EXCLUSIVE

By Beryl Varley, News Editor

Biased state authorities are disregarding evidence in the tragic party death of Daniel Whitman, it was alleged today.

In an extraordinary intervention by Sanctuary's veteran chief, Tad Bolt, the widely respected lawman revealed that investigating officer Detective Margaret Knight had asked him to 'hush up' crucial evidence.

Daniel died ten days ago, in circumstances still unexplained, at a start-of-summer party. A witness has claimed that witchcraft was used to attack him, causing his death.

New evidence

The *Sanctuary Sentinel* has seen photographs from footage filmed that night – which has been in the possession of the investigating officer for a week – that plainly shows inexplicable phenomena.

No arrests have been made. However, a number of voices are naming Harper Fenn (17), daughter of Sanctuary's only registered witch, Sarah Fenn, as a person of interest. Harper Fenn was formerly the girlfriend of Daniel Whitman – a relationship that ended shortly before the night of the party.

Death penalty

Should 'unnatural homicide' by witchcraft be proven, a quirk in Connecticut state law mandates the death penalty. Sanctuary resident and emeritus 'Little Ivy' law professor Malcolm Empson told the *Sentinel* he believes it is 'inconceivable' that current Connecticut governor, Democrat Tara Miller, would enforce the penalty.

As such, he says the only possible reason for not pursuing a clear case would be 'political correctness'.

Nonetheless, it appears that nervous state-level authorities are considering shutting the case down.

Chief: 'no confidence'

It's believed that two days ago Detective Knight returned to Middletown, the headquarters of Connecticut State Police, presumably to consult with superiors.

'I no longer have confidence in the state-level investigation,' says Chief Bolt. 'Therefore, I am formally recusing myself from any involvement and taking a period of leave from duties. This will enable me to actively support my son Jacob, and the Whitman family, at this painful time. Dan Whitman was a boy much loved in this town, and that's the sort of folk we are in Sanctuary – we protect our own.'

The *Sanctuary Sentinel* will bring you updates on this story as it develops.

39

Sarah

Bridget is helping Pierre repair the damage to my booth. He was furious at first, thinking it was another attack, like the house. I told him it was just a malfunctioning spell.

But was it? Was that explosion a divination gone wrong?

Or was it my answer?

I'm still woozy from the salvia preparation I drank. While Pierre boards up the shattered windows I move mechanically around my workroom, trying to empty my mind as I put things to rights. Bridget is in the garden, fingertip-searching for broken glass. Then she joins me and does the same inside: scouring corners, scrubbing benches. She keeps urging me to sit down and rest.

So I do, and I watch them, these two who have been my friends the longest. Even when we were at middle school, Pierre would gather offcuts from his uncle's lumberyard and build us dens and hideouts. Bridge would scavenge junk to add a finishing touch. A carpet. A chair with a busted-out bottom.

My role was to admire their industriousness and get swept along in their plans. Neither of them was ever much interested in my gift. To them, it was simply one more practical skill like their own, only less useful for our games.

I still remember Bridget's apprehension the first time I asked her to support me as I performed a spell. The quality of her energy was clear and dependable, like the natural strength you find in trees and plants. She never much relished being part of my magic, but as my friend and the person I trusted most, she did it.

It was much later when I met Abigail, at antenatal classes. Her interest grew as we hung out during baby play dates. She was intrigued by the craft objects in my house, and unlike reluctant Bridget, asked if she could participate in a spell. Her energies complemented Bridge's, and for nearly a decade I worked with the two of them: reliable Bridget and passionate Abigail. Their support enabled me to try more complex magic and ensured I never had to turn away a client in need.

Then, seven years ago, the Garcias moved to Sanctuary from San Diego. It was Beatriz and Harper who became friends initially. Julia first joined in my magic that desperate night a year later, and stayed a part of my circle thereafter. She loves the arcana and ritual, and responds with an artist's creativity.

The four of us were friends, despite our obvious differences. And we became a true coven. Bridget grounds me, Abigail fires me up, and Julia reminds me of the beauty of my craft. They all join my magic, despite having none themselves.

But can our friendship survive this? Can there ever be a way back for me and Abigail, after what she's said and done? I would expect Bridget to stand by me. Julia too, after the help I gave her when she came crying to me, suspecting Alberto of yet another affair.

I remember when I realized that the man both my friends had confided in me about – Julia's errant husband and Abigail's new lover – was one and the same. I kept that knowledge locked inside, to spare them both. What I did then, I did for all our sakes, and I brought us through it with no one the wiser. Surely I can bring us through this.

'I think I'm done,' Bridge announces. 'I'm famished and you still look terrible. Let me go grab you a sandwich and a coffee – or even some dumb quinoa bowl.' She raises her voice. 'Italian sub for you, P?'

Pierre yells his agreement from the yard.

While she's gone, I go into my office. The disaster in the workroom didn't affect things here, but I still feel compelled to check my cabinet and records. Governments always try to control what they neither understand nor trust. The less they trust and understand, the tighter they control. My whole livelihood depends on abiding by the rules laid down for us witches.

I lift the wards on my filing cabinet and my fingers go straight to the fold of cardboard bearing Dan's name. Both samples of his hair are there: the one from last year, when I worked on his injury, and the one taken six years ago.

Two samples, but – contrary to the rules – only one consent form.

I've always wondered if any of the kids saw what we did that night. If they sensed anything different about Dan afterwards. Because they'd all been so close, up till then. Piling into the same room for sleepovers. Having pillow fights and watching cartoons under the covers together. Just four normal kids.

Then it all stopped.

Izzy became a stay-at-home kid. Dan, of course, started getting serious about football. Harper and Bea still hung out, but they did group things, like going to the movies with other girls from school.

We never questioned it at the time. There were so many reasons why it was the most natural thing in the world. They were all reaching puberty, when boys and girls mix less and female friendships can acquire sharp edges. After Dan's talent was scouted, he got sucked into training. Izzy had to deal with her parents' breakup, and even though Bridge and Pierre did a good job of it, it was an emotional time for us all and Izzy struggled. She took to reading for hours with a box of cookies for company, becoming shyer and chubbier at just the time many girls start thinking about dating and dieting.

Childhood friendships seldom last into adulthood. I know me, Bridge and Pierre are exceptions. But all the same, I wonder about our kids.

They *can't* have seen it all. Would Harper have dated Dan, or Beatriz have wanted to, if they had? But Abigail's scream would have woken them. What might the girls have glimpsed before Pierre went and settled them down? My friend doesn't like to talk about that night.

None of us do.

And now here we are again. Only this time, there's nothing I can do.

I reach into one of the bags of Dan's hair and rub the soft, fine strands between my fingers. It's the earlier of the two samples, still the vibrant blond of childhood. I remember clipping it from his scalp with Bridget's kitchen scissors, while Pierre restrained Abigail, a hand over her mouth to muffle her screaming. I did it as I did everything that night – without pausing to think. Wanting only to end the nightmare.

Taken without Dan's consent. Though *of course* he would have consented, had he been able to.

Which is when a chill runs through me.

Something given for something gotten. That's our creed. My gramma drummed it into me. Abigail spat it at me just a few days ago, when she tried to bargain Jake's allegation against Harper for the impossible miracle of raising a boy a week dead.

Something given for something gotten. But that night six years ago, Dan *got*, without *giving*.

What if . . .

What if everything that happened at Sailaway Villa was what he *got* being taken back again?

What if there really *was* magic at the party? But not *used* by anyone. Merely the balance, righting itself.

What if *that's* the answer my scrying bowl just showed me?

40

Sarah

My train of thought is broken by low conversation in the yard, then an excessively cheery 'There you are!' – as if I'd be any-where else.

It's Bridge, back with a brown paper lunch bag. Pierre is hovering behind her in the doorway. They both look worried sick.

'I'm sorry, Sarah,' stammers Bridget. 'I took every copy in the deli, but there's gonna be more all over town.'

'I'll go find them,' says Pierre. 'Every fucking one.'

'What? What is it?'

Which is when I see Bridget has what looks like two dozen copies of the *Sanctuary Sentinel* folded under her arm. But the paper is a weekly. It only came out a couple days ago.

SPECIAL EDITION. Then: *WITCHCRAFT MURDER.* And somehow, incomprehensibly: *DEATH PENALTY.*

Everything slows down, as if I've taken a preparation of motherwort. A stillness more profound than valerian settles on me as I reach for the newspaper.

It's only a single sheet. News so urgent they couldn't wait to share it. The only time that happens is for elections or major accidents. It takes me a matter of moments to scan it and realize what's got Bridget horrified and Pierre incensed.

And when I do, I'm so furious I could explode my workroom all over again. Or preferably the *Sentinel*'s offices.

They're pinning it on my girl. On Harper. Publicly and unambiguously this time.

'Impossible.' I throw the thing to the floor. '*How* can it be Harper? Everyone knows she doesn't have the gift.'

'She doesn't, right?'

Bridget sounds anxious, like a child seeking reassurance.

'Of course she doesn't, Bridge. I determined it myself. Any witch would be able to do the same.'

'Then you sue these fuckers,' snarls Pierre. 'You sue that Varley bitch and take every dime off this rag so it has to close down. How do they think they can get away with it? The last piece was bad enough, but this one just comes right out and says it.'

Harper.

How do I keep Harper safe? Grief has made Abigail a monster, and Jake Bolt too, and I should pity them – but not when they threaten my child.

Dan's death could be a terrible, tragic accident. Or another witch could be involved.

It's just possible he died as a result of what we all did six years ago.

But it's completely impossible that my giftless girl had anything to do with it.

The last time Abigail and I met, I refused her impossible demand to bring Dan back. And now this. It's all her doing. By whipping up suspicion of Harper, she wants to force my hand.

I can't let it continue.

'Have you seen Abigail recently?' I ask Bridget.

Bridget is looking . . . guilty? Uneasy, certainly. And she spills it all. How Abigail summoned her and Julia and asked for their support.

155

Her story twists my gut, poisonous as a brew gone wrong. I feel like throwing up.

'She said *what*?' Pierre's shifting from foot to foot as though he's itching to swing a punch at someone, if only he could work out who. Bridget rounds on him.

'She was *grief-stricken*, P. Imagine if something happened to Izzy. What sort of state would you be in?'

'Not a trying-to-get-my-friend's-child-killed-too sort of state, for sure.'

He cracks his knuckles, but his anger has got nowhere useful to go.

'Pierre,' I tell him, 'leave this to me. Bridget, would you come with me to Abigail? This has gone far too far. I need her to come out and say clearly that she doesn't believe Harper did it.'

Even now, I can't hate Abigail if she's behind this. But that doesn't mean I won't fight her with everything I have.

And witches, after all, have magic.

41

Abigail

'Abigail? Abi? It's Bridget.'

I'd planned on ignoring the door.

Beryl Varley came by an hour ago to deliver some copies of the *Sentinel*'s special edition. We sat at the kitchen table and went through it. I wanted to know why there weren't any photographs from Jake's recording of that night, the ones that plainly show Harper using magic. Varley told me that they were being held 'in reserve'.

'You don't throw everything out there at once,' she said. 'Readers are only capable of taking in two or three facts at a time, and the facts they need here are "witchcraft", "murder" and "cover-up". Plus drip-feeding keeps pushing the story on. It builds confidence.'

She told me she expected the news to break out statewide in the next twenty-four hours and advised me to lie low. She and Tad and the Spartans and the people of Sanctuary would be a 'circle of wagons' around me, to protect me from intrusion.

So yes, I'd planned on not answering the door – but it's Bridget, and I'm so sick of being alone in this house. This empty, echoing house. No husband. No lover. No son. As she thumps the door hard and calls my name for the third time, I answer.

Except she's betrayed me, because Sarah is with her.

Before I can slam the door, Sarah sticks her foot in. Or I think she does.

'Sarah?'

Bridget sounds uncertain. Which is when I notice that there's nothing holding the door open except for Sarah's upraised hand, midair, about six inches from the door.

'Witch,' I spit with as much venom as if the word began with a B. 'How dare you.'

Sarah flinches, as if she can't believe I've used that word against her. But the door doesn't budge.

Bridget gulps. 'I didn't know you—'

'Consent.' And Sarah's wearing a grim little smile. 'She opened the door to me. And if she hadn't done, well, there are other ways.'

'Go before I call the police. They'll have you locked up alongside your daughter.'

'Stop it, Abigail,' Sarah says in that low voice of hers. 'Stop all this.'

She pushes her hand forward fractionally and the door edges wider, sliding me backward even though I'm now leaning all my weight against it.

'I'm pretty sure forcing entry by witchcraft is against the law,' I hiss.

'Forcing? Bridget, do you see me forcing anything?'

Bridget is hanging back on the step. What was she thinking, bringing Sarah here? And then she explains.

'You two have got to talk, Abigail. You can't honestly think Harper killed Daniel? I know you're . . . It's unimaginably hard . . . But you *can't* be sure about this.'

'I'm not. Discussing this. On the doorstep.'

I'm breathless. Expending so much of my strength on trying to keep Sarah out that I can barely speak.

'Fine. Inside, then.'

And with the merest thrust of the witch's hand against nothingness, my door flies open and I stagger backward.

Bridget gasps, shocked. As she follows Sarah over the threshold, she reaches for me. I shake her off and stand firm.

'Get out *now*, Sarah.'

'Not till we've had this out.'

At a wave of the witch's hand, the door slams. And despite myself, the hair lifts along my arms and something trickles cold in my stomach. Fear. Like a child seeing for the first time their pet dog bare its teeth and snarl. Realizing that something they've trusted and loved could actually harm them.

Copies of the *Sentinel* lie folded on the hallway table. Sarah holds one up.

'You see what it says here?' She points to the second column and reads. '*A number of voices are naming Harper Fenn as a person of interest.* Or here? *State law mandates the death penalty.* I know you understand what's on the line with these false accusations, Abi, because we've already discussed it. The *death penalty*? You're threatening my daughter's life.'

'At least you still have a daughter.'

At my words, I feel Bridget melt against me. Kind, soft Bridget. She's drawn to any suffering creature: beaten dogs and feral cats. The more wretched they are, the more her heart bleeds for them. She's stroking my hair like I'm some kind of wounded animal.

If it's a contest in wretchedness between me and Sarah, with my dead son I'll always win. Maybe Sarah's sensed that too, because with her next words she goes on the attack.

'Bridget, there's something I've not told you yet,' she announces. 'I'd hoped it was Abi's grief speaking, but you need to know what she's trying to do. What the point is of these accusations against my daughter. Last week, she confronted me and said that if I didn't attempt to bring Daniel's body – his charred,

159

days-dead body – back to life, she would frame Harper for his murder.'

Instantly, I feel Bridget's arms loosen around me. The suffocating warmth of her eases away. For once in my life, I don't want it to. I need her on my side.

'*My son's life for your daughter's innocence*,' continues Sarah. 'Those were your exact words. You even threw our creed at me: *something given for something gotten*. Well I'm sorry, Abigail. I can't give you that. And you *know* it couldn't have been Harper.'

What I know is what I've seen – Jake's video. His testimony.

Harper is guilty. She has to be, because it's the only way I'll get Dan back. My son, alive once again.

Once I have him, there will have been no murder. Harper will be free of suspicion and I'll never breathe a word of what she did to him. Daniel and I will be gone, far from here.

It's so simple. I *have* to make Sarah see it.

I start to cry.

'You did it before,' I say in a whisper. 'You brought Daniel back once before. Please do it again. *Please*.'

I sink to the floor, as if too weak to stand. I'm hardly even acting. I'm exhausted, kept permanently sleepless by this nightmare that just won't end.

Bridget crouches and gathers me up. As I sob, the hand is back, stroking my hair.

'You did, Sarah,' I hear her say. 'We all saw it. He died and you brought him back.'

'I . . . No. That was different. He wasn't dead.'

'Michael took his pulse,' Bridget says as I hunch in her arms, making myself very small, very wretched, very pitiable. 'There wasn't one. No heartbeat. Not for minutes. I think a Yale medical professor can tell if his own son is dead or not.'

'It wasn't . . .' Sarah is on the defensive now. 'Not a true death. People "die" like that all the time on the operating table, or after falling into frozen rivers, and they're *revived*. That's all it was.'

'His skull was broken, Sarah. Blood was coming out of his mouth. His nose. His *eyes*.'

I feel my friend's shudder.

'It was only minutes, Bridget. That's what matters. Not the injury but the *closeness*. And even then, I shouldn't have done it. It's forbidden for a reason. Not just by the law, but by my rites, too. It's . . . wrong.'

'Yet you made us all a part of it. Me, Julia and Abi.'

'You did it willingly. All of you. You did it out of love. That's the only reason I agreed. I didn't see how anything bad could come out of an act performed with such good, pure hearts.'

'But you're saying it's too late this time . . .'

And Bridget's tone isn't right. It's sorrowful. Accepting.

I push her arms away.

'It's *magic*,' I rasp. 'Yes, he's not a patient you can slap the defibrillators on and shock back to life, but isn't that the point of magic, to do the things that science can't?'

'Things like advance a husband's career? Give you a good life?' Sarah crouches down, her face close to mine, and she's got the gall to be crying too. 'Oh Abigail, if I could do this for you too, I would.'

'You won't try.'

'There's no point.'

'Not even to save your daughter?'

'I'd save her more easily by doing what you're asking, wouldn't I? Like you said – no body, no murder. But it's different to before, Abi. It's impossible. I'm so sorry.'

And somehow her regret makes it all real. The fight goes out of me. When I slump to the ground this time, there's no pretence.

Sarah's words are the perfectly placed blow of a knife, and what's leaking from the wound it makes is *hope*.

Everything inside me comes loose. The painted-on Abigail who has been fooling everyone – sometimes even herself – dissolves as I let my tears flow. Bridget rocks me, and Sarah kneels and smoothes back my hair. They both see me as I truly am. As what I've been denying I am, all this time.

The mother of a dead son.

I lie there breathing shallowly, and into the silence that falls Bridget murmurs comforting nothings, her hand stroking my back. I'm overwhelmed by jealousy of the broken, car-struck strays that she's comforted on the vet's metal table as a needle takes their pain away. If only she could bring me peace as easily.

Sarah's right. She gave me Daniel's life back once before. She'd do it again if she could.

But she can't, and I need to believe her.

I need to let go.

I draw in a breath that rattles to the bottom of my lungs, like *I'm* the one being brought back to life. There'll be a way through this. There has to be.

I wipe my face. Bridget is still warm against me, and I don't know how much time has passed when a phone goes. It sounds from Sarah's pocket, but she ignores it until it falls silent.

A moment later, it goes again. Then again. Finally the beep of a text.

Sarah pulls out her phone. Then she stands like someone lit a fire beneath her and runs out the door.

42

Sarah

Harper is pacing up and down the kitchen when I get home, summoned by her text. She's tall, having shot up over the last few years, but I'm suddenly aware of her strength, too. Those long, lean muscles, trained by her regular runs. She's a creature of the outdoors, and in this small room she's like a wild thing, caged.

My wild girl.

A copy of the *Sentinel* lies on the table between us.

'I got a text from Beatriz,' she says. '*Dear Harper, bummer to hear about the death penalty*, et cetera. The bitch. But she's not lying, is she?'

I've never felt so afraid in my life. Not since the moment they placed Harper into my arms when she was born. And even then, it wasn't like this. I looked at my newborn daughter and knew that I would protect her from anything. There's a reason why fairy tales tell us magic and a mother's love are the invincible combination.

But we don't live in the pages of a storybook. We live in Sanctuary. When Harper was little, I considered moving us to one of the witch towns: Summer Port in Oregon, Murdo in North Carolina, or even New Orleans. But I wanted her to know normal life as well, in case she chose not to walk the path. When I

163

discovered she was giftless, it only confirmed I'd made the right choice.

Until now.

I'll never forgive myself if she comes to harm in this place where my ancestors and I have helped and healed for so many years.

'I told you to stay away,' I tell her. 'To lie low. Why are you here?'

'Don't you think that under the circumstances my absence might look suspicious? How can I defend myself?'

'You don't need to defend yourself.'

She snatches up the paper and reads back the very line I read to Abigail just now.

'*Naming Harper Fenn as a person of interest*? Of course I need to defend myself, Mom.'

'You don't. It ends here. I've just been at Abigail's sorting it all out.'

'At Abigail's "sorting it out"?'

I can see her confusion. Abigail has been part of my daughter's life since she was born. Practically an auntie, when Harper was little. She knew Abigail didn't approve of her dating Dan, though she laughed and agreed when I said that in Abi's eyes no girl would ever be good enough.

'It's . . .' And I despair of being able to say this in a way that makes sense. 'Abigail's out of her mind, Harper. You know Dan was her whole life. She wanted me to use my magic to . . .'

'To *what*?'

'You can imagine what. Don't make me say it.'

'To bring him back?'

Harper stares, unswerving. I expect her any moment to laugh, to make some comment about how *magic can't do that*. But she doesn't. Instead, what she says makes me wonder all over again what she saw that night six years ago.

'You've got to be kidding, Mom. You *know* what they do to a witch even attempting that. Life in jail.'

She's not wrong.

The penalty for necromancy is brutal: a lifetime ban on magical practice, the seizure of all magical artifacts and a jail term up to and including life imprisonment. The Union lawmen who set the price during the Civil War were imagining all sorts of obscenities: reanimated soldiers sent to die over and over again as a tireless army of the dead, and the horror of enslavement inflicted even beyond the grave.

The last witch convicted of attempted necromancy was a pregnant young wife who lost her husband in a car crash. She failed and still got a cruel twenty years, her baby born behind bars then forcibly adopted. That was a decade ago, but I remember the case – and how there was zero public support for her. People prefer us to be soothing sore throats and mending marriages. Beyond that, they'd rather not be reminded of exactly what witches can do.

But why does *Harper* know this? My giftless girl, who never learned from me the harsh realities that I learned from my gramma about how witches must conduct themselves in the world. Who never went to summer camp to hang out with other witch kids of different magical heritages and absorb the rules we all live by.

She *must* have seen what I did that night. She must have researched what it meant. Is that one more reason for her coldness toward my craft? Not only that she doesn't have the gift herself, but that it can do something so unnatural?

Did she spend sleepless night worrying that the cops would come for her necromancer mom?

Is there any way in which my magic, and Harper's lack of it, hasn't blighted her life?

All this whirls through my head, but Harper's still standing before me expecting an answer. And right now, it's not my free-dom on the line – it's her *life*. She needs reassurance.

'Look, this is coming from two sources: Abigail, and Jake Bolt. Without them, these ridiculous accusations will simply go away.'

I tell her what I've just done. Bridget and me, confronting Abigail. I don't tell her how much it hurt my heart to do it to this woman whose life is so bound up with mine. But I'd do it again, ten times over, if that's what it takes to keep Harper safe.

I'd do worse.

'So you reckon Abigail's not going to accuse me of murdering her son? That's good of her.' Harper's lip curls. Any residual childhood affection for Auntie Abigail has burned away in the pale fire of her anger. 'What about Jake? That creep could never decide if he wants me or hates me. Looks like he's finally made up his mind. And now he's got his daddy on my case. So what can you do there? I know the chief comes to see you, so I guess you have samples – hair or something? You can do a rite to get him to drop the case.'

'That's not what I was thinking. Magic doesn't work quite that specifically.'

Fury flashes in Harper's eyes, and I feel it again, the sadness that never goes away, that I have to explain magic to my daugh-ter who has never felt it. I can only imagine how helpless and afraid she is, and how desperate, to be demanding something so unethical.

What must it be like, to see it printed in black and white that you're accused of a crime for which the sentence is death?

'Well, what *were* you thinking?'

What I'm thinking is blackmail. The chief's little problem? It's not something he'd want to get out. It could jeopardize his position. Not just the job, but his family's peace of mind and his standing at the church. Surely he'd put all those things before encouraging the fantasies of his grief-confused son?

It's never how I'd choose to proceed – it breaks witch–client protocol, and worse, it breaks every principle Gramma drummed into me. But both those fade into unimportance beside the necessity of protecting Harper.

'Never you mind,' I tell her. 'Because what you don't know, you can't be accused of being a part of.'

Harper nods.

'Anything, Mom, just not . . . Don't bring Daniel back.'

'I told you, I *can't* do that.'

She lifts a hand, but it's the way her eyes hold mine that silences me. Harper's pale, pale eyes give the impression you can see all the way down inside her. But you'd be wrong.

'What you don't say, I can't accuse you of lying to me about. No, you shouldn't bring Daniel back, because *he deserves to be dead.*'

43
Sarah

What does she mean? Each word is a little drop of aconite – five drops enough to make my heart stutter and stop.

'*He deserves to be dead*?'

'Yes. I didn't tell you, because we're good at not telling each other things, you and me. I wanted to deal with it in my own way. But Dan hurt me.'

Harper takes a breath, one of those deep ones that goes all the way down to your belly. Then she lifts her chin.

'He *raped* me, Mom.'

The word cuts deeper than anything I've ever experienced. More than Harper's giftlessness. More than my grandmother's death.

I've failed. I've failed in the one task I had during my time on this earth. Looking after my child.

And then my mind reels backward, to something I can hardly bear to think. Six years ago, I brought back to life *a boy who raped my daughter*.

My gorge rises and I grab the table for support. Aira shoots in, mewling loudly, and butts at my ankles. I pick her up and hold her painfully tight, but she doesn't complain. My sweet familiar and second soul. She wasn't at Bridget's that night. She was innocent of the crime I committed. The crime against my craft and against my grandmother's teachings. The crime against my morals. Against the law, and the laws of nature.

And now, I know, the crime against my child.

I should have left Dan there, smashed on the ground. I should have ignored Abigail's howls and screams, Bridget's begging, Julia's shock and disbelief.

'This makes me sick,' Harper says, snatching up the newspaper. 'Sanctuary doesn't know what he was really like.'

I pull out a chair and sit down. How long has my little girl carried this with her?

'I want everyone to know,' she says. 'This boy they're mourning? He was a monster. I was drugged. Someone else was there and filmed it. It's on the *internet*. Someone sent me the link today.'

She digs into her pocket for her phone. 'Unknown number' displays as she opens up a text conversation. It's only two messages long.

Happy memories? says one.

The other is a link to a website whose address doesn't conceal the sort of site it is.

'They played it that night at the villa party. It was up there on the wall for them all to see. Me being a slut, because everyone knows that's what witch girls are. It looks like I'm drunk, right? Looks like I'm putting on a good show for whoever's got the camera – maybe I wouldn't mind if they joined in? Well, Dan put something in my drink and it made me all floppy and weak. I couldn't control my body. My head was fuzzy. I couldn't do *anything*. Except . . .'

My daughter shoves her phone into my hand. She hits the link and rotates the device so I get a full-screen view.

'Listen,' she says, turning up the volume.

I'm about to tell her not to, when a catchy song I recognize blasts out.

Harper doesn't look fazed by the soundtrack.

'You get it?' she says. 'They wiped the audio. So you can't hear me saying *no*.'

I can't unsee it. My infinitely precious daughter, used as if she's of no value at all. Her mouth moving, mumbling, trying to form words that no one is listening to. I shove the phone back in her hand so I don't hurl it against the wall.

'When?' I croak.

'About four weeks ago. I broke things off with Dan last month. Things hadn't been great for a while. I did it quietly, and no one knew except his bros. They teased him, but he moved on pretty quick – you know he wasn't exactly short of admirers.

'Except that night – it was some football party – he told me he'd only gotten with . . . someone else to make me jealous. She didn't mean anything to him. Would I give him another chance? Now, I couldn't care less who he slept with. So I said as much, and that we were done. Which was when he apologized for being such a jerk and said we should be friends. He got a couple drinks, so we could toast breaking up like mature adults. They were shots, down in one.

'I knew as soon as I drank it that something was wrong. He pushed me up against a wall and was all over me. I could hear people coming by, asking, *Oh, that stuff about you two breaking up was wrong?* And him telling them, *Yeah, so wrong*. And I couldn't get the words out to say that *no*, this *was wrong*.

'He led me through the party. His bros were slapping him on the back, and he told them I'd apologized for being a stupid bitch and was going to make it up to him. I tried to pull away, kept stumbling and falling on the stairs, but he made out I was drunk. He basically carried me up and threw me on the bed. Then he just pulled my jeans down and did it. It went on for a while.'

170

As I listen to Harper, my stomach clenches and spasms use-lessly. I was fasting before attempting the divination, so there's nothing to bring up. Acid burns my throat. I want to beg her to stop. To say that I can't listen to any more.

And I want her to continue so that I know it all, know the worst — because *my* magic saved the boy that did this to her, and I need to know how deeply I've wronged her.

I need to fuel my fearlessness, to rip away any last scruples about what I might need to do to save her.

'When he was finished, he left me there and went back downstairs. I heard his teammates congratulating him. Saying that he'd brought me to heel. Showed me who was the boss. Had me gagging for it.

'I didn't know what to do, so I skipped school on the Monday and Tuesday, then the principal's office called and warned me about non-attendance. On the Wednesday, I went in and he found me in the canteen at lunchtime. He started talking loud in front of everyone. Said that I'd been begging him to let other boys join in, and that if that was what I wanted, he couldn't date me. He knew it was my witch heritage, and I couldn't help it, and that he hoped one day I'd be able to find the guy — or *guys* — who would be cool with it. Half the school was there, and I guarantee the other half knew all about it by the end of the day.

'I should have said it right there in the canteen — that he was lying and that he'd raped me. But I was blindsided. I remem-ber asking how he fucking *dared* say that, then walking out. I was shaking. I spent all week avoiding him and brooding about what to do. The next weekend was the party at Sailaway Villa. I knew he'd be there, so decided to confront him. But then some-one had the video of what he did to me and *projected it on the wall*, Mom.'

Harper's voice is wavering. Anger has boosted her this far

into her story, but it's finally all burned up and she's coasting only on pain.

'So this . . . *crap* here, about "evidence"?' She pulls the *Sentinel* special edition toward her and crumples it ferociously. 'That's Jake Bolt pointing his phone at me when I quite understandably lost my shit about the fact that my boyfriend *raped* me and someone *filmed* it and then it got *shown at a party*.'

And for the first time, her composure breaks. Her head hangs low. She's staring down at her hands, which are moving mechanically, ripping and tearing the newsprint. Can she ever forgive me that I let this happen? That I never even guessed it had?

That I worked a miracle for the boy who did it?

The boy she's now accused of killing.

And as the consequences join up in my head, I'm hushing her. Gathering her to me and pressing her face to my shoulder to comfort her, but also to keep her quiet. My eyes dart around the kitchen, checking for open windows. For any way that Harper's words might have been overheard by someone who could go running back to the newspaper for yet another special edition.

Because I can see the headline now: *ACCUSED KILLER WITCH HAS 'RAPE' CLAIM MOTIVE.*

44

Maggie

I called Remy. I had to.

I expected him to rage at me as I read the article down the phone, but it was worse than that. He was silent. Then he got in his car and drove to Sanctuary to rage in person. Now it's evening, and we're at my rental apartment rather than the police station, for obvious reasons.

'We agreed you were going to Shut. This. Down,' Remy yells. 'Do you know where I was when you called? Adam and I were at our daughter's ballet showcase. Normally, I'd rather do any-thing than watch a troupe of six-year-olds dressed like Disney princesses who fell in a cotton candy machine. Anything. Crash my car. Get revenge-stabbed by a perp. But I learned something new today. Because I would rather be *right back there* watch-ing the *twerking Sugar Plum Fairy* than here, in the middle of this.'

'We have a magical investigator on a plane right now,' I say, in the calm voice I save specially for when Remy's ranting. 'And we're gathering in everything else, forensics and the like, so that once the MI has confirmed there's no magic, we can focus confidently on identifying the real cause. It just has to be watertight, sir. The Whitmans deserve an honest answer, and it has to be *convincing*, too. Abigail Whitman has fixated on witchcraft. She'll never let it rest unless everything's set out so plain it can't be argued with.'

'Maggie, you came here on the understanding that this was an in-out job. It *theoretically* might be homicide and arson, so state police has to show its face, but *of course* it's just the usual story of a kid in an accident at a party. Box ticked. Back to head office. Instead, you're into your second week and this has snowballed from a routine inquiry to fucking *front-page news*. Just wait till the TV networks show up.'

Remy moans theatrically and throws himself into a chair, running his fingers through his slick hair. I've never seen him this bad, and that's freaking me out.

But hey, this is *my* case. And I'll be keeping the promise I made as I stood by Jenny Downes's grave on a bright, cold day last spring – I'll never let another girl come to harm because of my policing failures.

'I'm *dealing* with it, sir.' I tell him. 'The right way – by pursuing the investigation until we find the truth. That's what we agreed.'

'The governor will be down our necks, Mags. Your job's on the line here. And you know what? Mine is too. Give me one good reason why I shouldn't avert that particular calamity by throwing this to the Feds *right now*. It's a wet dream for the asshole that heads the New Haven field office. He'll hardly sleep, he'll be so excited about executing a witch.'

'That's *exactly* why,' I yell, before reining myself in. 'Jeez, Remy. You know what the law's like, how biased it is against witches – presumption of use of witchcraft, penalty uplifts, all that fun stuff.'

'Since when did you care about witches, Maggie?'

'Since when did you not care about justice, Remy?'

'Fuck you, Detective Knight.'

But he says it like the Remy I know. Like the Remy who could

174

have gone to law school, or Wall Street, and earned a salary ten times what he gets at state police HQ. Yet because he cares passionately about justice, and because he's a brown man and a gay man and he knows what it's like not to have authority on your side, he went into policing instead.

'Look,' I tell him, 'this town is a crock of shit soup that's been bubbling away for years. There's a whole bunch of interconnected families – not just the Whitmans and the Fenns, but others. Sarah Fenn has a coven and the dead boy's mother was part of it. There's also a sex tape that got shown at the party that night. Gossip and teenage hostilities. You name it.'

'A sex tape? Gossip? I thought this was a witchcraft homicide case, not fucking *Sweet Valley High*.'

'I'm pretty sure there weren't any sex tapes in *Sweet Valley High*, sir.'

Remy snorts. 'I missed a few episodes. But this tape? You didn't mention it before.'

'I wasn't sure if it was relevant before. No copy has turned up yet, just a screenshot that shows the deceased and the accused. When it got posted online, there was a caption that accused Fenn, the witch's daughter, of being a slut "and worse".'

'*And worse*? What's she like, this witch girl? What did *she* say happened that evening?'

'I haven't formally interviewed her yet, sir. We had a short conversation when she was discharged from hospital.'

'Hey, you hear that bouncing sound, Mags?' Remy cocks his head to one side. 'That's a ball dropping. Why haven't you interviewed her?'

'Believe me, I've tried. But she's been spending time outside Sanctuary – understandably enough.'

'Flight risk?' Remy barks.

'I don't get that impression. The mother implied it was normal behavior. But yeah, she's not been easy to track down.

There's plenty else I need, too. Because, at the moment, this whole so-called murder case is a he-said-she-said scenario. All I've got to suggest she did it is the testimony of the deceased's best friend, who is also the source of the video of her allegedly using magic . . .'

'. . . And also the chief's son, right? Yeah. He makes his allegations. She denies them. Not fruitful. And interviewing her creates a supposition of guilt that it wouldn't be healthy to encourage in the current climate.'

'Exactly. I thought it would be best to wait for the MI's assessment. If they tell me there's no magic at the house and all she's doing is waving her hands around because she's furious someone's showing a sex tape, then it becomes a completely different sort of interview.'

'Gotcha. So get the MI out to that house the minute the twigs of their fucking broomstick scratch Connecticut soil. Then, as soon as you know what you're dealing with, interview the girl. When we know there's no magic, that interview is just a formality: *What was the deceased's mental state? Was he real sad when you broke up?*, et cetera. If you want to get the mother to agree with minimal fuss to a case closure on accidental death, the hint that the alternative is a ruling of suicide could help clarify her options.'

Shit. It's a good thing I know from the Downes case that Lieutenant Remy Lamarr has a heart, because otherwise you might think that all there is inside that fancy suit jacket is an expensive shirt and a ribcage containing a tiny shard of ice.

'I need you to trust me, sir,' I say. 'I can get this done and give these people the truth about their kids. It's why we do this job, right?'

My boss opens his mouth, then closes it. And my heart's in my throat, because up till this moment, when Remy could still yank me off the case, I hadn't realized just how invested

I've become. I'm practically holding my breath when he finally speaks.

'Well, you keep pursuing truth and justice, Mags. Personally, I'm just here to pay my husband's tab at Brooks Brothers and keep my son in organic diapers. I'll monitor the media and want an update the minute your MI's done their woo-woo.'

He waggles his fingers mystically in a way that'd guarantee a disciplinary if anyone saw. Then, with a swirl of his trench coat around the door, he's gone.

And I'm back in business.

45

Maggie

New day. New start. And hopefully the beginning of the end for our case as Chester's car pulls up at Sailaway Villa with a witch inside. He's collected our magical investigator from the airport.

If Rowan's website photo was striking, then in person they have the impact of a meteor hit. Chester's wide eyes suggest he's ground zero. I've never seen that witchy megawattage at close quarters before. Does Sarah Fenn dampen hers down, or is she simply not as powerful?

As we shake hands, Rowan's grasp feels unusually firm and I glance down. Each finger is bound in coils. Most are metal, but one is sheathed in a spiral of what looks like bone or horn, which I realize is the inner whorl of a shell. Prickles run along my spine just looking at them.

I point out details of the burned shell of the house, and the witch's piercing gaze takes everything in.

'It's alleged that a crime was committed here,' I tell them. 'We need to know whether magic was used, and if there is any emotional imprint that might be a clue to intent or motive.'

'Understood. Before we begin, I need to perform a rite of readiness. I'll of course conduct the assessment using Moot-recognized magical procedures, but I prefer to prepare according to my tribe's traditions. So if you could wait in your vehicle.' It's not a question. 'And turn it away from the house. My craft isn't for the eyes of outsiders.'

The witch slips the strap of a satchel over their head and kneels to unpack it.

'I've found Rowan accommodation outside town,' Chester says, 'so there's no risk of them seeing any of Varley's articles about our case – or of Varley seeing Rowan.'

'Good thinking, Batman.'

But there's something uneasy in my sergeant's eyes.

'What's eating you, Chester? The magic? The fact that this case involves families you've known your entire life?'

'Both, I guess,' he says. 'I thought I knew what magic is – it's the small stuff. My gran goes to Sarah Fenn all the time and swears by her. And I thought I knew these people, too. Dan Whitman's a kind of local star and his dad's a really important guy. But this case is changing everything.'

'I understand,' I tell him. 'But that's what this job is. We see stuff that shakes us and confuses us, and it's our job to break it down into something that makes sense and that a jury will recognize as truth.'

Chester's nod nearly turns into a headbutt of the car roof when there's a rap at the window.

Rowan is ready.

They're carrying two sticks cinched with an iron ring. One half is bound by corded leather to form a handle. We duck under the incident tape, and the unbound prongs twitch in Rowan's hands as we enter the villa. Our feet scuff deep ash and crunch the grit beneath.

Then our investigator moans, sharp and anguished.

'Rowan?'

Chester is next to the witch, supporting their elbow. Rowan's breathing rattles, and they lean on my sergeant a moment.

179

'Are you okay?' I ask.

'This is . . .' Rowan wipes their forehead. 'This is *intense*.'

'Are you happy to continue?'

Their full mouth twists. '*Happy* isn't the word I'd use.'

Like a nervous new mom taking their kid to the adventure playground for the first time, Chester's eyes never leave Rowan. The witch's breath is coming hard.

And I'm getting a bad feeling about this. Because though I'm no expert, I'm guessing this isn't Rowan's reaction to normal, non-magically fucked-up places.

'Are you able to tell us what you're experiencing,' I ask, 'or would you prefer us to remain silent?'

'I . . . This . . . Right now I'm feeling the presence of all these kids. Adolescent emotion is so strong and chaotic. But there's something else, too.'

'Magic?'

'Anger. And fear.'

Fear. The fear of kids seeing their friend die in the middle of a party, in a crowded house that caught on fire? Maybe Dan's fear as he fell – or as he realized someone at the party wished him harm? Perhaps the fear of someone coming here to murder him, afraid of what they were about to do, and of being found out.

As we move into the atrium, the wood of Rowan's sticks starts to *thrum*. It's so like a tuning fork that I expect at any moment to hear an eerie note. The silence is somehow even more unnerving.

There is a force at work that I can neither see, hear, nor feel. It's like blind man's buff, which I refused to play as a child. I always felt queasy at the thought of stumbling around unseeing, arms stretched out for people who could be within your reach if only you knew. Or – somehow worse – be nowhere near at all.

Chester raises a hand and I glance over. He points to the ash carpeting the floor. It's swirling, as though birthing a dust devil. Rowan's eyes are fixed ahead. The witch hasn't seen it.

Which is riskier? To interrupt them, or not to do so?

Rowan advances. Half a foot, then another. And again, until they're standing in what the photographs tell me (though I've never told Rowan) is the exact spot where Daniel fell.

'It is,' they say softly. 'It definitely is.'

'Is *what*?' I whisper.

The writhing dust gives me the answer. *Magic*. Just as it appears to coalesce into a definite form, it dissolves again. As I watch, something like revulsion rises in me. It's as if an invisible hand is inscribing in the air every cruel and hurtful word I've ever had hurled at me.

'Oh,' breathes Rowan, in a tone close to wonder.

They're watching the shifting dust as if they've never seen anything like it, and I catch the moment their expression turns from wonder to horror. With one rapid movement they tuck their sticks away and raise their hands, moving them with practiced fluidity.

Then the witch freezes their gestures and utters a sound that's unmistakably a command.

I expect the dust to obey. To hang midair in some telltale shape. But it doesn't.

It explodes. I drop to my knees, choking and blinded, hands shielding my eyes. I feel my eardrums pop – from pressure, not sound.

In front of me, Rowan hits the floor.

46

Sarah

Journalists get to work early. The first knock on my door is at eight in the morning.

'Sarah Fenn? I'm Anna Dao from WCON-TV. Sorry to stop by so early, but I reckon it'll be a busy day for you after that piece in the *Sentinel*. Can I come in?'

She's caught me off guard. I stare at her, taking in the sprayed and backcombed hair, the camera-ready makeup. If I turn her away, will she stand on my lawn and repeat the lies that have already been printed about us?

'Ms Fenn?' the reporter coos sympathetically.

But I can see something at work behind her eyes that isn't at all soft sympathy.

Which is when I hear Harper on the stairs behind me and Dao practically leaps into the air to look over my shoulder for a better view.

'Miss Fenn? I was just having a word with your mom. Do come and join us.'

I pull the door closer, narrowing the reporter's field of view. But it's too late; Harper is at my back.

Dao turns to gesture frantically across the street, where a white van emblazoned with the WCON-TV channel logo is parked. 'Brett!' she yells, and a man in jeans who was leaning against the vehicle drops the cigarette he's been smoking and slams open the van's side. He emerges with a camera, a huge one, which he swings onto his shoulder, one hand already fiddling with its dozens of buttons.

'Harper,' says Dao, that sympathetic face turned back toward us, 'how do you feel about these shocking allegations that have been made against you?'

The cameraman is jogging across the road.

My daughter looks as if she's considering saying something. But there's nothing that'd be a good idea right now. So I slam the door, then flip the deadbolt and slide across the chain.

Dao is calling from the other side.

'Ms Fenn? Harper? We'd love to help you tell your side of the story.'

'Please move off my property,' I say, as loudly as I can.

'We'll be right opposite if you want us.'

Something scrabbles at the bottom of the door, and a moment later, two business cards are pushed under. I look at them lying there, knowing that this is only the beginning. Harper stoops to pick one up and shows me.

'She's eager.' Next to her phone number, the reporter has scrawled, 'Call me!'

How can I secure our home and protect our privacy?

Harper's reaching for the lock and I think she's got the same idea, but then I realize she's trying to open it. Which is when I register that she's wearing her running gear. The leggings and long-sleeved T-shirt that protect her skin from the sun. I slap my hand down to hold the door closed.

'You have to be joking. They'll be all over you.'

'I'm not under house arrest *yet*, Mom.'

And she's right. My free spirit. I can't let them cage her. Not in here, and not in a jail cell.

Not when *she's* the one who's been victimized, by Dan Whitman.

My daughter was raped. My daughter is falsely accused of murder. Those two unbearable facts stole my sleep last night.

To keep my girl safe, I need Abigail to state that she doesn't think Harper was responsible for Dan's death, and I need her to get Jake Bolt to withdraw his accusation. She told me that bringing her son back was the price for that. But it's impossible. Dan's body is charred and cold.

And now this. Abigail won't co-operate if I tell her what her son did to my daughter. It'll burn the last bridge between us. So keeping Harper safe means accepting that she'll never get justice for what Dan did to her.

And that *hurts*.

There are alternatives. I'm more certain than ever that what happened during my divination – that exploded bowl – is the answer to how Daniel died. That *magic itself* killed him. Death reclaimed the boy I snatched from it six years ago.

So I could come clean. Go public with how I brought Dan back that night, and how magic took him again at the party.

But my heart quails at the thought of the penalty for necromancy – imprisonment and magical forfeiture. My magic is my life, second only to my daughter. And it would be devastating for Harper. She's old enough to live independently rather than being taken into state care, but she'd be all alone and with the shame of a mother guilty of the most unnatural crime.

I'll do it if it's the only way to save Harper. But I'm not out of options yet.

The only way that doesn't involve yet more risk lies with Abigail. Yesterday, it seemed that she'd finally accepted that Dan was gone and was prepared to drop her allegations. Now I just need to make her do it. Could I get her here to speak to this reporter?

Harper's tugging on the door again.

'Earth to Mom? Or are you planning on keeping me indoors all day?'

I would, if I could. I wouldn't let her out – or even out of my sight – until I have this all fixed. But that won't be possible.

Going about our daily life will show them we've nothing to hide. And if the cameras can see how young Harper is, how she's just a girl . . .

'They'll be watching,' I tell her. 'WCON-TV could be just the beginning. There may be photographers. These people take hundreds of photos and use only one – the one where you're looking angry or dangerous, or smirking. Don't let them get that shot. Don't talk to them. Understood? And if you feel threatened or unsure at any time, you come straight home, or go someplace safe and call me, yes?'

Harper nods. I chuck her under the chin. I haven't done that for years.

'There's my girl. I'm going to Abigail's to end this. She's the one with the power to call it all off, and to make Jake see sense. I won't let this hang over you, darling.'

I try to show her my love and reassurance, looking deep into my daughter's eyes. But as ever, with Harper, I'm not sure that I see much further than the surface.

'Will you tell her what I told you?' she asks. 'What Dan did to me? After all this "perfect Daniel" stuff, I want her to know what her son really was.'

My stomach knots.

'That's not a good idea right now,' I say. 'It'll upset her. We need her to co-operate, at least until this is over.'

'So *I'm* the victim, but we stay quiet while we beg Abigail to *please, please* tell the nice cops that I didn't do it? That's what you're saying.'

'Darling, please, you can see why.'

Harper's lip curls. 'I should, what, be grateful to be off the hook for something I didn't do? *So* grateful that I keep my mouth shut?'

What can I say? That you can't get justice against a boy who's dead? That Abigail's suffered enough by losing her son, and that calling him a rapist would end her?

'Right now,' I tell her, 'your safety is the thing that matters. Abigail's on a knife edge. Unstable. Unpredictable. If she thinks you're attacking Dan, she'll go for you even harder.'

'Yet she's attacking me, and you're not going for her?'

Her accusation is like a slap.

I *would* fight for Harper. I *will*, if it comes to it. I'd do anything to save her.

But what my giftless girl doesn't understand is that witches can never strike first. They can barely even strike back. Gramma always told me that tolerance of us is a rickety bridge over a deep pit of fear and suspicion. We have to watch every step we take, in case there's a loose slat underfoot. I'll do this my own way.

'It's not . . .' I start, but Harper is wrenching the lock. I don't want to give the TV crew anything by dragging her back in or calling after her. So I just watch, feeling sick, as she bounds down the steps.

Across the road, the cameraman scrambles to pick up his kit again, but he's too slow, and with a flip of her ponytail Harper is around the corner and gone.

47

Abigail

'It's the right thing to do,' Bridget says, rummaging in cupboards so filthy, so disorganized that I wonder she can find anything. They're all full of brightly packaged, sugar-laden cereals, and she grabs an armful and piles them into the centre of the table.

I stayed here last night. After that awful scene with Sarah, I couldn't bear to be alone, so I let Bridget scoop me up and bring me to her house. I thought it would be comforting, but being in what is so unmistakably a family home scrapes at the open wound of my loss.

The fridge door is covered with papers and letters all bearing the Sanctuary High insignia. There's a Spartans pennant jammed over one curtain rail. The windowsill is cluttered with photographs, and somehow my eyes go unerringly to the one that shows the four of us – the witch and her bitches, as we'd joke – with our kids down on the shore. I look away.

'Izzy? Iz! Breakfast?' Bridget is bellowing up the stairs.

'No need to yell, honey.'

It's Cheryl, in a tailored suit and holding a smart Gucci bucket bag full of files. How can she bear to live in this house of cats and chaos? What on earth does she see in Bridget? Not for the first time, I wonder if Sarah had a hand in that. Love potions are a heavily regulated area of witchcraft. They're permitted when taken consensually within existing relationships. Husbands and wives who've lost a bit of sparkle but want to stay together. But magic isn't allowed to win someone's affections, or to end them.

Cheryl doesn't seem to need any encouragement as she pats Bridget's ass and plants a kiss on her cheek. She pats my arm too, as she leaves, and tells me I'm welcome to stay as long as I like. Then, brushing cat hair from her sleeve, she's out of the door.

'Izzy!'

Bridget's exasperated bellow is cut short as her daughter appears. Isobel is in a slovenly onesie. The girl sees me and shrinks back in the kitchen doorway. That shouldn't hurt, but it does. It's happened countless times by now. For every person who crosses the road to hug me and offer sympathy, someone else looks away to avoid eye contact or hangs back to prevent our paths crossing.

I know that it's embarrassment, or a desire not to hurt me further by saying the wrong thing. But how could anyone feel that an awkward word would inflict pain, after the agony of Daniel's loss? I *want* people to talk to me about him. To praise his talent, his good looks, his kindness. To never stop talking about him, as if he's just upstairs, or out at practice, and will be home soon.

Bridget corners Isobel before she can slink back to her room. 'It's okay,' I hear her say quietly. 'Come and chat. She's lonely.'

She pities me. *Bridget* pities me. And I know that I've toppled from the top of our friendship group to the bottom.

'Just do it, young lady.' And Bridget practically pushes her daughter into the kitchen.

Defeated, Isobel creeps in, tucking a strand of frizzy hair behind her ear. It seems impossible that she's only a year below Daniel at school. There were rumors that Beatriz bullied her, and things got tense between Julia and Bridget for a few months, but it must have gotten resolved eventually. I always felt proud to be the mom of a boy – they're so much more straightforward and honest. Girls can be sly, slinking things.

'Good morning, Abigail, I'm sorry for your loss,' Isobel mumbles robotically, as if someone just pressed a button in her back. Bridget gently maneuvers her into a chair and pours her a large glass of orange juice. Dan never drank OJ – it's pure sugar.

'Have something to eat, darling,' Bridget coaxes, selecting a cereal and tipping what is plainly twice the recommended portion size into a bowl. The chocolate dusting on it turns the milk brown as she pours it in. 'Izzy's finally getting over her mono – aren't you, sweetie?'

The girl listlessly spoons cereal into her mouth, and for a few minutes the only sound in the kitchen is the wet noise of her eating, and the mewing and scraping of cats underfoot. I'm relieved when she trudges back upstairs and Bridget suggests we sit outside on the terrace. It'll be good to escape the stink of cat food and litter trays.

Except as soon as we step outside, I freeze up. My heart takes off at twice its normal speed, and I grip the door frame.

'Abi? Are you okay?'

Bridget's face looms in front of me as she asks her foolish question. Of course I'm not okay. And then realization dawns on her.

'Oh God, here, where we all . . . Abi, are you having a panic attack? Let's go back in.'

It feels more like I'm having a heart attack. Bridget's voice is reaching me over the deafening sound of my own frantic pulse.

But it's not that either. My long-ago therapist training taught me what this is. It's adrenaline: the fright, flight or fight response to a threat. Only the threat isn't to me; it's to my boy, and I'm powerless to help him because it's already too late.

This is where Daniel died the first time.

And this is where I sat just a few weeks ago, in the last moments I was happy, while we all ate dinner and drank wine as our kids were fleeing for their lives from a burning building. Only my son was already dead.

Bridget is trying to coax me back inside. Instead I unclaw my hand from the door frame and step out. The outdoor table and chairs are still in the exact same place. They rest on decking now.

I glance up at where he fell – and see Isobel's bovine face watching me from the window, confused by what her mom's making all this fuss about. Bridget gestures at her impatiently and she steps away, pulling the curtains.

'Abi? If you won't go back in, come and sit down.'

I let Bridget steer me to a chair. I feel dizzy, like I'm in two places at once – or two *times*. Then and now.

If losing a child is the worst thing that can happen to you, what did I do to deserve losing mine twice?

'Do you remember that night?' I ask her. 'Do you remember what happened?'

48

Abigail

Daniel fell without a sound.

The kids had been messing about, playing. It was past their bedtime and we'd blithely assumed they were all asleep. Beatriz's older brothers had stayed at home – they were about to start their senior year and found our tribe of twelve-year-olds too 'babyish'. So it was just Daniel and the girls upstairs, and us moms downstairs. Michael and Pierre were there, but Alberto was away in the city.

Dan hit the ground right *there*. Just meters from us.

And I can't help it, I get up and crouch and touch the spot. I stroke the smooth decking, imagining that beneath it a tiny speck of my son's blood seeped down between the original paving and into the ground. That it's still there, warm within the soil. Living.

My recollections of what happened next are a mess, though we worked out later that the whole thing took no more than twenty minutes from beginning to end – or from end to beginning. From the moment my boy lay dead at my feet to the moment we carried him inside to the sofa, his heart beating again and his chest rising and falling.

Michael got to him first. I've never loved my husband more than in that moment as he knelt by our son's motionless body.

It was only a second-story window. Kids fall from that height and merely break an arm or an ankle, or even walk away un-scathed. But we could all see from *how* Dan fell that it was bad. He'd landed head first. The paving was stained dark be-neath him, and blood was trickling from his nose in a thin red stream.

Michael did all the checks, but our son's eyes didn't open, he gave no verbal reply. His body didn't even make a reflex response – I think that's when I finally screamed.

'No,' Bridget says. She's lowered herself beside me and is holding my hand. 'No, you were screaming from the moment he fell. You sounded like a stricken animal. Pierre was the only one of us strong enough to hold you.'

As she says it, I remember. Pierre's arms so tight around me that I couldn't move, couldn't go to my broken boy.

'Michael wanted you to keep back,' says Bridget. 'He said that with head trauma the slightest wrong movement of the patient could be fatal.'

I remember Michael performing the checks again with crisp precision: fingertip force. A pinch to the collarbone. A touch above the eye.

We could all tell from his face that he wasn't getting the re-sponse he needed.

'That was when you turned to Sarah,' Bridget prompts me. 'You begged her. You sort of slumped in Pierre's arms and he told me afterwards that he thought you'd fainted, but you were actually trying to get on your knees. Literally begging on your knees. Oh God, it was unbearable.'

She's crying. My friend is sobbing as we sit on her deck reliving it all. Now I'm squeezing her fingers and comforting *her*.

Because there's no reason to cry about that night. It ended with my son whole and alive in my arms.

'I remember what you said,' Bridget gulps. 'I'll never forget it. You said: *Will you offer them me instead?* I'd never heard anything so awful or so beautiful.'

I remember it too. I didn't know who *they* were. Angels. Demons. I didn't care. I would have let them peel off my skin and bottle up my soul in exchange for my child's life.

But of course there is no *them*. There was only Sarah.

She told us it was impossible. Then she told me she'd try anyway, and that it was the web of our love, the coven's strength, that made her even consider it.

'I got the knife from the kitchen,' Bridget says. The flesh beneath her chin quivers as she wipes at the tears streaking her face. 'It was the sharp one we keep for special – Thanksgiving turkey, birthday cake.'

We both laugh, a hiccupping, despairing sort of hilarity.

'I sprayed it with hand sanitizer and brought it out.'

And then Sarah did it. All four of us did – Julia joining in for the very first time. The ritual that brought Dan back to me.

The disbelief of the moment when his body jerked upwards, as if magic had dropped a hook into his chest and fished him back up from the depths. That tiny moment of almost not wanting it to be true, because if it was, it meant hope, and if that hope was false, it would have been the end of everything.

How the four of us, utterly drained, watched as Michael repeated the checks. How Dan's eyes opened and he nodded in response to a question. Then Pierre scooped him up – my son was taller and heavier than me, even at age twelve – and carried him indoors to the sofa.

'That was when we heard the police siren,' Bridget interjects. 'Someone had heard you screaming. Pierre and I were on the rocks by then, and we both knew some folks were taking a more than neighborly interest in our business. There was one

193

old busybody who'd never liked having a black guy live across the street. Well, she got an Asian lesbian in exchange. I think the shock finished her off.'

We laugh properly at that, and it feels good – honest and cleansing. It's the first time I've laughed since Daniel died. And although that thought brings a wave of guilt crashing down on me, I somehow don't drown. Bridget's hand anchors me. She was there for me that night. They all were. Sarah most of all.

It was Sarah who took command again when we first heard the siren. She knew that what we'd all done was illegal. I remember insisting that it was worth going to jail for the rest of my life, whereupon Julia slapped me to snap me out of it. Daniel would need me. All our kids needed us. All it required was a simple story.

Sarah knelt by Dan and told him what to say – that he'd come downstairs for cookies, hadn't switched the light on so as not to disturb the girls, and had slipped on the unfamiliar stairs. She made him repeat it over and over.

'She was insistent,' Bridget adds. 'And I remember you getting angry with her. But it was the right thing to do. Then she just collapsed into the chair. We were all exhausted from that spell . . .' She shudders, and I remember the bone-deep weariness that didn't shift for weeks afterwards. 'Pierre went upstairs to check on the girls. Told them that Dan had fallen down the stairs, and to tell anyone who asked that they'd been asleep when it happened. Then the cop turned up. Thank goodness we'd got our stories straight.'

I don't really remember the cop, only that she kept suggesting that Dan go to hospital to be checked over. I was sitting on the sofa with him, holding his hand, and you would have needed the strength of ten Pierres to pry me away from him.

Michael handled all that. Pulled the Yale medical faculty card, and the cop backed down soon enough.

And that was that. No police follow-up. No questions. Just my boy, given back to me thanks to the love of my friends.

My tears start up again. Quietly at first, but soon I'm hunched over, bawling my eyes out. And these tears are something new. It's not heartbreak and loss over Daniel, or contemptible self-pity. It's shame and remorse for how I've treated Sarah. The threats I've made against her.

'I'm a monster,' I gasp, curling away from Bridget's comfort that I don't deserve. 'What I've said to Sarah, and what I've done. Oh God, what am I?'

'You're a woman who's suffered something none of us can imagine,' Bridget says. 'And whose friends love her.'

'How can you? I threatened Sarah. Told her that I believed what Jake said about Harper. I *did* believe it. But it can't have been Harper, can it?'

'No, it can't,' Bridget says.

'Sarah must hate me.'

'She doesn't. Shh, she doesn't.'

My friend gathers me in like Pierre did that night, and rocks me.

'We understand. *Sarah* understands. It's all going to be all right.'

Will it? I'm torn in two. I know Dan's not coming back.

I know Harper couldn't have killed him by magic.

I don't know where we go from here.

But in this moment, my friend's strong arms and her comfort are enough.

49

Maggie

Chester reacts first, dragging Rowan backward to the doorway. I hawk and cough blackened spittle into the ash, then wipe gritty gobs from my eyes.

When I can see clearly again, I make my way unsteadily outside. Rowan is squatting in the churned dirt, coughing. I've never been so relieved to hear someone sound like they're regurgitating lung.

Chester scuttles back to the witch's side with their satchel, and Rowan fumbles for a water bottle. It's a good few more minutes until they stand up, and when they do, it's by leaning on Chester's shoulder.

'So, the answer to your question is pretty obvious,' Rowan says. 'Yes, magic was used in that house. And it was powerful. So much so that even its *traces* have power.'

'You mean the villa is still under a spell of some kind?'

'Not actively bewitched. Think of a bonfire. Even long after the flames have burned out, the embers are still hot. Well, this villa is still magically "hot". Whatever happened here was done by someone extremely gifted.'

I look back over my shoulder at the villa, half fearful that those smoky symbols might swirl out the gaping window and choke us, clogging our every breath. What we felt in there was

. . . wrong. The mere memory of it makes the house somehow obscene.

But what did I tell Chester? It's our job to break this down into something that makes sense.

'Is there any way you can identify who did it? If I introduced you to a person, or gave you a thing belonging to them?'

'That's an ethical gray area, Detective, like obtaining a DNA sample without someone's consent. But in this instance there's something else. How can I put it? Magic is *personal*, like finger-prints or handwriting. But this? It's like something typed instead of handwritten. Like fingerprints without any whorls. It's just *magic*. I got no sense of where it came from or whose it is.'

'What if it was done by more than one witch?' suggests Chester. And I'm impressed, because that's a smart idea. But Rowan is shaking their head.

'I don't think so. It's illegal for witches to craft magic with another magical practitioner. We have to work alone with non-magical assistants – that's how Moot defines a coven. I saw it once down in Kentucky, though. Triplet witch sisters, fourteen years old, who were their own illegal coven and got their kicks by hexing livestock on farms belonging to their daddy's rivals. Unpicking it was tough, but I figured out that even though it felt like one spell, there were three separate sources. Here, it's almost as if there's no source at all.'

Rowan sways and Chester helps them lean against his patrol car.

'Are you going to need medical attention?' I ask. 'Chester can take you.'

'I don't use commercial medicine. Never have, never will. Let's see how I feel tomorrow.'

The investigator looks beyond physically exhausted. I don't want to press for more information, but I have to.

'Just one more thing before Chester takes you to rest up. I'd like to show you something. Is that okay?'

We get in the patrol car and sit side by side; Chester, in the back, cranes over the seat as I place a screen in Rowan's lap and hit 'play'.

The witch watches attentively, wincing as the video reaches its conclusion: Jake's awful cry as he sees the body of his friend. But they make no comment on Harper.

'That's it?' they ask. 'The boy who's fallen, is that the act supposed to have been caused by magic?'

'You mean you're not seeing any magic being worked in what I've just shown you?'

'No, I've seen two kids arguing. Or rather, I've seen one kid, the girl, who's shouting at whoever is recording this. I presume that's his voice we hear at the end.'

'And her . . .' I pause, not wanting to ask a leading question. But Rowan Andrews is no fool. They'll be fitting together the pieces to get a clear idea of the scenario I'm investigating. 'Her hands? Are they . . .?'

Rowan restarts the video, slowing it right down. Frame by frame. Then again. And a third time.

'What am I doing?' they ask, moving their hands in the way Harper does in the tape. Their gestures are choppy, tense, angry. There's no flow to them. No purpose that I can see. Chester and I look at each other, at a loss.

'I'm giving someone a piece of my mind,' Rowan says, eventually. 'I'm suppressing the urge to strangle them with my bare hands. I'm probably calling them a motherfucker. But I'm *not* doing magic. The only thing these hands are channeling is anger.

'I'm presuming the scenario is this – you don't need to confirm. The girl has been accused of magically causing the boy to fall. And it's easy to see why. Her hands are perfectly in sync with what happens.'

Rowan backtracks and takes us through the crucial few seconds. Harper's hands come together and push downward. A few beats pass, then the first scream, as someone realizes Dan has fallen.

'It's a strong gesture,' the witch concludes. 'Suspicious to someone untrained in magic. But believe me, when hand movements are used in our craft, it isn't like that. In some traditions, it's flowing and fluid, like conducting music. In Western European magic, which is dominant among white New England witches, it tends to be controlled and precise. But there's no tradition where gestured magic looks wild like this.'

I exhale. So it's *not* Harper.

That tallies with what the school principal told me about the girl not having the gift. Her mom told me that too.

Except that leaves the *mom* as the only known person of ability in Sanctuary. I think back to the scene at Fenn's workroom – the blasted-off door and blown-out windows. There's one other place I've seen blown-out windows recently, and it's the ruined villa right behind me.

Could *Sarah* Fenn be responsible?

It was plain that she wasn't being completely honest about what happened at her booth. Is there anything else she hasn't been telling me?

I recall the half-painted pentagram, the paint slashing across the facade of their little wooden house in the twisty streets of The Cobb. I'd linked it to the accusations against Harper, but it could just as easily have been because of her mom.

But why might she want to harm her daughter's boyfriend – the son of one of her oldest friends?

What if the answer lies in another part of this puzzle? The other video filmed on some high-schooler's phone. The sex tape that was playing on the wall at the party.

What if Sarah was angry at Dan for allowing it to go public, humiliating her daughter?

That's a reason for her to lash out at him – though it doesn't seem motive enough for her to intentionally kill a boy she's known his entire life.

A mother's anger. A tragic accident. A boy left dead. It's plausible.

Chester is silent, waiting for my instructions. I ask him to get Rowan to their accommodation to rest up after what just happened.

While they head out of town, I head in, to the historic quarter where the Fenns live. There's a goddam WCON-TV news crew parked outside their house. The reporter hurries over as I pull up. Anna Dao. Does the court beat, and we all know her by sight.

'Routine visit, Anna,' I tell her before she can get a question in. 'Sorry, no story for you today.'

Dao pouts and instructs her cameraman to film anyway as I knock on the door. When there's no response, I figure that Fenn knows there's a journalist on her doorstep, so I add that it's police, and soon afterward the chain rattles and the door cracks open all by itself. At first I wonder if it's magic, before I realize that Fenn is tucked behind the door to avoid the camera.

'Good technique,' I tell her, and receive a frazzled smile.

'How can I help?' she asks, leading me through to the kitchen. Despite that smile, I sense wariness in her voice.

This time around, I'm noticing everything. The house is like some museum of witchcraft, with weird objects on every surface and wall. That thing on the mantelpiece – is it just a twig, or could it be a shriveled finger? Is that mirror for doing makeup, or for seeing visions?

What just happened at the villa is making me jumpy. Everything in here is acquiring a sinister aura.

'Did you work out the mistake?' I ask.

'What mistake?'

'The one you made in your divining rite. The one that wrecked your workroom.'

She grimaces. 'Magic is extremely complex, Detective – that sort of thing especially so. There are literally a hundred mistakes I could have made.'

'You were able to secure your booth, though?'

'Yes, thank you. Though I had to call Pierre out again. Is that why you're here?'

'Mainly to make sure that you've not been subject to any further trouble after that special issue of the *Sentinel*. I'm going to be visiting Beryl Varley today, to remind her of reporting standards and advise that there is a duty of care in respect of your daughter, seeing as she's a minor.'

'Varley published lies about my daughter and claimed she'd be executed if they were true, so I'd like her to get rather more than a reminder of reporting standards. But I can't tell you how to do your job.'

'Understood. Ms Fenn, can you think of any reason why someone might wish to harm Daniel Whitman on your daughter's behalf?'

The question is unexpected, as I intended it to be. Fenn controls her reaction well, but not so well that I don't spot it.

She lies.

'No, I can't, Detective. I'm sorry. And honestly, I've yet to see a single good reason why anyone is even linking my daughter's name to Dan's death.'

I let that pass, as I must. Then: 'Ms Fenn, are you the only witch or magical person in Sanctuary?'

'Yes.' She pauses. 'That I know of.'

Something changes between those two responses. What is it? The first sounded genuine. So why add the second? Has Fenn

201

got wind that Rowan is in town? Did she sense them at work at the villa?

If she's responsible for the magic at the party, and knows there's an investigator who'll confirm its use, is she preparing to shift the blame onto some mystery witch?

'There could be one that you're not aware of?'

'I would have thought that was unlikely, but with everything that's happened, it's certainly not impossible. Why are you asking about magic? Do you have proof that it was used at the party house? I mean, proof beyond whatever Jake Bolt thinks he saw?'

Her expression is shrewd, and it occurs to me that it's not for nothing that witches were called 'cunning women'. I fleetingly consider telling her *yes*. Her reaction would be revealing.

But those words Remy threw in warning – *flight risk* – stop me. If Sarah Fenn is behind whatever happened and she knows I have proof of magic, she'll also know it's only a matter of time until we can connect it back to her. She might leave town.

For now, I sidestep her question by offering advice on dealing with the news crew, and telling her again to get in touch immediately if she or Harper feel threatened in any way. So, of course, when I finally take my leave, the news van has gone.

Fenn looks relieved. As she closes the door behind me, I hear her pick up some keys from a dish in the hallway.

Flight risk.

Don't run out on me, Sarah Fenn. Or I'll have no alternative but to believe you're guilty.

50

Sarah

That was close. Too close for comfort.

Any reason why someone might wish to harm Daniel Whitman on your daughter's behalf? the cop said, just tossing it out there.

Are you the only witch in Sanctuary?

What has she figured out? What has she heard – or what is she guessing at? Does anyone else know that what Dan did to Harper was rape?

Did she phrase the question like that to trap me? Because what it really means is: *Did Dan do something to Harper that deserved revenge?* I was tempted, just for a moment, to tell her the truth. To say, *Yes, he did. He raped my daughter.* But while Harper's still prime suspect, I'm not handing them anything that pins a motive on her.

And why was the detective asking about magic? Has she brought in a magical investigator who has found its presence at the villa, just like I did?

Time to finish this.

I need to speak to Abigail. I've been trapped in here waiting for the news crew to leave, but now the coast is clear. Time to make her keep her word and come out publicly behind Harper's innocence.

Except Abigail's cell phone rings and rings with no answer.

I call the house phone instead, but still she doesn't pick up. Frustration almost chokes me.

Well, there's someone else to speak to. Another accuser I need to help see the error of their ways.

I head to my car, with a stern reminder to myself to park it in the alley out back from now on, where I can slip in and out unobserved. I don't know the exact address I'm going to, but I'll recognize it. And I have a landmark to guide me – the huge white box of the Black Hill Beacon Chapel.

If the chapel folks knew I was driving by, they'd probably convene a prayer ring to try and pray me away.

I've nothing against religion. In fact I admire people who hold firm to their values. Many of those within the three Abrahamic religions of Christianity, Judaism and Islam have made their peace with witchcraft, even if it's an uneasy peace. But all faiths have those who'd happily vote to outlaw us if offered the choice at the ballot box. Luckily, politicians don't have the appetite for it – we're pretty watertight under the First Amendment.

And all faiths have those who'd go further, and return to the days of persecution if they could. While that's not the official stance of Beacon Chapel, several members of the Black Hill congregation would as soon light a bonfire under me as shake my hand. When my house got attacked last week, my thoughts went to them. But they're mostly old men, and crabbed letters to their representatives are more their thing, rather than spray-can graffiti.

The chief's wife is a pillar of the congregation. I don't know where Mary-Anne Bolt stands on the matter of witchcraft. But I'd bet my gramma's crystal ball her husband hasn't told her he's a client of mine.

Their house is two streets away from the looming church. A drive-by tells me instantly which it is, among these identical suburban homes. 'Summer's Coming!' says the sign in the front yard, featuring a kitten and a puppy rolling on a beach. I've heard Mary-Anne changes it every season, the kitten and puppy gamboling tirelessly through leaves in fall, snow in winter, and flowers in spring. Through the open window wafts the smell of baking, doubtless destined for a church sale.

All around are signs of a home that's raised four boys, from the outsize vehicle garage to the basketball hoop screwed to the side of it.

Jake is the only boy still at home. His mom and pop have turned out three upstanding sons: one gone to the military, one to the ministry, and one following his father into law enforcement. The eldest is married already, and rumor has it that the Bolts will soon be grandparents. But the automatic smile drops fast from Mary-Anne's face when she answers the door and finds me standing there.

'Sarah Fenn,' she says, wiping her floury hands on her apron. 'Team Jesus' is printed on the front in a swooshy sports font. 'Can I help you?'

'I was looking for Tad. I think I read something in the newspaper about him taking leave of absence from the station during a current investigation . . .?'

I'm trying to appear as unthreatening as possible, but she doesn't react to my attempt at humor.

'He's out back, doing yard work with Jake.'

'May I go around? I just want a word.'

'It's hardly appropriate, I would have thought.'

'Why's that?'

Mary-Anne won't say. She's evidently considering whether or not to shut the door in my face. Finally, she sighs.

'It's a free country. But there's something I could use Jakey's help with, so give me a moment.'

She pulls the door halfway, and I hear her at the rear of the house calling out to her son, summoning him indoors. Two things strike me. One: we moms are all the same beneath the skin. We'd do anything to stand between our child and danger. And two: that's what Mary-Anne Bolt thinks I am – a danger.

It's a strange, prickling feeling.

Up till now, and excepting the usual hardcore bigot, I've believed that my neighbors consider me and my services to be a good thing. They might not all consult me – though goodness knows, enough of them do. But they like having that option. Back pain? Go see the doctor, the acupuncturist – or the witch. Relationship problems? Pick from the divorce lawyer, the counselor – or the witch. To those who don't need me, I'm an irrelevance. To those who do, I'm a help, a friend, a guide.

The suspicion bristling off Tad's wife is a novel experience, and an unwelcome one. Has everything that's happened poisoned how I'm seen in this community? Or has she always felt like this, and now believes it's acceptable to show it? Neither thought is comforting.

I find Tad vigorously turning over some raised vegetable beds. When he sees me, he slams the fork down so hard its sharp tines thud into the bottom of the container. His face, already red from his exertions, looks thunderous.

'What can I do for you, Sarah?'

I gather my courage. 'I wanted to tell you that Abigail and I spoke yesterday, and she no longer believes Harper had anything to do with Dan's death.'

Tad grunts, as if I've raised something trifling.

'I'm off the case, Sarah. It's nothing to me. I'm supporting my boy in this, and I know what he believes. He was the only person right there, after all.'

'In a house that was pitch-dark and noisy, when he was most likely drunk.'

'Jake knows what he saw.'

'If we're talking about what people *know*, then I know quite a lot myself. Don't I?'

The chief's eyes narrow as he works out whether I'm saying what it sounds like I'm saying.

I am.

It's painful to do this. Psychically — almost physically. To make even this veiled threat goes against every principle instilled in me by my grandmother and the women who trained me. We witches use our art to support and uplift people.

And I've supported Chief Tad Bolt with his addiction. It's one that shades from 'barely legal' all the way into 'criminal'.

I've helped him with it for years, now. A carefully crafted ritual to suppress his cravings, and it *works*. The problem is that each time he goes for months without a blowout, he puts it down to his strength of will and the power of prayer, and gets complacent. It doesn't help that the ritual flattens what he calls his *lawful urges*, as well, which causes strife with Mary-Anne. So he often neglects to keep his four-monthly appointments, with the inevitable result.

If it got out, he'd lose his job and position in the community — and most likely his wife and the respect of his God-fearing sons. I see him thinking this through. His eyes flick back to me with a mixture of fear and fury. Time to defuse the situation.

'No one wins from this turning into some kind of show trial,' I tell him. 'Least of all Jake. There was a news crew outside our door this morning. If Jake sets himself up as a star witness, they'll be outside your door tomorrow. So I'm asking you, for the good of all our children, get him to see that this isn't the way. There are things I could do . . .'

Tad's arm flashes out. I flinch, but he's already checked himself so the blow never lands. It's so close, though, that the air itself slaps me.

'Get out,' he snarls. 'Stay away from my son and my family.

It's like I said in my statement, Sarah, I trust in the law of the courts and the law of the Bible. My son has sworn on the Good Book that he's telling the truth, so it's up to me to make sure the law takes its course. If Harper's innocent, then so be it. But that's not what Jakey believes, and I believe *him*.'

Have I frightened him enough to comply? Or angered him so much he'll plough on just to hurt me? Tad may be full of bluster, but he isn't stupid.

But given the threat of what I know about him leaking out, I'm quietly confident that a few more hours of yard work and reflection will bring him to the right conclusion. And when Abigail withdraws her accusation, that will make it easy for him and Jake to do the same.

And this whole nightmare swirling around my daughter will end.

Back in my car, I drive to a quiet street nearby and try Abigail again. No reply. Then I remember that Bridget took her home yesterday. Perhaps she knows where she is.

I dial, and the call connects.

51

Maggie

Spots of sunlight through the leaves dapple the Garcia place, but they can't disguise what it is: a glass sandwich made with two slices of concrete. It's more like an auto showroom than a home.

A glass house. Will Beatriz Garcia throw stones? My first interview with her was cut short. Now I have more questions – specifically what was going on between Harper and Daniel, and who knew.

Beatriz opens the door and frowns up at me, politely hostile. She yells over her shoulder for her mom. A smell wafts out from the house that's almost overwhelmingly sweet. At first I think it's one of those sickly celebrity perfumes that teens love so much, but then I see behind Beatriz what looks like an entire store-worth of roses stuck in a vase. So many that there's no pretence at arrangement – their number is all the statement they need to make.

'Somebody's birthday?' I ask, as I hear Julia stirring in the recesses of the house.

The girl takes a swig from the peach Coke Zero in her hand and looks at me, eyes narrowed. She evidently decides the answer doesn't require her to have a lawyer present.

'Mom's favorite. Dad buys them for her all the time.'

'Detective. How can I help?'

Julia Garcia is in her usual monochrome attire. Her hair is swept up in a bun and the fancy glasses on her nose look like they cost a month's cop salary.

'I just wanted a talk with Beatriz, if that's okay with you both? To get a better sense of the dynamic between Harper Fenn and Daniel Whitman.'

'*Dynamic*,' says Beatriz, mockingly.

I see her mother considering whether to make an excuse: a deadline, a client call, or Beatriz's schoolwork. The two of them exchange a look. I'm exasperated. This pair are supposed to be close friends – best friends, even – of those on both sides of this case. I get that they'll be feeling conflicted, but don't they want to help all involved find resolution and relief?

'If now's not a good time, maybe Beatriz would prefer to come by the station?'

That electrifies them both.

'The station? Well, I don't think . . . Come in, Detective.'

I'm shown into the living room, that great circular space overlooking the woods. No offer of tea this time. Beatriz settles on the couch. Her mom sits at a slight distance in a wooden armchair designed for looks rather than comfort.

'How would you characterize the relationship between Harper Fenn and Daniel Whitman?'

Beatriz Garcia rolls her eyes. In the light from the vast windows, the skin around them is still flushed and taut. Perhaps she's only getting two hours' sleep a night revising for her exams. Or perhaps she's still grieving.

'A bad idea.'

'Why's that?'

'You never met Dan, but he was . . . everything. Good-looking, yeah, but smart, funny, popular. People *liked* him.'

'And Harper?'

'She wasn't any of that. I mean, hot, yeah, if eyeliner and tattoos are your thing. But she made no effort with Dan, or anyone else.'

While I've heard that Beatriz was sweet on Daniel Whitman, her tone feels more intense than a crush's resentment of the official girlfriend.

'Why did she date him, then?'

Beatriz's expression hardens. 'I've no idea. Maybe because she could. He wanted her, and she thought: *Why not?*'

'Were they still a couple on the night of the party when Daniel died?'

'No. He'd finished it weeks earlier. She was furious.'

'Do you know why he ended the relationship?'

'Well, because she wasn't giving him respect. And because she was like all witch kids are, you know.'

'No, I don't know.'

The girl narrows her eyes, and her tone is venomous. '*Slutty*, Detective.'

'Beatriz, language,' interjects her mother.

I try not to betray my interest by edging forward on the couch.

'How do you mean?'

'You know the reputation they have. Well, Harper was all that. She was never around to spend weekends with him, so it's pretty obvious she has another guy out of town. Dan told her he wanted to break it off. Date someone who was better for him. Who was just *better*.' She tips her chin up, defiantly, and a suspicion forms in my mind. 'But she couldn't just let him go and be happy. No, she tried to reel him back in with that thing she did at the football party.'

'"That thing at the football party"?'

I'm pretty sure I know what *that thing* is, but I want Bea to tell me.

'She said she wanted to make it up to him. To prove how much she loved him.'

'What did she do, Beatriz?'

The girl pulls a face. 'I'd rather not say, but it shouldn't be too hard to find online.'

'Online?'

'Once something's on one phone, it gets onto *every* phone, sooner or later. And then it gets everywhere else, too. A search on the right sort of website for "high-school witch slut" should—'

'Bea!' Julia is on her feet, outraged at her daughter's coarse language.

'It's only the truth, Mom. I mean, everyone knows what she did. What she *is*. And when Dan ditched her because of it, she *murdered* him.'

The girl's poise breaks down. Her chest is rising and falling. She's on the verge of tears, and her mom will throw me out of this house any minute.

But that's okay, because although it sounds like she's just backing up Jake Bolt's line that Harper killed Dan after he dumped her, Beatriz Garcia has actually just told me a whole bunch of interesting things.

Harper Fenn has some sort of second life.

Harper dated Dan despite not being into him, which is kind of a peripheral detail, but intriguing all the same.

And Beatriz has twice used a word that I've come across before in my inquiries. I think back to the screenshot of the sex tape. The person who posted it called themself *SanctuaryslutXposer*. And they described Harper as *a slut and a liar. And worse.* Jake Bolt trash-talked Harper too, but he used a different slur.

As Bea's mother pulls her up for a hug, I see the girl's oversize smartphone tucked where she was sitting. She had it in her hand the first time I stopped by.

When a phone starts ringing, I jump, thinking it's Bea's and wondering — nonsensically — if I've set it off just by looking. Julia squeezes her daughter's shoulder before hurrying to answer. She stands, listening to whoever is on the line, making *uh-huh* noises like she wants to speak but feels she shouldn't. Presumably because I'm here.

'Got it,' she says eventually. 'No, it's just that someone's here right now . . . Yes, as soon as I can . . . Okay, bye Bridget.'

Julia rejoins us but doesn't sit down. Beatriz is curled on the couch, hugging a cushion. She's picked up her phone again, though she's not looking at it, as if just holding it is a comfort.

'Will that be everything, Detective? It's just this is all very hard on Bea, and now I have to head out . . .'

'Of course. This has been helpful. Just one thing, if I may, Mrs Garcia. You've known Harper from quite a young age. Has it always been the case that her mother believes she can't do magic?'

Beatriz sniffs and looks up, her eyes red-rimmed and her expression indignant. Julia lifts a hand, calmingly.

'You heard the question, sweetheart. If you're going to be a lawyer, you've got to be precise about what's being asked. It's not about whether or not Harper *did* magic that night. It's about whether *Sarah thinks* she can.'

She turns back to me. 'I got to know Sarah after we moved from California. I'd had a regular practitioner there who helped me with some ongoing health issues and my eldest kids' allergies, and finding a town with a good witch was one of the criteria when Alberto and I relocated. Sarah and I discovered our daughters were the same age, eleven, and we talked about them a lot. It was what made us friends, not just practitioner and client.

'At first, Sarah would tell me how excited Harper was about becoming a witch. The next year, I became a member of her

213

coven with Abigail and Bridget. We all knew that a witch's gift comes in by her thirteenth birthday – a kind of magical puberty. There's a ceremony for it, and usually a big family party. Well, Sarah never mentioned throwing one for Harper. And one night, when we'd all had a few drinks, Abigail asked when it was going to be. That was when Sarah completely broke down. I've never seen her so distraught, before or since, not even . . . Well, she said that she'd already conducted the rite and it had shown that Harper was giftless. We never spoke about it again.

'So to answer your question, Detective, to the best of my knowledge her mother believes that she can't do magic.'

'She's a liar,' says Beatriz, flatly. 'Or Harper is. They're both liars.'

Harper Fenn is a slut and a liar.

And worse.

I look at them both, mother and daughter. Bea has already picked up her phone and her thumbs are busy on the keypad. Texting Jake Bolt, to tell him the cop doesn't believe him?

Or maybe putting up another post with a lurid photo of Harper Fenn?

I'm nowhere near the truth of all this yet. All I know for sure is that Bea Garcia is yet another devastated kid convinced that Harper killed Dan Whitman.

'Thank you both for your time,' I say.

The scent of roses nearly chokes me on the way out.

52

Abigail

I've somehow slept the day away.

After Bridget and I sat on her deck and relived that awful, wondrous night six years ago when Daniel fell and broke, and Sarah and the three of us put him back together, I was exhausted and drained. But drained of a poison. Purged. We therapists call it a healing crisis.

As my thoughts clear, I find that I'm lying on a couch beneath a soft blanket. My shoes have been placed neatly alongside, together with a glass of water. The outside of the glass is wet, but the water's no longer cold. It's been there for a while. The sun is low enough to lance through the window.

In times of extreme emotional distress, the body can simply shut down. Grief sends people to their beds for days, weeks, even months. I've seen it in others, as patients, and now its gentle oblivion has washed over me. Bridget's kindness and this house so unlike my own allowed it to happen, and I am overwhelmed by gratitude.

Not even the realization that this sofa is the one on which we laid Daniel all those years ago, before the cops turned up, disturbs me. Instead it brings a strange peace. A circularity. He was here, and now I am here, and he was a part of me and still is.

My beloved boy.

I get to my feet, a little wobbly, and haven't reached the door before Bridget pops her head around.

'You're up!'

I don't resist as she ushers me into the kitchen and prepares soup. Cheryl has just got home, and she's at the table, eyes darting between a mound of papers and Isobel's progress with homework sent to ensure she doesn't fall behind.

'So,' Bridget says, settling herself next to me as I eat, 'I've had a call from Sarah. She's been trying to reach you, was wondering if she could come over so you two can talk. I said I'd let her know if you were feeling up to it. What do you think? I reckon it'd be a good idea. Perhaps Julia as well? But maybe you'd find that too . . .'

Too painful, she means, given the last time the four of us were here together.

But it's that circularity again. For us to be *together* and *here* feels right. Sarah, Bridget and Julia gave me that precious extra time with my son. Though I'll never have stories to tell of in-laws who aren't good enough, or grandchildren to dote on, these women share my memories of Daniel, and when we reminisce about our kids' childhoods, my boy will be as present as the others.

'I'd like that,' I say.

Bridget goes to call Sarah and Julia while I freshen up. In the time before they arrive, I sit quietly and prepare what I want to say. I ask Bridget if we can go back outside, the four of us on the deck just as we were that night.

Julia arrives first. The breeze is gusting up from the shore and we light candles, even though it's barely evening. Bridget, inevitably, brings out a bottle of wine, though she's the only one who drinks. I talk and weep and let myself be comforted by these women.

Then the doorbell sounds again, and it's Sarah.

Cheryl brings her out to us, before disappearing back inside, and Sarah stands there, not taking a seat, but rigid and upright as if she's on trial. I can't decipher the expression on her face. Fearful? Hopeful? But sleeplessness and strain are etched on it, just as they are on mine.

Will she be able to forgive me? It's time to say my piece.

I stand too, and we're facing each other as though we're exchanging vows – or maybe renewing them.

'I need to apologize to you, Sarah,' I say. She makes a noise, as though to protest that it's not necessary at all, but I'm having none of it. 'I was mad. The things I said and the thing I asked you to do. Will you forgive me? I never wanted to hurt Harper. Or rather, I think I wanted *everyone* to hurt. Everyone to suffer like I was suffering, and that was so wrong of me.'

'Of course I forgive you, Abigail,' Sarah says, and her hands reach for mine. Clever hands that once wielded enough power to pull Daniel back across death's threshold. My wonder-working friend.

There are tears in her eyes too, but I see her look at Bridget and Julia as if to check that they're listening before speaking her next words. She looks unbearably tense.

'Harper had nothing to do with Daniel's death. You know that, yes?'

I nod.

'I need to hear you say it, Abigail. And I need to know that you'll tell them all. Tad Bolt and his son, the reporters, even the Spartans. Because they're all trying to put the blame on my girl. Someone attacked our house. We've got a news crew on our doorstep. Harper isn't safe – she won't be until you tell *everyone* that you know she didn't do this.'

I hesitate. Sarah sees it, and her anguish is plain. She's my friend. She gave Daniel back to me once before, even if she can't

217

do it again. Could someone so good have a child so bad as to do what Jake's accused Harper of? Surely it's not possible.

'I'll tell them,' I pledge, solemn as any marriage vow.

'Thank you,' she says, her whole face relaxing. 'Thank you, Abigail. I know how hard this is for you.'

I'm all out of words. I mutely squeeze Sarah's fingers, and she reaches out and embraces me. Julia and Bridget join us, the three of them enfolding me. This is true magic: the comfort of friends.

We jolt apart when the French doors bang open.

'You all need to come inside right now,' says Cheryl.

She looks deathly, and I free-fall to the moment she came back from answering the phone on the night of the party. Has she news of another fire? Another one of our children dead? The thought is both absurd and somehow not at all impossible.

In the living room, Cheryl's been watching the news while she does more paperwork. Sheets have been scattered all over the floor by her haste to come find us. It's the local news on WCON-TV. I recognize the reporter, that Dao woman, sounding breathless as she asks, 'Witchcraft?'

SANCTUARY 'WITCH' DEATH ALLEGATIONS reads the banner across the bottom of the screen. I assume that when we see the interviewee it'll be Jake Bolt, and I feel guilty that I've let Sarah down already. I turn to explain that I didn't know he was planning this and am so sorry I couldn't stop him.

But it's not Jake. It's Harper.

'Do you know the truth about Daniel Whitman?' the girl says. 'The so-called victim in all this? The whole town's acting like he was some kind of saint. The sports star. The kids' coach. Mr Popularity. But the truth is that he drugged me and abused me while one of his friends filmed it. He *raped* me.'

There's a low moan beside me: Sarah.

What is this? *Rape?*

I look at Sarah, expecting to see her as stunned as I am by her daughter's filthy lie. But she's not. I see it in her face. She looks appalled. Desperate.

But not surprised.

She *knew* about this.

And I can't believe that I was taken in by her for even a minute. She's been covering up for her daughter. She's probably bewitched *me*, to get me to listen to her these past two days.

Harper killed Daniel once – and now she's killing him twice. Desecrating his beautiful memory.

I snatch up Cheryl's mug of tea and fling it at the television. Half the screen blacks out as it rocks on its base, back, forward, back . . .

. . . and falls.

Standing in the doorway from the kitchen, Isobel is pitching into hysterics. Bridget goes to her. Julia is motionless. Rigid with shock.

My gaze and Sarah's meet. My empty, useless hands twitch – there's no power in them, unlike those of her whorish daughter. If there was, I'd strike her dead where she stands.

But there's power in my wrath, perhaps. Enough to make Sarah stifle a cry and rush from the room. The front door slams behind her.

The witch nearly had me agreeing to bury my son and bury myself in grief. She was so close to tricking me into shutting this whole thing down.

You failed, Sarah. It's only just begun.

53

TRANSCRIPT OF NEWS ITEM AND INTERVIEW BY ANNA DAO WITH HARPER FENN, WCON-TV *CONNECTICUT TONIGHT*
Prepared for legal and editorial standards review

DAO: The small town of Sanctuary is a quiet sort of place, a favorite of Yale professors and vacationing Manhattanites. It's fair to say that violent crime isn't common here. And neither – at least for the past three hundred years – are accusations of death by witchcraft.

But that all ended this week, when in an extraordinary step, local newspaper the *Sanctuary Sentinel* published an article all but naming a high-school student as the murderer of her ex-boyfriend.

That young woman is Harper Fenn, and she's here with me now. Harper, thank you for agreeing to speak to me.

FENN: [. . .]

DAO: So, Harper, tell me how you're feeling. Frightened, maybe?

FENN: Frightened?

DAO: Your house was defaced last week. Did that make you fear for your safety?

FENN: Whoever did it probably hoped it would, yeah. But they're the ones that are scared.

DAO: Of what? Witchcraft?

FENN: Of the truth. And do you know the truth about Daniel Whitman – the so-called victim in all this? The whole town's acting like he was some kind of saint. The sports star. The kids' coach. Mr Popularity. But the truth is that he drugged me and abused me while one of his friends filmed it. He *raped* me.

DAO: [crosstalk] Harper, I need to stop . . .

FENN: [crosstalk, inaudible] . . . me.

NEWSCASTER: Anna, I have to just interrupt and say that no charges have been brought against either Harper Fenn or Daniel Whitman – or anyone else.

FENN: Let them try and kill me. I'm innocent.

NEWSCASTER: And I'm afraid that's all we've got time for this evening, Anna. Again, for viewers at home, no allegations in this case have been substantiated. We'll continue to follow the story as it unfolds.

Now, it's good news for holidaymakers heading to Kettletown State Park. Officials have confirmed that the campgrounds will be open for the upcoming holiday weekend. [. . .]

54

Sarah

Oh, Harper. Oh, my darling girl.

Couldn't you have let me take care of this?

What have you done?

55

Maggie

I swing by the pad thai place on the way back to my rental apartment. I've a lot of brainwork ahead of me and it'll need fuel.

I have to call Remy, like I promised, to update him on Rowan's findings. But first I have to work out what the hell I tell him, because today dumped a bunch of new information and ideas in my lap. Unfortunately, not only does none of it solve things for me, it makes this investigation even more tangled.

Our magical investigator confirmed the presence of powerful, untraceable magic at the villa. But they also said Jake's video *doesn't* show Harper using witchcraft. So who *was* responsible, and what exactly did they do?

My skin still crawls just thinking about what happened at Sailaway Villa this morning.

Apart from Sarah Fenn, upset at a sex tape of her daughter, there's still no one I know of with a clear reason to harm Dan. There's no way I can put this to Remy. I've not forgotten what he said about both our jobs being on the line if I mess up.

So I keep things brief, telling my boss that Rowan's still tired from their flight. He's just asking if there's been progress elsewhere when I get a call incoming. Now, there's nothing you should interrupt a talk with Lieutenant Remy Lamarr for, not even a booty call. But the number is Chester, which means it might be important. I throw my boss a quick apology and take the call.

'Ma'am!' Chester sounds panicked. 'Turn on the TV, now. WCON-TV *Connecticut Tonight*.'

Filling the screen is Harper Fenn.

'Stay on the line,' I tell Chester, and I hear his groans of horror as we watch the report unfold.

Rape. Harper has stepped forward and alleged that Dan Whitman raped her.

And although this makes my hot mess of a case a good deal messier, something inside me settles and calms.

Because I believe her.

I know what she's referring to. The incident shown in the screen grab Varley sent me. Which I'll bet shows *that thing at the football party* that Beatriz Garcia told me about earlier. *A search on the right sort of website for 'high-school witch slut'* . . .

I tell Chester to have a watch put on the Fenn house through the night, in case the folks who trashed it last time come back for more after this. Then I grab my laptop and check that the 'safe search' function is switched off. Honestly, someone should come up with a browser for cops that does an 'unsafe search', taking you straight to the dark corner of the web where the scum we deal with live. I tap in those four words, then hit the 'videos' filter on the results page.

The screen fills immediately with thumbnail images. Luckily, I don't have to inspect them all, because one is a close match for the grainy screen grab. I see it again lower down in the list. And again. All different sites. I click on the first thumbnail and it connects to one of the biggest hosts of user-uploaded online porn.

The video's there, ready and waiting, all two minutes and forty-eight seconds of it. It's been given a title, the sort of crude, titillating thing that hooks in the creepers who use sites like this: *High-school slutwitch begs for it.*

I check the name of the user who uploaded the footage. It's not SanctuaryslutXposer, though, but a person calling themself Anaxander. Which strikes me as an unusual choice for a site like this. I google it – anything to delay the moment of actually having to watch this – and get results for a music group and a Wikipedia reference to some ancient king.

Ah. A king of *Sparta*. Jeez. Dan played for the Sanctuary Spartans.

Gotta hit 'play', Mags.

Sometimes I really hate my job.

The video is horrible. It would be even without having just heard Harper confirm that what it shows is rape.

The quality is poor. It's been filmed in low light, and smoke drifts through the frame. There's a bed, but the room beyond is indistinct – nothing I'll get an ID off.

Harper told the reporter that Dan Whitman drugged her. She's conscious – she's tossing her head from side to side, and her mouth is moving. But there's no audio, only music – a sample of several songs, everything from Taylor Swift to what sounds like Swedish heavy metal. The video has already racked up several thousand 'likes' from the pervs who use 'high school' as a search term on sites like this. Tomorrow I'll get a copy stored on our database and a take-down notice issued to the site.

My heart aches for Harper Fenn, even though she's not the first raped girl I've seen and she won't be the last. Jenny's frail, starved face comes back to me, pale against her hospital sheets. Despite all she'd endured, she was radiant with gratitude that we'd rescued her.

Harper Fenn on the news blazed with righteous fury.

Not everyone thinks that 'believe the victim' is the right way to proceed. But I believe this girl, because in coming forward with this accusation against Daniel, she has given herself a motive for his murder. So with her life on the line if it came to a trial, she must be either a very, very confident liar or very, very innocent.

Which makes sense, because magic *was* used at the villa that night – and Harper doesn't have magic.

But her mother does. And experience has taught me that the person most likely to take revenge on an abuser isn't the victim – it's the victim's parent. Usually fathers, taking a swing or even a potshot at their daughter's abusive or unfaithful partner.

I specifically asked Sarah Fenn earlier if there was a reason someone might want to hurt Dan on Harper's behalf. And Sarah told me *no*. I sensed that was a lie when she said it. Now I *know* it was. She knows Daniel assaulted her daughter – she knew before Harper told the entire state on live TV.

So have I just solved my case? *Boy rapes girl. Girl's mother kills boy.* Seven small words to sum up something so huge and painful.

Rowan's findings mean I should add two words to the end of that, though. Two crucial words: *by witchcraft*. That means the death penalty. For avenging her raped daughter, Sarah Fenn would die.

If I make one false step, a woman will be executed for a crime that every parent in America would consider, in her shoes.

So: no missteps, Mags.

The bulletin's just uploaded to the news station's catch-up service, so I watch it and rewatch. The third time around, I notice something interesting.

Harper's still talking right after she makes her allegation. But the interviewer is talking *over* her, trying to shut her up after the compliance shitstorm she's created for the program exec back in the studio.

All I can hear clearly is . . . *me*. The word before it might be *just*? The cameraman turned full frame on to the reporter after Harper launched her allegation, so I can't try and lip-read it.

I'll ask her – if I can find her.

Which conjures up a whole other nightmare. When she realizes the consequences of what she's just done, will Harper skip town permanently? That'd be a disaster. But I can't imagine how bad it'll look if I arrest her – a seventeen-year-old-girl who's just stated that she was raped.

I scribble down my to-do list. It's pretty straightforward: *Harper. Jake Bolt.*

Then I take a deep breath and call Remy back to explain what the hell just happened.

Funnily enough, I don't get the best night's sleep.

As early as is reasonable, I call the Fenn house. The phone rings off and the answerphone kicks in. I told Sarah yesterday to screen her calls, but frustratingly she doesn't pick up as I leave a message that I urgently need to interview Harper.

As an afterthought, I call back to ask if she caught what Harper said when the reporter was talking over her. But the line's now engaged – so she is there – and after a couple more tries I give up.

Jacob Bolt is my next mark. His father answers.

'Would have thought arresting that little bitch would be your first priority,' he says, before brushing aside my assurance that Harper was the first person I've tried to get hold of this morning.

He sounds furious, which is understandable. Harper Fenn just told the entire state of Connecticut that his son's best friend was a rapist. And I wonder if he's thinking about who the 'friend' was who filmed it.

'Jake's under the weather this morning, Maggie,' he tells me.

'Maybe coming down with this mono that's going around. I don't think he's in a fit state to attend the station.'

'If it's mono' – which I don't for a minute believe it is; more like a chronic determination to avoid hard questions – 'it'll get worse before it gets better. So we should get this done.'

'It'd better be about what she did to Daniel, and not that crock of crap she talked on the television last night. If you're not going to arrest her for murder, I'll happily pick her up for slander.'

He can't, of course. You can't defame the dead. But this isn't the moment to point that out. Instead, I reiterate that as Daniel is unable to put his side of the story across, only Jake can do that.

'You'll be getting me too,' Bolt growls, before slamming down the phone.

56

POLICE TRANSCRIPT: JACOB BOLT
Interviewing officer: DETECTIVE KNIGHT, MARGARET
Attending: BOLT, THADDEUS (father)

DET. KNIGHT: Thank you for coming in today, Jacob.
  Let me know if you need to stop this interview
  at any time.
BOLT: This is important, Detective.
DET. KNIGHT: As a minor attending the station
  voluntarily, you have elected to have an adult
  present, who is your father, Thaddeus Bolt. For
  the record, Mr Bolt is the chief of Sanctuary
  but is attending today in a parental capacity.
  Please confirm this is correct, Mr Bolt.
PARENT: Correct.
DET. KNIGHT: Now, since we first spoke, things have
  moved on. I'd like to show you a screen grab
  from a video that has been available online.
  We have masked the identity of the two primary
  figures, but I'd like you to tell me if you
  recognize this scene.
[The footage can be accessed in the digital

evidence database, ref. IB-9-02360. Restrictions apply.]

BOLT: What the fuck is this? I thought we were going to be talking about what Fenn did at the party?

DET. KNIGHT: Are you saying that the two people in this photo are—

BOLT: Yeah, that's Dan and Harper. Anyone at school could tell you that. What a complete ho. He dumped her the day after.

DET. KNIGHT: Okay. So, what's the occasion here? When was this filmed?

BOLT: How would I know?

DET. KNIGHT: You weren't there?

PARENT: Plainly the only people there were the two seen on camera and whoever was filming. And as you know, Detective, that person would be guilty of making indecent images of a minor. Next question.

DET. KNIGHT: Tad, that's ... So, Daniel breaks off his relationship with Harper the day after this video was filmed. Did he discuss that decision with you?

BOLT: Not really. We didn't exactly talk much about girl stuff.

DET. KNIGHT: But you were his closest friend?

BOLT: Yeah?

DET. KNIGHT: So, I'd imagine a guy about to break things off with his girlfriend might tell his best pal.

BOLT: Guys don't gossip like girls do, Detective.

DET. KNIGHT: If you say so. What explanation did your classmates, or the school more widely, put on this breakup?

230

BOLT: He'd been getting bored of Harper for a
    while. She acted so entitled, never came to his
    games, wasn't there to hang out at the weekends.
    Dan had half the school after him. Simple as
    that.

DET. KNIGHT: So it wasn't to do with the evening
    shown in this video, then? Help me here, Jake —
    I'm confused.

BOLT: It was and it wasn't. What she did that
    night, everyone reckoned it was because she saw
    the breakup coming, decided she wanted to hang
    on to him after all, so let him make a sex tape.
    Dan said she was begging him to let the rest of
    the team join in. What a ho.

DET. KNIGHT: Less of that language please, Jake.

PARENT: She's right, Jakey.

BOLT: But ...

PARENT: Just keep telling the officer what
    happened, and soon you'll be able to call her
    what she really is: a murderer.

[BOLT laughs. Laughter turns into coughing. BOLT
    becomes breathless.]

DET. KNIGHT: Jacob? Jake, are you okay? Interview
    suspended.

[Recording halts. Resumes.]

DET. KNIGHT: Jacob, you can stop at any time if
    you're feeling too unwell to continue.

BOLT: Fucking mono.

DET. KNIGHT: Let's move on. So, this sexual
    footage that I have just shown you — this is
    what was projected on the wall the night of the
    party when Daniel died. Correct?

BOLT: Yeah.

DET. KNIGHT: Let's talk about that night. Can you describe for me where the projection appeared to be coming from? Close by you, or further away?

BOLT: Further away. Higher.

DET. KNIGHT: Further away and higher. So maybe somewhere like the landing where Dan was?

BOLT: Probably, yeah? That would make sense.

DET. KNIGHT: Okay, so, you and Harper are on the stairs? In our earlier interview, you described Harper as 'yelling'.

BOLT: Yup.

DET. KNIGHT: What was she saying, exactly?

BOLT: It was really loud, Detective.

DET. KNIGHT: You said she was swearing, so you could obviously make out a few words. Could she have been angry about the tape? Maybe making the allegations she made yesterday on TV?

BOLT: If I'd heard her say 'rape', I would have done something about it. My mom raised me to be chivalrous toward women, even if girls these days are too skanky to appreciate it. So I didn't hear her say it then, and don't you think it's pretty convenient that she's crying rape now? She's trying to distract from what she's done, or maybe get a lighter sentence. She must have found out about the death penalty and is running scared.

DET. KNIGHT: Just the facts, please, Jacob. Did you see Daniel fall? Actually go over the bannister?

BOLT: [...]

DET. KNIGHT: If Harper's shouting in your face, you probably wouldn't immediately notice something happening on the landing, right?

BOLT: I was kind of looking back and forth between them. I wanted to check whether he'd noticed her. [Coughs.]

DET. KNIGHT: Feel free to take a drink of water. We're almost done.

BOLT: I don't need any water. I just don't feel great.

PARENT: Speed this up, Detective.

DET. KNIGHT: So you saw Dan fall, or not? It's just that throughout the footage, your phone follows your line of sight, but you don't capture the moment he falls, only when he's on the floor below.

BOLT: I was filming Harper with the phone, just holding it up, you know, but watching Dan.

DET. KNIGHT: So how did he fall?

BOLT: I don't remember.

DET. KNIGHT: You don't remember? Jacob, you didn't see the moment Dan went over the bannister, did you?

BOLT: It was a party. It was dark, full of people. No one could see anything, really. But it doesn't matter that I didn't see him fall. I got the important thing: her hands. The moment she used her filthy magic.

DET. KNIGHT: Have you ever seen Harper Fenn use magic before, Jacob?

BOLT: I ... Well, I guess.

DET. KNIGHT: You guess? It'd be pretty easy to spot, surely?

BOLT: It's not like she's making brews in chemistry class, Detective.

DET. KNIGHT: So what have you seen?

BOLT: Well it's pretty obvious how she got Dan in the first place.

DET. KNIGHT: You think she used witchcraft to make Daniel Whitman date her?

BOLT: Why not. Yeah.

DET. KNIGHT: It couldn't have been very good if he dumped her. Why wouldn't she use it to win him back, instead of agreeing to make a sex tape at a football party?

BOLT: I guess she liked what she did at the party. Witches do.

DET. KNIGHT: Were you in that room when it happened, Jacob? Was it you filming it?

BOLT: It wasn't me, absolutely not. [Coughs.]

PARENT: Final question, Detective. This boy needs to get home to bed, not sit here answering these bullshit questions.

DET. KNIGHT: Okay, final question. Were there any adults at the party the night Dan died? Anyone's parents? Or anyone else you didn't recognize?

BOLT: Well I didn't know everyone, but I kinda knew them by sight. The usual party crowd. And parents? That was the whole point of it being at the villa, rather than someone's house.

PARENT: And you're done.

DET. KNIGHT: Yes — yes, I am. Thank you, Jacob. I appreciate you coming in. It was good to talk again.

BOLT: I wish I could say the same, Detective, but my mom raised me never to lie.

57

Maggie

'Seemed like a PB&J kind of day,' Chester says, setting a box on my desk along with a strong coffee. The donuts glisten enticingly through the film lid.

'Your baked-goods-buying skills are coming along as nicely as your investigational skills,' I tell him. 'Pull up a seat.'

I left him out of the interview room for a reason. He'll be working under Bolt long after I'm gone, and I don't want to make things awkward with his boss. As I take him through the interview, his face screws up with concentration.

'Jacob's got a point,' he says, anxiously. 'If Harper never told anyone about this "rape" before now, surely it's suspicious she's only mentioned it *after* Daniel's death?'

'Chester, do you know what percentage of women who have been raped report it? Around a third. Hardly any cases are prosecuted, and even fewer get convictions. Ninety-nine out of a hundred perpetrators of sexual violence walk free in this country. Now, would you like to ask me that question again?'

Chester doesn't. He sits thoughtfully as I explain what caught my attention in the interview.

'Jake admitted he didn't see the exact moment Daniel fell. And that matters, because he's been saying that her hand movements are her using magic to *make him fall*. But if he never saw Dan fall, then that sequence of events is his conjecture. Plus, Rowan said that Harper's gestures aren't those of someone working magic. So his account doesn't stand up.'

I expect Chester to congratulate me on my deduction, but he goes quiet.

'Maggie – ma'am – don't take this the wrong way, but you seem very eager to prove that Harper didn't do it. I thought our job was to be building a case.'

'Not building a case against someone who's *innocent*, Chester,' I snap back.

But his words sting, because there's truth in them.

I don't want this teenage girl to be guilty of her boyfriend's murder, by witchcraft or any other means. The witch's daughter, who carries all of the stigma that still hangs about magicals but none of the gift that would provide solidarity and reassurance.

I don't want to let down another girl by not being a good enough cop. Remy gave me a talk after the Downes case. He said every cop has a case like it – one regret, the one that got away. *The One.* But just like in love, he said, you can't fixate on The One or it'll wreck you for all the others. Is that what I'm doing here?

I spent a fruitless hour last night thinking of other possibilities. Who might want Daniel dead? A bitter ex-colleague of Michael Whitman's, or a spurned lover of Abigail Whitman's? Who might want the Fenns accused? Someone Sarah Fenn disappointed, perhaps? But those are fantasy scenarios. Just speculation.

'Rowan's input is what's screwing this case,' I tell Chester, who frowns, but listens. 'They're telling us there was magic at the villa, but that Harper wasn't using it – or at least not in the minutes Jake caught on camera, which are also the minutes in which Dan falls. What we're left with should be the easiest thing imaginable: solve a crime perpetrated by a witch, in a town where's there's only one witch.'

'*Sarah?* She's been part of this place all my life,' Chester says. 'My grandma's a client. Swears by her. I get that she has a motive, if Harper's telling the truth about the rape . . .'

'Sarah might have lied to me about that, by the way.' I explain how the witch denied knowing any reason for someone to harm Dan.

'But she just seems so . . . *kind*. And witches have this whole non-violence, do-no-harm thing, right?'

'It'd be a crime of passion. A mother's outrage. No murder intended, quite likely, just some kind of fright or shock.'

'Hmm.'

'I don't suppose there are any other witches in Sanctuary that it's slipped your mind to tell me about? The coven – from what Rowan said, they don't have magic, right? Could you put feelers out about whether anyone else in town has ever been rumored to have ability?'

Chester nods and heads out. When he's gone, I pick up the phone to WCON-TV and get a mobile number for Anna Dao off a sulky news desk co-ordinator. When the reporter answers her phone, she sounds harried, but also chastened.

'I hope I haven't screwed up your case, Detective. I've already been chewed out by my bosses. It was meant to be a how-are-you-feeling piece, to show the human impact of this death-penalty threat. I mean, jeez, she's a *high-schooler* – and in *Connecticut*. We'd discussed what she might say. I had literally no idea she was going to come out with the rape stuff. Complete nightmare. I can only apologize. Anyway, is the case progressing okay?'

Hah. Digging even when apologizing. Dao's a good one.

'I can't comment on that, Anna. But I've a question for you. After Harper came out with that allegation, and you had to close it down and started talking over her, what was she saying? The camera's not on her, so . . .'

'God, no idea. I was just thinking about shutting her up. But maybe my producer . . .? Hang on.'

The phone is muffled with a hand, then a different voice comes on.

'Detective Knight? I'm Anna's producer. I think she's told you how sorry we are about that screw-up yesterday. The Harper on camera was like a different girl from the one we spoke to beforehand. You're asking what she was saying when Anna acted – as per editorial guidelines – to terminate the interview. I have to stress this is not for attribution and I'm telling you what I *think* I heard. Understood?'

'Understood.'

'Right, so, what I heard Harper say was . . .'

I write down four words. And the crazy pinball machine of this case takes another tilt.

Last night I was frustrated that I didn't know of any reason why someone might harm Dan, other than revenge by or for Harper, or something connected to jealousy and breakup dramas.

But the producer's four little words have given me exactly that.

She heard Harper Fenn say: *It wasn't just me.*

Wherever Harper is, I need to speak to her *now*.

58

Abigail

Julia went after Sarah. I won't forget that.

Bridget looked after me. She phoned Michael and he came down from New Haven immediately. I'm not fool enough to think it was on my account. I heard Bridget speaking to him. 'Something's happened and Abigail needs you' wasn't enough – she had to spell out what his son has been accused of to get him agreeing to return.

There's no going back from this, for me and Sarah. My son is innocent – I know it, and everyone who knows him knows it.

All the way home, I talked Michael through what we should do.

'A lawsuit against the news channel for broadcasting such gross falsehoods. Damages pursued. A lawsuit against Harper . . .'

My husband nodded, listening. I can't remember the last time he was so attentive when I spoke.

'Those are the legal means,' I continued. 'But we can do more than that. Sarah knows everyone's secrets. But I know *Sarah's* secrets.'

I tallied them in my head, trying to remember each thing she'd told us or that I'd witnessed that might cross the line. The magical infringements: illegal charms, use of restricted

239

ingredients, craft performed for minors. And the technical ones: breach of confidentiality, retention of harvested human ingredients.

'The right lawyer could cobble something together from all that,' I told Michael. 'But there's a better way to use it. Sarah likes to preach about unity and oneness as though they're her witchy superpowers. But they'll work equally well *against* her. By the time I'm done, Sanctuary *will* be united – in seeing Harper and Sarah destroyed.'

I was talking so much I hadn't noticed that we'd reached the house and the car was stationary on the driveway.

'We'll sort this,' Michael said. 'Rest, and we'll make plans in the morning.'

I accepted the sleeping pill he gave me, because I'd never have slept otherwise, and I need my strength for what's ahead. When I woke, the horror of Harper's vile, lying interview came back to me and I rushed to the toilet to vomit. But now I'm finally washed and dressed and have stumbled downstairs, I see all the proof I might need of my son's beautiful innocence.

The living room is full of Spartans. I stand in the door for a moment watching them, inhaling that wonderful odor of teenage boys – a light tang of sweat, the faintest whiff of training shoe, all incompletely masked by body spray. The smell still lingers in Dan's things. The dirty clothes I pulled from the laundry basket and zipped in a storage bag to preserve his scent on them as long as possible.

Freddie McConaughey is here, and his dad Mitch, who manages Sport on the Shore. Here's Coach, his expression determined, like it is before any match. This is Dan's team – they're still his teammates. *Spartana semper* – always a Spartan.

'Come and join us, Abi,' Michael says, patting the space next to him on the sofa. 'I've invited the guys here to make plans. Something public – something big.'

'Boys,' I say, taking my place. 'You can't imagine how much this means to me.'

An attack on one is an attack on them all. They understand that. These boys will be my wolf pack as we hunt Harper down and tear her apart.

59

Sarah

Harper didn't come back last night. Where does she go to? How could she not want to sleep wrapped up in my charms and spells?

How could she not want her mother's protection?

My girl has become a mystery to me, and it pierces like glass in my heart. For weeks, she carried around the secret of what Dan did to her. Yes, she told me. But only a few hours before she told a reporter and the entire state.

That's a selfish sadness, though. The only thing that matters is keeping her safe. The cops now have a motive to pin on her. The detective rang first thing this morning, in between the reporters calling. I didn't answer, just listened as she left a message asking where Harper was. However sympathetic she seemed before, she'll be after my girl now.

And Abigail . . .

Abigail will never forgive this. I saw her face. She smashed the television, but she wanted to smash the world. If Harper had been there, Abi wouldn't have snatched up a mug to throw – it would have been a knife from the kitchen.

There's no chance now that this will end. At first, I thought Abigail was convincing herself that Harper killed Dan to have something to bargain with for his resurrection. But now I think she truly believes it.

So what do I do? My overwhelming urge is to look for my daughter. To hold her and know that she's in one piece. But rituals of finding rely on people's memories, identifying the last place something was seen. They're for objects that people have lost, not for people who've chosen to get lost. Otherwise there'd be no such thing as missing children or runaway spouses.

Wherever she is, I have to trust that she knows what she's doing and is safe.

My task is to shield her from the consequences of what she's just shared with the world. Jake will double down on his accusation, which means Bolt will double down. He'll close ranks with Abigail. My visit to him will have been useless. So what do I do next?

There's a rap on the door. It'll be more journalists. I've ignored the nonstop ringing of my phone this morning, and their knocking. Peeping round the curtains, I've seen three TV crews outside, and after what they did yesterday, my fingers itch to hex the lot of them. There's more banging, which I ignore, until I hear a voice that I *can't* ignore calling my name.

It's Cheryl.

Why is Bridge's wife here? Does she have news of Harper?

I open up. Cheryl is looking authoritative and composed in her pantsuit. A couple of cameras have swung in our direction, perhaps uncertain who this official-looking visitor is. Plain-clothes FBI, perhaps. Or Child Protection, come to take my girl.

She hesitates, and I urge her in. I don't miss the little shudder as she ducks under the bundle of twigs hung above the door. Her gaze roams around the hallway, absorbing everything.

I'd forgotten that she's never been in here before. It both-ered me at first, that my oldest friend's wife didn't want to step inside the house of a witch, but I trained myself not to take it personally. Told myself it was nothing more than someone with allergies avoiding a dog- or cat-owning home.

It still hurts, though.

'Bridget sends her love,' says Cheryl, like it's a formality to be hurried through, 'but I wanted to speak to you as Sanctuary High's principal. Obviously, things are going to be difficult at school after what Harper's claimed . . .'

'After what Dan *did*, you mean?'

'Sarah, my heart goes out to you, it really does. But it's not up to us, me and you, to decide what happened. That's for the police. And given that Dan's dead, it's not like this rape allegation will ever go to court, so we'll never know the truth.'

'*I* know the truth. It's what my daughter told me.'

How dare she stand in my home, talking like this? But Cheryl has obviously realized she's not handling this right.

'Look, I don't want to sound unsympathetic. It's just that I have a duty of care to an entire school. Hundreds of kids. They're already traumatized from Daniel's death, and this is going to rock them all over again. My concern has to be for their welfare. But while I can't take sides in any of this, I had to stop by and reassure you and Harper that I'll do everything I can to ensure she feels safe at school. It's just she can't afford any more absences. She's already dipped below ninety percent attendance, and if that gets worse, we'll have to include it on her student record.'

One day off school every two weeks. I wasn't aware of that, but I'm not going to tell Cheryl. My girl has just revealed that she was raped by her boyfriend, and the principal is hassling me about her attendance?

'Given what you now know, I'd say there's a pretty clear reason why she's not been feeling safe at school.'

Cheryl looks conflicted.

'Yes, of course, I . . . Sarah, I'm saying this for Harper's own good. I know that for people like you, education maybe isn't a priority, but it's my belief – it *was* my belief – that your career route isn't an option for Harper. We want her to graduate, but she has to turn up. I'll do all I can to make sure she feels supported.'

Cheryl is trying to help, I know it. But there's so much wrong with what she just said that I don't know where to begin. Education not a priority for *people like you*? She means witches. Because in addition to being slutty, we're also stupid? And what was that correction about formerly believing that being a practitioner isn't a career open to Harper? Cheryl knows that Harper doesn't have the gift. She's always known that. Nothing's changed.

'Thank you,' I say, pasting a smile onto my face. 'Of course Harper's graduation is a priority. Without the gift, she needs to make her way in the world somehow. I'll let her know that she can count on your backing.'

'I'll assign her a dedicated counselor,' Cheryl says quickly. 'As principal, I have to remain . . .'

I nod, but inside I'm incensed. Cheryl was a campaigner in her youth – 'just your basic angry feminist' she said once, with an uncharacteristic flash of humor. But now her job means she can't take the side of a girl who was raped by her boyfriend?

As I show her to the door, I figure that pretty soon Harper and I are going to learn who our friends really are.

I'm so afraid they'll be fewer than we think.

But the magical community will always have our back. There couldn't be a clearer case of discrimination than the way we're being treated. An innocent, giftless girl being victimized without evidence, just because her mom's a witch?

I can go to my own kind for help.

Perhaps one of the Moot Council could conduct a Rite of Determination on Harper, to prove she has no ability? Yes, evidence obtained by magic can't be used *in court*. But we all know the police use magical investigators while evidence-gathering. Surely with something that unequivocal, the cops would abandon their inquiry before it gets to court.

It's almost office hours, and on the stroke of nine I call the Moot and ask to speak to their legal counsel. The bored-sounding receptionist asks if this is my first time making contact about my problem, and when I say yes, he directs me to an online form to complete.

'This is about the Connecticut murder-by-witchcraft case you may have heard of,' I say through gritted teeth. 'I'm the accused's mother.'

He gulps and transfers me immediately.

But the minute the counsel comes on the line, I sense the Moot isn't going to be the solution I'm hoping and praying to the goddess for.

'Yes, the Moot is aware of the case and is monitoring the situation,' she says flatly to my initial introduction. And it gets worse from there, as I relate the madness happening in Sanctuary.

'Let me stop you, Ms Fenn,' the counsel says eventually. 'I can tell that you're upset, but there are two key things. One, your daughter is not a witch, and as such falls outside the scope of Moot assistance. Imagine if we were asked to intervene in the case of every non-magical person accused of witchcrime to prove their innocence.

'And two, the intervention you are proposing – that a prominent member of the Moot conduct a Determination of your daughter to prove that she does not have magic? Well, that's exactly the sort of mindset that first led to the rules about magical evidence not being admissible in law. Witches covering up for each other.

'We have fought tirelessly from our inception *against* those sorts of preconceptions. You know the Moot's origin, campaigning for witches' rights when our craft was still illegal and being the public voice of our kind since decriminalization. We were created by and exist *for witches*. You know our mission: Positive Advocacy for Witches.'

I do know the Moot's PAW slogan, and its stupid badge: a cat familiar's pawprint. We bend over backward to make ourselves unthreatening, and still, deep down, people fear us anyway.

'So I'm sorry, Ms Fenn. Your daughter's case isn't something the Moot can support.'

And the call ends.

I stare at the phone in my hand before slamming it down. I want to keep slamming till it breaks.

Will *no one* help us?

I had Abigail and Bolt so close to giving way. Why did Harper have to ruin everything?

Sudden self-disgust breaks over me and I sink to the floor, hugging my knees. After all my poor girl went through, I'm blaming *her* for something she did? What's wrong with me? No wonder she keeps things from me.

No, Harper understood that the course I was taking would hush everything up. That Daniel's crime would die with him, because the investigation into his death would make it too risky for her to tell the truth about the sort of boy he was.

And she was braver than me. Stronger than me. She stood up and told her truth anyway.

I know what I need to do. I need to fight alongside her, to back her up no matter what. Because I can see what this will turn into — a witch hunt, of the kind Sanctuary used to relish. It'll be the word of Jake, Tad and Abigail against my seventeen-year-old daughter, who is not only not guilty, but the victim in all this.

I won't let them win.

I wash my face and change my clothes. I pick my outfit carefully – which is to say conservatively – apply minimal makeup,
and leave the house. I moved my car out back, but leave by
the front door anyway, because I have to give the reporters
something. I want to give Harper something, too – a public
declaration of my belief in her. Then maybe she'll come home.

The journalists are on me immediately.

'Ms Fenn, how is Harper?'

'Where is your daughter, Ms Fenn?'

'Harper is staying with a friend,' I tell them. 'Meaning no
disrespect, you can understand why she wouldn't want to come
back to a house with all of you camped outside.'

'Ms Fenn, did your daughter kill Daniel Whitman?'

'You should be asking: "Did Daniel rape Harper?" And
the answer is "Yes, he did." My innocent seventeen-year-old
daughter suffered at that young man's hands and is now suffering again because of these false allegations made against her.
Think about your part in all this. That's all I have to say.'

I don't linger to see what sort of reaction that gets. I need to
get to my booth. Only work can fix this.

Magic performed on anyone without their knowledge or
consent is always a Bad Idea, but I've done it, of course. For
Abigail. For Julia. The end justifies the means.

Never more so than now.

60

Maggie

No one answers at the Fenn house – the reporters are on me, and I have to bellow 'off the record' and make them lower their cameras before I exchange a few words. They're disappointed – they think they're getting something from me, whereas in fact I get from them all I need to know: Harper Fenn hasn't been seen, and her mother says she's staying with a friend.

In exchange, I give them a little lecture about harassment of a minor who has just stated that she's the victim of a sex crime.

'So you believe her?' one of the reporters asks.

'It's not my job to "believe" anything,' I tell them. 'It's my job to gather evidence around a suspected crime. And for the record, what I'm investigating is the death of Daniel Whitman, nothing else.'

'So you're saying Whitman's death *was* a crime?'

'My words were "*suspected* crime".'

'You've been here well over a week. Seems to me you don't think it's *not* a crime.'

I narrow my eyes at the reporter. I don't know him, but I recognize his face – he's from the regional bureau of one of the national networks. Shit. The nationals.

'I'm not making any comment.'

'Is your "no comment" on the record, or off the record, Detective?'

Screw him.

It's not Harper's mom I need, it's Harper herself. Her absence is like a closed door, behind which I've a hunch all the answers in this case are shut.

How do I find her? Her mom either doesn't know or isn't saying. Could Rowan help me? Witches find stuff, don't they? And I should make sure my investigator is doing okay after what went down at the villa.

I turn my car onto the coastal road and am a few miles outside Green Point when I see her, running.

Cops have a second sense for people running. We register them automatically. It's almost always a jogger, and our attention simply slides over them – which is what mine does, until it snaps back when I register that *this* jogger is Harper Fenn. It feels like my first lucky break in a long time.

I perform what would be an illegal road maneuver if I wasn't police – hey, perk of the job – and pull ahead of her. She speeds up.

'Need a ride back to Sanctuary?' I call out the window.

Harper stops when she hears a woman's voice. She maintains a wary distance, though, as she says 'no thanks' and turns away.

'Wait, it's Detective Knight,' I say, sticking my head out. 'I'm glad to see you. Are you okay? That was a big thing you did yesterday. Harper, I really *do* need to talk to you.'

'Do I *really need* to talk to you?'

She doesn't sound hostile, exactly. She's certainly not afraid. I don't know what to make of her tone.

'It might be helpful for both of us. At any rate, stopped by the road here like this we're going to draw attention, and I'm guessing that's not what you want.'

'I can run on.'

'And I can keep trailing you, because that'll be really discreet.'

'And I can run off *that* way, where you can't follow.' She points into the scrubby woodland, which must lead to the dunes and down to the shore.

But she doesn't run.

'Touché,' I say, with a smile. 'But Harper, you know we have to talk sometime. Isn't it better to do it here, away from Sanctuary? There are news crews outside your house.' That brings a scowl to her face. 'Wouldn't you like to see them gone? To see this over with?'

She considers my words, then nods, opening the passenger door and unshouldering her small backpack. She directs me back the way I was going, then down a small rutted track to a makeshift parking lot behind a grassy dune. It looks like the sort of place kids would come for a BBQ, or simply to hang out and smoke and do all the things young people do away from their parents' eyes.

'You know this area?' I ask. 'You stayed round here last night?'

'I know it. I have friends out this way.'

I remember what Bea Garcia said, her eyes red-rimmed and her voice poisonous. *It's pretty obvious she has another guy out of town.*

'You *run* to go visit with them?'

'I like running. Sometimes I get a ride partway back. I needed to get away, Detective. I knew Mom would make a fuss after what I did yesterday.'

'Is it true? What you told the reporters.'

Harper's eyes flash with anger. 'Of course it is. I'd be pretty dumb to give myself a motive for murder if it wasn't.'

'You know nothing can be done now Daniel's dead. Dead

people can't be prosecuted. Police can't even say if they would have been charged.'

'Why do you think I did it? I knew I'd never get heard otherwise.'

I cast a look at her, this frank, clear-eyed girl, and think back to the first time I met her at the hospital. There's something not quite right about her response to everything that's happened, and yet I can't put my finger on anything wrong.

'When we met at the hospital, I asked if you thought Daniel's death was an accident. You said that it certainly wouldn't have been suicide over a . . . a girl like you. Did you not think of murder as a possibility – or that you might be the accused?'

'Of course I didn't think of murder. And no, I couldn't imagine anyone accusing me, seeing as I was nowhere near him at the time.'

'You didn't kill Daniel Whitman that night, by witchcraft or any other means?'

'No, I didn't.' A smile ghosts her lips. 'By witchcraft or any other means.'

'So what's your explanation for what happened?'

'He was drunk and he stumbled and fell.'

'But Dan was an athlete. Would he have been drinking?' Forensics have told me there was hardly any alcohol in the boy's bloodstream, but I can't tell Harper that.

She tips her head, considering. 'You're right. Maybe not. I mean, he certainly drank *sometimes*, but not as much as the others. And a *lot* less after getting his scholarship. So the tape, then. Pretty distracting, right, having a film of yourself raping someone projected onto a wall at a party.'

'But you can't tell it's rape. There's no sound. None of the kids who saw that projection described it as anything other than a sex tape or implied there was anything wrong with it.'

Harper bristles, her anger almost tangible. But there's

something more in her eyes as she asks her question. Is it shame?

'You've seen it?'

'I have.'

No, it's sorrow. And it pierces me. You see often, in victims of sexual assault, a whole range of emotions. Guilt and shame. Incomprehension and disbelief. And, yes, sorrow.

'*He* knew it was rape, Detective. *I* knew. And whoever filmed it knew. It doesn't matter what it looked like to anyone else.'

'Did you see who it was filming it?'

'No, it was dark, I was semiconscious; I couldn't even control my muscles enough to lift my head.'

'On the television yesterday, after you made your accusation, you were saying something when the reporter talked over you. Could you tell me what it was?'

Harper's mouth twitches. 'Sure. I was trying to tell the whole state. I said, *It wasn't just me.*'

'What did you mean by that?'

'There are other girls Dan attacked. But he was clever about it. They're not ones who'd speak out – or be believed if they did.'

'Will you tell me who they are?'

'Will you believe them?'

'I . . . For a cop, it can't work like that, Harper. But it's in your interest. A parent whose daughter was assaulted by Dan could conceivably have a motive for hurting him.'

'By pushing him off a landing in the middle of a party full of teenagers? No offense, Detective, but that's the dumbest thing I've heard in a long time.'

This conversation is going nowhere I expected. Harper is more composed than I could imagine any girl being under these circumstances. Which could be suspicious – or could simply be because she's telling me truth after truth.

She has engaged with all my questions and has revised her

own ideas. People who are lying tend not to do that. They have their script and stick to it. Every instinct I have is telling me she's innocent.

'What if it wasn't that? If it was some other way?'

'Some other way?'

'Witchcraft.'

'Witchcraft?' She looks at me blankly. 'My mom is the only witch in Sanctuary.'

'Well, what if it was your mom? She'd have a motive, after all.'

And despite the bluntness of my question, Harper relaxes. I see the tension go out of her.

'It wasn't her. I only told her what Dan did to me a couple days ago. The day before I did the interview. She was horrified. So upset. She wasn't faking that. There's no way she'd known about it before.'

'And no one else in Sanctuary possesses magic? None of your mom's coven? No one she's ever said she feels might have it?'

Harper shakes her head. 'Coven members don't have magic. That's the whole point. No, the Fenns are the only witches there've been in Sanctuary, for generations back.'

I nod. My brain is frantically trying to process everything she's said, so I can jot it down once she's gone. If there's any more, I won't be able to keep a hold of it all. So I thank her for her time. Solemnly, Harper thanks me back and climbs out of the car.

'Watch out for the news crews at your house,' I tell her.

'I'll drop by Izzy's for a bit. Lie low till they've gone.'

'If you feel unsafe at all, contact me immediately.'

I jot down my number and tear it off. She tucks the paper into a waistband pocket on her leggings — I get a flash of tattooed midriff as she lifts her top — then she's off, feet kicking up the parking lot's dirty sand, braid bouncing over her shoulder.

And I'm scribbling in my notebook like my life depends on it.

When I'm done transcribing our conversation as best I can, I read it back.

Harper's story is simple. And one thing life as a cop teaches you is that ninety-nine times out of a hundred, the simple explanation is the correct one. The husband killed his wife. The junkie robbed the store. The secretary embezzled the accounts.

Dan was startled by the sex tape, because he knew that what it really showed was rape.

He fell.

It was an accident.

But then what about the magic?

I call Chester with my good news – I've finally spoken to Harper Fenn. But he's got news for me. Everything's bustling at the station because an event has been organized for tonight and they've requested police presence.

The Whitmans are staging a vigil for their son at the Sport on the Shore club.

'It's even got a hashtag,' Chester says, like that's the worst thing about this. 'JusticeforDaniel.'

61
Abigail

As the light thins to evening, Michael and I make our way to the shore. The Spartans have turned out for Daniel. In fact, they've spent the day ringing round and on their social media, making sure *everyone* turns out.

Hundreds of people are here. Giant photographs of Dan line the shoreside running track, each with candles in jam jars in front. One of the Spartans' fathers owns a chain of grocery stores and donated for a BBQ, and the smell of roasting meat drifts on the breeze. The team marching band is playing. It's almost a party atmosphere, a carnival. The only thing that reveals the event's true nature is the giant banner across the clubhouse: *#JusticeforDaniel*.

There's no better proof that Harper's grotesque claim was a lie than this show of love and support. First we clear Dan's name, then we bring his killer to justice.

Several television cameras and people with microphones and recording equipment are circulating among the crowd. I go brief them that something is planned for later.

Moving on, I spot Tad. Technically, he's still on leave, but he called in orders to send some of the local uniform boys and girls along.

'Where's Jake?' I ask, as he huffs his way over.

'At home. He's laid up with that mono some kids at the school have. I blame the stress of all this bullshit.'

I lay my hand sympathetically on his arm. It would have been good to have Jake here, but he's already done his part. It's someone else's story I'm telling tonight.

The banner flaps in the breeze. Any number of the Sport on the Shore parents come up to me with condolences. Several of the moms are in tears. I am their worst nightmare. I smile and thank them – and in a small corner of my heart I hate every one of them for their healthy, happy, living children.

'Dan did so much for this club,' sniffs one. 'He was always generous with his time. My daughter was so looking forward to joining the junior girls' soccer and was actually kind of heartbroken when he had to stop volunteering at the club. I think she was a bit in love with him. She cried for a day when we heard what happened.'

I give the woman a comforting hug. So many tears for my son. Of course her daughter was in love with him. They all were.

Moving on, I spot a few of the cops in uniform tucking in to sauce-slathered wings and beer. And there's the detective, talking to Pierre Martineau. I'm surprised Pierre is here, given how close he is to Sarah. But then he's part of Sport on the Shore too, running their boxing classes.

I'm glad the cop is seeing all this – she needs to understand how loved my son is. How innocent.

How badly she's failing.

There's Bridget with Cheryl, over by the drinks stand. She waves, but doesn't leave her wife's side. I know she's still conflicted, pulled by her old friendship with Sarah. But it's only a matter of time before she's mine.

Julia's not here. I called her up, but she refused to choose between us, saying she owed Sarah too much. When I argued that potions for her older kids' allergies hardly counted, she said it went deeper than that. And once she explained exactly what sort of debt she owed Sarah, well, suddenly a lot of things made sense.

If Julia had been here tonight, if she had come out to support me, then the speech I'm about to make would have been different. But as it is, she has only herself to blame.

Freddie McConaughey bounds up to me.

'Shall we hand out the candles, Mrs W?' he asks.

Under his arm is a box full of tapers, and other Spartans hold more. Just as well. There are hundreds of people here, spread out across the playing fields, the running track and the shore. I'm glad of the PA system that Mitch has rigged up. No one must miss a word.

'Go for it, Freddie.'

The sky is darkening and I check my watch. It's time.

Across the club grounds, tapers are being lit. Points of light spread from person to person. As I ascend the few steps to the platform, the perspective changes. Instead of individual flames, I see a whole sea of light. Sanctuary is blazing with love for my son.

Now I have to turn that love into rage.

62

REMARKS BY ABIGAIL WHITMAN AT THE #JUSTICEFOR
DANIEL VIGIL, POSTED TO SANCTUARYFORDANIEL.COM

I wish this was simply a celebration of my son's life and
promise. But as you all know, Michael and I cannot mourn
our beautiful boy. We cannot bury him with dignity or let
his spirit go in peace.

There has been no justice for Daniel.

The truth about how he died is being suppressed.

And last night we saw vicious lies hurled against his
reputation on statewide television. By the person – you
all know who she is – most directly involved in Daniel's
death.

It was like watching him murdered a second time.

It was worse than murder, because it aimed to kill that
thing of Daniel that still lives – his reputation. His beloved
memory.

I'm sorry. Please give me a moment.

It's so hard.

There's not a day I don't wish it was me who died. Me
being attacked. When it's your child, and you can't protect
them . . .

So here's what I wanted to say. Witchcraft. We're used to thinking of it as something harmless. Something helpful. We've all done it – or have thought of it. A charm to prevent the dog peeing on the carpet? Yes please. A token to stop your husband snoring or your wife nagging? Wouldn't that be great.

I know that since this all happened, some people have been asking: but can witchcraft *kill*?

Most of us don't really know what it can do. But I do, because for years I counted as a friend the witch whose daughter killed my son twice over, once at the villa and again on live TV last night. I know exactly what witchcraft can do.

Here's an example. Just one, though I could tell you many more – and I will, if the authorities fail to act in my son's murder. A woman – let's call her 'J' – told Fenn that her husband didn't love her any more. He'd fallen for someone else. This was true: the man loved this other woman madly. Pursued her. Bombarded her with messages and calls.

I know this because *I* was the woman this man was obsessed with, although I never returned his feelings. I was happily married to my amazing Michael.

So 'J' demanded that Fenn magically force her unhappy husband to remain faithful to her.

Now, you might be thinking: is that even possible? I'm telling you, it's possible. Though of course it's illegal.

Fenn used her power to override that man's will. To make him do her bidding.

That's the truth about what witches are capable of. To them, other people's rights – their loves and lives – are things their magic can alter on a whim.

A few spells. A ritual. A brew. That's all it takes to change a life – yours or mine.

Or to *end* a life, like Daniel's.

Thank you again for coming tonight. I'm more grateful than I have words to say.

63

From: soccergirlsdad@outlook.com
To: m.knight@csp.hartford.gov.us
Date: 28 May, 06:55
Subject: Dan

Detective,

I heard there was some big party down at the Shore club last night 'celebrating' Dan Whitman or some such. I wasn't there. Figured you maybe oughta know why.

Dan used to coach my girl. He coached the whole junior girls' soccer team. Which you might think is weird given how he's a football player, but then girls don't play football, do they?

My daughter was thirteen when Dan picked her for the team.

First off she loved it. She went every Saturday and to special coaching on Tuesday nights. Turns out sometimes 'coaching' was trips to the bowling alley or beach BBQs.

Then she didn't love it any more. Eventually she told me and her mom she wanted to stop playing. Took a while longer for her to tell us why.

I'm not gonna put it all down in an email. We never went to the police 'cos my girl was worried it'd get traced back to her and folk would find out. Sanctuary's a small place, Detective. I wanted to break every bone in that boy's body, but my girl begged and begged me not to.

My daughter woke me and my wife up crying after the Fenn girl's interview on TV. Seems all the kids were talking about it on their social medias. When we gave her a cuddle, she said, 'If I'd said something, Daddy, maybe he wouldn't have hurt that other girl.' She was crying again all last night.

So yeah, I don't reckon there was justice for Daniel. 'Cos justice would have meant that shit being called out for the sort of boy he is. Was. I don't reckon that witch girl's lying and neither should you.

Angry Dad

64

Maggie

So here it is — proof of Harper's *It wasn't just me*, delivered to my inbox.

It's clear what Angry Dad is saying, even if he doesn't spell it out: he believes Dan Whitman molested his kid when he coached her team.

And if there was Harper, and this guy's daughter, there might be others. Molestation often manifests as repeat offending behavior. We all know the cases where abusers secure positions that give them easy access to victims.

Dan's dead, so he can never be tried for any crime. But what he did — or may have done — is still part of my case, because it gives me another line of motive for his death. What if he died, deliberately or accidentally, in a revenge attack by a parent?

But as Harper said, how would a parent pass unnoticed in a party of teenagers? So, maybe an older sibling . . . I'll get Chester to check who in the girls' soccer team, this season or last, had a brother or sister at the villa that night. And we'll need to talk to Angry Dad himself. I fire back an email requesting a conversation.

It'll be a busy day ahead. But first is making sure the Fenns don't come to harm because Abigail Whitman stirred up the town last night. I head to the station to tell the desk sergeant that walk-by checks must be made on their house and Sarah's booth.

There's a surprise waiting for me. An angry and unwelcome surprise, albeit handsomely packaged.

A man wearing sharply tailored trousers and a charcoal-gray sweater that looks knit from the belly hair of baby alpacas weaned on Rogaine is sitting in the waiting area. He's drawing on his expensive-looking phone using a stylus. One foot – yeah, his shoes look dead expensive, too – is tapping the floor.

'Detective Knight?' he says, springing up before my butt has even cleared the doorway. 'I need to speak to you urgently.'

I wonder if this is Angry Dad, father of the soccer-playing girl, but this dude's swanky appearance doesn't match the email's homespun style. He's got a Californian accent and hair that's longer than you usually see on East Coast guys, worn in a smooth slick salted with gray. His dark eyes glare behind small rimless glasses.

'I'm sure you're aware my current investigation is keeping me rather busy, sir,' I tell him.

I know this sort of man – and woman, because entitled ass-holery is a gender-equal pastime. My death-penalty witchcraft homicide case be damned. He probably got a speeding ticket and wants me to know that his nanny, not him, was driving at the time.

'I'm very aware of it, Detective. My wife is Julia Garcia. I'm Alberto, and I want to discuss what was said last night.'

Oh.

Suddenly a minor puzzle slots into place. The anecdote Abigail used – the unfaithful husband and the wife named 'J'? What if 'J' is for Julia?

But that makes no sense. Alberto's a plainly adoring husband. I remember the photos all over the house. The huge vase of roses.

And – *ahhhh*. I get it.

'Follow me.'

Alberto Garcia looks contemptuously at the strip lighting and carpet tiles as I lead him through to my scrappy HQ. When I offer him a chair, he looks round as if to check I've not got one of those fancy Aeron ones hidden in a corner.

'So how can I help?'

He takes out a folded piece of paper that looks like something printed off the internet.

' "*J*" *demanded that Fenn magically force her unhappy husband to remain faithful to her,*' he reads, his expression grim. '*Fenn used her power to override that man's will.*' That was Abigail Whitman speaking last night, Detective. "J" is my wife Julia, and the man is *me*.'

He puts the paper away and sits back, looking at me expectantly.

'And, Mr Garcia . . .?'

'*And*, Detective, this describes a plainly illegal act, and I would like to know how you intend to investigate it.'

Is he for real? My case has a teenage girl's life at stake – a girl who must have played at his house, dined at his table, discussed first periods and first boyfriends with his daughter. And Alberto Garcia wants me to drop it and investigate Sarah Fenn's Love Potion Number 9 that his wife asked for because Albie got the hots for his wife's friend?

That impatient foot starts tapping again. He's for real.

'I was called this morning by that dumpy little witch from the *Sentinel*, Beryl something, the news editor. They're going to lead on this story and she wanted an interview, or at least a quote. I told her she'd get a lawsuit if she didn't back off.'

'I'm sorry, are you saying that Beryl Varley is a witch?'

'I don't know if you're being funny or stupid, Detective, and I'd say it's in your best interests to be neither.'

266

Ugh, this guy. And his wife seriously used magic to keep him?

I explain, patiently, that I am in Sanctuary to investigate one case, and one case only – the death of Daniel Whitman. And given everything riding on that, including a death penalty and state-level interest from the media plus police and government authorities, I unfortunately have neither the time nor the dispensation to pursue side cases. But I'll get one of the uniforms here to take a statement.

'You people just don't get it,' Alberto says, sliding his glasses up his nose. I remember he's an architect, and picture him presenting plans for a steel-and-glass box to clients who asked for a cozy family home and saying the exact same thing when they protest.

'Abigail may be crazy – for the record, it was a consensual affair and *she* pursued *me* – but she's got one thing right. This *is* your case. A witch who's prepared to mess with someone's life like this plainly has no boundaries. How do you think it makes me feel?'

'Are you telling me that you don't love your wife, Mr Garcia?'

'Of *course* I do. I adore her. I buy her a hundred roses every week. The whole house fucking stinks of roses. I'm allergic to flowers, so why would I do that if I didn't love her? Unless . . .'

I look at him. A pulse is throbbing in his forehead. And somehow, despite myself, I get what's eating him. In a world where it often feels like not much is within our control, one thing that everyone expects to have free rein over is what they do with their heart.

'I'm sorry,' I say. 'I do wish I could help. Let me find someone.'

It takes time to locate someone to speak to him, as it's barely office hours and no fewer than three of the guys have rung in sick. They were all patrolling the Sport on the Shore gathering last night, and I'll bet they're suffering from a bad case of undercooked chicken wings washed down with too much free beer.

That also means the station will be too short-staffed to send officers by the Fenn place. A quick visit to warn Sarah that resources are spread thin today will give me an opportunity to ask about Garcia's accusation, too. Because Alberto, asshole though he plainly is, has a point. What Abigail alleged was a dark and manipulative magic. I can't believe Sarah Fenn capable of it.

I don't *want* to believe Sarah Fenn capable of it.

65

Sarah

I'm jumping every time someone knocks on the door, but I've come to recognize that firm *bam-bam*.

The detective's face is all sympathy. She's still on my side – for now. Would she be if she knew what I spent all yesterday and most of the night doing? I doubt it.

'You heard about the vigil?' she asks as she watches me prepare tea. 'The nature of Abigail Whitman's remarks?'

I tell her I did. Pierre came by after to tell us everything, then insisted on staying the night. He slept on the couch and drove Harper to school this morning. The cop is pleased he's watching out for us and explains that the station is short-staffed today.

'But how are you feeling? Those were strong allegations Mrs Whitman made, and from someone who's been close to you for many years.'

And the question is so unexpected, so hard to think about, that I put the teapot down before I drop it.

How do I feel?

I feel exhausted, and just so frightened and sad – for myself and for Harper. For the friendships I've counted on for years, that won't survive this. For this town, where my daughter was born and where my ancestors brewed and bound, that is ready to turn against us.

Pierre told me there were hundreds of people at the vigil last night. I know they were there to support Abigail in her grief, not to take sides against me and Harper, but that's what it feels like.

'Sarah?' The cop pulls out a chair and presses me into it.

I've been solving other people's problems my entire life. And now there's one problem that's mine to solve, and mine alone, and I'm terrified I won't be able to. What if what I'm doing isn't powerful enough? Or goes wrong?

I can't let that happen. I need to get back to my workroom.

'I'll be fine,' I tell the cop. 'I just want this to be over. Now don't let me keep you.'

'Before I go, Sarah — Ms Fenn — I'm sorry, but I do have to ask and take some notes. Did you, through magical means, cause Alberto Garcia to cease his involvement or infatuation with Abigail Whitman and resume a marital relationship with his wife?'

The detective has switched into formal police-speak, masking her thoughts.

I wonder if she can imagine my divided loyalties last summer. First, Abigail's confession that she was in love with a married man, then Julia coming to me in tears, convinced that her husband was having an affair. When I scheduled a coven gathering for a weekend Alberto was supposedly at a conference, and Abi said she couldn't make it because she was visiting her cousin, I knew I was dealing with one problem, not two.

How could I choose between them? I know how loveless Abigail's marriage is. And yet she could have set her sights on anyone. Why did it have to be the husband of a woman who had risked so much to help her the night her son fell from the window?

Julia told me that Beatriz was acting out and neglecting her schoolwork, and there were terrible fights between Alberto and

270

their two older kids, twin boys now away at college. Abigail said she didn't think she could leave Michael, in case it hit Daniel too hard at such a crucial time in his football career.

So I made my choice. I made it with love in my heart for both women. And I kept my coven united.

'Love magic is highly restricted,' I tell the detective. 'You know how fundamental the concept of consent is to our craft. To administer a draft to an unknowing subject to procure affection? I hardly need to point out what that sounds like.'

'Narcotics- or alcohol-facilitated sexual assault,' the detective says, and then winces, presumably as she thinks of Harper.

'Abigail's been very clever, Detective. The allegation my daughter has laid against her son, she now lays against me. Do you see?'

Knight nods.

'But did you do it, Ms Fenn?'

And I have to tread carefully. So carefully.

Because of course I did.

66

Sarah

Luckily, that's not the story my record-keeping tells.

I knew that either Alberto would need to consent, or I would have to bend the rules by bending his will. So we had a heart-to-heart after I slipped a gentle disinhibitor into his drink. I steered the conversation on to his indiscretion, and as expected, he got defensive, blustering about how much he loved Julia, how much their family meant to him, how he was 'only fooling around' with Abigail, that she had initiated it, et cetera, et cetera.

It was the usual sort of protest from a caught-out adulterer. But it was sufficient for my needs. I recorded the conversation in my notes, tabbed under *Garcia, A.*, as if he was a separate applicant from his wife, *Garcia, J.*

Witches are permitted to create a low-level affection-altering brew, if this is taken 'by mutual agreement within pre-existing, legally recognized relationships', as the law book has it. *Client Garcia, A. shows a clear desire to be reconciled with his wife*, I wrote, leaving out the fact that I hadn't asked him if he wanted me to use my magic to achieve this.

I reported back to Julia, who was of course overjoyed. The only thing I omitted was that I didn't believe a word he'd said. All I needed to do after that was document her desire for the same outcome, then I could prepare the brew.

My records are regretful that an unexpected work engagement for Alberto meant that I handed the potion over to Julia only. She signed a receipt that the treatment protocol had been explained to her.

Alberto got a strong dose in his evening tea every night, and before the week was out, he was whisking Julia away to Paris for a romantic weekend and placing the recurring order for roses that, if she'd known the truth of it, would have won me the gratitude of Sanctuary's florist for evermore. Abigail never knew why he suddenly ended things, and it was tough to see her broken-hearted. But I never doubted that I'd acted for the best for all involved.

Needless to say, Detective Knight gets a heavily edited version of this tale, and she seems to be swallowing it.

'So you have records of your conversations and a signed protocol?' she asks. 'And you could take me to your booth and show me those right now?'

That catches me off guard. I don't want to take her to the booth – not with what I've got set up in there. She won't know its purpose, of course, but there are only so many more stories I can spin without getting my threads hopelessly tangled.

I like the truth. It can never catch you out.

But sometimes lies are necessary. I can manage another one.

'I'd be delighted to.'

'Then let's do it. I can share that with Mr Garcia and hopefully he'll back off. There's only one thing I don't get. Why would he come storming into the station denying all knowledge of your intervention when, as you've just told me, he asked for it?'

The detective looks genuinely puzzled. I don't sense that she's trying to trap me, only that she was paying more attention than I thought. It's an uneasy realization. I still feel like she's on

273

side for me and Harper, but here's one more reason to hope she stays that way.

'Abigail's account of his pursuit paints him in a bad light, wouldn't you say? So what better way of deflecting attention than to seize on the other thing she said, and claim to be the victim of magical coercion?'

'It's a common strategy,' Knight agrees. 'The guilty claiming that they're the victim.'

Then she falls silent and I realize who she's thinking of.

Oh.

Can she be having doubts about Harper's testimony? Harper told me the cop ran into her yesterday, and that they spoke. And the way Detective Knight keeps checking in on our safety has been reassuring.

Should I simply tell her everything? About the raw, form-less magic I sensed when I made my divination, and my belief that it's connected to what happened six years ago. That Dan's death at the villa was him being somehow reclaimed, after we brought him back that night.

It needn't be a confession of necromancy after all. Surely I can tell the story well enough – Dan was on the threshold. Not actually dead. Merely close.

But I remember how, just now, she went straight to that one discrepancy in my story about Alberto. She'd work it out – or talk to magical experts until she did. Death can only re-claim those it's been cheated of, not those it never had in its clutches.

I can't go down that route, not yet. Not until it's the last card I have left to play. The ritual I'm preparing in my booth will work. It has to. And I'll have the car journey over to come up with an innocuous explanation for the detective as to what the apparatus is all about.

'Right,' I say brightly. 'Let's go show you the Garcia records.'

A lone photographer skulking outside, doubtless on commission from the *Sentinel*, runs over, bulb flashing, as we head to the cop's car.

'Smile,' Knight mutters. 'And play with your hair so it's obvious you're not cuffed. Then get in up front, next to me, not in the back like a perp.'

We're over the bridge and out of The Cobb, heading for Main Street, when my phone goes.

'Ms Fenn, it's Anita here, the principal's secretary at Sanctuary High. We have an incident ongoing with your daughter and I'd like you to come in right away.'

'I'm with . . . Wait a moment . . .'

'Ms Fenn,' the secretary persists in my ear, 'whatever you're doing, you should drop it *right now*.'

'Can we?' I ask the detective, as panic rises within me. And mercifully, she nods and turns in the middle of the road and we speed toward Sanctuary High.

67

Maggie

Sanctuary High is plenty swanky. I'd wondered why kids like Dan Whitman and Bea Garcia, whose parents are loaded, came here when they could attend private schools, but now I see. The central building is historic in a good way, not a falling-down way, and it's flanked by new buildings, all smoky-glass windows and high ceilings. Every kid is in uniform, with few concessions to teen style: girls' skirts reach over their knees, boys' pants all cover their ass. As kids mill in the corridors, I see no facial piercings or colored hair.

No wonder Harper skips school.

'Sarah.'

As we turn a corner, Cheryl Lee steps forward. A pursing of the principal's mouth suggests she isn't pleased to see me.

'To what do we owe the pleasure, Detective Knight? This may be an unpleasant little incident, but it's hardly a police matter.'

'Sarah was with me when your call came, so I brought her straight over. And obviously after last night I need to know that the school is safeguarding Harper adequately. Now what's going on?'

'It's over, just about. We're trying to find Harper some spare clothes.'

'Why?' Sarah asks, panicked. 'Is she hurt? Blood?'

'Nothing of the sort. Only water.'

'Water? Who did it? *What* did they do?'

'Sarah, this really is a private matter. I wish you'd let—'

'I want Detective Knight to hear, Cheryl. If someone is trying to intimidate my daughter, it's relevant to her investigation.'

It's lucky that part of my job is ignoring the fuck out of people who'd rather I was somewhere else, because Principal Lee is glaring daggers at me. When she speaks, I understand why.

'It was Bea Garcia. She and a few others dunked Harper into the fountain.'

Sarah makes a wounded noise. The window of the room we're in cracks from side to side with a loud, clean sound that makes us all jump. No question what caused it. Sarah Fenn looks like she could punch her way through a wall. The principal is horrified, and her hand reflexively goes to the dainty crucifix round her neck.

'Take me to my daughter,' Sarah says.

We hear Harper's voice before we reach the counselor's office.

'I'm not having my mom see me like this. Your sweater will do.'

There is a sound of protest and scuffle, and when we enter the room, Harper is sitting there wearing a man's knit sweater, while a flustered guy in a striped shirt flattens down his hair. He nervously introduces himself as the school counselor.

Water is pooling on the floor beneath Harper's chair, where her hair's dripping. The limp cuffs of her white school shirt poke out from the counselor's sweater sleeves. The shirt itself must be practically transparent from the soaking. How could they expect her to sit like that in front of an adult male, counselor or no? I'm disgusted. It's clear that Harper's being treated like the problem here.

Sarah goes to her at once, and Harper doesn't push her away.

277

She clings. Her mom smoothes the wet hair back from her daughter's face.

'I am so sorry this happened to you, darling. I won't let them get away with it. I *won't*.'

'You said the fountain?' I ask Lee. 'There could be all sorts of contaminants in water like that. This girl needs a hot shower, dry clothes and some space. Ms Fenn, you should take Harper home right now. Principal, get your secretary to call a taxi.'

Cheryl Lee bridles. She's not used to being given orders in her own school. Well, screw that. How could she have let this happen?

'You do realize,' I tell her, 'that while a "dunking" is arguably common assault, a "ducking" done to a person linked to the magical community is a hate crime? It's what was done to test premodern witchcraft accusations.'

That shocks her into acting. I guess hate crimes don't go down well in school annual reviews to the board of education. We escort the Fenns to the taxi, and as it pulls away, another car rolls up. It's Julia Garcia, looking no less anxious than Sarah did, and like she's not slept since . . . well, since Abigail's revelations about her husband, I guess.

'The traffic from Anaconna was terrible, but I drove as fast as I could. What's happened, Cheryl? Is Bea okay?'

'She's in my office and she's fine, Julia. But we need to have a talk. Come with me.'

I hold a hand out and stop them.

'Technically, I could ask to be there,' I tell Lee. 'But I think you'll have a more constructive conversation without me. However, I presume your counselor is going to prepare a report of this incident? I'd appreciate being sent a copy before the end of the day.'

'Certainly, Detective,' Lee grinds out between clenched teeth.

Julia's head swivels to look back at me as the principal leads her away. She's harried and bewildered, and I think of her husband sitting wild-eyed in my office just a few hours earlier, claiming that Sarah Fenn bewitched him. What went down in the Garcia household last night? Is that why Bea's been acting up today?

This whole town is starting to come apart at the seams. And far from stitching it back up, every conversation I have is ripping it that little bit harder.

68

INCIDENT REPORT, 28 MAY
Prepared by school counselor Samuel Damasio, MA, NCC

Cause

Incident occurred during mid-afternoon recess, arising from a conversation between Beatriz GARCIA and Harper FENN as they left a tutoring session.

FENN says GARCIA alleged that her mother was responsible for bewitching GARCIA's father, and that FENN herself was a 'slut' who bewitched the late Daniel Whitman and then 'cried rape'.

GARCIA claims that FENN was 'gloating' over remarks made yesterday by Abigail Whitman, about her mother's magical manipulation of GARCIA's father.

It seems unlikely that we can establish an accurate picture of this conversation.

Incident

By the time the two girls had reached the inner courtyard, they were audibly combative, using language prohibited under Section 7b of the Student Code of Conduct. A small group of onlookers had gathered, including Freddie McConaughey, Oliver Welland and Dale Hamilton.

Witnesses report that both girls appeared 'angry', 'worked up' or 'furious'.

All onlookers agree that FENN attacked first, lunging at GARCIA. GARCIA admits that she was using provocative language but denies abuse. FENN claims that Garcia employed hate speech, including terms such as 'stick-hopper', a listed slur of sexual promiscuity applied exclusively to the magical community.

No onlookers support FENN's claim that GARCIA used hate speech.

GARCIA pushed FENN away, and FENN stumbled back into the fountain. GARCIA states that this was an accident. FENN claims that it was GARCIA's intent all along, which was why she had picked a fight and then escalated it at this particular location on campus.

Onlookers corroborate that FENN went into the fountain as a result of physical force from GARCIA.

Still standing in the fountain, FENN made a threatening gesture toward GARCIA, described variously as a 'clenched fist' or 'choking' gesture.

GARCIA claimed that she felt her airways constrict and was fighting for breath. Witnesses saw GARCIA fall to her knees, gasping and clawing at her throat, and heard her blaming this on FENN.

FENN states that GARCIA was 'entirely faking' and reiterates that it is common knowledge that she does not possess magical abilities.

GARCIA insists that the choking sensation she experienced was real. The school nurse suggests it was a panic attack.

FENN claims that GARCIA then directed McConaughey, Welland and Hamilton to restrain her in the fountain, while GARCIA taunted her that they would test if she was a witch by ducking her.

FENN points out that the three boys are all members of the football team and were close friends of the late Daniel Whitman. She claims that this proves the entire incident was a premeditated assault orchestrated by GARCIA with the foreknowledge of the named boys. She further states that GARCIA had no problem speaking when urging the boys to 'duck' her under, making nonsense of her claim to have been 'choked'.

GARCIA says that she did ask the boys to go to FENN, but in order to 'get her out of the fountain and away from me'. She states that she was 'genuinely terrified' of what FENN might do next.

McConaughey, Welland and Hamilton all agree that they took hold of FENN but did not lift her from the fountain immediately. They describe her as 'kicking', 'scratching' and 'thrashing about'. McConaughey says he told her to calm down so that they could lift her out. FENN did not comply and in their struggle to restrain her, she slipped and fell deeper into the water.

FENN states that this was a forcible ducking.

At this point, faculty member Casey Hodiak (Geography) intervened. Mr Hodiak says that he heard considerable noise from assembled students as he approached the scene, which died down immediately when his presence was realized. He ordered the boys to lift FENN from the fountain basin, which they did right away. He describes both girls as 'overexcited' and 'aggressive'.

He sent GARCIA to the nurse's room, with instructions that she was to report to the Principal's office once discharged, and brought FENN to me, Jeremy Damasio (School Counselor). Both sets of parents were immediately notified.

Conclusion

This was an ugly episode, involving students with mostly excellent prior conduct records. FENN is the only one with identified issues, chiefly unauthorized absences and numerous dress-code violations. GARCIA is a prominent student leader (class president in grades 9 and 11) and committed to her intended course of politics and legal studies. All three boys are starters on the school football team.

All involved were close to Daniel Whitman, whose tragic passing has affected this school's community so deeply. There are ongoing tensions around claims made in the aftermath of that death.

In light of this, I recommend leniency for all parties. See attached action plan.

Signed: Samuel Damasio, MA NCC

Submitted to Principal, VP, and filed

69

Abigail

Mary-Anne Bolt answers the door. Her thick body is trussed in apron strings like a ham in twine, and her face somehow looks both puffy and hollow.

If she's surprised to see me on her doorstep, she doesn't show it. There's a robotic quality to her politeness as she asks how she can help.

'Is Tad here?' I ask. 'I need to speak with him.'

'He's with Jake. Upstairs.'

'Can I come in?'

Mary-Anne is standing in the doorway, seemingly unable either to invite me in or turn me away.

'Mary-Anne? Is everything okay?'

And something releases. The chief's wife breaks into weeping that's helpless as a child's. I lean in to comfort her, using the opportunity to step across the threshold and nudge the door shut behind me.

'The doctor came last night,' she sobs, 'and said it's just another case of mono and all Jakey needs is rest and fluids. But he's so bad this morning, Abigail. He refused breakfast, and when we tried again to get him to eat, we couldn't even rouse him. When you rang the bell I thought maybe you were the paramedics already. But that doesn't even make sense.'

I want to slap her and yell that it's only mono, not murder, and that she needs to pull herself together. But I can't antagonize the Bolts. I need the chief wholly committed.

'You don't want an ambulance,' I tell her. 'They'll only take him to the local hospital, and I know from Michael they have poor outcomes. Very poor.'

Another wail from Mary-Anne.

'Michael's at home. Let me call him.'

The chief's wife is nodding dumbly at me like the milch cow she is. I can hardly bear to be in this house, surrounded by photos on every wall of her grinning, robust sons, but the opportunity is too good.

Michael agrees to come right over. He understands that Jake and the Bolts are our allies. I hurry Mary-Anne up the stairs to tell the chief that help is on its way, and to broach a conversation about ditching the detective and cracking on with a proper prosecution of the two witches.

Jake is in bed, Tad holding his son's hand.

'Mary-Anne?' he croaks, not turning round.

'It's Abigail. I've called my husband and he'll be here any minute. He'll get Jakey well again,' I tell him.

Tad swivels on Jake's desk chair, which he's dragged to the side of the bed. His fleshy haunches bulge beneath the molded plastic arms, but it's the expression on his face that shocks me. Tad Bolt isn't a man in his prime, but he always radiates vigor. Now his eyes regard me listlessly.

His son's sickness is plainly taking a toll on him. It's so frustrating. I need him fired up if we're to bring everything to its proper conclusion. Why did Jake have to pick now, of all moments, to fall sick?

And I freeze.

Why now, of all moments? Why now, when he has evidence of Harper's wrongdoing. When he was the first one to speak up;

the best and most credible witness to Harper's crime; the source for Varley's reporting in the *Sentinel*?

What if it's not mono that's responsible for Jake's wrecked state? Could it be Sarah, removing her daughter's prime accuser *by witchcraft*?

And even if it isn't, wouldn't it be convenient if Tad and Mary-Anne *thought* it was?

I need to plant the seed carefully. I speak to Tad rapidly, insistently, praying that enough of what I say is registering in a brain preoccupied with his son's condition.

'The detective's used to tackling gangbangers and drug dealers,' I say. 'She might even be good at that, though I doubt it. But this is outside her remit. Witchcraft – and the way Sarah and her daughter have misused their power. Who knows what else they've been responsible for?'

I let my gaze fall sadly on Jacob, and reach for the boy's other hand, lying limply on the bed. Let Tad draw the obvious conclusion.

'These are crimes against our community,' I press. 'As such, they need to be investigated and prosecuted by our community. And that means *you*, Chief. Sanctuary needs you. Come back on the case.'

That connects with Tad. I can see it in his wretched eyes. One more step and he'll arrive at the same conclusion. Maybe that'll come when Michael's bag of medical tricks fetches up short on fixing Jacob. Then everyone will see it – that the chief's son, like my son, like Alberto, is one more victim of the witches.

My thoughts stray to Alberto as we wait for my husband. It's strange. I loved him so much; then, when he ended it without a word, I had to unlearn all that love. To teach myself to hate him instead.

And now I know the truth, thanks to Julia's confession of her debt to Sarah, never realizing that the affair she asked Sarah to end was with *me*. It was never Alberto's choice to walk away from me at all.

When he understands that, when news of what I said last night reaches him, what will he do? Will it break Sarah's spell and bring him back to me? Or have I ruined everything by painting him as a man manipulated by his clinging wife and a witch?

Do I even care? It feels like my heart got stuck partway through that change from love to hate – and then Dan's death burned it to ashes. I can't think about Alberto now.

When the doorbell rings, it's a welcome interruption. Back to business. I leave the Bolts at Jake's side and go let Michael in.

'It's probably only mono,' I tell him. 'But wouldn't it be useful if it was witchcraft?'

Michael's gaze meets mine and I see a gleam there. We've understood each other better these past couple days, united in protecting Dan's memory, than we have in years.

I watch as he runs through the standard battery of tests. I saw him do them once before, to our son, the day he fell from the window.

'I'm sorry, Tad, Mary-Anne.' My husband's voice has that quelling tone that doctors use for breaking bad news. 'What I'm seeing is alarming and I'd like to give Jakey an immediate shot of antibiotics.'

Mary-Anne lets out a sob, wringing her hands in her apron as Tad nods curtly. I try not to shudder as Michael draws a slender hypodermic from his bag and tests Jake's arm for a vein. Who knows what's in the vial he upends? I shrug off a shiver of misgiving at how readily he has seized on my suggestion.

'He needs to be in a hospital right away. I'd like to get him admitted to my R and I unit, if you agree. We'll start with emergency intervention to stabilize him, and begin investigations immediately. Tad, your insurance will be good for everything.'

'R and I?' the chief asks.

'Rare and Infectious. My area of specialism, and the Yale team is second to none. Jake will be getting care from the best minds in the country.'

'Yet you don't know what this is?'

'I'll admit it's like nothing I've seen before. If I was inclined to superstition . . . but no. I'm a man of science.'

He's playing his part perfectly. But then we're both good at that – we've acted the perfect family for so long.

It's Mary-Anne who first takes the bait.

'You're saying it's magic?' she asks, fearfully. 'Witchcraft?'

Michael spreads his hands. 'I can't say it's not.'

Mary-Anne whimpers and crosses herself.

But Tad? Tad Bolt comes back to life, as anger flashes in his eyes.

70
Sarah

I didn't want to leave Harper alone, but she's gone up to her room and gone to bed. We had a tense, hushed conversation in the taxi on the way back from the school. When I asked if she had felt afraid, I got a brittle laugh.

'Those losers don't scare me.'

'But do you feel safe here, after what Abigail said last night? Should we get away from Sanctuary – maybe go someplace else?'

'I'm not running. I want to see their faces when they realize I'm innocent. I want to hear them say sorry – for this investigation, for everything we're going through, and for what Dan did to me.'

Mary-Anne Bolt joining my coven feels more likely than Abigail ever acknowledging that her son is a rapist, but I didn't say that.

'But maybe we should think about it?' I pressed. 'Someplace new, where you won't have this label of "witch's daughter". I could get another job – a normal one. Not practice for a few years. It must be hard for you.'

'You know what's hard, Mom? Seeing you, with so much power, working yourself to the bone for people who secretly fear and hate you.'

And that *hurt*. I help people. I mend their hearts, their bodies, their minds. It's a privilege. And it hurt because I fear that Harper doesn't see how incredible, how astonishing she is even without the gift.

Because I worry that words are driving us apart, I said nothing, just reached out a hand and wound our fingers together. She didn't snatch her hand away, and I counted it a victory, of sorts.

'I'm going to have a bath,' she announced when we got home. 'Maybe a nap after.'

I heard the water running and the bathroom door close.

I don't want to leave her, but the urgency of what I have to do is overwhelming – even more so after Beatriz's attack today.

The rite I've decided upon requires the creation of a perimeter. Witches have performed such spells since earliest times: defensive wards around a traveling encampment, a girdle of fertility for a field the whole village relies on, a rite of protection upon a house in time of plague.

And there's another class of spell with a long and honorable pedigree. We call them sunstone rites, for the mineral that Vikings used to set a course by even on overcast days. We witches use them to bring clarity in times of confusion, to resolve disputes and settle arguments.

Laypeople imagine they're 'truth spells', but it's nothing so straightforward. Magic is the art of doing things the crooked way, not the straight. Sunstone magic helps people see the gleam of truth amid the clouds of prejudice, ignorance and lies.

Combine the two, the boundary and the sunstone rite, and I think – hope, pray – that I can bring Sanctuary to its senses.

But to create the boundary, I need help. It requires four people, as many spell templates do. We call it the Power of Four: four can draw an enclosure; four is the smallest mathematical root; there are four cardinal points of the compass and four elements. That's why those witches who, like me, use covens generally work with three other people.

Except my coven is now one short. Abigail is lost to me. And after what Abigail said about Alberto, and what's just happened with Beatriz, I don't know how much longer I can count on Julia.

Three can still create a boundary. A triangular one. And because Sanctuary is bounded by the shore to the south, if I set points east and west along the coast, then position the third far enough north, the town will be contained within the triangle it forms.

I need to get back to my booth and finish my preparations. It won't take long, just a few hours. Maybe Harper won't even know I'm gone. I make a sandwich for her and write a note, like I did when she was little.

My booth is still in one piece, but as I pass the front, I see eggs have been thrown at the window.

Well, that's common enough if you're a witch – or anyone in a position of authority. I remember a kid at school once doing the same to a disliked teacher's house. If that and today's bullying are the worst fallout from Abigail's speech, Harper and I will cope.

The heap of dog shit left on the yard step isn't wholly unexpected, either, but is more upsetting in its sheer, rank offensiveness. I cringe, but at least my neighbor is a pet salon, so they'll have something for scooping it up. I pop into their yard, and as always, the staff working there turn toward me.

Except today, there's none of the usual friendliness in their faces. No one offers me a glass of wine or brings over a customer they've just clipped to show me their handiwork. One girl, the chattiest, silently bends back over the spaniel she's brushing. The others follow her cue. The yard is muted, apart from the yapping and huffing of the animals. The manager comes out of the salon, and when I explain my request, she fetches me a scoop bag then turns away without a word.

What's caused this? Harper's interview? Abigail's accusations last night?

As I close the yard door and let the latch drop, I hear talk resume. *Gives me the creeps knowing that's next door*, says one. *It'll hurt business*, adds another. *If we lose our jobs because of that—* says a third, using a slur for witches that we're all familiar with, even though polite folks pretend no one would dream of using it any more.

As I scoop up the poop, I tell myself they're just worried. Nothing more.

I don't believe it, though.

Taking down the wards, I unlock my workroom. The red light of the answerphone is flashing in the darkness of the office beyond. With a sinking feeling, I know I should ignore it. But what if it's important? What if it's Harper, or the cop, or Bridge or Pierre? Or someone calling to tell me my mom in Florida has had an accident?

All those people have your cell phone number, my brain insists, as I press the button anyway.

Six messages. The first two are from long-standing clients. They're warm and sympathetic. They heard Harper's interview and hope she's doing okay. They believe her and send their love. And then the hatred kicks in. One male voice, ranting about how stick-hoppers like my daughter are corrupting good American boys.

Two from women, rambling and abusive, one whose husband left her, which she has now realized is somehow all my fault. Another man informing me courteously that I'll burn in hell.

I take a deep breath, then a few more. Calmer, I switch off the answerphone. The little red light winks and dies.

292

The sooner I can complete this rite, the better.

The brew is progressing as it should. No more ingredients to add now. Just a slow steeping and infusing.

I can prepare the three sunstones, though. Carefully I oil them, lay stalks of clary sage and dried evening primrose petals across, and wrap them in clean linen cloths. The chart I've selected is rolled into a leather tube.

Then I pick out everything else I'll need to prepare the sites. Herbs for the rite must be dry enough to burn but fresh enough to have vigor, so I clip them from the yard and spread them across my drying racks. Small crystals I pick out and net. They'll hang from tree branches.

With a whetstone, I sharpen my silver sickle. My skin tingles at the thought of it, but it has to be done.

When everything's ready, I lock up tight and layer a strong deterrent charm onto the booth and yard. It's *too* strong. The grooming salon next door will be all but deserted until I lift it again tomorrow, but I think of those girls, so quick to bad-mouth, and squash my guilt.

The site preparation I'll do now. I place my bag, heavy with the sickle, onto the back seat. Aira curls around it, keeping it safe as I drive, as though she knows what's at stake.

Each site centers on a tree – the anchors of my spell. Oaks are the most congenial to my tradition of magic. With my sticks, I etch sigils into the soil around each trunk. I loop the nets of stones from low branches and clear a space of bare earth where the herbs will burn. Both Bridget and Julia know how to spark the flints witches use instead of matches or lighters. Then I take my sickle in hand and draw it across the back of my forearm.

Blood amplifies magic. And this spell must cast its net across miles, must whisper sense into the ears of thousands of people. So I grit my teeth and cut deep. The blood runs down my forearm into the cup of my palm, where I consecrate it to the work before flinging the drops wide.

By the time I'm driving from the third site, the fingers of my left hand are numb and nerveless on the wheel. There's nothing more to do now except wait. The brew should complete tonight, and I'll go speak to Bridget and Julia in the morning.

For now, what Harper and I need most is normality. Perhaps a mother-daughter movie night in our PJs, with Aira purring alongside us. I do a run-through of Harper's favorite snacks.

When I get home, though, she's not even touched the sandwich I left. My note is unread. The house is quiet. She's sleeping, I remind myself. Nothing to get alarmed about.

But I can't stop myself going upstairs to check, and I half know what I'll find.

Her bed is empty. Her window is open – she must have thought I was still downstairs.

And Harper is gone.

71

Sarah

I get up repeatedly in the night to check if Harper's come home, but her bed is still empty when I rise for the last time at 7 a.m.

Again I tell myself not to panic. For all her bravery about not being intimidated, after the disgusting school incident it makes sense that she wants to get away from Sanctuary. I'm glad I didn't have to tell her about the girls at the grooming salon, the hateful messages and the eggs on the window.

It's time to set this town to rights before it tips too far against us.

I know Cheryl leaves for work at seven thirty, so I head straight to Bridget's. As I park up, I become aware of faint voices in their yard. Cheryl hasn't gone yet. I head for the side gate, but as my hand is on the latch I hear something that stops me in my tracks.

My name.

'. . . has Sarah done for you that you're not telling me about?' Cheryl says. 'If she'd do something like that for Julia, when *you've* been her friend since grade school . . .'

'Nothing. Honestly, nothing.'

Bridget sounds distressed, and I want to throw open the gate and tell Cheryl to butt out of what doesn't concern her. But my friend's wife is relentless.

'Are you sure? What about your business – would that do so well if you weren't bosom buddies with a witch? Or my pay rise? It was going round in my head all yesterday. Everything I've achieved in the past few years, that I've worked so hard for and was so proud of. Did I deserve *any* of it? What about the "windfall" that paid for Izzy's therapy and bought you that ridiculous car? Was that *really* some generous great-aunt whom you'd never mentioned till then?'

'You *know* it was. It was an inheritance. Ask the lawyers. As for my business, that's because I worked my ass off for years. What – you think because I never got a college degree I'm too stupid to make a success of my life? Is that what you think of me?'

Then, tears. I can't tell from which of them, though my money's on Bridget. My tender-hearted friend.

'Babes. Darling,' says Cheryl, in a caressing tone that I'm sure no kid at Sanctuary High has ever heard. 'Don't cry. I'm sorry. It's just . . . yesterday. You didn't see them. Harper is so wild, and Sarah . . . They've got that cop eating out of their hand in a way that's really unnatural. She wasn't even interested in Beatriz's side of the story.'

'You know that Bea's been jealous of Harper since forever.'

Cheryl snorts. 'I'm perfectly aware. Bridge, darling, I'm sorry I said all that. I went too far. But promise me you won't get any more involved than you already are. Abigail is off her rocker, stirring things up. Now Julia's husband has been dragged into it. I don't want our family to be the next sucked into the storm.'

I wait to hear Bridget launch a passionate defense. To remind her wife of our three decades of friendship. Above all, to insist on Harper's innocence. But she does none of those things. Instead, she sniffles.

'I hate it when we fight.'

'Me too. Me too . . .'

They fall quiet. I imagine them embracing. Perhaps Cheryl petting Bridget like she's a pooch at the salon.

'You've wanted me to step back from the coven ever since we got serious,' Bridge says. 'You're not just using this as an excuse, are you?'

'You know how I feel about witchcraft. My faith . . . None of that's changed. But this is because I worry about *you*, darling. These are big accusations. Who knows what dark deed of Sarah's will surface next? I don't want you – or Izzy – hurt as collateral when it does.'

Bridget doesn't reply. She'll be thinking of the same dark deed that I am. The one that took place right where Cheryl and Bridget are standing now, and which has haunted us all ever since.

But if I don't confess, no one will ever know about that. Alberto wasn't there. Pierre's too loyal. Julia and Bridget were a part of it. And Abigail and Michael are hardly likely to tell the world that their golden boy owed his life to something so unnatural.

Lost in my memory, I almost don't hear Bridget's murmured response, punctuated with a kiss.

'All right, darling. No more magic – for now. Though I'll be there as a friend for Sarah whatever happens. Now get back to bed. I'm not letting you go in with a migraine and auras – we both know how those develop. I'll call the school.'

Another kiss.

'Thank you. I know it's hard, but it's for the best – for now.'

For ever, I think bitterly, if Cheryl has her way. But I won't let it come to that.

Then I realize just how screwed I am – because how can I work my sunstone rite now?

My thoughts circle like a fox trapped in a shed, searching for a way out. A crack of light. I wonder who else I can rely on. Who has stood by me unquestioningly.

There's only one name – Pierre. He's never been part of my coven, and he's a man. But he's my lifelong friend, so I should be able to connect with his energies, and Sanctuary born and bred, which makes him a good bet for magic worked upon our community. Julia and Pierre will be enough.

Julia will be furious with Abigail for what she said. She has a good heart. How could she not want to help me with a rite to soothe our troubled town?

I don't want to get to Julia's too early, so I can be sure that Bea and Alberto are gone. He drops her off at school before heading to the train station on his city days, and I bet he's having a city day to escape the gossip swirling around Sanctuary. So I take a leaf out of my daughter's book: some quiet time in nature, to get my head straight. The trails out toward Anaconna are lonesome and lovely.

I'm leaving the town limits when something catches my eye in the rear-view mirror. I pull over and walk back.

It's not subtle. And I'd bet whoever did it was responsible for that first attack on our house, because I recognize the red paint. They've sprayed three words onto the sign that proudly displays the town insignia and the name SANCTUARY. There's a 'MAKE', above it, and 'WITCH FREE' below.

MAKE SANCTUARY WITCH FREE.

Whoever did this has become bolder. They held back from completing the pentagram that would make their graffiti into a crime. But there's no restraint here. This is hate, in letters a foot high.

I've programmed the detective's number into my phone, so I call it. When she doesn't answer, I leave a message. I consider trying the station, but decide they might simply paint it out, no questions asked. Instead I snap some photographs. I'll send them to the Moot later. If they won't help me one way, I'll make them help me another.

When I get back in the car, my hands are shaking on the wheel. I need to get myself together. There are lots of cafés around the trailheads. One will serve me a hot chocolate, for a little sugar boost.

But when I turn in at the first place I see and go in to its fake-log-cabin interior, there on the counter for patrons to read while they eat is a stack of *Sentinel* special editions. The guy behind the counter looks up with an eager-to-help smile. It fades as he recognizes me. He lifts the countertop and steps out.

I know what's coming. I turn and hurry away before he asks me to leave – or maybe even throws me out.

In the parking lot I sit behind the wheel and sob, snottily and without ceasing. All I've ever tried to do is use my gifts as my gramma taught me: to help and to heal.

What did I do to deserve this?

Will it cost my daughter her life?

72

Sarah

I've pulled myself together by the time I'm standing in front of the Garcia house. I can still make this happen. I can't afford not to.

But anxiety screws tight within me as I watch through the glass as Julia approaches. She looks a mess. In pyjamas and a robe, hair tied messily on top of her head. As she nears, her face is pink and blotchy, eyes puffy. She looks like she hasn't slept all night, and the hours that should have been spent sleeping were spent crying instead.

She hesitates on the other side of the door, before opening it.

'Why are you here, Sarah?'

It's not the greeting I'd hoped for. We regard each other warily.

'Julia, are you okay?'

'It's been as bad as you might imagine,' Julia says. 'Worse, actually. Alberto left early this morning and I don't know where he's gone. To see a lawyer, maybe. And Bea is an absolute state. Your daughter *attacked* her.'

I bite back my retort – that Beatriz set a pack of Spartans on Harper and half drowned her in the school fountain. Recriminations won't get me anywhere.

'We can set it all right. I've prepared something: a simple

ritual that will help everyone in Sanctuary come to their senses.'

'A *ritual*?' My friend's laugh is bitter. She wipes her streaming nose. '*More* magic? Are you crazy, Sarah? Magic is what caused all this in the first place. I was vulnerable when I found out about Berto. You should have given me a shoulder to cry on and the number of a good couples therapist, not brewed an illegal potion.'

'Julia, you *begged* me. You told me that you'd tried to talk to him when he'd strayed before. That you'd suggested counseling, and he wanted nothing to do with it. You said I was your "last hope" – those were your words. I did it because you were desperate, and because you mean so much to me and I couldn't bear to see you in pain. It all looks perfectly proper in my records. No one can accuse you of anything.'

'It's not about looking innocent, Sarah. I *love* him. I would have put up for ever with him cheating, as long as he didn't leave me. But you know what he's like. His pride. I think this is it, this time.'

She tugs her dressing gown sleeve over the heel of her hand and hides her whole face, sobbing. I reach to comfort her, but she lashes out. Her blow connects with my cut arm and I stifle a cry. Not entirely, though. Julia studies me through misery-swollen eyes, and I see what she sees. The bandages I wrapped around my arm are stained through with blood. I cut deep to make this spell take hold.

'What the hell have you been doing, Sarah?'

'It's the rite. A sunstone incantation. It sheds light – makes things clear. Helps you find your path. I just need you and . . . one other, to create a boundary around Sanctuary and—'

'*Around Sanctuary?*'

'Yes. Everything's got so stirred up. So confused. That's all it is: confusion, not malice. And we can fix it.'

Julia takes a step back, and the look on her face I recognize, too late, as fear.

'You want to bewitch the *entire town*?'

'Not *bewitch* it. Just . . . help it calm down. Help all of us.'

'I don't think anyone needs that kind of help, Sarah. Please leave.'

And slowly, deliberately, she closes the door in my face.

She stays there a moment, looking at me through the glass. Then my friend turns away.

73

Maggie

I've sent Chester off to talk to Angry Dad. I figure a local boy might get more out of him in an initial conversation. Meanwhile, I'm making a quick detour to someone else with links to Sport on the Shore.

I was surprised to see Pierre Martineau at the vigil when he's such a friend of Sarah's. Turns out he's the club's boxing coach. An apology for not being straight about when we'd first met went partway to thawing him toward me. Then when I phoned this morning and asked if I could stop by for a chat, he readily agreed. Seems Sarah had told him about what happened at the school, and he's decided I'm giving her and Harper a fair hearing.

Pierre's loading up his van for a job, but he brews me some coffee and we sit side by side on his back step and talk.

He's a reassuring presence, with his calloused hands and paint-splashed coveralls. I envy him his work. He builds things from brick, wood and mortar. Solid structures that will last for decades. All I build are flimsy theories that hardly last from one day to the next.

'Do you remember when Dan Whitman stopped coaching the girls' soccer team? And why that was?'

Pierre blows on his steaming drink as he casts his mind back.

'Maybe a year and a half ago. I remember Mitch getting stressed 'cos it happened partway through the season. Kinda abrupt. But I reckon Dan was upset about it too.'

'Why so?'

'Because his dad was the one who put an end to it. Had a couple of meetings with Mitch, and Dan wasn't there. It was about the time it became obvious that Dan had a shot at pro one day. You know what Michael Whitman is like. Ambitious ain't the half of it. We all reckoned he'd made his kid give up anything extra to focus on his own training.'

'And that was it?'

'Most that I ever heard it was. Why, you heard differently?'

I exhale, setting my coffee down on the stoop.

'Just trying to make sense of a bunch of things, Mr Martineau. Things that don't make much sense as is. Can I ask one more question: do you believe Harper Fenn, what she told that reporter?'

Pierre scratches his neck. He's thinking carefully.

'Harper, she . . . You know her dad was never on the scene. I never even met him, though Sarah and I go way back. So I've been like an uncle to her. And she's always watched out for my Isobel. So yeah, I believe her.'

Those dark eyes of his are troubled, though, and I wonder what he's not saying. Is he hurt that she never confided in him? Or is it more than that? Is he confused about why she didn't speak up earlier? Wondering, despite his loyal words, if he really can believe her?

I've heard enough for now.

'Thanks so much, Mr Martineau. And I'm sorry again for not being straight with you about the first time our paths crossed.'

'The night Dan fell out the window? Yeah, well . . . Abigail Whitman found out who her friends were that night, and Sarah was chief among them. It's a shame she's forgotten.'

304

So Sarah has got at least one staunch ally. But when I pick up her voicemail, it's plain that she might need rather more than one. I drive over to check out the town sign, and it's a disgrace. I ring the station and give them an earful about getting it photographed, then cleaned off. As I'm scratching for a sample to compare with the paint that sprayed the Fenn house – I don't trust Bolt's goons to do that properly – a car pulls up and a guy with a camera and a press badge from the *Sentinel* starts snapping away.

'Tell your boss Varley she'd better run this with the right sort of headline,' I warn him. 'Something like "Witch-hate shame", rather than "Best idea ever". I'll be watching.'

I take a few photos myself, and am walking back to my car when my radio crackles. It's Chester. I can hardly make out what he's saying. It's not my radio on the fritz, though. He's babbling with excitement.

'Deep breath, Chester, and say that again at half-speed.'

'I'm in Green Point. I'd just finished up with Angry Dad when I got a call from Rowan, who's still feeling rough. So we've driven to the nearest witch booth outside Sanctuary, which is here. It's a sleepy sort of place. You know: gets fat on tourists every summer, then minds its own business the rest of the year. Couple gift shops, surf school and tattoo shop, beach café – and the witch's booth.'

'Sounds charming. I'll go on my next day off. Oh, wait – what's a day off? *And?*'

'And she's here. Harper Fenn.'

'What?'

Gee, won't that girl stay put at her mother's even one night? I know she's a wild free spirit and all that jazz, but she's also accused of murder and an accuser of rape.

Then I think of Beatriz Garcia and the Spartans ducking her in the fountain. The classmate who filmed as she was raped, and those who shared pictures of it online. The trashing of her home, and the local newspaper splashing accusations. Abigail Whitman telling the world that Harper murdered her son. Even this loathsome graffiti on the town sign, which makes it plain that she and her mother are no longer welcome in the place where she was born.

And I think of the death penalty that hangs over her.

I should be grateful she hasn't absconded across state lines or fled the country altogether.

Then another set of possibilities lights up in my brain.

Green Point is Harper's bolthole. Which explains why she was jogging from that direction the day I saw her. *I have friends out this way*, she said.

And Green Point *has a witch*. Could *this* be the person whose magic Rowan sensed at the party villa? The person whose magic surely murdered Daniel? Because why would you conceal your identity when working witchcraft, unless you were doing wrong?

Perhaps the witch is Harper's friend. Or maybe they have a son who is a secret boyfriend (Bea's allegation of *another guy out of town*), and who begged his mother for revenge on her behalf. Or a loyal girl. One who, unlike Harper, inherited the gift and was prepared to act on her wronged friend's behalf.

'Make sure your patrol car is out of sight,' I radio Chester. 'We don't want her to spook. I'll be right over.'

This feels like a break. At last.

74

Maggie

In a roadside picnic spot outside Green Point, Rowan and Chester join me. The witch sits up front – they're not suffering too awfully, but have been experiencing what they call psychic depletion – while Chester explains.

'The booth doesn't open till ten, so I went into the café to get us a drink – that one on the beach. It's pretty busy, 'cos the paddle-boarders all go in the water early. And there she was, looking toward the sea as if she was waiting for someone. So I radioed you right away.'

'You're sure it's her?'

'Definitely. Though she looks a bit different from usual. You'll see . . .'

'Well let's get right back,' I say, starting my car. 'Here's the plan. We'll leave the patrol car here, and Chester, you're too conspicuous in your uniform. Stay put in this vehicle and be ready to tail Harper if she heads out. I'll go into the café and observe.

'Rowan, I'd like you to go to the booth for your treatment but try and engage the practitioner in conversation about Sanctuary. Find out if they know Harper. Maybe present yourself as a witch vacationing in the area and anxious about the news, wondering if it's wise to stick around these parts. Is that something you feel comfortable doing?'

Rowan's smile shows their sharp white teeth.

'Sure. It beats checking whether a client's noisy dog has been hexed by the pissed-off witch next door, or if a gifted former girlfriend has cursed her ex's dick. Both true cases,' Rowan adds, laying a hand on my assistant's arm. 'Remind me to tell you about them some time.'

Chester has turned that beetroot red again. Thank God all I've asked him to do is stay in the car.

The café is loud with the noise of the barista machine, and there are at least six different milks for my coffee, only one of which involved a cow. The menu is fifty percent 'superfood' and eighty percent vegetarian. Standing there trying to make head or tail of it gives me ample opportunity to scan the interior for Harper.

And there she is. Unmistakable, just as Chester said, and most definitely 'different from usual'. She's wearing a skinny-strapped vest top and she's absolutely *covered* in tattoos. I stare, fascinated, despite myself.

The inking is like a garment, stretching down to her wrists and up to her collarbone, but almost nowhere that would be visible when she's fully clothed. Everything I've heard or thought about Harper's 'modesty' now makes sense. Why she wears long sleeves for sport and took the school counselor's sweater when her white shirt was soaked transparent. Even why she pulled the hospital curtains tight that first day.

Not the self-harm that Cheryl Lee worried about, or abusive bruising. The opposite. Harper has made her skin into art. There's something outrageous about so much ink on a girl so young, but at the same time, the designs are absolutely beautiful. It's hard to take my eyes off her. But I have to, because she's with someone.

He's your clichéd beach dude. Dirty-blond curls that are slick with seawater. Perhaps mid-twenties – young enough that his complexion looks sexily tanned, rather than merely weathered. And he's covered in tattoos too. Celtic knots curl around his bulging biceps. A mermaid adorns his right pec and a winking sailor his left.

Harper is leaning across the table toward him, smiling as if she doesn't have a care in the world. Like she was never accused of murder. Never raped. Never bullied. Not living in fear of judicial execution.

It's an extraordinary transformation, and now I understand why this girl comes here so often. To be someone different. Not the witch's daughter or the athlete's girlfriend. Not the giftless one.

'I said, *what can I getcha*?'

I say the first words that catch my eye on the drinks list, which unfortunately are 'turmeric chai latte'. I carry my beverage to a discreet table, try not to gag as I sip, and continue to watch the pair by the window. I'm concerned that this guy is some kind of sleaze or druggie, but there's nothing predatory in his body language or strained in hers. Maybe he just doesn't know how young she is?

Other wet dudes and gals come into the café. Several stop by the table. One guy peels back a waterproof dressing to show Harper what looks like a recent tat on his arm. She checks it over with a professional scrutiny, then nods approval and covers it up again. The arm's owner pats Harper on the back – he's so hefty she's winded by the blow – and they bump fists.

What *is* this? One thing is plain: Harper is a part of this community like she's never been back in Sanctuary. I think of everything I've heard about her growing detachment from schoolwork, the distance that opened up between her and Beatriz even without the Dan Whitman issue. Julia Garcia's remark about *different aspirations*. And no wonder, if she's found her place here. Green Point's locals couldn't be more different from a designer-label-loving overachiever like Bea Garcia.

Is *this* the story I've been searching for?

Harper outgrowing her friendships in Sanctuary as she chooses a different kind of life. Trying to break it off with her jock boyfriend, Daniel. The alpha boy of Sanctuary not wanting to lose face, drugging Harper and having sex with her while his friend recorded it to humiliate her.

Harper set on confronting him at the party, ranting angrily just like Jake said, but unheard amid all the noise and music. Maybe a Green Point pal – one of these burly guys – coming along as support. Dan, alarmed, stumbling over the balustrade and falling to his death.

An accident. Just an accident after all.

It's a story that doesn't account for the fact that the villa reeks of powerful witchcraft.

But I think I prefer it.

I pull myself together. Like I told Ches, we're law enforcement. We don't get to decide who's guilty and who isn't.

The case that I have requires a witch, and Green Point has one of those. Maybe she's a surfer and doesn't open her booth till she's had her daily dip in the sea.

This little shoreside community is where my answers lie, I'm sure of it.

When the pair get up, I tail them out and along the board-walk. We pass the witch's booth, a cute little place, all sky-blue paint and calligraphed signage: 'Siobhan Maloney – registered witch. Consult a fully licensed practitioner. *Works like magic!'*

A ship's bell hangs to one side of the door for customers to announce their presence, and a blind is drawn down in the glass window. 'Witch at work!' reads a card that's been flipped over. Rowan's in there. Good.

Harper and her friend, meanwhile, have gone into a store three doors further along. And surprise, surprise: it's the tattoo shop.

Canvas, the place is called, its name gorgeously painted in coiling letters across the large window. Framed photographs hang either side of the entrance, displaying the talents of its proprietor. There's a newspaper article reproduced. It's a photo of Harper's friend giving a thumbs-up alongside a heavily inked man.

'Tat's brilliant' is the headline. 'Green Point artist Jonny Maloney scoops first prize in statewide tattoo contest.' I don't read any further. That surname gives me all I need to know. Harper's friend is related to Green Point's witch. A son, brother or husband.

I take a few photographs with my phone. I'm worried about being spotted, but the pair inside are busy. Harper moves around confidently, preparing tools and instruments, syncing a phone so music starts up, low and growling. She produces a sketchbook from under the counter and shows something to Maloney. He evidently has suggestions, and they discuss the design.

Maloney heads out back and I watch as Harper props a mirror alongside the medical-looking couch where the tattooist's clients submit to his needle. She tugs off her vest top and turns this way and that, inspecting herself. Beneath her bra, her midriff is swathed in coiling designs.

She fits a needle carefully to the ink gun and lays it back in the metal dish. Then she pulls around a spotless curtain and hides herself from view. Jonny Maloney is nowhere to be seen. A moment later, just audible over the music, the needle starts to buzz.

And I realize those tattoos on Harper aren't just beautiful – they're her *own* handiwork. No wonder she feels at home here.

Just along the boardwalk, the bell rings outside the witch's booth and Rowan exits. I hurry after them back to Chester's car, eager to hear what they've learned.

Eager to finally fit everything together.

75

NOTES BY MAGGIE KNIGHT OF ROWAN ANDREWS' (RA)
CONVERSATION WITH SIOBHAN MALONEY (SM), GREEN
POINT WITCH

- RA presented self as a vacationing witch struck with a
  headache.
- SM age 50-ish. Performs approved assessment of RA.
- RA raised topic of Sanctuary & Harper Fenn.
- 'A bad business, it's got all the Connecticut witches
  fearful,' says SM. 'Of course, it's not witchcraft at all.'
- Does SM feel anxious so close to Sanctuary?
- 'Yes & no. The girl who's accused has friends here. Known
  to Green Point locals. She's a very nice young lady. No
  magic to speak of.'
- Has SM spoken to her?
- A little. She's friendly with SM's son. Since the case blew
  up, SM has kept her distance, so no one can link the girl
  to a magical practitioner.
- And she's definitely not a witch?
- 'No way.' SM believes the Whitman death must be 'just a
  sad accident'. No witchcraft at all. Expresses sympathy for
  Sarah Fenn, who she 'knows only a little'.

- SM concludes diagnosis of RA – an adverse reaction to recent magical exposure. Performs aura cleanse ritual & prescribes premix potion.
- RA compliments SM on her booth & practice. Is her son a witch to carry on the tradition?
- SM laughs. 'He's a surf bum. Not a magical bone in his body – though rather good with a needle.'
- RA pays & leaves.

76

FROM THE *SANCTUARY SENTINEL*

Front page

UNDER THEIR SPELL?
LOCAL MAN IS WITCHES' LATEST ALLEGED VICTIM

By Beryl Varley, News Editor

Sanctuary has been rocked by fresh outrage about the actions of witches in our midst.

It is claimed that a local man – named by sources as Alberto Garcia, 48, of Anaconna – has unknowingly been subjected to magical compulsion.

When asked for a comment, a spokesperson for the US Moot, the national body of magical practitioners, said that 'The United States prides itself on having some of the most stringent guidelines for the practice of witchcraft of any country in the world. Anyone found to be operating without regard for these guidelines will be stripped of their license and, where relevant, may face prosecution.'

In light of the latest development, Chief Tad Bolt has exclusively told the *Sentinel* that he is reversing his decision to step back from the investigation into the death of Daniel Whitman.

'I cannot stand by and permit the failings of a state-level detective to thwart any chance of obtaining justice for Daniel and his parents,' said the popular local lawman. 'And I will not let people lie awake at night, terrified of malevolent forces at work in our town. Here in Sanctuary, we deal with our problems ourselves.'

Alberto Garcia has been approached for comment.

77

Sarah

My daughter has gone. My coven is broken and disbanded. Abigail has turned on me, Julia blames me, and Bridget is keeping her distance.

The sunstone rite I needed to end this madness is impossible now.

I have to leave the ritual spaces intact – once an offering is made, you can't take it back. But I can clear up my workroom. The smell of the brew still pervades the space: pungent sage and the stale, greasy reek of evening primrose oil. But as I wash and purify the vials, cleanse the stones and pack them away, I begin to wonder if I shouldn't just keep going. Pack it *all* away, even my ingredients and sticks. Sell the lot – or donate it to the Witches' Benevolent Fund so some young and impoverished magical can benefit.

Move far away from here. Perhaps go see my mom and her third husband down in Florida. Mom always hoped that, like her, I wouldn't have the gift, and our relationship was never the same after my grandmother's talent showed up in me. Now the same thing is happening with me and Harper. My girl's lack of ability is driving a wedge between us. Perhaps spending time with her equally giftless grandma will help my daughter settle.

Could I make us disappear?

An enchantment would disguise us. Would let us cross the country unnoticed and lie low in Florida until this has all died down, my daughter's name has been cleared, and we can make a calm decision about whether to return to Sanctuary.

In my heart of hearts, though, I know that if we leave, we'll never return. They'll say we fled for a reason.

I go to a small cupboard in the corner. Behind my business's more mundane supplies – toilet roll and printer paper – is a safe that Pierre installed for me. I cycle through its combination: 05261647, the date the state of Connecticut hanged Alse Young for witchcraft. She was the first witch in the Thirteen Colonies to die, and her body swung for days in Hartford's Meeting House Square nearly five decades before Salem. My gramma always said we can never be sure it won't happen again.

I wish she was here now to advise me.

The safe contains only one thing: a book. Or, technically, a grimoire.

It was printed more than two centuries ago, after witches supposedly rehabilitated themselves by proving their courage and loyalty in the Revolutionary War. The new American state recognized us – though it took another two hundred years to formally decriminalize us – and the result was a flowering of our art like we've never seen since in this country.

A coven in the town of Starcross, Pennsylvania, worked for a decade to assemble what they titled the *Standard American Book of Lore*, but which soon became known as the Starcross grimoire. They had a patron, a rich landowner who paid for copies to be made. These were freely given to magical families of 'good heritage', and some were acquired by those without the gift, who were fascinated to learn more of our art.

But the achievement of Starcross, the incredible detail it contained, was its – and our – undoing. Its pages revealed that we can make people fall in love, waste away, do our bidding. It

318

even hinted at acts like that I used to bring back Daniel. Within a year of its creation, reprinting of the grimoire was forbidden.

And then, inevitably, the crackdown began. In a country trying to establish the rule of law, power that could neither be seen nor defined was viewed with suspicion. The body that eventually became the Moot co-operated, not wanting the public to learn and be frightened by the full extent of our powers. Volumes of Starcross were confiscated and burned.

A handful, of course, survived. Among them one possessed by my family.

It's a crime, even today, to reproduce or sell copies of the book now in my hands. Any fragments that find their way online are taken down, and even universities and national libraries are barred from digitizing it. No one knows how many originals still exist. But up here in New England there's more than one family, like ours, with a grimoire treasured more carefully than an old family Bible.

I carry the book to my workbench, savoring the feel of it, the leather worn butter-soft by the hands of the women and men who cherished it before me. The binding is loose, fragments dusting into powder at every turn of a page. I studied the grimoire the day after I brought Dan back, to check how closely what I had done matched the clues and hints recorded in its pages. I'd had to compress a painstaking rite into ten minutes of frantic work, so what I'd done was an approximation, but Starcross reassured me it was close. Close enough.

The aromas that rise from the pages are the smell of magic itself. Incense, herbs, blood and iron. Sweet, bitter and salty. And something *felt*: tingling across my skin and lifting the hairs on my arms.

Harper was obsessed with Starcross when she was little. She loved the history and anecdotes, the long lists of potion ingredients. But above all she adored the illustrations – the woodcut pictures of witches at work, of ingredients and objects. She'd copy them onto art paper and color them. She'd ask all the time when her magic was going to come in.

She couldn't wait to be a witch.

It's only when a water stain appears on the crinkled page that I realize I'm crying.

I couldn't give Harper magic. But I'll use everything I have to give her the life she chooses. The book in my hands would be worth a considerable sum to a private collector not bothered about an illegal acquisition.

The grimoire is my family's past. But if I have to sell it to secure my daughter's future, I will.

I stroke the pages, and then turn to the section on 'Spellworke for hiding of a person, power or object'.

Which is when my phone rings. I frown at the number. It's not Harper, the school, the cop, or Pierre, Bridget, Julia or Abigail, so I let it go to voicemail before listening to the message.

It's a woman's voice, pleading, and she sounds absolutely broken.

78

Sarah

Securing the workroom and hurrying out, I spot her right away, standing distraught and bewildered in the small central park on Main Street. She couldn't find my booth, even though she's standing almost directly opposite it, because of the concealment charms I laid.

I want to hasten her inside, not stand in public like this. But it's too late.

'You did it, didn't you?' shouts Mary-Anne Bolt. 'You did. To punish him.'

What's she talking about? Has something happened to Tad?

'When you came to our house. You came that morning and he got sick that afternoon. You *cursed* him.'

She's crying hysterically and her finger is pointing right at me. It's mid-afternoon and Main Street is busy. At least half a dozen people just heard that accusation.

'I did nothing to Tad, Mary-Anne.' Nothing except threaten him, anyway.

'Not Tad. *Jake*.'

'Jacob?'

'He's in a *coma*. Michael Whitman came and had no idea what's wrong. My boy's breathing failed in the ambulance on the way over, and now some machine is all that's keeping him alive. And you did it, didn't you? To shut him up.'

Words fail me. My craft fails me. I have no idea what to say or do, because no option is good. We're drawing a small crowd of onlookers.

'It's not just Jake. Some of Tad's boys have gotten sick, too. The ones who were on duty at the vigil for Daniel. Only them. You did it. *You*.'

And with a scream, arms flailing like she wants to claw my eyes out, Mary-Anne launches herself at me.

I grab her wrists to fend her off. She's strong but uncontrolled, and twists in my grip. There's only one way to calm her down quickly, and that means working magic on the chief's wife, in front of an audience. But if I don't, who knows how long this will continue, drawing stares.

I've no choice. I make the sign for pacification – that one I use on bitey dogs – and murmur the accompanying cantrip, all the while praying to the goddess that the *Sentinel* photographer isn't hiding behind a tree, snapping away.

But somebody spots my fingers working in the air.

'Magic!' calls a voice from those gathered on the sidewalk. 'The witch just cursed her!'

A small child shrieks and runs away. Someone spits. Unable to evade in time, I watch disbelievingly as it spatters my sleeve.

Mary-Anne is quieter. Her struggles are weaker. But I've no idea what to do with her. Several of the spectators have followed the child and fled. But the few who are left edge closer. Panic bubbles inside me. To lay the cantrip on them all, here in the middle of Main Street, would be madness. But what can I do? They'll be on me in a moment.

'Get your hands off her, witch!' snarls one man, bolder than the rest.

Which is when Bridget appears, out of breath after jogging over from her salon.

'Come on, Mary-Anne. Come and have a sit-down. What are you looking at?' she snaps at the gapers. 'Can't you tell when a woman feels faint? It's nothing serious.'

'It's magic,' says the man. His fingers are clenching as though he'd just love to take a swing. 'The witch did it.'

Bridget ignores him, leading the chief's wife away to her pet salon as I stand there uncertainly. But Bridget hasn't forgotten me. She bellows back over her shoulder for me to follow them, so we can all 'have a drink and a quiet chat'.

The huddle parts to let us through, but I don't miss the slur words. The threats. As I pass, old Nikos from the deli where I pick up baklava makes the fig sign for warning off the evil eye. Their fear and hatred weighs me down. It's ironic that Sanctuary is panicking about how powerful I supposedly am, when in truth I've never felt more powerless.

Bridget leads us to her little office and lifts a box of dog shampoo off a chair so Mary-Anne can sit down. She shouts for one of her assistants to fix us all a glass of wine and some cookies, and I don't miss the girl's disgusted glance as she brings the tray. Mary-Anne's shoulders are shaking, but she's quieted. Bridget presses a glass into her hand, makes her take a few sips, then coaxes the story out of her.

And it doesn't look good for me. Apparently right after I visited the Bolt house, Jacob started feeling unwell. They assumed it was mono, but he went downhill fast. Michael Whitman took him off to the university hospital for evaluation, and Mary-Anne's been there all day, coming apart bit by bit as her son's indicators went from bad to worse.

Eventually, Michael gave her some sedatives and sent her home to rest. But she didn't. She came to find me.

'Why did you do that, Mary-Anne?' Bridget asks.

The chief's wife looks groggy, and Bridget frowns. It's a side effect of magical pacification, but given Cheryl's judgment of me, I'm not going to tell Bridget what I just did and fuel that fire.

'Must be the sedatives,' I say, as we watch her struggle to speak.

'She's managed the rest of her story.'

And, okay, I may have made the pacification stronger than a simple 'calm down'. The scene she was causing was getting out of hand.

But I plainly didn't make it strong enough.

'Sarah *cursed* him,' she gasps. 'I came to ask her to lift it. And she cursed the cops who were at the vigil. She's going to curse the whole town, to punish us.'

'Hush now, Mary-Anne,' Bridget says. 'Calm down. I've known Sarah all my life. She wouldn't do that.'

But when my old friend looks at me, I see a question, and that question is: *Did you?*

'She did. *She did*,' the chief's wife insists, rocking back and forth. 'My son's going to *die*.'

'Mary-Anne, that's enough.' Bridget gives the woman's shoulder a little shake. 'You know lots of folk have been getting poorly, long before this happened. The kids with mono, like my Izzy. Even Cheryl's off sick, and let me tell you, that woman has an iron constitution.'

'Of course Cheryl's sick,' gasps Mary-Anne. 'Everyone knows she's not expelling any of the boys from school. So she's been cursed too.'

'Absolutely not,' I snap. 'Bridget, tell me you don't believe that.'

'Of course I don't.'

But I see it again, that little flicker of doubt in her eyes.

There's only one way to fix this. I get on one knee beside

Mary-Anne, to make myself look less threatening, and reach for her hand, which quivers in mine.

'Mary-Anne, our kids have grown up together. I've never wished harm on any of them. I can try to help Jacob, but I have to see him to make a diagnosis. You know that.'

She snatches her hand back. 'No! I know what you're trying to do. You tried to kill him, but Michael rescued him, so now you want to finish the job. You're not going anywhere near my boy. You cursed him, so you can lift it.'

'I didn't, so I can't, Mary-Anne, truly. It'll be some normal physical sickness.'

Mary-Anne's hand flashes up and slaps me so hard my head rocks back. I'm sent sprawling on my butt, clawing at boxes. She crouches over me.

'Witch!' she hisses. 'Murderer! You and your witch daughter. First we'll burn you. And then you'll burn in hell.'

79

Abigail

Bridget called to tell me about a scene between Mary-Anne Bolt and Sarah on Main Street. She asked if I could try to talk sense into the chief's wife.

I'll do nothing of the sort. The whole episode couldn't have been more perfect if I'd suggested it myself. Sarah using offensive magic *in public*? She's practically announcing her own guilt.

So when the phone rings, I expect it to be Mary-Anne giving me her own update. But it's not – it's the school. Cheryl Lee's vice principal, in fact. He asks me to come in to discuss an 'important matter', but won't say what.

Once, such a call would have filled me with dread, imagining the worst: a football injury, my beautiful boy strapped to a board in a neck brace, his life utterly altered. It can't be that now. So it must be something about Harper. Perhaps they've found further evidence against her.

'Mrs Whitman, thank you for coming in,' says a man who introduces himself as the school counselor. He's a prim guy in his thirties who looks like listening to his students' romantic troubles is the nearest he's ever come to having sex. The other man is Cheryl Lee's deputy. The principal is off sick, he explains.

'Is that so?' I tell him. 'She's not the only one suffering. Jacob Bolt is in intensive care. Several police officers working on the Fenn case are also poorly. And now Ms Lee. A strange coincidence.'

But the vice principal isn't as quick to take the bait as Mary-Anne was, saying it's nothing more than one of Cheryl's sporadic migraines.

I may be imagining it, but the atmosphere is cool. I've always been treated respectfully, as befits the mother of a sports star and the wife of a Yale professor. Since Daniel's death, people have been falling over themselves with solicitude, and that's only gotten more noticeable since Harper's disgusting allegations. These two ought to be pulling out a chair for me and asking how I am. Something's wrong.

A small tablet sits on the counselor's desk. The sort of thing kids use to stream TV. Daniel had several.

'I confiscated this earlier from Freddie McConaughey,' the counselor explains, fingers framing the device like a cop trying not to contaminate evidence. 'Yesterday, a tenth-grade girl said that she had seen Freddie showing some of her classmates inappropriate material.'

I keep my face blank. I'm not Freddie McConaughey's mother. He was Dan's teammate, no more.

'The girl is a credible student, so I alerted Freddie's homeroom and subject teachers, and between classes one of my colleagues saw fit to confiscate this. There are several unpleasant videos on it, but one of them . . .'

I'm still silent. What has this got to do with me? The vice principal clears his throat, a nasty, moist sound.

'Us asking you to come in is irregular, Mrs Whitman, but I hope you'll understand why. We'll be discussing this matter with the police next, and given the recent terrible events, I thought . . . That is, we . . .'

So I was right. It is more evidence against Harper.

'From the party? I've already seen it. Or rather, Jake's version of it.'

'You have? And yet you—'

'The more the police have, the better. I mean, no version could be clearer than Jacob's. He was right next to Harper when she did it. But he doesn't catch the actual moment Daniel falls. Or what was happening on the landing beforehand. Whatever Freddie filmed can only help.'

The two men exchange glances. The counselor has gone bright red – a classic anxiety flush. The vice principal appears to be losing all powers of speech, though he manages it eventually.

'Forgive me, Mrs Whitman, it's not *that* party.'

Not that party?

'The video in question appears to be the original of footage that the school authorities have been aware exists online in an, ah, edited version. The same footage that was shown on the night your son so tragically lost his life.'

'The sex tape?'

The deputy leans forward in his chair. He's an unprepossessing man, the front half of his head almost entirely bald, but now there's something in his eyes that tells me how he got this job. That he's capable of putting the fear of god into disobedient or slacking students. I shrink back. Whatever he's going to tell me will be worse than anything any student has ever had to hear in this airless little office.

'I'm afraid that wouldn't be the correct term, Mrs Whitman. You see, in Freddie's footage the audio hasn't been edited. There's no music track. It shows your son having sex with Harper Fenn, yes, but she can be heard saying – not clearly, but repeatedly – "please stop" and "no".'

As quick as reflex, I reach out to grab the tablet and hurl it against the wall, shattering it into pieces that no forensic geek will be able to put back together.

But the counselor is faster, pulling it toward himself.

'I'm truly sorry to be the bearer of bad news, Mrs Whitman,' says the vice principal. 'But I hope you can use this time to prepare yourself. We'll be handing this to the police tonight.'

80
Maggie

The recording on Freddie's tablet? It's *bad*. Harper's soft and slurry, but when she says 'no' and 'stop', there's no mistaking it.

Chester has to get up and walk away as we watch, looking like his breakfast will be putting in a reappearance.

I peer at the screen. There are ten minutes of this, not the cut-down version on the porn site. Boys hoot drunkenly and yell encouragement from the other side of the door. At one point someone hammers on it and cries, 'My turn next!' Nothing to prove they know what's happening on the other side is a rape, but sickening all the same.

And Harper had to see them all at school, every day.

'Christ,' Chester says when it's all over, his face pale and sweaty.

'Yup. No doubt now what happened. So, we have a narrative, of sorts. A rape. Leading to a confrontation at the birthday party. And Dan dies, accidentally or with premeditation. By magic, or not by magic. And at whose hands, do we think?'

'I guess we're ruling out the dad of the girl who Dan . . . who *says* that Dan . . . No, no . . .' Chester's face screws up as his police impartiality wars with his revulsion at what he just saw. 'He really did molest that girl, didn't he? If he's capable of *that* . . .'

'Certainly looks that way.' I turn the tablet face down so neither of us has to look at it. 'Tell me again how he seemed when you spoke to him.'

Chester reminds me of the main points of Angry Dad's testimony. The account the man gleaned from his daughter, hint by fearful hint, culminating in a distraught revelation of everything Dan did. Each inappropriate touch, from standing too close as he showed her how to kick a ball, to a brush of hands at the bowling alley on a team evening out. How those hands later found their way under her skirt.

'He said he was going to go to the cops, but his daughter begged him not to. She thought all the other kids at school would turn on her. Plus, the mom goes to the same church as the Bolts. This is such a small town and Dan was so popular that the kid was terrified of what it would mean for them all. You should have seen her dad – he was in pieces just telling me about it.'

'Right. But if he didn't go for Dan then, why would he go for him now? So perhaps put him low on the list. Harper too, because if she did it, then why would she go public with a motive? Plus—'

'*Plus*,' says Chester, finishing my sentence, 'there's the *magic* thing. Rowan and I were discussing it on the way to Green Point. They're frustrated that they can't tell what it was used for specifically, but it was used with violent intent.'

'No shit. It nearly blew Rowan's face off. Did you see it . . . swirling? That wasn't just me imagining things, was it?'

My colleague shakes his head with the emphatic *uh-uh* of a child.

'But Harper sort of needs to be higher on the list, doesn't she? Because even if she couldn't do the magic herself, she

331

could have asked someone to do it. Like the Green Point witch, Siobhan Maloney.'

'Or her son, Jonny,' I add. 'We only have Siobhan's word that he has no ability. And if you suspect your son of unnatural homicide, you'd hardly tell a random stranger that he's a witch, would you? Maybe Harper asked one of those two to work magic on Dan. Perhaps one of them chose to do it without her instigation. Harper looked pretty tight with that community. If she confided in them about what Dan did to her, Jonny or his mother may have decided to act on their own initiative.'

'But they weren't there. The first thing we did was compile a list of who was at the party. I gave it to you myself.'

'Tell me, Chester, who's in this station this morning?' He looks puzzled, so I prompt him. 'Here. Right now. Their names.'

He reels off the names of the four colleagues in today – one of them an old dude brought back from retirement to cover the three that ate themselves sick at the BBQ.

'Okay. Good. But you forgot the two folks sitting out front waiting to speak to an officer.'

'But they . . . I wasn't sure if they counted, and I don't know their names.'

'Exactly.'

I watch his face as he grasps my meaning. The party attendees came from several groups: Sanctuary High seniors, but also football bros from across the state and girls from the private school outside town. No one could have named *all* the kids attending. So, everyone just mentioned the names they knew.

'If someone was there who *no one* knew,' he says, 'no one would have told us about them.'

'You're flying, Chester. We gotta ask those party kids about people they *didn't* know, and specifically anyone who didn't seem to fit a particular set.'

I secure the tablet, then run off a few photocopies of the guest list, and we head out. I ask Chester to recruit the colleague he rates highest from those outside, and he taps a good-looking dude in a nicely spruced-up uniform.

'Can't help ya, Ches,' the cop says, snapping gum in his mouth. 'Chief's orders. None of us are to go near this shitshow of a case. In fact, when he's back from checking on his kid in the hospital, where that witch put him, he's gonna pull you off it, too.'

'Wait, wait,' I interrupt. '*In the hospital, where that witch put him*? What do you mean?'

'Exactly what I said.' The cop's gaze is low-key hostile, like he's challenging me to disagree. 'The witch cursed Jake. Maybe even tried to kill him, to stop him giving evidence.'

What *is* this madness? What's happening in this town is bad enough, without the chief stirring it up worse with claims that the witch cursed his sick kid. Jeez.

'Seems you're in need of help,' says a slow voice behind me.

The old boy brought in as cover has hauled himself out of the desk chair. His uniform barely fits any more. It bulges around the hips, and a second soft belly spills over his belt. He looks like he'd keel over with cardiac arrest if he was called to get a kitten out a tree, let alone chase a perp.

'Bin a few years since I was on patrol,' he continues. 'But I ain't never heard of a uniform refusing to do police work when it needed doin'. Tad Bolt was a greenhorn fetching my coffee when he first joined. What's the worst he can do – retire me?'

The old fella gives a hoarse laugh, both his guts jiggling. He picks up his badge and follows me and Chester out.

I'm glad to get out of the police station, and brief Chester and Old Fella as we head to the school. I explain myself to the vice principal, and see my guys installed in small cubicles. The secretary will call the party attendees in one by one, and my colleagues will go through their recollections of anyone at the party they didn't recognize.

I'd bet my last donut someone will remember seeing the tanned and tousled form of Jonny Maloney.

81

Maggie

I leave them to it and go hunt down Mr Maloney myself on the police database. But I'm scratching around. There's a warning for cannabis possession, several years old and due to disappear off his record any day.

Nothing else. This dude has never got in a brawl or pulled a knife on someone – not that the cops ever heard about, anyway. Nothing to give me a clue as to whether he has a temper or is prone to violence. I wasn't getting bad vibes off him in the beach café, but there are plenty of people who flip like a switch.

I run back over what I saw of him and Harper in his tattoo shop, but again, no clues. She was at ease, proficient with that needle. As someone who winces just putting on a Band-Aid, I never imagined someone could tattoo their own skin. And he left her to it.

He's got to be responsible for *some* of her inking. As she's a minor under eighteen, state law calls for a $100 fine or up to ninety days' imprisonment. But again, if Mr Maloney has got a thing for illegally tattooing schoolgirls, it's left no trace in the records.

I go to ask her mom what she knows of her daughter's out-of-town bolthole. But the sight that greets me at the witch's house is shocking. Sarah Fenn is a shadow of herself.

She trails back to her kitchen table and sinks into a chair. There's a bandage from wrist to elbow on her right arm that wasn't there before. She looks suddenly very small sitting there, elbows up. As if she's a child and life is a meal she's being forced to eat.

Is anyone looking out for this woman? I can't imagine what it feels like to have your whole town turn on you. Of the three women closest to her, one is now trying to destroy her, and one – Julia Garcia – must be ambivalent at best. Is Perelli-Lee still on her side? At least Pierre Martineau is. I make a mental note to ask him to check in on her.

Then I gently question her. How much does Sarah know of where her daughter goes outside Sanctuary, and her friends there?

The answer, frustratingly, is almost nothing. Fenn gives her daughter a lot of autonomy and trust. It appears that's the witch way of childrearing. I wonder how she feels that her daughter doesn't return much of that trust. Not sharing the details of her life at Green Point, and not even (if Harper told me the truth) telling her about the rape.

'I couldn't give her magic,' Fenn says, sadly, 'but I can give her the space to work out who she is, given that she's not a witch. I thought that growing up with ability was hard – the way people judge you. But it turns out that growing up without it is harder. I show my daughter respect, Detective, and I do that by allowing her freedom.'

I suppress the urge to tell her that her daughter has found a place nearby where she fits right in, and when my radio crackles I'm guiltily relieved at the interruption.

'Ma'am,' says Chester, formal as ever. 'Can you swing back to the school? There's something rather interesting . . .'

I'm glad to shut the witch's door behind me.

*

'We haven't spoken to everyone,' Chester explains when I'm sat down opposite him and Old Fella. 'Several of the kids aren't in today.'

He reads off three names: Freddie McConaughey, Oliver Welland and Dale Hamilton. The boys from the fountain incident. They're sick, just like Jake and some of Bolt's cops. What *is* this?

But that's not what Chester wants to show me.

'Nobody's reported seeing anyone who matches Maloney's appearance. All the partygoers were school age. When they described people they didn't know, they could still identify them as part of one group – *I don't know those girls, but they're from that posh school*, et cetera. But there's one name that wasn't on our original list that got mentioned several times. They'd almost forgotten she was there, or they weren't *certain* that they'd seen her.'

'And?'

Old Fella spins round the copy of the list that he's been annotating with student responses and taps a name he's scrawled at the bottom.

'Isobel Perelli-Martineau,' he says.

Izzy? Who's had mono and not attended school for weeks?

Her moms believed she was in bed asleep that night. But plainly Isobel crept out to the villa. She must have escaped the party in time to avoid injury from the fire, then made her way home. In the chaos of the news that Dan was dead, and Harper and others had been taken to hospital, no one would have worried about the one child certain to be safe – the one at home.

Those four kids – Harper, Dan, Beatriz and Isobel – all grew up hanging out together. It's only natural she wouldn't want to miss this party just because she was poorly.

'So, a kid sneaks out to a party,' I tell my officers, skeptically. 'They do that all the time.'

'Thought you might say that.' Chester nods, smiling grimly. 'But here's the thing: all the kids that reported seeing Isobel? They say she was upstairs. On the landing.'

He doesn't need to say the last bit.

The landing from which Dan fell.

82

MYSTERY SICKNESS STRIKES SANCTUARY
WITCH CURSES CHIEF'S WIFE IN STREET

Chief's son hospitalized, other victims reported

NEW PICTURE EXCLUSIVE

By Beryl Varley, News Editor

Jacob Bolt (18), youngest son of local lawman Tad Bolt and his wife Mary-Anne, has been rushed to hospital, where his condition has been described as 'life-threatening but stable'.

The youngster, a senior at Sanctuary High, fell sick a few days ago. After his condition deteriorated overnight, Sanctuary resident and Yale rare-diseases specialist Professor Michael Whitman, MD, ordered immediate admission to a specialist intensive care unit.

It is not yet clear what has struck Jacob down.

However, reports have emerged of a number of other Sanctuary residents also mysteriously stricken. These include several players on the Spartans football team, three members of Sanctuary's police division, and high-school principal Cheryl Lee.

Meanwhile, onlookers report an angry confrontation in Main Street yesterday between Mary-Anne Bolt and witch Sarah Fenn.

'It's plain what the witch is doing,' said one witness, who did not wish to be named. 'That boy is the one who saw what her daughter did to Dan Whitman. She wants to shut him up.'

After Mrs Bolt made her allegations, Fenn cast a spell on her. This can be clearly seen in footage shot by a witness at the scene.

<<EMBEDDED USER VIDEO_FENN/BOLT MAIN STREET>>

'It was terrifying,' said the onlooker. 'She used her hands and the chief's wife just stopped talking. She was struck dumb. It's like what they say she did to that poor man.'

A few days ago, Ms Fenn faced accusations of unnaturally influencing a local man by means of magical compulsion.

Her daughter, Harper, has been accused of murdering Daniel Whitman by magical means. Video shot on the night of Whitman's death shows Harper Fenn using her hands in a similar fashion. The *Sanctuary Sentinel* has obtained images from that video, which it publishes here for the first time.

<<EMBEDDED USER PHOTO_HARPER FENN PARTY SPELL>>

Fearful locals may be forgiven for asking themselves if there is more to this strangely selective 'sickness' than meets the eye. And for asking why the investigating state detective has made no move to arrest either mother or daughter.

Is she too under their spell?

What will the witches do next?

83

Abigail

'This video is obviously something Harper *staged*,' I tell Michael. 'You know what girls are like these days, doing the sort of things that only porn stars did ten years ago. She probably set it up so she could hold this over him. You know how devious witches are.'

'What if she *didn't* stage it?' my husband says, his voice unnaturally calm.

'Of course she did! Jesus, Michael, do you *want* your son to be the sort of boy who forces girls?'

Michael's hand, his strong, steady physician's hand, lashes out and catches my wrist, pinning me to my seat. And with a reflex born of long experience, I go limp.

'That's exactly the sort of boy he was. I should know, I had to go around tidying up after him often enough.'

'What?'

'Some girl on the club soccer team was the closest call. Why do you think I pulled Daniel from coaching?'

'Dan stepped back to focus on his training.'

Michael scoffs. 'He quit because I told him it'd blow up in his face otherwise. He'd brought her *back here* one night. You'd gone to bed, but I came downstairs and found them. You don't have a hand over the mouth of someone who enjoys what you're doing to them.'

'Don't be ridiculous. Dan could have any girl he wanted. Why would he force himself on someone? Let alone a child barely in her teens with no tits or conversation.'

'Twelve,' Michael says.

'What?'

'She was twelve when it started.'

I hunch in the chair. Why on earth is Michael talking like this?

'He was just giving her extra attention because she was a promising athlete,' I hear myself pleading. 'And why would Dan rape Harper when she was his girlfriend anyway?'

Michael shrugs. 'Maybe he enjoyed it.'

I can't bear it – neither Michael's words, nor the cold detachment with which he's saying them. I explode, hands clawing, arms flailing.

Something – a fist, a vase – slams into my chin and my head snaps back with such force I'm sure something breaks.

I black out.

When I come to, I'm in my own bed. The curtains are drawn, the light dim.

I see a shape in the armchair in the corner. Michael, asleep.

Who *is* this man I married?

I need to get away, to think clearly about everything he said last night. I'm practiced in tiptoeing around him, and ease myself up from the bed.

'We need to talk, Abigail.'

My heart races. Michael's not asleep after all. He drags his chair over and I shrink back against the pillows. My husband cups one of my hands between his, not touching, but confining, like a bird in a cage.

'Are you saying all this because you're jealous of Dan?' I ask, fear making me reckless. 'You are, aren't you? You always were.'

His hand strikes upside my jaw so hard that my teeth clash and I taste blood.

'Shut up, Abigail, and listen. You *know* Dan did those things, and now there's a video to prove it. So, our son was a rapist. That's what everyone will say. I said *shut up*.'

He wrenches my wrist again, because I'm sobbing loudly. He's right. He's so right and I can't endure it. Those sisters Dan offered to babysit for? The girl down the road whose puppy he always stopped to play with? How proud I was of my charming, helpful son.

Was there a moment when I *chose* not to understand?

'Think about how it will reflect on us,' Michael continues. 'All those years I've put in. For nothing. I'll just be "that rapist's dad". How will I be able to hold my head up with the faculty? Who will collaborate with me? What will happen to my research? My legacy?'

He's looking at me intently as he rants about his career, and it's wrong. So wrong.

Then I *finally* realize what I'm looking at.

It's Sarah's work again.

I begged her, all those years ago, to make Michael successful. To give my diffident husband drive and ambition that matched his talent. And she did it.

She did it *too* well. And now that's all Michael is. No love for me. No pride in our son. If he's cared about either of us or done anything for us, it's because of how our actions reflected on him.

He *knew* our son was rotten to the core, and he covered it up. He summoned the Spartans to organize the vigil, a huge public statement of how popular his son was, to make sure that any slurs on Dan's name died with him. It was always all about *Michael's* own position.

Is there any part of my life Sarah's magic hasn't touched and ruined?

'If this video gets currency, there's a chance some of those other girls might come forward.' Michael is still talking. 'So we have to shut it down. Some explanation that makes it *her* fault, not his. Maybe what you were saying before about Harper staging it to hold something over him, or to extort money from us. Or perhaps it's just racy play. Teens experimenting. Witches are like that, and half the town thinks she's a whore anyway.'

But I'm only half listening, because suddenly everything has joined up.

Sarah worked magic on Michael, and changed him.

Sarah worked magic on Alberto, and changed him.

And Sarah worked magic on Dan. On my darling boy. *And she changed him.*

Yes, technically Daniel may have done those things. The soccer girl, and those others. The rape. But none of it was his fault. None of it was *ever* his fault. Our boy died when he fell from the window at Bridget's. And whatever Sarah did to bring him back, she *twisted* him in the process.

'No,' I tell Michael calmly, laying a hand on his arm. 'This is what we say. Yes, Daniel did that to Harper. But he couldn't help it. It wasn't his fault – it was *Sarah's*. We reveal everything about what she did that night six years ago. How she brought him back. But we say she brought him back *wrong*. That's insurance against *any* allegation. No matter *what* comes out, Daniel is the victim. Sarah is to blame.'

It's more than just a convenient story. It's the truth. I feel it in my bones.

Sarah spoiled my husband and my marriage.

She spoiled my son.

And now the world will hear what she did.

84

Maggie

It takes heavy-duty knocking and yelling 'Police!' through the door to get Bridget to open up.

'Detective? Can I help? It's just that Cheryl's not doing well and Izzy is still—'

'I just need a moment of your time.'

Reluctantly, Bridget lets me in, talking half to me, half to herself about her wife's condition. Then she stops and turns so abruptly I nearly walk right into her.

'It's not magic, is it, this sickness? I know Sarah wouldn't . . . But that article said some cops and those football boys are ill too, and you know that Cheryl had to untangle that nasty incident with Harper and Beatriz, and she worried that Sarah felt she wasn't being supportive of Harper . . . She does get migraines, but this one's real bad. She's in bed, curtains drawn, can't eat and in too much pain to sleep. Oh *God*, I can't believe I'm even thinking it. I should just ask Sarah, but she'd be devastated that I even imagined . . .'

And right there in her hallway, Bridget Perelli-Lee bursts into tears. She does it quietly, so as not to disturb her family, and swipes at every tear as soon as it spills. I gently touch her shoulder as she cries it all out.

'I'm sorry,' she sniffs. 'I'm sorry. It's just, I'm scared for

Cheryl. I'm scared for all of us. I was in Sarah's coven. The last couple of days, my salon's been real quiet. What if no one's coming because they think I'm mixed up in it too? I was thinking I should shut it down for a few days. I saw what was done to the town sign, before it was cleaned off. You know we were always taught in history class that during the persecutions, innocent folk were driven out along with the witches. Anyone suspected. I've done magic with her for *years* . . .'

Her voice trails off. I'm startled and saddened by how distraught she is. Fearful for her wife. Fearful that it might all be the doing of her oldest friend. Fearful that the town's suspicion could fall on her.

When I tell her why I'm here, she'll be in bits that suspicion is falling on her daughter too.

'I'm still standing, aren't I?' I offer, in hopes it'll raise a smile. It doesn't.

'Take a seat,' Bridget says, steering me toward the kitchen table. The room is full of cats playing hide-and-seek in the empty box of a new TV, or curled up on kitchen surfaces. With Cheryl laid up in bed, the house is plainly reverting to its natural state.

'Shoo! Down!'

Bridget swats a cat from the table. At the last minute it daintily evades her, and she sends a stack of workbooks and folders cascading to the floor, where they scatter among loose cat litter.

Bridget swears. She's worn to a frazzle.

'I'll get them,' I say. 'It's no trouble, if you wouldn't mind fetching Isobel. It's her I'm here to see.'

'Izzy?' Bridget's voice rises in alarm. She looks at me like one betrayed. I figured that if I mentioned on the doorstep that it's her daughter I'm here to speak to, she might not have let me in. Looks like my hunch was right.

'It's just about something she may have seen. I'm sorry if she's sleeping. Just a quick word.'

Bridget gives in the way animals do, resentful but obedient. I stoop and pick up the books. It's Izzy's school stuff that she's been working on from home. I pile up the texts, then reach for the last book. It's a daily planner, pastel and covered with rainbow stickers. It landed spread-eagled, and as I flip it over, the pages fan – and I see something I could never have expected.

Hastily, I pull out my phone and snap some pictures. I turn a few more pages. Another.

Snap, snap, snap.

My heart stutters when I see the last one.

'Are you all right, Detective?'

Bridget has returned with Izzy. I murmur some excuse about having a bad back and kick the journal further under the table before straightening up, groaning. When they find it later, they'll think I simply overlooked it.

Izzy stands before me in a rumpled onesie. She looks sweet and hesitant, with her mom's round face and her dad's gappy teeth.

'Come and have a seat, Isobel. I'm sorry to get you up. Don't be alarmed, it's just we're going back to everyone who was at the party the night Daniel died, and—'

Izzy has barely touched the chair to sit down before she springs out of it as though electrified. Bridget looks pissed off.

'You've obviously forgotten, Detective, but Isobel wasn't at the party. She's been sick for weeks.'

'Oh, right.' I feign confusion. 'Okay. I didn't compile the initial list of attendees, but when we were going over it with kids at the school this morning, four students confirmed seeing you, Isobel, so I thought . . .'

Izzy looks terrified.

'I *wasn't* . . . I . . .' She's shaking her head, that springy hair flying.

'Detective, we're all having a difficult time right now and I could do without this. Izzy wasn't at the party, so she won't be able to help you.'

'Of course, of course,' I murmur, getting to my feet. 'My mistake. Thank you, Isobel. Glad to see you looking better.'

The kid's staring at me like I'm her worst nightmare come to life and standing in her kitchen.

As I'm stepping over the threshold, I turn back to Bridget.

'Sorry, I should make a note for my records in case anyone queries it. The night of the party, what was the last time you checked on Isobel? And did you check on her again later?'

'I don't know, Detective. You can imagine what that evening was like. I certainly checked before making dinner. Then the whole thing went to hell with the phone call, the texts from Harper and Beatriz. I did look in on Izzy before I went to bed, but I've no idea what time that was.

'There's no way she could have been there, though. Kids at that party were taken to hospital, talked to by cops. You've seen how sensitive Isobel is. She couldn't have simply crept home and into bed as if nothing had happened.'

'I get it. Thank you. And I hope Cheryl makes a quick recovery.'

Bridget can't shut the door fast enough behind me.

I can't make sense of it, but I wouldn't deserve the name of cop if I didn't recognize in a heartbeat what Izzy's reaction was just then.

Guilt.

I pull out my phone, swipe through the images, then compose a quick email to Chester.

Get back to the station – leave the Old Fella to finish the interviews. And bring Rowan.

85

Maggie

'They're the Old Signs,' Rowan says, frowning at the photos on my phone as the three of us study them. 'Ancient. Powerful. Also: banned.'

'What the hell are they doing in a schoolgirl's journal?' I ask. 'Where might she have seen them — online?'

'Nope.'

Chester fidgets uneasily.

'These are from a text called the *Standard American Book of Lore* — all witches know it as the Starcross grimoire. It's two and a half centuries old, and Class 1 restricted. Starcross can't be copied, loaned or consulted. Whoever drew these has technically already committed an offence. In fact, *you* have, just by taking these photos. You shouldn't email them, print a copy or store them on your database.

'During the fight for magical decriminalization, the movement that became the Moot attempted to track down and destroy copies of Starcross to reassure people that witches and witchcraft aren't threatening. So they're super-rare. They've usually been quietly handed down in families for generations.'

'This sign, though? It's like . . .' I point to the third picture, the last sign I saw in the jotter before Bridget interrupted me. If you didn't know it was magic, looking at it would make you think you need spectacles, because it slips and writhes on the page. It's as if the letters of every vile word imaginable got broken into bits and jumbled up, and now they're trying to re-form all by themselves, straights and curves out of place. As if the one word they'd form would contain every awful thought ever written or imagined.

Rowan hasn't answered my question. They're holding one hand over their eyes, as if to shield them or to ward off evil. So I finish my sentence myself.

'It's what we saw in the villa. The dust, twisting just like this . . . before the explosion . . .'

I sit back in my seat, exhaling hard. How is this possible? That the terrifying magic we've been looking for belongs to onesie-wearing, sweet and innocent Isobel Perelli.

Isobel, who's been out of school for most of the semester, giving her ample time to plan an attack on Dan. Who has been hidden in her bedroom through all these weeks of investigation, able to do goodness knows what behind its closed door.

Isobel – whose only friend that anyone has ever mentioned is Harper.

Is she our mystery witch?

Could she *really* have killed Dan?

'You say Starcross is rare?' I ask Rowan. 'Might a family with no known magical pedigree have a copy?'

'Impossible. You'd be looking for an unbroken line of magical practice going back to the post-Revolutionary War era when it was printed.'

In other words, the Fenns.

Could Sarah have been secretly teaching Isobel? Is the witch too loyal to tell me about her young apprentice, even when it's been plain that I'm sniffing around in search of a magically able suspect?

I've told myself that there's not a single person in Sanctuary that Sarah Fenn would cover up for, if by doing so she put her own daughter at risk. But Izzy Perelli is surely the one exception. I'd bet that Sarah would keep Isobel's secret right to the point where Harper was heading for the dock. Possibly even then. She'd probably go on the run with her daughter rather than incriminate the child of her two best friends.

I come clean with Rowan about the identity of the person who drew the sigils.

'Izzy's mother is a member of Sarah Fenn's coven,' I tell them. 'Fenn has always said that none of them have any magical ability, but what if Bridget Perelli does, and has managed to conceal it? I mean, she's always had an affinity with animals.' A stray remark drifts back to me across the weeks. 'I remember her wife saying Bridget had enough cats for a coven.'

Rowan tries to smile. 'Go carefully with that. Accuse women with cats and you'll have half the female population under suspicion. That's a tactic from the persecutions. And no, Bridget wouldn't have to be gifted. Ability often skips a generation. With people living longer, we're even seeing it skip two, so one of the girl's grandparents or great-grandparents would be enough for it to show up. Although . . .'

The witch's gaze slides unwillingly back to Chester's phone. Rowan had flipped it over, to avoid even glancing at the pictures, but now they pick it up and study the images again.

'Although what?'

'I'm not a hundred percent up on Starcross,' they explain. 'It's a Thirteen Colonies, white thing, though it steals and stuffs in bits from all over, usually inaccurately. But I was able to read a copy when I worked for the Moot. It's the only place licensed to have one for consultation by the council, because there's all sorts of cultural lore in there too.

'I don't know the precise meanings, but this one' – they expand one of the other images from Izzy's planner – 'is something to do with *hiding* or *concealment*. If this sigil had been cast at the villa, it could account for the explosion. A reaction to my attempts to reveal the magic at work.'

'An explosion,' I say, because more links are forming in my head. 'And concealment. That's how Sarah Fenn described it when her booth blew up. She said she'd been scrying to discover what happened to Dan, but rather than seeing anything, her bowl shattered. It took the windows out.'

The three of us fall silent, trying to process it all. So many links are forming. If I can just keep joining up the chain, there at the end of it will be my answer, I know.

'There's one massive problem,' Rowan says, breaking the silence. 'No witch in America would teach these sigils to a child. Sarah Fenn would have shown Isobel how to make brews and perform simple charms. Not had her copying banned sigils that even witches have tried to forget exist.'

'What if she taught herself?' Chester says. 'I mean, her parents are both friends of Fenn's. What if Bridget or Pierre borrowed Starcross for Isobel to study – without Sarah knowing about it?'

Rowan scoffs. 'Every copy of Starcross is kept under lock and key. And most likely powerful wards. Borrowing one wouldn't be like checking a novel out of the library.'

'Why would they not tell Sarah?' I object. 'That makes no sense.'

'Perhaps they only discovered Izzy's ability after Bridget met Cheryl, so kept it quiet given Cheryl's views on witchcraft?' Chester suggests. 'Or, you say the girl's super-shy. Well, she would have seen the attention her friend Harper received as a witch's daughter, and maybe she didn't want that for herself. Maybe she's frightened of her ability and asked her mom and dad not to tell anyone.'

'Self-taught witchcraft is extremely dangerous,' says Rowan. 'That's one reason why registration is mandatory, so the Moot can confirm that every magical person is properly instructed.'

'Boss?' Chester asks. Because I've gone quiet. Something Rowan said a moment earlier has prompted a few more recollections to link up.

Every copy of Starcross is kept under lock and key. And most likely powerful wards.

I remember the day Sarah's workroom blew after her scrying attempt. Bridget and Pierre on the scene.

Bridget, who has a talisman that enables her to get into the workroom despite Sarah's protective wards. And who spent a suspiciously long time inside.

Pierre – charming, gap-toothed Pierre – who repaired Sarah's workroom. Who built it in the first place, as he told me on that first town tour he gave me.

They'd know exactly where Fenn kept any copy of Starcross. And they'd be able to get to it.

Shit.

Shit. Shit. Shit.

I have seriously *had enough* of this godawful little town, its lies and its feuds. And in particular, I have had enough of this messed-up case of witchcraft and murder that's going to end my career.

'Ma'am?'

Chester is eyeing me warily. And he's right. I have to pull myself together.

No matter how delightful, Pierre is simply the latest Sanctuary resident to come into my crosshairs – along with his oddly innocent daughter, who has been doodling her rainbow jotter with eldritch sigils so powerful a magical investigator can hardly look at them.

'Guess we'd better talk to Pierre,' I say, scooting my phone back across the table. 'Thanks so much, Rowan. We may be needing you again later, but for now, the mood being what it is

353

in Sanctuary, I'd suggest a taxi back to your apartment. We'll be in touch. Come on, Greenstreet.'

We never get to Pierre's, though. As I'm driving, the radio crackles and Ches answers. I hear the drawling tones of Officer Asshole through the static.

'Something's turned up,' he says. 'Unfortunately a TV crew's got there first. They're planning a broadcast tonight. You're gonna want to drop everything for this.'

And he's right.

86

TRANSCRIPT OF AS-LIVE* NEWS ITEM AND INTERVIEW, WCON-TV *CONNECTICUT TONIGHT*
*pre-recorded after compliance concerns with previous
  broadcast*

NEWSCASTER: The investigation into a potential witchcraft death in Sanctuary has been rumbling on. The latest claim to rock this town is that a spate of sickness may be unnatural in origin – and connected to the case.

And now a dog walker may have stumbled across a vital piece of evidence. Anna Dao is on location outside Sanctuary.

DAO: Yes, thank you Jeremy.

Well, as you can see behind me, the police have now secured the site and have asked us to remain at a distance. But I saw it with my own eyes, and I can tell you it was disturbing.

The only way to describe it is as a ritual, maybe even a sacrificial site.

With me is the lady who found it, Jennifer Blum. Thank you for joining us, Mrs Blum. Can you tell me what you discovered?

BLUM: It was Rocket here who found it. Wasn't it, Rocket? He's a beagle, you see. Excellent sense of smell.

DAO: And what was it he smelled?

BLUM: Well, blood. We were on the track, here, when he ran off over there, and when I found him he was licking it off the tree.

DAO: From what we've seen, police are taking samples right now. But that's not the only thing you saw, was it?

BLUM: No. The branches were tied with red wool. There were little bags of crystals. But then, on the ground . . .

DAO: What did you see on the ground?

BLUM: Nasty signs. Marks. All horrible and wriggly, sort of drawn into the soil with a stick or something.

DAO: And how did you feel, Mrs Blum. Standing in that space daubed with blood?

BLUM: Well, not very nice. Not nice at all. In fact, after a minute, Rocket got so spooked he ran right out of there.

I could tell right away it was nothing natural. Which is why I called you. There's supposed to be this investigation, but we hear nothing about it. It's like they're doing nothing. And now people are getting sick. I'm telling you, Sanctuary is frightened. Very frightened indeed.

DAO: Thank you so much.

We'll wait to hear if the investigation moves forward after this grisly discovery. In the meantime, back to you in the studio, Jeremy.

87

Abigail

The square is full to overflowing.

After the news report about the ritual site, Michael and I knew we had to move quickly. People will be terrified that Sarah has worked magic on the town – I've no idea what she thought she was doing, but it couldn't be better for our purposes. It's the perfect moment to reveal what she did to Daniel all those years ago. And if we leave it any longer, the video of what Dan did to Harper might leak before we can get ahead of the story.

So it's tonight.

The Spartans put the word out on social media. Everyone I spoke to rang two people, who rang two more. One of my fellow Yale faculty wives is sister to the guy who does the evening talk show on Smooth Sound FM, so we're cropping up in their discussion all night, which is bringing more people to us. The TV crew that was talking to the dog walker? We reached them before they turned their satellite truck round for Hartford. We've even got the blood-licking beagle.

Tad Bolt is grim-faced as he works the crowd, putting his chief's authority behind our gathering. I don't like that we're deceiving him about Jake's condition – a simple case of mono being doctored by Michael to look like a witch's curse. But this opportunity is too good to pass up. Mary-Anne is over on the other side of the square, surrounded by members of her congregation. And not just her own church. Sanctuary's Christian community is here in force – I forgot that Cheryl Lee is one of their number too. Several hold hand-lettered banners.

By your magic spell all the nations were led astray (Rev. 18:23) reads one.

Anyone who does WITCHCRAFT is DETESTABLE TO THE LORD (Deut. 18:12) is another.

It's not just the Christians. I don't know anyone who attends the mosque on the outskirts of town, but there's a neat-bearded man with a sign that says *Sihr = haram*, and what must be the same words written in Arabic script. A few like him stand nearby, some in long prayer robes. My fears about needing a more confined space to make this gathering look good are unfounded. There are more people here than at the vigil.

All those waverers who might have thought our dead son was our problem? They're now afraid for their own kids.

'Mrs Whitman? Mrs Whitman!'

It's Beryl Varley, tugging at my sleeve. Her usual fawning expression has been replaced by a frown.

'What is it, Beryl? I'm just getting ready to speak.'

'I need a word.'

The pudgy little journalist won't let go. The only way I'll dislodge her is to listen.

'I need you to tell me,' she hisses, 'seeing as I've supported you all the way in this. A little bird tells me that the school authorities have handed a recording to the police. The original of your son's encounter with Harper Fenn.'

So, word *is* slowly leaking out.

'You're worried about what it shows? Concerned that you've picked the wrong side?'

The journalist's eyes widen, but I press on.

'You haven't. You'll hear it all in just a minute, I promise. Have faith.'

It's time for me to tell my truth – and see Sarah and Harper finally face the consequences of their deeds. They've walked unchecked among us for far too long.

I press my hand solicitously over Varley's, then turn and cue the Spartans marching band to strike up the team anthem. Mitch McConaughey has assembled the podium the sport club uses for medal ceremonies. As I mount it, it feels appropriate. Because tonight is when I *win*, Sarah.

'Thank you all for coming. Thank you. I know this is short notice, but today's terrifying discovery of some kind of *blood rite* worked upon our town means that waiting any longer is too risky. People are falling sick for no reason at all. People who were well yesterday are confined to their beds today. Three of my son's teammates. His beloved best friend. Even three of the officers investigating my son's death.

'In the weeks since Daniel died, we've all learned more about how magic can be abused. As many of you know, *I* was once one of Sarah Fenn's coven. I lent her my support as she worked her magic. It's not something I'm proud of. In fact, it's a decision I bitterly regret.

'Do you want to know why I did it? You have every right to that answer. I did it for the same reason many of you are here now. Because I was afraid. Wretchedly, utterly, afraid.

'I'll tell you why that was later. But first, you need to hear from people other than me about how magic is preying on our town. Please reach out to uplift Carmel, the wife of one of Sanctuary's officers struck down because he's working for justice against the witches of this town. And to comfort Mary-Anne, whose son Jacob lies in intensive care where brilliant scientists are doing all they can to keep him alive. Carmel, Mary-Anne, please join me.'

Wiping at tear-streaked faces, they do.

Carmel, it turns out, hardly has two brain cells to rub together. She mostly just stands there and cries. But she's pretty – and even better, she's pregnant. The spectacle of her is absolutely piteous.

And then comes Mary-Anne Bolt. And goodness, you can tell she's a preacher's daughter. Maternal love, rage and brimstone. She pours it all out. Details I hadn't known, like how Jacob fell sick right after Sarah came by their house.

The crowd is in a frenzy by the time she's finished. From my elevated position I spot several of the boys at the back of the crowd peel away, a few tugging down hoodies or wrapping scarves over their faces. The lads must have more mischief planned.

I hope they do.

But then comes something I hadn't expected. Tad shoulders his way forward and stomps up to take the microphone. Something inside me clenches with anticipation, like when I used to watch Dan running with the ball.

He pays tribute to his four kids and Mary-Anne. But then it's not Jacob he begins talking about, but himself.

'I've tried to walk a righteous path, as a chief, as a husband and a father. But the Lord knows that, like many of us, I've been tempted. And like many of us, I've sought help with those temptations. Unfortunately for me, I went to Sarah Fenn.'

The crowd is on tiptoes, craning for a look. What on earth is he going to say? Surely not that he had an affair with Sarah?

But it's better than that.

'My temptation is gambling. You may think that's not a bad one, as they go. My pa liked a game of cards, and his pa before him. Maybe some of you do too. But let me tell you, when you've four fine sons to put through schooling, anything that takes even a cent away from their futures is a sin. And then there's the temptations that follow on from gambling. If you win, you celebrate in unrighteous ways. If you lose, you drown your sorrows in unrighteous ways.'

The crowd is murmuring, shocked. The chief is being juicily non-specific, and we're all picturing Tad Bolt being 'unrighteous' with bourbon, hookers and drugs.

'After I gave in to my weakness a couple times, I went to see Sarah. This isn't something you can fix with pills or therapy. Spilling your guts in some little room? That isn't me – it's what I get suspects to do.'

A ripple of amusement runs through the crowd at the joke. And then Tad slams his touchdown.

'I went to the witch to be *helped*. To be *cured*. And she laid her wiles on me and made it *worse*. So much worse that I'm ashamed to speak it in front of my beloved wife. It was Sarah Fenn's doing, but by my weakness I put myself in the way of making it happen.'

Mary-Anne is holding Tad's hand in a death grip, tears running down her face.

'That witch forced me to dishonor the badge that it's been my life's privilege to wear. She made me dishonor my marriage bed.' He's choking up too, now. His sobs burble across the square, amplified by the microphone. 'Because of her, what had been a one-time thing became a habit. A compulsion. And I never knew why – until now.

'Like most folks here, I never had any reason to think bad of Sarah or her daughter. Her booth's been a fixture of Main Street as long as I can remember. But sometimes familiarity means you can't see the evil right in front of you.

'Because what did Sarah do with that knowledge of my frailty? *Blackmail*. Mary-Anne's told you how she came to our house. She did so to threaten me. She swore to reveal all if I didn't get my son to abandon his testimony.

'And when I told her that it wasn't my choice to make? That Jacob was a righteous boy and I would support his truth? She cursed him. And now my son's fighting for his life in a hospital bed.'

Tad breaks down weeping, the microphone drooping from his fingers. I step forward to take it and watch the crowd heave with emotion as the lawman shakes and sobs, comforted by his wife.

I couldn't have asked for a better curtain-raiser.

But just wait till they hear what comes next.

'You've maybe heard the accusations Harper Fenn made on TV against my son,' I say, looking out across the sea of faces.

A ripple runs through those gathered. Shock, perhaps, that I've even acknowledged it.

'You're probably expecting my next words to be a denial. Well they're not. He did it.'

88
Sarah

My phone buzzed a few hours ago. A message from Bridget, telling me what was just said on the news about the dog walker's discovery. It couldn't be worse timing.

I'd hoped the blood would fade and the marks disappear before anyone stumbled upon any of the sites. But it wasn't to be.

My phone vibrates again on the table. Another text from Bridget.

Somethings happening in the square. Abigail, Tad, Mary-Anne all there. Im worried for u Sarah. Think u shd get out, stay somewhere for a few days. Maybe call Pierre?? Take care. B xoxo

I go to the window and open it. I live several blocks from the square, and I can hear the noise faintly on the wind. A voice, amplified by a microphone. Mary-Anne Bolt? And the restless sound of people gathered together.

What is Abigail up to now?

Should I take Bridget's advice? I'd worried that running would look like an admission of guilt, but I don't have many options left now. I've still no idea where Harper is, though. I wonder about a blood rite, something to enable my blood to call to hers. It'd take some figuring out.

And when I go for good, I'll need the things in my workroom

– above all, my charts and my copy of Starcross. I'm still not sure if I could bear to sell the book, but whether as an asset or simply a link to my ancestors, it's the most precious thing I own.

The booth is much better protected than this house, particularly since I layered those extra spells on. I'll lie low there and make my final preparations. Call the detective to reassure her that I'm merely heading out of town until things cool down a little. Promise to stay in touch every day, so it won't look like a guilty run.

Then once I've prepared everything for me and Harper – *bouf*! We disappear.

It'll be the work of fifteen minutes to pack the essentials from this house and go. I run upstairs to my room and drag my travel bag out of the closet. Then it's a case of ransacking drawers and cupboards for the things I can't replace.

In a box in the closet, the jewelry my grandma left me. Her expensive jewels went to my mother, but I got the heirlooms: a tarnished copper ring said to have passed down through our family from the age of persecution. An old deer antler pendant, whittled by an enlisted Fenn during the Civil War. I remember my mother taking up the silk-lined box of Gramma's pearls, and her diamond engagement ring, and looking enviously at these dirty homemade objects.

I'm rummaging through drawers for the blanket Gramma knitted Harper when she was a newborn when I hear the brick go through the window downstairs. Catcalls and hoots from the street are loud through the hole it's made.

My chest tightens, but only briefly. I'm a witch. And though I'm not permitted to defend myself aggressively with magic, I can use it in subtler ways if they try and get in.

'We know you're in there, *witch*,' calls a voice. A young male voice. Maybe one of the boys Dan boasted to after he'd hurt my daughter. Hatred rises up and chokes me.

The things I could do to these young men.

I could do the thing they're accusing Harper of. I swear to the goddess I could. And worse.

My hand goes back into the drawers and I start pulling things out heedlessly. It's only what they'll do anyway. In a flash, I see it – though is it imagination or the craft? – a vision of my little house, burning.

A second smash. Another brick.

'Feel free to try and stop us,' taunts the boy. 'Show everyone what you are.'

'Witch!' calls another.

How close to the surface it lies, this hatred of us. What people don't know or understand, they fear. It's always been this way – even here in America, the country to which my ancestors fled seeking haven.

I find the blanket and tug it out. Harper's baby booties, too. I have everything I want. Is there anything of Harper's I should take? I cross the landing to her door.

Something thuds through one of the smashed windows downstairs and a roar goes up. It's not the jubilant kids outside, though. It's fire, which must have caught the curtains immediately. Once it reaches the stairwell, this old wooden house will burn like kindling.

'Fire's the only thing that gets rid of a witch,' taunts the voice below. He's shouting loudly, to make sure he's heard. Doesn't he realize what a risk he's taking? He'll be recognized – reported. You can't burn a house down and get away with it.

Or maybe he can. Perhaps there is no law here any more – none to protect *me*, at any rate. Above the crackling fire, I can hear the rally in the square, and the voice speaking now sounds like Tad Bolt.

There's no help coming.

I shoulder open Harper's door. But I don't know where to

start in here, or whether I even want to. This is her space. Whatever is most important, she presumably has with her in her hideaway.

Which is when my eye falls on a recent picture of us, from Thanksgiving, when Harper incinerated a nut roast. We're curled up on the couch clutching cartons of takeout noodles, grinning at my phone like loons as I take the photo. I loved it so much I had a copy made for each of us.

It's tucked into the rim of her mirror. Harper didn't take it with her.

It's unimportant.

Tears are coming again, but not of laughter. I wrench the photo from the mirror frame. It's important to *me*. I turn to head downstairs and out the back door, then remember the route my daughter often takes from this room and shove up the sash window instead.

It's not a long fall into the yard. I let the bag go, then drop down after it. My knees jar and I roll. No harm done – which is more than can be said for my home. One of the windows and the pane of the back door are red with raging fire.

I dash for the gate that lets out into the alley where I parked my car so I could come and go away from the eyes of the journalists. I'm glad of that now. Tossing the bag onto the passenger seat, I slide behind the wheel, trash crunching beneath my feet. I reach down to swat it and come up with a half-empty bag of cat treats.

Which is when I nearly puke over the wheel.

Aira. My darling. My more-than-pet. My second soul and familiar.

Where is Aira?

A vehicle pulls in to the far end of the alley. It might be blocking my exit, but there's no time to think about that. I scramble out and back through the yard gate.

Surely my familiar is here somewhere. She would have shot through the cat flap. Or maybe she's fled further from danger. She's probably five houses over by now, or on the other side of the street altogether.

But one look tells me the worst. Behind the back door with the cat flap is an inferno. Aira couldn't have gotten out of there unless she went before the flames took hold.

She must have. She must have. She . . .

She's at the kitchen window, scrabbling desperately at the glass. It's the only window downstairs not gouting flame, because the kitchen door is closed – a gust when the first window broke must have slammed it shut. But as I run toward the house, fire begins to lick up the frame.

Aira sees me and batters the windowpane in a frenzy. I'm overjoyed because she's still alive, and so afraid because what if the fire is faster than me?

And once I smash that glass, the inrush of oxygen will cause the inferno that's surging against the door to flare up in a fireball that will take us both.

Unless I do something about it.

89

Maggie

The TV crew has long since packed up and moved on before forensics call it a day at the bloodstained tree. Chester and I watch them going about their business, scraping and photographing.

Scratched into the dirt are more witch signs. But they don't look like the three in Izzy Perelli's jotter. They're elegant curlicued markings. I'm not sensing that crawling wrongness of the villa.

'How does it feel?' I ask Chester, to check it's not just me.

'Not like . . . that,' he says, understanding what I'm asking. 'It's *creepy*, but not *scary*. Does that make sense?'

'Perfectly. Same here.'

But it should feel scary, shouldn't it, if this site is responsible for the sickness in Sanctuary, like the TV report suggested? I guess that's a question for Rowan in the morning.

'Nothing more to see here tonight,' I tell Ches. 'Let's head home.'

Back in the car, I turn on the radio – I always stay tuned to the local channel when I'm working a case. It helps me get the sense of a place. But Chester leans forward to turn up Smooth Sound FM at the exact moment I do when we realize what we're hearing.

We listen in silence for a few minutes.

'Why the *fuck* weren't we radioed about this?' Chester says. It's the first time I've ever heard him cuss so filthily. 'A rally in the square? *Chief Bolt's there?* They must have deliberately not told us.'

I switch course and step on the gas. We've just hit The Cobb when Chester points.

'Over there. Isn't that where Sarah Fenn lives?'

On the horizon, something is burning, smoke pluming into the sky.

In the distance, a siren wails — someone has alerted the fire department, at least. But we're nearer. The rally can wait. I tear down the street to the front of the house, which is a scene of utter destruction. The entire facade is in flames, boards falling and collapsing.

Fenn's neighbor is hurrying three tearful small kids out of his house. The buildings here are set close and made of wood.

'Have you seen Sarah?' I yell out my window.

The man shakes his head and spits on the ground.

'Hope she's in there,' he says. I'm stunned for a moment.

'Round the back.' Chester grabs at the wheel. 'If the fire started at the front, it may not have reached the back. These places have alleys; you can go in through the yard.'

We spin around. Chester's out faster than I am, and we sprint toward Fenn's yard. There's a car pulled over with its interior light on, one door open.

'Sarah's,' Chester says. 'She must have gone back to the house.'

Through the gate, the scene is apocalyptic. The house has been reduced to a crude child's drawing done in red, yellow and orange. The outline is still there, but the structure is made of flame rather than wood. My face scorches even at this distance.

Closer, far closer — *impossibly* close — is Sarah Fenn. Her hands are moving commandingly in the air. She pauses, then smashes a window with the heel of her hand.

369

Any cop can tell you what will happen next. But it's too late. Before Chester or I can scream out a warning, flame has erupted from the shattered window, surging outward with a horrible roar.

I go rigid with shock. This is how it ends for the witch. Something as simple and awful and ordinary as this, after all these weeks.

Until Ches grabs my arm and points.

Walking out of the flames unharmed, the cat in her arms lashing its tail with furious life, is Sarah Fenn.

And I find myself thinking, unwillingly, of Izzy Perelli – who was at Dan's fatal party, yet came out of it with no breathing problems or burns at all.

90

Abigail

'You've maybe heard the accusations Harper Fenn made on TV against my son,' I say. 'You're probably expecting my next words to be a denial. Well they're not. He did it.'

The crowd recoils. Good. It's time for Sanctuary to hear the worst.

Tad Bolt's seedy testimony couldn't have prepared the ground better. The chief has just explained to everyone how Sarah Fenn's magic can take a person and twist them into a dark distortion of themselves.

'I'm going to tell you *why* he did it. The answer's simple. It was because of Sarah Fenn.

'There is a secret I've carried for six years now. It's about the day Sarah performed a miracle that turned out to be more monstrous than you can possibly imagine. When he was twelve, my son Daniel fell from a window and landed head first. His precious skull cracked like an egg . . . and he died.'

A ripple of shock runs through the onlookers. Up here, on the podium, I actually see it: a pressing together, a lift and surge, a sway.

'It was during a dinner party at a friend's house. The kids were supposed to be asleep upstairs. Sarah was there, and others who'll back up this story. My husband is a medical professor at Yale. He did everything he could, but our boy was gone.

'In my grief, my madness, I begged Sarah to do something unthinkable. You would all have done the same. A mother whose only child has just died isn't in her right mind. No, the person who needed to stay calm, to say "I feel your pain, but I won't do that", was Sarah Fenn.

'She didn't. She said *yes.*'

They're with me, this crowd. The people of Sanctuary. I feel their rapt attention as if it flows in my veins. Is this what it feels like for Sarah, all the time, having reserves of power at her command?

How dangerous she is! How have we let people like her live among us like normal citizens? Allowed them to be our neighbors – called them our friends?

Our ancestors had it right. *Thou shalt not suffer a witch to live.*

But it's too soon for that. The time for that will come when the law has run its course.

'She did something savage – terrifying. And I helped, and the other women helped. Every awful moment of it is sealed in my memory until the day I die. And at the end of it, my son's chest shuddered and he drew in a breath. His eyes opened. My son came back.

'But you've all watched the movies, or read the books. You're probably imagining what I didn't dare admit to myself. That Daniel hadn't come back the same.

'Outwardly, he was still my sweet boy. That was who Dan *truly* was. The boy I hope you'll all remember. But every now and then, a crack would show. I'm his mother. I loved him. I couldn't let myself acknowledge the truth – that this wasn't my Daniel any more. There was a darkness in him, biding its time . . .'

I'm making it sound like demonic possession. Sarah always

refused to discuss the spirit world, and I still don't know if she reached out to it that night. But the crowd listening to this can think what it will. Not being certain is even more terrifying than knowing.

'You all know that *something given for something gotten* is the witches' mantra. I don't think life comes cheap. And it was my poor boy, not Sarah, who paid the price.

'Occasionally, very occasionally, this thing inside Daniel drove him to hurt people and to hurt himself. And when he realized what he'd done, he'd weep and cry and ask me what was wrong with him.'

I made that up. There's no one now to call me a liar.

Just a few more lies and this town will be *mine*.

'Each time this happened – and it happened fewer times than you could count on one hand – Dan promised me he'd be stronger. Better. That it would never happen again. And I couldn't betray my little boy's trust, because *I* had asked Sarah to save him. *I* was the one responsible. I supported and prayed for my son. Prayed that together we could beat the darkness inside of him.

'I thought Sarah had given me my life's greatest gift when she brought Daniel back from the dead. Instead, it was a wicked, *wicked* curse that's blighted lives. She knew what she was doing and she did it anyway.

'My son's not here any more to accuse her – and he was only an innocent child of twelve when she broke him. But *I* accuse her. I accuse Sarah Fenn of forbidden, unnatural acts. I accuse Sarah Fenn of every hurt my guiltless boy ever perpetrated. And I accuse Harper Fenn of his murder, in order to keep the secret of her mother's dreadful deed.

'I call for their trial. I call for the death penalty. The Bible and the law of this land demand it. And a mother's broken heart demands it.'

The crowd heaves again. Not away from me in shock, but *toward* me in support. In compassion.

In fury.

'Go home,' I tell them. 'Go home and rest, and pray, and prepare. Because we must be brave enough to do as our ancestors did. To take back our town. To free it from the evil of witchcraft – and make it once again a sanctuary.'

91

Maggie

Chester is tailgating me, driving Sarah Fenn's car. In his place, strapped into my passenger seat, are a frightened, angry witch and a livid familiar.

After her house was torched, I reckon Sarah Fenn was ready to bolt. But I can't let her go. So I dangled the one hold I have over her – that I've discovered the whereabouts of her daughter. I'll get her to a safe place, then bring Harper there.

But we can't agree where's safe for a witch in hiding.

'Your workroom won't do, Sarah. It'll be the next obvious target.'

I don't want to tell her that after today's discovery of the bloodstained tree and the ritual site, I'll also need to have it searched.

'There are things I need in there, Detective. Personal, family things.'

'Like your copy of Starcross?'

Her head whips around. 'Who told you about that?'

She sees it in my face. It was a guess, and she's just confirmed for me that she has a copy. You see that trick all the time in cop shows, but you know what? The old ones really are the best ones.

The cat hisses. Its fur smells singed. Helluva pissed-off feline.

'Is there anywhere else you could go?'

'Pierre,' she says eventually. 'There's really only Pierre Martineau.'

Aaaand . . . It takes me a moment to weigh up whether that's a good idea, or a really, really bad one. I currently have *his* daughter in the frame for the crime of which *Sarah's* daughter stands accused. I want to know if Sarah's been teaching Izzy witchcraft, or if the girl's parents have been sneaking out Starcross for their kid to study by herself.

I decide it's a good idea. I'll speak to them both, together. I'll put my questions to Pierre in Sarah's presence, and then question her. That way I'll know they've not had a chance to put their heads together and come up with a story. While I'm talking, Chester can watch to make sure no looks or glances are exchanged between them.

I radio him with our destination.

Pierre flashes a smile at seeing me on his doorstep after dark, and I momentarily wish it was just me with a takeout pizza and beer. But I have a scorched witch and her familiar in tow, and Pierre swiftly pushes past me to wrap his friend in a bear hug. He asks her what happened, and ushers us all inside.

That open face grows fiercer by the minute as Sarah and I unfold the day's events. Pierre's been working on a job out of town, and all of this – the dog walker's discovery, the rally of townsfolk, the destruction of Sarah's house – has passed him by.

Then Chester – who was tuned in to Smooth Sound FM in Sarah's car – gives us the full details of what happened in the square, and I realize that everything is about to spin out of control.

'She said' – and my boy visibly gulps – 'she said that Daniel died in an accident, six years ago, and that Sarah brought him

376

back to life, but wrong, somehow. So he did bad things occasionally, but those were all Sarah's fault.'

Jesus Christ.

Now you'll never hear me take Jesus's name in vain. I was raised better than that. But honest to God, this has gotten ridiculous. Rape and murder are run-of-the-mill crimes. The only unusual thing in this case is that witchcraft is involved.

But bringing a boy back from the dead? Abigail Whitman has officially tipped over from credible witness into frothing lunatic.

A *resurrection*? How could that stand up in court?

Which is when I notice that Pierre Martineau and Sarah Fenn have gone quiet.

And I remember that evening, six years ago, when I was called to the Perelli-Lee house after a woman had been heard screaming and got told some story about how it was just a false alarm, a kid falling down the stairs. A kid who was Daniel Whitman.

I remember sitting with Pierre on his doorstep discussing Harper's accusation. How Pierre mentioned a night when Abigail found out who her friends were. A night when Dan fell . . . What did he say? Something about the conversation struck a false note, but at the time I couldn't put my finger on why.

A night when Dan fell *out of the window*.

I was there. They all lied to me. Dan hadn't slipped on the stairs in the darkness going to the kitchen for cookies, as I recorded in my incident log. He'd fallen out of the window.

Why would they have lied to me about something so trivial?

Unless Abigail Whitman isn't a lunatic after all.

Unless the boy on the couch who I spoke to that night hadn't just come round from concussion — but had come back from the dead.

I can't help it: my hand checks instinctively for my gun. I know Chester has his, too. So why do I feel so vulnerable?

I need the truth, and I need it now.

'Let's talk,' I say.

The hard lump of my weapon digs reassuringly into my side.

92

Sarah

Once we're sat in Pierre's living room, the cop takes off her jacket and removes her gun from its holster, setting it right beside her.

'Can't be too careful,' she says, noticing me looking at it. 'Things have gotten pretty hairy out there. Do you want to tell me what just happened at your house?'

I do, and she and Chester listen grimly. Pierre looks like he wants to smash something – probably the faces of the boys that did it.

'Must be the same folks that sprayed the sign on the house,' Chester suggests to his boss. 'And sprayed the sign. The town sign, I mean. And on the house, the pentagram sign.'

'I get it, Ches.' The cop holds up a hand to silence him. She looks exhausted. We all are. Exhausted and at our wits' end. All except Abigail, who is growing stronger every day.

'I need to ask you both about what Abigail Whitman was saying in the square this evening,' Knight continues. 'About events six years ago. Pierre knows this, but Sarah, I'm not sure if you do. I was the officer who attended that night.

'I checked my old log a few weeks ago, when I made the connection. Everyone's story back then was that Dan fell down the stairs. But he didn't, did he? Pierre, you let that slip when we spoke about it, and Abigail said the same thing tonight. Dan fell out of a window and was badly injured. But did he . . .? Was he really . . .?'

The cop's throat works. She doesn't even want to say the words, and I don't blame her. It's wrong.

So, so wrong. I know that now. But those I love have always been my weakness. Whenever they came to me hurting, I tried to make things right.

But the law doesn't flinch when it comes to necromancy, no matter how compassionate the motive. I think again of that young mom, the last person convicted of it, even though she failed. Her baby taken away for adoption. Her witch's sticks broken. The decade she still has to serve in a federal prison. The magic she'll never use again, under penalty of life in jail – even though to have magic and not use it is a life sentence in itself.

It'd destroy me.

No matter how sympathetic this cop has appeared, her job is to uphold the law. I couldn't admit to something as grievous as necromancy and expect her to forget I ever said it.

Has the moment come yet when I *need* to confess? To explain about the magic at the villa and how Dan died – that it was simply death reclaiming him – in order to save Harper?

No, we're not at that point yet.

So what *do* I say? I doubt the detective will buy a flat denial. 'I'm not Michael Whitman,' I tell her. 'I can't give you Dan's medical status at that moment. But he was unconscious. Unresponsive. And Abigail was desperate. I couldn't let her suffer without trying to set it right.'

Knight nods. She almost looks relieved that I've not confessed.

'And what about this other thing Mrs Whitman claimed? That this act you performed somehow made Daniel . . . *go wrong*. She's saying that Harper's rape, and other violent behavior by her son, are a direct result of what you did. Is that possible?'

I shift unhappily and Aira writhes too, clawing and ripping

at Pierre's couch. This detective asks questions to which, in witchcraft, there are no easy answers. Nothing that doesn't sound like equivocation at best or lies at worst.

She's right, of course. It *is* possible.

Our entire craft rests on consent. Where there isn't true, open and informed consent, things do . . . go awry.

Look at what I did for Julia, with Alberto. Or for Abigail, with Michael. If those men had known about and consented to my use of magic to modify their behavior – whetting Michael's ambition, rekindling Alberto's faithfulness – their wills would have worked with my art to produce a perfect result.

But without their consent, my magic had to do all the heavy lifting. And the results overshot: Michael's obsessive careerism and Alberto's absurd devotion.

Could Abigail be right?

I already feel responsible for what Dan did to Harper, by the mere act of bringing him back. But is it *worse* than that? Did my magic *change* him?

I can't bear the thought of it.

Harper violated. Dan twisted. *Because of me*? I would rather have pulled out my tongue that spoke words of power over Daniel's broken body. Cut off these fingers that traced marks of strength and binding on his pale skin. Emptied these veins that spurted my life-giving blood between his numb lips.

I'd burn my copy of Starcross and spit on its ashes.

I hear Aira's howl before my own. My beloved familiar is convulsing on the carpet, screeching with pain. And it's *my* pain that's doing it to her. But I can't help it. Horror consumes me from the inside. I'm tied to the stake of my own guilt, and burning.

Through my misery, I hear a rattling. I notice, distantly, that the objects on Pierre's mantelpiece are shaking. A framed photograph that takes pride of place topples forward and smashes.

The glass shards spray across the floor and a sharp, clean hurt stings my ankle.

Behind me, something crashes. Aira screams. A cold wind gusts in from somewhere.

'The table – oh God, it's . . .' Greenstreet is moaning, terrified.

In the corner of my eye, the detective reaches for her gun.

Someone's shaking me, calling my name. A male voice.

Pierre. My friend. The only friend I have left.

'Sarah,' he says again, urgently. 'Sarah, stop this.'

I don't want to stop this. I want this house to burn too – and me with it. Because I've been wrong all this time. Daniel Whitman isn't the monster. I am.

I am.

I throw Pierre off, somehow unnaturally strong. He staggers and falls, winded, against the wall. The cop moves her hand over her gun and lifts it.

'No,' shouts Pierre. He lunges – but not for the cop. For me. Holding me tight.

'Stop it, Sarah,' he yells. 'You didn't do anything. Daniel was *always* bad. He was bad *before*.'

93
Maggie

At Pierre's shout, the table — which has been frikking *floating* — slams back to the floor. I yelp like a puppy. It feels as though every hair on my head is standing straight, and I'll find some witchy white streak running all the way through. I don't know what the fuck that was, but it was *unnatural*. And it was absolutely fucking terrifying.

My arm is extended, the gun in my trembling hand all ready to shoot Sarah Fenn clean through the head. Anything rather than endure another moment of whatever was building up just then.

On the carpet, the cat has been frothing and snarling like it caught the world's fastest case of rabies, but it suddenly goes still, floppy as a shaken baby. Is it dead?

Did *Pierre* do that? Is *he* the witch, who passed his ability on to his girl Isobel?

But maybe he just brought calm the old-fashioned way, shocking Sarah Fenn into silence, because she sits there stunned, her chest rising and falling as she breathes hard.

'It wasn't you,' Pierre croons, drawing his friend's head against his shoulder with those strong arms. 'Daniel was bad *long* before.'

He's stroking Sarah's rust-red hair like a parent comforting a child.

Chester and I look at each other. My boy's all pale and sweaty, like he's made of wax and melting. He motions me to lower my gun.

'Pierre?' I scrape every shred of my cop authority into that word. It's not much. 'Care to explain?'

And as he does, everything joins up.

At long last, *it all joins up*.

'When we spoke, Detective, you asked me whether I believed Harper. And I said I did, but really I was thinking: *didn't she trust me or her mom enough to tell us?* It wouldn't quit bothering me. I figured she might have confided in Izzy. But my baby didn't want to talk about it, just insisted that Harper was telling the truth. I could tell there was a *reason* why she didn't want to talk, though, so I persisted.'

Pierre's whole body heaves with the breath he draws in, as if worried he might any minute forget how breathing's done.

'The room Daniel fell from that night six years ago? It was my daughter's. Izzy had gone to bed early and the other three were watching a movie. Except Dan decided to pay her a visit.'

As Pierre talks, I try to fit it all together. Izzy would have been eleven. Daniel twelve, the age boys start to shoot up and fill out. Testosterone kicking in. Already on his way to that athlete's physique. But Izzy would still have been a child.

Was Angry Dad's daughter an attempt to recapture that thrill? Were there others? Shy ones. Young-for-their-age ones. Molesters who seek opportunities to be close to their targets – like sport coaching – rarely confine themselves simply to looking.

'He was touching my girl under her nightdress. Had her pinned against the wall by the window, one hand over her mouth to prevent us hearing her struggle. Because she *did* struggle. She wriggled out of his grasp, and as he went to grab

384

her, she ducked to one side and he went out of the window.'

Rage twists Pierre's handsome face. Rage at Daniel, but also, it's plain, at himself, for never having suspected what his child suffered. For not having been there to prevent it.

'So that's how Dan fell. It wasn't just him leaning out eavesdropping, like the kids all told us that night. Swear to God, if I'd known, Sarah, I would have told you just to let him die. That little shit. *Both* our daughters.'

Pierre almost chokes as his wrath dies in grief. And now he and Sarah are comforting each other. Two lifelong friends who've raised their children together, have been through the best and worst of times together, and now have one more unbearable thing in common.

I tune them out. They deserve privacy. And I have something else to focus on.

Means, motive and opportunity. For the longest time I never imagined that Isobel Perelli had any of those. Yet now I know she had them all.

She wanted revenge for Dan's assault on her only friend — and on her, all those years before. The crowded party and her illness were the perfect opportunity and alibi. She sketched the runes in her jotter as she planned it out: that dark one to kill him; another for concealment to hide her traces. And there on the balcony, while Dan was distracted by the rape tape playing on the wall, Izzy used magic to send him falling to his death.

She surely thought of a *fall* because she'd seen that once before.

I lean back against the couch and close my eyes. I'm feeling suddenly dizzy, because while my brain is racing along one track, my heart is on another. *Focus*, Mags.

It's plain Pierre doesn't know about his daughter's ability, or he would never have told me the story he just has, knowing that Jake's allegations rest on Dan being killed by witchcraft.

I'd thought it was him or Bridget illicitly borrowing Starcross for her. But now I realize there's an even more obvious candidate – Harper.

Maybe Harper encouraged Isobel to share the fact that she has ability, but when her friend didn't want to, Harper took her to Fenn's workroom or sneaked out the grimoire for her to study. With no one to guide her, Izzy soaked up all of it. From the innocuous stuff to the terrifying sigils that even trained witches can scarcely look at.

So what do I do now?

I inhale deeply and open my eyes. Chester is looking at me. It's plain from his face that he hasn't yet made all the connections I have. But he's likely working toward them.

'Greenstreet, a word outside, please?'

Because my heart has just caught up to my head.

If Isobel Perelli used magic to kill the boy who molested her when she was a little girl, she'll die for it.

If Sarah Fenn brought a friend's only child back to life, she'll go behind bars and lose her magic for life.

Because that's what the law demands.

94
Maggie

Smoke and ash drift on the night breeze as Chester and I stand in Pierre's yard, speaking so quietly we can hardly hear each other. There's a distant blue light from the fire truck that must even now be hosing down Fenn's house.

I lead my sergeant through the connections I've just made that point to Izzy Perelli.

'Surely Harper has the same motive and opportunity?' objects Chester. 'Molested by Dan. Present at the party.'

'Yes, but I saw those sigils Izzy drew. They were clear, no hesitation. Jotted down in such a casual way. She's the one who was at the party secretly, when Harper was there for everyone to see. She was right near Dan on the landing, when Harper was far away. Okay, we've no proof that Izzy does have magical ability, but we know that Harper *doesn't*. And you didn't see Isobel's reaction when I asked where she was that evening. It was guilt, I know it.'

'You *know* it?'

'Gut instinct. You get a feel for it after a while. A colleague of mine trusted his and it helped him save a girl's life when I failed her.'

'But you won't be saving a girl's life here, ma'am.' Chester's so quiet I have to strain to hear him. 'Quite the opposite.'

And that's my problem. Now that I've finally solved this case, I desperately wish I hadn't.

But there could be another way. Will Chester agree? I'm taking a terrible risk even discussing this with him. But I've come to trust him. I've seen him make good call after good call. Be discreet and loyal. There's how he is with Rowan. And if I really *am* going to do this, then it's not like I have a choice anyway. I do it with him, or not at all.

'Let's try this another way. Forget everything we've just been discussing and tell me, hypothetically, what if there was never any witchcraft?'

'But Rowan said . . . And at the villa, we saw . . .'

'You and I and Rowan are the only ones who know what happened at the villa. What if Rowan had detected no magic? What conclusion would we have drawn?'

'That Dan wasn't killed by a witch.'

'Keep going. So how would he have died?'

'An accident,' Chester breathes. 'Maybe like Harper said, he was startled by the tape and he fell.'

'Yes. And if it wasn't murder, then there'd be no need for a motive. All this talk about what Dan may or may not have done becomes irrelevant. No one digging into whether he was a rapist – and therefore no discussion as to whether or not Sarah Fenn broke him in the act of bringing him back from the dead. No necromancy. So who gets a happy ending that way?'

My deputy exhales.

'Everyone, pretty much,' I continue. 'No death penalty for Izzy. No prison for Sarah. No one calling Abigail Whitman's dead child a rapist. No justice for Harper Fenn, of course . . .'

'Dan's dead. I'd say that's some justice.'

'Closure, at least. If we choose, we can end it like this, Chester. Abigail will fight all the way, but when I think of the alternative . . .'

'What about Rowan?'

And there I pause. Because *yes*, what about our magical investigator?

'You don't think they'd agree, given the fate that awaits Izzy if she's convicted?'

'They told me that they regard any use of magic to do harm as abhorrent,' Chester says. 'That's got to include murder, no matter how justified. And you saw how shocked they were by those sigils. Just the pictures on your phone really freaked them out.'

I nod. I have the same fears. It'd be ironic if our attempts to protect two witches were thwarted . . . by another witch.

Surely Rowan would accept that a girl untutored in witchcraft, and ignorant of the heinous nature of the magic she's used, shouldn't be judged as harshly as someone knowingly reaching for banned magic to do harm?

And what about the risk to the magical community of a full-blown trial? I've lost count of how many times Rowan has decried the biased way the law treats witches. They'd understand that what we're seeing here in Sanctuary – this multiplying fear and hatred of witches – could flare up nationwide if this case goes to trial.

I explain this to Chester, who nods. It looks as if we've reached a decision. My chest is painfully tight as I consider what I'm about to do.

Why did I join law enforcement if I ignore the law when it doesn't suit me? Because there's something higher than law. *Justice*.

I think of what Remy said when he waved me out of his office that day. *You keep pursuing truth and justice, Mags.*

Here in Sanctuary, the path has split, and I can pursue only one of them.

I've made my choice which.

95

Sarah

'What do I do now, P?'

'No idea, Magic Girl.'

Pierre wraps his arms around me as I huddle against him. The pair of us have cried ourselves empty, while the cops gave us some privacy. I'm so exhausted that all I want to do is sleep. But across town Abigail has been whipping up the crowd against Harper and me.

'Should I run? The detective says she'll bring Harper to me, so the pair of us can get out of town and lie low. Can I trust her, or is she planning on taking us both to a cell?'

'I don't know. But I do trust her – I think.'

'Yeah, me too. Is she really the same cop who turned up that night?'

'The very same.'

'How on earth do you remember? I don't recall a thing other than the magic, the spell work. And Dan himself. I don't think any of the others recognized her either.'

'Shorter hair,' Pierre says. 'Little heavier. But cute don't change.'

'Pierre!'

I smack my friend's bicep and he gives a faint chuckle. It's one of my favorite sounds in the world, and it's a small comfort.

'Should I tell the detective that magic *was* used at the villa? I never shared that, because while Jake was insisting that Harper had magic it seemed like a really bad idea. But maybe I should have, because she *doesn't* have it, even if I can't prove that. Except will I look bad for having withheld what I knew . . .?'

I trail off unhappily. Ever since the party, I haven't stopped trying to find ways to prove Harper's innocence, and to discover what happened to Dan. But it feels as though everything I tried was the wrong way to go about it.

'You're tying yourself in knots,' Pierre says, stroking my hair. 'I have faith in this cop. She's thorough. She will have called a magical investigator in already – or be planning to. She'll get to the bottom of this.'

The yard door opens and I startle upright. But it's not a lynch mob headed by Abigail. It's only the two police coming back inside. Pierre's words reassured me, but now I'm scared all over again, because the detective's expression is absolutely bleak. She lowers herself to the couch opposite and Chester Greenstreet takes out his notebook. My heart rate quickens.

'Just for the record,' the cop says, 'so please answer truthfully: your daughter Harper Fenn has no magical ability?'

Her tone is flat, more like a statement than a question.

'She does not.'

'Isobel Perelli has no magical ability?'

What is this? *Izzy?* I dart a look at Pierre, who's plainly troubled by the question.

'She does not.'

'Can you confirm that, Mr Martineau?'

'She definitely doesn't.'

'Ms Fenn, do Bridget Perelli-Lee, Julia Garcia or Beatriz Garcia have magical ability?'

'They do not.'

'Thank you so much. That'll do, Chester.'

Greenstreet snaps shut his notebook.

'I'll need those answers on tape at a later date, Ms Fenn, but for now that will suffice. It's my conclusion that no magic was involved in Daniel Whitman's death. The probable cause was an accident due to his being startled by the projection of a tape showing a sexual act between him and your daughter. That act, while it may appear to have non-consensual elements, was in fact consented to by your daughter.'

'What are you . . .? *No.*'

I don't understand. What is she saying? The first part is everything I've desperately wanted to hear. But the rest? Harper was *raped*. I stare at the cop. She looks absolutely sick as she repeats herself.

'I'll recap. Daniel Whitman's death was an accident. Your daughter consented to their sexual encounter.'

Then I *do* understand. I moan, because it hurts so much, and Pierre's arms tighten around me.

I remember Abigail in my kitchen when this all began, wielding grief that was sharp and deadly as my sickle. *My son's life for your daughter's innocence,* she said, as she tried to make me resurrect the horror that would have been Daniel's days-dead and burned body.

Now the cop is making the same offer, but it's all back to front. *Your daughter's life for Dan Whitman's innocence.*

If we stick to the version of the story that she just set out, this will all go away.

'Abigail will never agree,' I tell her.

Harper will never agree, I think to myself.

'Leave Mrs Whitman to me. I need to know that you can answer for Harper.'

Aira leaps to my shoulder and kneads me with fierce paws.

'Why should she say that?' I demand. 'Is there really no other way?'

The cop is silent. Her wretchedness at our situation is plain in her face. But I'm furious. Time and again, society demands this of us. Keep quiet. Play along. Don't push back.

Our silence is the price we're expected to pay for peace.

When I said I'd do anything to keep my daughter safe, I never imagined this.

I give no guarantee on Harper's behalf. But I nod, and the detective sags with relief.

'Thank you, Ms Fenn. I'm going to step into the next room and call my boss. After that, we'll leave you until morning, when we'll return and take you to Harper. We'll get the two of you to a safe place out of town until things have calmed down. No one knows you're here tonight, so you'll be safe. Chester will take you through some practicalities.'

I listen with one ear as Chester explains how they'll take my car away to a secure spot so no one connects it with me being here. With the other ear, I'm straining – we all are – to overhear the detective's conversation.

I hear her repeat 'mass hysteria', then 'mob mentality'. She's unsparing about Abigail.

'The woman's been claiming all this time that a witch killed her son. Now she's saying that he's already died once before, six years ago, and a witch resurrected him. I mean, which is it gonna be, lady?

'And not only is the chief, Tad Bolt, not helping – he's part of it. This evening he stood up and told everyone he was a gambling addict who used prostitutes. And guess what? The local witch made him do it. I'm not blaming Bolt exactly; he's under a lot of stress with his son being sick. But he's certainly not competent. And yeah, that sickness? That's because of witches, too. This whole place just took a one-way ride back four centuries, Remy.'

I can't follow her boss's side of the conversation, though I do hear frequent cussing. And then the crucial question – she asks permission to take me and Harper outside Sanctuary to a safe location.

And her boss gives it.

It's done.

The cops take their leave, promising to be back at 7 a.m. to drive me to Harper. My bed for the night is Pierre's spare room – the one Izzy uses when she sleeps over with her dad. It's full of childish decorations: Disney princess posters, boy-band and teen-actor photos cut from magazines.

Though I'm worried I won't be able to sleep, I find my eyes closing as soon as I slip beneath Izzy's cheerful pink comforter. And when I wake, this nightmare will be over.

96

Abigail

A sound wakes me in the night. I check the clock: 3:30 a.m.

It's someone moving around in Michael's bedroom. Quickly, I come to full alert, reach for my robe and slip out of bed. Adrenaline is flowing. Do I stay put, or try to flee?

I hear the closet door slide back. Now would be the moment.

But I'm undone as I step onto the landing. I'd forgotten how squeaky our antique floorboards can be. As one of them creaks unignorably loudly, I'm paralyzed with fright.

Until, in an instant, my husband's voice unfreezes me.

'Abigail? Is that you?'

Michael steps onto the landing – fully dressed.

'Darling! It's only you. You scared me.'

Truth be told, there's something about him that scares me still. In the oblique moonlight through a window, his face is half dark, half bright. It makes his expression impossible to read. In his hand is a tiny medical monitoring device, its screen dully illuminated.

'Where are you going?' I ask, when he doesn't respond.

'To the hospital. To check on Jake.'

'Surely he's asleep. Can't it wait till the morning?'

'The morning will be too late.'

'Too late? You mean he's getting worse?'

'I mean he's getting better.'

Michael bends to brush a kiss an inch from my cheek, then lopes athletically down the stairs. His words make no sense at all. I'm still puzzling over them when I hear his car start up. The gleam of headlights rakes the walls in an arc as he pulls down the driveway.

It's only once I'm back in the darkness of my bedroom that I understand.

In the car on the way home from the rally, I'd been rejoicing at how fired up everyone was. How full of revulsion at Sarah's filthy works. How ready to act against her and Harper. Michael, though, had sounded a note of caution.

'But will they wake up angry?' he'd said. 'Will they wake up afraid? That's what we need.'

That's what we need.

I scrabble for my phone and dial his number. It goes to voice-mail. I cut the call and dial again. Voicemail. And again.

On the fourth call I open my mouth to speak – then swallow the words just before they come out.

He's acting under a magical compulsion. Nothing I say will make any difference. A voice message from me could only incriminate both of us.

I end the call. Switch off the phone.

Try to sleep.

Fail.

97

Maggie

Surf boys and girls are creatures of habit, and at eight o'clock on a sunny morning I'm catching the rays with Chester on the Green Point boardwalk, watching their tanned bodies race through the water. One of them, upright and carefree on a paddleboard, sleek in her wetsuit, is Harper Fenn. She hasn't noticed her mother yet, though the witch is pacing the sand barefoot.

The world feels different this morning. Hope has crept back in. Hope that a fresh start is possible for this mother and daughter. That acceptance and closure will finally come to Abigail Whitman, and tranquility be restored to Sanctuary.

The path I've chosen is to do the wrong thing in the eyes of the law, but it sure as heck feels *right*.

Sarah talked excitedly about Harper all the way here, and I imagine the pair of them happy in a place like this – though, ideally, far from Sanctuary. Chester has been extolling the pleasures of Oregon, which he's doubtless heard about from Rowan.

My conversation with Rowan last night was difficult. But I pushed through it to a place I feel good about. I laid out my theories – and my fear about how inflamed Sanctuary has become in this short time. What the consequences might be nationwide if this case went to trial.

The investigator understood me right away.

'One guilty witch gets away with murder, so that our kind doesn't have to walk in fear. That's what you're proposing.'

'Technically, Isobel *isn't* guilty,' I said, 'because all accused are innocent until guilt is proven, and the case would be closing before anything's proven either way.'

Rowan studied me as though I were a bird whose plumage they had thought was familiar but on which they'd just spotted unexpected new markings. Eventually, they nodded.

'One innocent witch. I understand.'

I held my breath, not wanting to push their consent to my proposal. But I had to make sure that by saving Izzy and Sarah, I wasn't putting more people at risk. So I had one more question for my investigator.

'Sarah's told me that what the dog walker found was for something she called a sunstone rite. But the media is linking it to this sickness. Can I believe her? Or could Izzy be responsible for the sickness? It's only been affecting people linked to the case.'

'Sunstone spells promote clear thinking in times of confusion. The photos of what was found at the site match the usual ritual form. It's a creative, rather elegant idea that might even have worked. As for the sickness, witches aren't capable of smiting whole towns. That's persecution-era propaganda.'

So it's not Izzy causing it. It's simply what I told Remy – panic and hysteria.

'Isobel will need urgent remedial instruction to make sure she masters her abilities and knows the right and wrong ways to use them,' Rowan had concluded, sternly. 'I could take care of that myself.'

So we made plans to sit down with Izzy and her parents as soon as the Fenns are safely over the state line. Meanwhile, Remy will issue an official statement that the investigation is under review.

That review will continue for a few weeks, to give Sanctuary time to calm down. I will make Abigail understand that pressing her case will keep the spotlight on her son, and that not everyone will believe he only molested children because a witch made him do it.

If she doesn't fall into line, then much though I don't want to threaten a grieving mother, I'll have to play hardball. Point out that her statements at the vigil and last night's rally could constitute hate crime. Note that the two attacks on the Fenns' house coincided with public gatherings for Daniel and inform her that the Supreme Court takes a dim view of 'fighting words' that incite others to violence.

Once all the loose ends are tied, and the TV crews lose interest, the case will be formally dropped.

Chester nudges me. Harper has peeled her wetsuit down to her hips, revealing a thin vest, and is paddling back to the shore. She looks good here. Her hair tousled and her body ink of a piece with the rest of the surfers. If she chooses this life, her talents will be in demand wherever she goes. A few years from now, I can picture a pair of booths side by side, like Jonny Maloney's tattoo shop and his witchy mom's storefront.

I hope that vision comes true. This mother and daughter deserve it after what they've been through. The hostility in Sanctuary has been frightening these past few days. I remember the illustrations of witch persecution displayed at Sanctuary's Old Square, and what was done to Sarah's home. If you burn a person's house, then you've already accepted the possibility that you're burning them in it.

A shout snaps my attention back to the Fenn reconciliation down at the water's edge. It's not getting off to a great start.

Harper has zipped her wetsuit back up and hoisted her paddleboard under one arm, storming off toward a boathouse. Sarah is standing at the water's edge, looking shocked and shaken.

'Go make sure Harper doesn't disappear,' I tell Chester, nudging him. 'I knew their conversation about retracting the rape allegations was going to be tough. I'll tell Sarah to keep calm. We've got this.'

As Ches trots off across the sand, my phone rings. Remy's number.

'Hey, we're nearly done here, boss. We have the Fenns together and we'll be leaving shortly.'

As Remy replies, everything falls apart.

'Nearly done? Too fucking right you're nearly done. I've just had a call from some white-coat douchebag at CDC. Not good news for you, Margaret Knight. Sanctuary's been quarantined.'

'What?'

'*Quar-an-tined*. Comes from the Italian, meaning *forty days*, which is how long they used to isolate ships in port to make sure no bastard had the Black Death. Or, in the case of Sanctuary, killer witch flu.'

'That's not funny, Remy.'

'Damn straight it isn't, Maggie. Jacob Bolt, the chief's son, who you told me last night had nothing more serious than broken-heart-itis? He's *dead*. Died early this morning. And right after that, those Yale pointy-heads rushed half a dozen others into the emergency isolation unit – *schoolkids and cops*. Witchcraft is beating bird flu and closing in on fucking Ebola.'

I sink to my haunches in the sand, phone pressed to my ear, trying to talk down this madness.

'It's *hysteria*, Remy. If it's witchcraft that's striking people down, then why is Abigail Whitman still walking and talking? And *her husband* is the one taking folk off to hospital. I'd say that's a bit of a coincidence.'

'You're saying the Bolt kid died of hysteria?'

'Of course I'm not. But you know, people do die suddenly for perfectly straightforward reasons.'

'Not when they're prime accusers in murder cases, they don't. Look, the kid could have choked to death on Tootsie Rolls for all I care. But this has escalated to a Grade-A-for-Assfuckery incident and we can't just walk it back like we discussed last night. My next call is going to have to be the governor, to tell her that I've relieved you of your badge and am sending in my best people to sort this out. And you can't take those witch women anywhere.'

'No, Remy, I—'

'We'll bring them into state custody. I'll make sure they're safe. But we've got to be seen to do this right. This is going to bring the national media to our doorstep. The whole fucking three-ring circus plus popcorn.' He pauses. Sniffs. 'At least it gets me out of being my daughter's ballet chauffeur for a couple weeks, so there's that. Sorry it had to end like this, Mags. Wait at Green Point till the guys turn up, then get your ass back to HQ.'

He cuts the call. My wrist goes slack and I stare at the sand. This can't be happening.

Jacob Bolt, *dead*?

And I'm *definitely* not handing over the Fenns.

I go to Sarah. She's standing on the waterline looking bewildered and shell-shocked. She and Harper must have had harsh words. She doesn't even respond at first. Not until I shake her arm does she look up. Her eyes are haunted. Did she overhear my conversation with Remy?

'Come on,' I say, shaking her again, gently. 'Time to get you both out of here.'

'I don't . . .' Fenn says. She seems confused. 'I . . .'

There's a yell from over by the boathouse. Shouting. Which is when I notice a patrol car parked up by the café.

Not one car. Three. And one of them has the word CHIEF on the side.

Officer Asshole has Harper Fenn by the hair. She's changed into a flowing dress and stumbles over the hem as he twists her neck painfully.

In his other hand, he holds a gun at her head.

What the fuck is this?

Someone is striding toward us across the sand. The light glints off his badge.

When Chief Tad Bolt reaches us, he punches Sarah Fenn in the face. The witch goes down without a sound beyond the audible crack of an eye socket.

I snarl and position myself between him and her slumped body.

'That's two counts of assault, Bolt. One from you, and one from your boy over there. He needs to let go of Harper right away.'

Bolt smiles, and it's so damn wrong I have no words. His face has fallen in on itself, like an apple gone bad on the inside. His skin is a slaughterhouse pink, and each blunt bristle on his chin looks stabbed painfully into its follicle. His eyes are more red than blue.

I hear the click as he raises his gun and holds it two inches from my forehead. And I am honestly ready to shit my pants, because I've realized too late that this man knows no rules or laws any more except those of wild grief.

'You shut your face, you dumb bitch. If you'd arrested these witches weeks ago, my boy would still be alive.'

Then he twirls the pistol. It's a curiously graceful motion, and the arc of his hand continues until the gun butt slams into the side of my skull and I crumple.

98

LIVE BROADCAST, NPR, *MORNING EDITION*

EVANS: It's eight thirty, and you're listening to NPR's *Morning Edition*. Now, breaking news just in from Connecticut of a town that has been placed under quarantine by the CDC – the Centers for Disease Control and Prevention, the nation's health protection agency.

Over to our health correspondent Stephanie Geller for more details.

GELLER: Thank you, Bill. Yes, this is very curious news coming out of Connecticut. Sanctuary is a small town, population nine thousand or so. And it's been making headlines locally during the past couple of weeks for a string of accusations about witchcraft, including the alleged murder of a young star athlete. Connecticut news yesterday carried a story on the discovery of a so-called ritual site, and in the town there has been widespread speculation about what its purpose may be.

Now there has been a confirmed death overnight, that of a young man named Jacob Bolt, who was admitted to a rare and infectious diseases facility on the Yale campus several days ago. Bolt, the youngest son of Sanctuary's chief,

Thaddeus Bolt, was the primary witness and accuser in the murder allegations, pointing the finger at the daughter of the local witch.

Beside Bolt, a number of others involved in the case have reportedly been taken unwell. By imposing a quarantine, is the CDC really saying that Sanctuary is seeing America's first witchcraft-caused epidemic for, well, centuries? Luc Porowski, a CDC spokesperson, says not.

POROWSKI: We are absolutely not speculating as to the origin of the symptoms manifesting in Sanctuary. The purview of the CDC is clear. Our Division of Global Migration and Quarantine is empowered to detain and medically examine individuals suspected of carrying a communicable disease.

One of our eighteen quarantine stations is in Boston. The Boston team was contacted yesterday by the medical faculty at Yale, who shared their concerns, and our station chief visited the hospital to assess the individuals admitted. Their decision to impose a temporary quarantine on the town of Sanctuary pending further investigation was not undertaken lightly, and we look forward to lifting the restrictions once we are able to determine that there is no risk to the public.

GELLER: What about those who say that the only thing wrong with these people is hysteria caused by rumors of witchcraft? By intervening like this, couldn't you be making things worse?

POROWSKI: One young man has tragically died, although the cause of death is as yet unconfirmed. Our priority at this time is to prevent further loss of life.

GELLER: The Moot – that is, the national body representing witches and the magically able – has issued the following statement.

We are surprised and disappointed that the CDC has chosen

*to stoke prejudice by this ill-informed decision. There has been
not one scientifically verified incident of witchcraft-induced
mass sickness in the entire history of the United States. We
strongly urge people to use their common sense regarding
reports of this quarantine in Sanctuary.*

That's all for now, but we'll keep you updated. We understand that, at this time, roadblocks are being put in place
and movement into and out of the town is restricted.
EVANS: Thank you so much, Stephanie. That was health
correspondent Stephanie Geller.

99

TWEETS FROM @POTUS – OFFICIAL TWITTER ACCOUNT OF
THE PRESIDENT OF THE UNITED STATES

@POTUS 8.45 a.m.
Witches killing people in Connecticut is result of
Democrat craze for 'tolerance' and 'integration'.
Witchcraft = unnatural and UNAMERICAN. CDC right to
set #quarantine
💬8.4 k ♻7.9k ♡37k

@POTUS 9.02 a.m.
No new regulation of witches EVER introduced by
liberal Supreme Court. We will end this NOW. I am
ordering immediate inquiry into #Sanctuary #witchcraft
#quarantine
💬9.1 k ♻10k ♡42k

100

Abigail

'Got 'em,' Tad announces. Police and guardsmen flatten themselves against the wall to make room as the chief strides into his office where we're gathered. 'They're in the cells.'

When Michael and I told him about Jake's passing this morning, I saw that this was the moment from which there was no going back. Tad Bolt's despair could turn inward, as grief, or outward, as rage.

I needed him to rage.

'Arrest the Fenns,' I told him. 'They've killed both our children. They have to pay.'

Michael emphasized that the whole town was at risk from the witches, and told Tad he'd ordered ambulances to take the three cops and the Spartan boys to hospital. When he suggested a quarantine, I knew it would be perfect. We could put a lid on Sanctuary and bring it to a boil.

Michael's creepy golfing buddy, who runs the CDC Region 1 office in Boston and tells dinner party stories of inspecting prostitutes for rare sexual diseases, delivered on that. Which meant Tad could call the detective's boss in Middletown to get her off the case and probe for the whereabouts of the Fenns — which turned out to be Green Point.

NPR picked up on the quarantine, so we're national news.

And once the President tweeted? Well, that's practically an executive order.

Now the witches are in our custody – and I'm in control. Tad's in no state to think. His grief whips him on to do, do, *do*. Michael's played his part. The finale is in my hands.

One last act of justice.

I had Tad call in the National Guard and they're prepping the football stadium.

'Mitch McConaughey's guys are assembling the stage and a podium for the accused,' says one police officer, a handsome young man with dazzling badges. 'And Pawson's Hardware had the other thing we needed.'

'What about the witches?' someone adds, anxiously. 'Will it be safe having them out in the open?'

'Have they made any attempt to escape since they were brought in?' I ask the sergeant who oversees the station's cells.

'Nope. They're shackled wrist and ankles, and we've taped their fingers so they can't use their hands. They seem weirdly calm.'

'Are they talking to each other? Could they be making a plan?'

'Not that we've seen. They've been ordered not to speak.'

'But are they telepathic?' the anxious man persists. 'Could they be, like, *mind*-speaking.'

'Or mind-*controlling*,' someone else adds. 'Like they did to that dude. What if they hypnotize us and make us set them free?'

'Enough.' Tad slams the desk so hard it jumps and rattles beneath his fist. 'They're *witches*, not superheroes. They're cuffed. Each witch has a guard, and both men have their guns drawn.'

'What if they make them shoot each other?'

'Shut. The fuck. Up.' Tad punctuates his words with his fists.

'They are contained. And in just a couple hours, all this will be over.'

'One question,' says another officer, raising his hand. 'What about the media? We've had reports of TV crews trying to cross the roadblocks. They say the quarantine is public interest news.'

'Absolutely not,' I snap. 'They'll obstruct our preparations. And if they see inside the stadium, you can bet the governor will try to step in. That can't happen. This trial is our *right*.'

If one thing will screw this up, it's the presence of the press. People have second thoughts when they know their actions are being recorded for posterity, and we can't afford any second thoughts.

Besides, what we're embarked upon feels almost . . . sacred. This is how things always were. No calculatingly selected jury members. No lawyers to twist arguments. Just people speaking truth for their peers to hear and pass judgment.

Just a community meting out justice.

101
Maggie

I come to on the sand at Green Point to find Chester by my side.

'I told Bolt I was gonna drive you straight to Middletown,' he says, after fussing to make sure I'm okay. 'So how do you feel about riding back to Sanctuary in the trunk, because I think something bad is going down.'

'What?'

I listen groggily as he explains what's happened. The CDC has closed the town, no vehicles going in or out. A public gathering in the football stadium. All officers needed.

'A public gathering?'

My brain runs through all sorts of scenarios, but there's only one that fits. That Sanctuary is planning some kind of show trial of the Fenns. I suppress panicked laughter, because you'd have to be insane to think such a thing possible. Trials happen in courts, in front of juries. You can't just seize a couple of people and hurl accusations at them. That's not how law's been done since back before we told the king of England where to stick his crown.

But then I remember Bolt's face as he punched Sarah Fenn and clubbed me with his pistol. At some point in the night, I'm guessing right when his son died, Tad Bolt's sanity took a hike, and it won't be home for a while.

'Whatever's planned, we've got to stop it,' I tell Chester.

I pull out my phone and dial Remy. He answers on the second ring.

'Mags.' His tone is flat and clipped. 'You'd better be calling to say you're in the lobby ready to brief me on what the fuck is going on.'

'I'm still in Green Point. Someone's about to drive me to a clinic. I'm *concussed*. Bolt knocked me out and grabbed the Fenns. I think he's going to stage some kind of show trial, Remy. You have to send your boys in there and get them.'

'I'm glad you've just said you're concussed, Maggie, because that explains why you're making no sense. Bolt contacted me himself. With the CDC quarantine, I can't send anyone to Sanctuary, so he's taken the Fenns into custody and our guys will collect them as soon as we have the all-clear.'

'And you *agreed* to that? I told you *he's* the threat—'

'Maggie. Calm down. You've gotten too invested in this case, and you know that's never a good idea. This is twenty-first-century Connecticut. No one reset the clock to the Dark Ages while we weren't looking.'

'Remy, *please*. Surely you can see how bad an idea this is? Bolt thinks the Fenns killed *his* son too. I'm asking you, just send someone in to get them.'

'And break a quarantine?'

'And break a quarantine.'

'Maggie, this lockdown isn't Bolt playing at Wild West justice. It's been called by the C-Damn-C. The President is tweeting about it.'

'What *doesn't* the President tweet about?'

Remy gives a bark of laughter, but his tone is all seriousness.

'I understand your concerns. I explained to Bolt *very* carefully that I wanted the Fenns safe and secure, and that our boys will be on his doorstep the minute the roadblocks come down.

He's not dumb. He knows there'll be repercussions if he doesn't comply.'

'Remy, *sir*, I don't think his head's in a place where—'

'Go get *your* head looked at, Maggie. Then get back here. We'll work this out.'

My boss hangs up. I'd love to believe he's right.

But I don't.

'Let's get going,' I tell Chester. My deputy is hunched over his phone, tapping on a map.

'Just looking for the nearest clinic – for your concussion?'

'I'm fine. Just needed to give Remy an explanation why he might not be seeing me for a while. We're heading right back that way.'

And I point along the road to Sanctuary.

102

Sarah

I sit on the thin metal bed as far as I can get from my daughter, who leans against the wall. I watch through one eye – the other has swollen shut – as Harper glances at the two guards on the other side of the bars.

The pair have been standing watch, guns drawn, since we were thrown in here. One weapon is trained on me, and the other on my child.

When Harper looks at them, and particularly when she smiles, the two cops fight their instinct to step back. They think they're trying to avoid the wiles of an attractive teenage detainee. But are they attracted to her – or are they afraid of her?

Or is it both?

What if they're responding to the signs that writhe across my daughter's skin. That have been etched into it by a needle. Because there's no mistaking what I saw on Harper's body when she unzipped that wetsuit and the thin vest she wore beneath rode up and bared her stomach. I know now why she has hidden her body from me this past year and a half. Why she started wearing long sleeves and jeans. Why her bedroom door is always shut.

Of course I glimpsed some of the art that unfurled across

her skin as Harper became an exquisite canvas. A snake coiled around one ankle. A feather balanced along each collarbone. But I never saw her midriff. And now I know why. Because there among wreathed vines and flowers hang dark, rotten fruit. The Old Signs.

I saw the sigil for *Command*. The ones for *Ruin* and for *Obscurity*.

The one for *Undoing*.

Some witch traditions use tattoos to enhance their powers, although mine does not. But no witches, anywhere, mark themselves with such abominations. Those sigils are the reason Starcross was banned. Yet they're etched into my daughter's body.

I lean back against the wall, pulling up my knees and looping my cuffed wrists and duct-taped hands around them. It brings me no comfort.

'You – witch!' The cop whose weapon has been pointing at me steps closer. He raps his gun against a bar of our cell. The metal on metal makes a hard, sharp sound. 'Hands where we can see them.'

'Jeez, calm down,' Harper mutters.

'And you – don't say anything!' His voice is panicky.

'Don't get so close to 'em,' warns his buddy.

Harper scoffs at him. I was worried she'd be afraid, but she's showing the fearlessness and defiance that has flashed out in the past few weeks. Going to that TV reporter by herself. So confident when I told her Jake's accusation was of murder by *magic*, because she has none. Despite my warnings about the way the law works against witch folk, she believes her innocence protects her.

But no one will believe she's innocent if they see what's inked on her. The sigils may be small, and artfully concealed amid the blossoms and branches of the larger design. But to those of us who recognize them, they affront the eye as much as if they'd been cut into her skin with a knife.

It must be the work of the Green Point witch's son, the tattooist. I don't know him. I only know his mother slightly. Siobhan Maloney and I have talked about our craft a few times, over a pot of dandelion tea. But we're not close and our magics have nothing in common. She and her family are true travelers. They came from Ireland a few generations ago and settle nowhere for longer than seven years.

Theirs is the transient magic of the hedgerow and the bonfire. Their grimoire is written in falling leaves and spiraling smoke. Their spells are the breath of the wind. To witches like Siobhan, nature itself is magic.

The traveling tradition scorns all written lore. The Maloneys are not a Starcross family.

And so I doubt Siobhan would know what she was looking at if she glimpsed Harper's secret beneath her wetsuit. If her son knew what *he* was doing, he would never have etched those sigils, blacker than ink, into Harper's pure skin.

Harper must have asked him to. It's the only explanation. She must have taken the designs to him. These tattoos are her choice. Is this her way of claiming a little piece of my craft for herself after all? Tattoos often memorialize our losses: a loved one's name, or a comrade's death date.

Harper has memorialized something that was never hers to lose.

My eyes fill as I think about it, though with the cop's gun on me I don't dare raise my hands to wipe at them. The salt tears burn my bruised flesh.

The only comfort is that those sigils are nothing *more* than tattoos. There is no power in them. No magic animates them. They're inert and empty, like Julia's elegant copies of my charts. Thank goodness they were done by Maloney's son, and not by

415

the witch herself. Even if she didn't know what she was inscribing, her ability would have given them life.

I can't imagine what the consequences of that would be. Of marking with magic a body incapable of containing it. When we bespell objects, if the item isn't prepared carefully enough, it can shatter beneath the magic laid upon it. Done by a witch, those tattoos might have killed my daughter.

As it is, they still might.

Harper could hang for Dan's death because those sigils mark her out as unnatural.

And it's even worse than that. My one defense of my daughter, the thing I've clung to as our last resort – to confess that *I'm* the one responsible for Dan's death at the villa, because I cheated death of him six years ago? That's useless, because now there's *another* dead boy. Jake Bolt.

If I take the blame for Dan, they'll still pin Jake's death on Harper. I saw it in Tad's eyes.

Tad and Abigail have both lost their children. How can they do this? Hand me and my child over to the authorities, knowing what awaits us?

Where is the detective I thought was on our side? Has this sickness convinced even her?

How did Jake Bolt die?

I stare at the ceiling, willing myself to calm down. There's still a way out – there must be.

But right now, I can't see it. Shackled and with my fingers taped, without my sticks, without my charts and tools, there's nothing I can do.

Perhaps when they move us, when they take us upstairs for interview, I'll have my opportunity.

I try flexing my fingers inside the duct tape. All five have been bound together like a Maine lobster's claws tied before they're tossed into the pot. The tape is wrapped as far as my wrist. The cops have done their job well and there's no wriggle room.

They said they'd shoot us if we spoke. But I've lived here my whole life. Everyone knows me. I'm gambling on the fact that a young local cop will find it difficult to shoot point-blank someone he knows. Besides, Tad will want to keep us alive so he can bring us to court. Grief demands closure.

'I want a lawyer,' I say loudly, my heart pounding in my chest.

'I said shut up! Or I'll do it – I swear I will!'

The riled young cop darts back to the cell door. His hands are shaking as they grip the gun. If only *my* hands were free, I could try the force charm that I used to push my way into Abigail's house. Then we'd see who holds the more powerful weapon.

But after days spent anticipating this moment, preparing spells and pondering escape strategies, disaster fell on us too swiftly for me to react. There was only Tad's punch on the beach, and when I came to, I was already restrained and bound. The bruises across my daughter's face tell me those animals did the same to her.

'You can't keep us here without a lawyer and without a charge,' I say, emboldened that my last outburst didn't put a bullet in me. If I can just get them used to the idea of me speaking, then the moment I work my fingers loose . . .

'You won't be needing a lawyer, Sarah.' Abigail stands at the bottom of the stairs that lead from the station above. 'Bring them up. It's time.'

'Wait! Abi!'

Those dainty shoes Abigail wears even fieldside at football games rap the concrete floor as she halts just beyond reach of our cell. Somehow, amid all this, her makeup is immaculate. Did I ever see her without it, even once in all our years of friendship? Did I ever know the woman underneath?

'There's no point begging,' she tells me. 'Either of you. Sanctuary made its choice centuries ago. There's no place here for your kind and the evil you do.'

'The *good*. I only ever did *good*. You know that. And Harper's innocent – you know that too. You can stop this madness, Abigail.'

Inside the tape, my fingers are working desperately. My mind runs through half a dozen spells. But thoughts aren't enough. A musician can know every note in a piece, but she needs her instrument to play it, and I have neither free hands nor sticks.

And Abigail has noticed.

'Stop that!' she barks. 'Guards, take them out.'

Harper steps to the bars. I want to yell at her to stay back. I imagine Abigail striking my girl, spitting at her – maybe even grabbing one of the guns and shooting her.

My daughter's gaze is gentle.

'I'm sorry for your loss, Abigail,' she says. 'I'm so sorry you never got to see him one last time, to say goodbye.'

Abigail sways a moment. This is the first time these two have met since the night Daniel died. The first time Abigail has seen the girl she's accused, and looked into her eyes.

I hold my breath. Could this be all it takes? A simple voicing of sorrow to remind Abigail that we all share in her grief. Are Harper's words working their own kind of magic?

'Bitch,' says Abigail. 'The rope's too good for you. If I'd had my way, it would be the fire.'

She turns and hurries up the stairs. Disappointment burns through me and the last of my hope curls up like ash and drifts away.

103

Maggie

It's stifling and sweaty in the trunk of Chester's car as we speed toward Sanctuary. I suck in a grateful breath when we finally halt and the lid springs open. My deputy and Pierre Martineau look down at me.

'Am I glad to see you,' Pierre says, and one of those strong arms hauls me out like a sack of cement.

The three of us agree that Chester will head back to the station and play at being a loyal cop – he'll call me with anything he discovers. Pierre and I will do recon to find out just what the heck is going on, where the Fenns might be and how much danger they're in.

I need a change of wardrobe, but my options aren't great. Pierre offers me one of his own hoodies and a pair of his daughter's sweatpants. I take them uneasily. My conflict of interests is off the scale. I might as well toss my police badge in the trash compactor right now. I tell myself that involving Pierre is only fair. If his daughter is responsible for the crime Harper is accused of, the least he can do is help me try to rescue her. And he'd want to anyway – Sarah is his oldest friend.

Please let there be some kind of rational explanation for all of this. Please let me not have to arrest Izzy Perelli for killing one boy at a party and somehow striking down another.

I strap my handgun to my side, making sure I can reach it easily beneath the baggy hoodie, and stow my phone. Pierre fastens his workman's belt around his waist. Stuck into it are a claw hammer, a chisel, a long screwdriver and a pair of bolt-cutters.

'In case we need to cut 'em free or anything,' he says, shrugging on a canvas jacket that covers the lot. I try not to think about what that *or anything* might include.

We go on foot toward the stadium. As we cross into the historic district, the first thing I notice is that half the premises are shut up. Pierre stops to help the elderly proprietor of a gift store struggling to put storm shutters on her windows.

'It's only for the tourists,' she says anxiously. 'I don't mean anything by it. I'll be getting rid of it all first thing tomorrow.'

I wonder why she's so worried, until I glimpse the window display. To one side are historical witch-themed souvenirs like you see in half a dozen towns across New England. Mugs and key chains showing witches on broomsticks. Candles in the shape of black cats and skulls. 'Relaxation Potion'-branded bubble bath. As Pierre locks the final shutter in place, the woman barely squeaks out a 'thank you' before scurrying off.

A few blocks further along, a godawful noise blares from one of the residential side streets. It's a van with a PA system.

'*Important information about the quarantine,*' intones a woman's voice. '*Please gather at the football stadium. Important information about the quarantine . . .*'

The van rolls slowly on. Further away, I hear another one repeating the same script. People are being drawn out of their homes and the streets are filling up. Don't they realize that the last thing you should do during a sickness is gather together?

Which tells me that they don't think this is any normal sickness. They believe it's witchcraft.

The noise intensifies, and in scraps of conversation audible above the hubbub, people sound afraid, uncertain, angry. Carried along by the pressing crowd, we approach the stadium. The gates are wide open and I glimpse what's inside.

And it's bad. It is *extremely* fucking bad.

I pull out my phone and dial the TV reporter, Anna Dao.

'Do you guys have a helicopter,' I ask, when she picks up. 'Because there's something going down in Sanctuary that the world needs to see.'

104
Maggie

I've barely hung up, promising to send pictures, when Pierre and I are jostled forward into the stadium. In the centre is a platform that I see from a weather-beaten logo is property of Sport on the Shore. It's painted white, neatly trimmed in a bright red that I *finally* recognize. The same paint that sprayed Sarah's house and defaced the town sign.

Facing the stage is a small podium. It's where medals are awarded at athletics meets, but I can imagine its purpose today. A dock. Guardsmen are dragging metal barriers in place to fence it.

Most rows of bleachers are near full already. An elderly couple sit with blankets over their knees and a brown paper bag of sandwiches, as if ready to watch their grandkid's soccer match. Half the tier along one side has 'reserved' signs laid neatly on each seat. The people occupying one front row have wrapped a long banner the length of the stand. It's inscribed with Bible verses.

Another tier is draped with the Sanctuary Spartans colors, and teenage boys and girls fill it, chatting, flirting and drinking cans of soda. Mostly, though, the faces all around are grim and frightened. And that frightens *me*, because if there's one thing that works on people even better than anger, it's fear.

At a distance around the stage, speakers are being set up.

You'd think it was the setting for a cute small-town celebration – Founder's Day or Thanksgiving or something – were it not for what's down one end.

Because dangling from the crossbeam of a goalpost are two lengths of rope, fashioned into nooses.

I snap pictures. But just as I'm about to send them to Dao – and also to Remy, because he needs to have people in here *now*, quarantine or no quarantine – my phone is snatched from my hand. It's a young National Guardsman, his face open and friendly.

'I'll need that, ma'am.' He points to the LED scoreboard, which is flashing a 'no phones' symbol. 'Apologies. Give me your name and it'll be available to collect tomorrow. Yours too, sir.'

He holds out his hand. I think for a moment that Pierre will refuse, but then a second guardsman trots over, his hand visibly on the holster of his gun. And Pierre does what every black parent, heartbreakingly, teaches their kids to do the minute they see lawmen reach for their guns. He complies instantly.

I give false names – only to have our cover almost blown by a voice behind us.

'Oh, P!'

As the guardsmen amble off to confiscate phones from more people streaming into the stadium, we turn. It's Bridget Perelli-Lee. Alongside her, muffled up like it's December, is Isobel.

'Bridge, babes,' Pierre says. 'What are you doing here? You'd better not be part of this shitshow?'

'No – no, of course not. I've come to try to speak to Abigail. She's driving all this, with Tad Bolt. I tried to get Julia to come too, but she's so scared. She says that if Abigail can turn on Sarah, she can turn on us next. But I thought . . . Oh, Detec—'

We both shush her.

Izzy's round, trusting face looks back and forth between us – and sudden apprehension rises in me. I've been spinning theories. I've even convinced others of them. But now that I'm back in Izzy's presence, it's hard to imagine she's been responsible for anything worse than dropping crockery when she empties the dishwasher. She pats her mother's arm.

'Mommy, I need to tell her.'

'No,' Bridget hisses. 'No, you say *nothing*.'

'But I—'

'*No*, Isobel.'

'Hey, hey, easy now.' Pierre crouches down in front of his daughter. 'What's up, poppet?'

'Pierre, don't . . .'

'Izzy?' Pierre coaxes.

'*I* did it,' Isobel says in the smallest of voices.

'What?'

'It's bullshit, Pierre.' Bridget looks frantic. 'Some fantasy she's just dreamed up to save them. Don't listen to her, Detective.'

'*I* killed Dan,' Izzy says, jutting her lip. 'I went to the party and I pushed him. For Harper. And for *me*.'

'Don't joke, Iz. Don't go making stuff up.' Pierre shakes his daughter gently by the shoulders.

'You *know* why, Daddy,' Isobel says, a little louder now. 'I didn't mean to *kill* him. I just wanted him to go down the stairs and break a leg or something, so he couldn't use his football scholarship. But then he saw that tape Bea put up, and stepped forward just as I did it, and he fell *all wrong*. It was an *accident*. Then the fire started.'

Wait.

What?

Izzy *pushed* him? It doesn't take witchcraft to push a boy.

The girl is sniffling into her giant muffler, her words caught in its soft folds. No one else has heard them but us.

424

They're words that change everything.

I stare at the kid's distraught face. No wonder she looked terrified and guilty when I was at her house. She must have bottled this up, hoping my investigation would find it was all an accident. Trusting that Harper was safe in Green Point, and knowing that she was innocent of witchcraft. But now it has spiraled to this, so fast, and Izzy is desperate to save her friend.

What she's just admitted isn't murder, but it's *definitely* a crime. She's only seventeen, though, and there are mitigating circumstances. The courts would be lenient. If I arrested her right now, would her sentence be a reasonable price to pay to stop the madness building up in this stadium?

Someone has started singing a hymn – I recognize it from my childhood as 'A Mighty Fortress Is Our God' – and more voices take it up. As I look around, I see that the seats are all filled, and I've a dizzy intuition that this has tipped too far for any arrest, any official action of mine, to make a difference.

'She's just upset,' Bridget says. 'None of it's true. She was sick. At home. She was never at that party. I don't know why anyone told you she was.'

'Why the fuck did you bring her here, Bridge?' Pierre has balled up his hands. 'Do you want our little girl up there next to Sarah and Harper? *Do you see what they're going to do?*'

He stabs with his finger at the dangling nooses.

'*And though this world, with devils filled, should threaten to undo us . . .*' rises a woman's soprano. It's Mary-Anne Bolt, standing opposite the stage. Her supporters have joined hands all down the row, and as I watch, the whole stadium does the same. '*We will not fear, for God hath willed His truth to triumph through us.*'

Bridget is sobbing and Pierre reaches for her – for his family – and draws them into a muffling hug that's designed to silence as much as comfort.

I'm watching Izzy Perelli's shaking back.

She just admitted she killed Dan. But she only meant to push him down the stairs. He was distracted by the sex tape. And Izzy just pinned *that* on Beatriz, which explains why Bea has been acting so cagey. Freddie filmed the rape, and his on-off girlfriend must have posted it online and played it the night of the party. With Bea's position atop the school social pecking order, no wonder all the kids conveniently failed to notice her doing something so conspicuous.

Who knows why Bea did it. Maybe she wanted to impress Dan by joining in his humiliation of Harper. Maybe she was hurting that even after he'd broken up with Harper, he still didn't want *her*, and she wanted to embarrass both of them. I don't want to believe that she knew it showed rape. Maybe Freddie wiped the audio on the version he sent her. Perhaps he told her that Harper was play-acting.

I hope that's how it went.

Has Beatriz been devastated by Dan's death because she's terrified that *she* was responsible – that her projection startled him and made him lose his footing? In a way, she was, because the distraction she created gave Isobel the chance to act.

Two guilty girls, haunted by their roles in a boy's death – while an entire town gathers to condemn one innocent girl.

Except . . .

Except where's the witchcraft in this version of events? Where is the power that blasted us at Sailaway Villa? Whose dark magic was at work that night?

What am I missing?

'Izzy,' I say, crouching down beside her. 'Those things you doodled in your jotter. What were they?'

Izzy looks blank. 'My jotter?'

'Detective?'

Bridget is frowning at me. Pierre looks suspicious. I reach for my phone to show Izzy the designs she drew – the Old Signs, terrifying witch marks – but of course the guardsman just took it.

Damn. *Damn.*

'The swirly shapes,' I say. 'The ones like . . .' I consider sketching them in the air with my finger, but remember Rowan's horror at merely looking at them.

But Izzy's shaking her head. Those childlike eyes are vacant.

And I feel it in my gut: she's no witch. Not even an accidental, untrained one.

'You can stop with the questions now, Detective,' Pierre says, his voice gone cold.

A marching band starts up, instruments blaring. Feedback shrieks through the loudspeakers. The crowd suddenly heaves – it's doubled in size these last few minutes – and down a path left open by metal barriers, Sarah and Harper Fenn are marched at gunpoint.

105
Sarah

They lie.

I see horror in the eyes of the spectators as, one by one, people I've spent my whole life caring for ascend the stage with a microphone and damn me and my daughter with their lies.

It feels as if half of Sanctuary is here to spit in my face. The old man from the Greek deli. The once chatty girl who works at Bridget's grooming salon. Alberto, telling his story himself and painting me black as pitch. Their faces are tight with fear and hostility. Every pain and sadness I've tried to ease, I'm now accused of *causing*.

What did I do to deserve this?

Who did I offend?

Mary-Anne Bolt tells her story again, but it has an unbearable new ending: Jake's death in the hospital in the small hours of this morning. Once she's done, she collapses to the ground as if her heart has given out. In every sense that matters, it has. An awful noise goes up from the crowd, a groan of pain at the death of another of Sanctuary's children. Tears are hot on my face, too. How could such a thing have happened?

Tad stalks back and forth in front of the podium where Harper and I stand shackled. His gun is in his hand and he stares at us with more hatred than seems possible can fit inside a human-size skin. It's only with the barest restraint that he hasn't shot us both where we stand. All that's stopping him is the promise of a sweeter, crueler punishment. The nooses dangle from the goalpost crossbeam.

This is how it'll end for me – just as it has done for women like me for ever. There's no comfort in the thought. It's a grim sisterhood of death. I feel their bony hands reaching out through the years to clasp mine.

But I can't let them have Harper too. I *won't*.

We've been told that at the slightest movement, we'll be shot. But time is running out. Abigail is preparing to take the stage, and I know that her accusations will be the last. After her, Tad will invite the people of Sanctuary to judge whether or not we are guilty of *murder by unnatural means*.

And when we are found guilty – because of course we will be found guilty – we will be hanged.

Thou shalt not suffer a witch to live.

So: death by bullet, or death by the noose. Better to risk a bullet with a last attempt at magic to save my child. And if I fail, at least Harper will see that when the time comes, she can feign magic as they tighten the rope, and so take that kinder way out.

I can barely move my fingers inside the tape. But I've been working them, wriggling them looser ever since we were led from the cell. I tried snagging them on walls and door frames as we passed, under the pretence of keeping myself upright in the shackles. As everyone watches Abigail rise from her seat to go speak, Michael passing her the microphone, I try twitching my fingers in the familiar gesture of pacification. If I can just sway the guard who levels his gun at me, then maybe I can try a bolder movement, a stronger spell . . .

Which is when a deafening roar erupts from the centre of the stadium.

It's not human voices, though, but hungry fire. The stage has burst into flames.

Have they decided hanging isn't dramatic enough, and they want us on a pyre instead? I remember the words Mary-Anne Bolt hurled at me in the street – that we'd burn now, then burn in hell. And Abigail telling Harper that she deserved not the noose, but the fire.

I glance at my daughter. I can't bear the thought of her fear. But she's staring at the fire with naked fascination. Reflected flames dance in those pale eyes, and I feel like I've lost her already. My girl of secrets.

There's hammering high overhead. A helicopter swings into view above the stadium. My heartbeat ramps up again, faster than I thought was possible. Is this a rescue? Will commandos rappel down to pluck Harper and me to safety?

But then the chopper banks and I see the insignia of a news channel emblazoned on its side. They're here to *watch*.

The townspeople are applauding and cheering now. The parade of accusations and confessions has stirred their blood, and the presence of an audience in the sky excites them. In the stands, many are on their feet. '*Jus-tice, jus-tice, jus-tice*,' they chant. The tier full of Spartans waves #JusticeforDaniel signs and flags.

Why doesn't Abigail start speaking from where she is? I long for her to begin, so that all this can end, one way or another. Instead, she's motionless, transfixed.

In the building frenzy, the officers guarding me and Harper are risking the occasional glance around, trying to make sense of what's happening. I have a chance. Just this one chance.

Then a howl bursts from the speakers around the field, amplified to a blood-curdling, hellish pitch. I've never heard anything like it – or not since the night Abigail hugged twelve-year-old Dan's dead body as Michael set down his son's pulseless wrist.

Abigail is still staring at the burning stage, and the howl is coming from her throat. Her finger is pointing straight ahead to the flames.

The noise takes shape, as one word: *Daniel*.

And despite myself, mesmerized, I look at where she's pointing. In the middle of the flames, I see a writhing, staggering form.

It looks like Daniel Whitman.

'*Daniel!*' Abigail screams. '*No!*'

She runs toward the fire.

'Abi – stop!'

A man darts forward. It's Alberto. But something holds him back. His own cowardice – or maybe the last traces of my fidelity spell? His arms are outstretched, but nowhere near close enough.

Abigail stumbles to a halt before the burning stage. Whatever she sees, she's looking at it like it's everything she's ever hoped and longed for. The flames are still twisting, but I can no longer make out the flickering human form I thought I saw. Only the hungry heart of the fire.

'Daniel!' my enemy – and old friend – cries. Her voice isn't horrified any more. It's joyful.

She sets one foot upon a flaming step and throws herself into the inferno.

As one, the crowd starts screaming. Then all hell breaks loose.

106

Maggie

The crowd churns behind the barriers. Half want to get closer to the grisly spectacle of Abigail Whitman's self-immolation, and the other half want to get away as fast as they can.

Abigail's hair has gone up like a torch. I can no longer see the figure that, for a fleeting moment, seemed to be moving in the flames. She called her son's name, but she is making no coherent sound now; just shrieks of agony. Those nearest to the bonfire are calling out, begging her to jump. But Abigail Whitman doesn't have legs any more, only roots of fire.

There's another roar, a crack and a clatter. The far tier of seating – the one filled with Spartans – has collapsed and is burning. Kids are throwing themselves off the back of the stand, scrambling over the side, as the seats begin to melt.

Everyone's running for their lives as smoke thickens the air. The smell intensifies: scorched plastic and paint, and the charred-fat stench of a human burning to death. Screams go up as people are separated from loved ones, or stumble and fall.

With a clang, the metal barrier nearest to me is pushed over. People go down, trapped under it or their ankles caught between the bars. But the surge of those fleeing doesn't stop, trampling those on the ground.

Sending up a prayer of thanks for my training in riot and

crowd control, I slip through the worst of the turmoil toward the stage. Someone needs to try to give calm instructions. But Tad Bolt has beaten me to the microphone.

'Stay where you are,' he bellows. 'Nobody move. We're not done here yet.'

The mic in his hand sparks, and he roars and staggers back, fingers across his face. It sparks again, with a hiss and crackle, and his body jerks like a fish on a line. He drops to the ground.

I glance up. Sarah and Harper Fenn are watching it all. The two cops guarding them are conferring about what to do.

Bending over Tad, I reach for the keys on his utility belt. They'll include the master key for the cuffs. Then I tug up my hoodie, try to pitch my voice higher than usual, and scream at the two cops, 'Your boss is gonna die here, boys!'

He's already dead, every fingerprint melted off his hands, but they don't know that.

'Those witches won't be running nowhere,' I cry, as the pair still dither. Then, as they make up their minds to come to Tad's aid, I slip back into the crowd and take their place.

'Stay calm,' I tell Sarah, as I find the cuff key and unfasten her ankles, her wrists. The chief's boys have taped up her hands in some barbaric way, like I've only ever seen sadists do to their victims. That's what the law did to these women.

I find a frayed end and tear a strip. It's enough for Sarah to take in her teeth and unravel the rest. I'm on to Harper.

The girl's wearing the same floaty dress she changed into on the beach this morning. Her arms are naked, sleeved only in ink, and she holds out her cuffed wrists for me to unlock.

Harper Fenn's clear blue eyes look into mine, and it's like looking into water, transparent and oh so cold.

And she smiles.

As I crouch to free the girl's ankles, I tell Sarah where Chester parked her car last night, how he taped the key beneath the tow bar.

I pull off the hoodie I'm wearing and thrust it at Harper.

'You're too recognizable. You'd better cover up.'

The girl's bruised mouth curves a little wider.

'I'm used to that.'

Then they're off, into the smoke and panic.

I straighten up with a groan and turn to see what I can do to help amid the chaos.

High overhead, the WCON-TV helicopter blades beat the air. I summoned Dao's team here to bear witness, and in the hope that their presence would force the residents of Sanctuary to restrain themselves. Now I'm hoping there was too much smoke for the news cameras to see anything at all. Certainly not that rescue.

I lift a one-finger salute to it, skyward, then turn to the cries of the injured.

107

TWEETS FROM @POTUS – OFFICIAL TWITTER
ACCOUNT OF THE PRESIDENT OF THE UNITED
STATES

@POTUS 8.54 p.m.
Quarantine lifted and order restored in Sanctuary thanks
to firm action by @NationalGuard @SanctuaryCTdept
GOOD JOB!
💬11.1 k ♻9.2k ♡51k

108

Maggie

It's bright and early, and I'm packing up my rental apartment to get back to Hartford and face whatever music Remy plans on playing me – prediction: it won't be Sinatra – when there's a knock at the door.

I said my goodbyes to Chester last night in our favorite sad Starbucks. So whoever this is, I don't wanna see them.

Until a low voice says, 'I know you're in there, Detective Maggie,' and I decide that I do.

'Came back for that hoodie you borrowed,' Pierre says when I open the door. 'That's all, I swear.'

'Lost it. Sorry.'

'No problem.' He grins, then flips serious again. 'They get away?'

'They did.'

'You know where?'

'I don't know. Didn't ask. Don't *want* to know.'

Pierre shakes his head. 'That figures. Listen, I owe you an apology. Those last words we exchanged in the stadium? I was afraid for my girl when she started saying that stuff. You know she's a goofy kid and doesn't think about half the things that come out of her mouth. I spoke to you in anger, and I'm sorry.'

I wave it away. 'Nothing to be sorry for. You might not believe this, but in my time in this job, I've seen more than a few parents worried for their kids.'

'I bet. But here's something else. Izzy wanted me to tell you – that thing you were asking about? The doodles? She realized later what you meant. They were tattoo designs. She's been obsessed with them for ever, keeps nagging her mom and me for one – as if.' He rolls those eyes. 'The doodles were inks that Harper has. She'd always show my girl her new ones.'

My hands pause in their folding of clothes. Then resume as Pierre keeps talking.

'She does them *to herself*, if you can imagine. Izzy begged her for one, but Harper refused. She's a good kid, and I can't thank you enough that she and Sarah got away. I've never wanted to hug a cop before, but . . . may I?'

I nod and turn so those arms can go around me. Pressed against Pierre's thick body, I smell his sweat and the smoke from the stadium that still clings to him. I find him attractive, this strong, decent man, and under other circumstances I might have made a bold move right now. But in my head swirls an image hazier than smoke. Shifting and pulsing.

A drawing in a schoolkid's jotter.

A tattoo on a girl's skin.

A shape made of ashes, taking form, dissolving and reforming in a burned-out villa where a boy died.

Magic.

'Anyway,' Pierre says. He steps back, and I let him go with mingled relief and disappointment. 'I just wondered what you were planning on telling your boss, or anyone else, about what Izzy said . . .'

His large brown eyes hold mine, expressing more than his words. *Are you going to tell anyone my girl confessed to killing Dan?* they ask.

'You know,' I tell him, 'things were awfully loud in that

437

stadium. The marching band. The hymns. The helicopter. I remember your daughter saying something, but I didn't catch it all. She was worried for her friend. That's the main thing I remember.'

'Is that so?' says Pierre. 'Well, I guess that's fine then, Detective. You know how kids are. They say a deal of things that aren't true, just 'cos they feel they ought to.'

'That's the truth.'

I resume folding my clothes, even though I've pretty much never folded a T-shirt in my life. I've had too many conversations like this in the past couple days. Too many things left unsaid or ignored. That's not how I like things to be. I'm *law enforcement*. But I made my call on this one and I'm going to stick by it, whatever the consequences.

I was prepared to let Izzy get away with murder when I thought she killed Dan by witchcraft. So I can turn a blind eye to involuntary homicide when I know all she intended was to break his leg.

Pierre's standing there watching me. He just came to make sure I'll let his daughter off the hook, right?

Or maybe not.

'So, Maggie, if you ever need, yeah, a handyman, you let me know. You got my number, and Hartford isn't far. I know those poky city apartments, always something in need of fixing. Not that I'm saying yours . . . Okay, diggin' myself a hole here. If you ever want to reach me for any reason, you know where I am.'

'I do,' I say. I find that I want to be bold after all, and lift myself on tiptoe to kiss his cheek. 'You take care of yourself, Pierre. And do what you can to help this little town put itself back together.'

'Putting things back together is what I do.'

He gives me that gappy grin, then disappears out the door.

I throw the T-shirt down. Their damn necklines never fold straight anyhow. I stuff the lopsided heap of them into my holdall.

How is this town gonna fix itself after this? It's like it really was bewitched, but by fear and paranoia, not by magic. By the time I met with Chester last night, emergency services had cordoned off the ruined stadium. Forensics will go through the ashes for human traces – the remains of Abigail Whitman. The body of Chief Bolt had been hauled into an ambulance.

Chester told me that Cheryl Lee discharged herself from Michael Whitman's hospital, saying there was nothing wrong with her except a crippling migraine. In the isolation room alongside hers, she had heard the three Spartan boys laughing and joking. Her hunch is that there was never anything wrong with them, and they were faking, under Michael Whitman's instructions.

And the cops? Well, maybe that really was spoiled chicken wings – or perhaps Michael had a hand in that too. Either the cops were also faking, or the not-so-good doctor's 'treatment' for a simple bout of food poisoning ensured they stayed sick as long as was useful.

What will an autopsy find Jake Bolt died of? My hunch is something that can be labeled 'medical error'.

So it's plain the supposed sickness wasn't witchcraft. And given Izzy Perelli's confession, neither was Dan Whitman's death.

And what went down in the stadium? There's an explanation for all that too, of course.

The stage went up in flames thanks to some faulty wiring. Those speakers had been rigged up in a hurry after all. Sparks must have drifted to the far bleachers.

Abigail Whitman cracked because her son had died in a fire and the blaze triggered her trauma. She'd probably watched

Dan die a hundred times in her nightmares. No wonder she seemed to see him there, twisting in the flames. No wonder, in her desperate grief, she tried to save him.

Chief Bolt was electrocuted by a dodgy microphone clasped in sweaty hands. Or maybe it was simply a heart attack – it's pretty well documented that bereavement raises your risk of cardiac arrest.

This is what I'll be telling Remy, and whoever else needs to hear it as this whole case is investigated: *a boy lost his footing at a party, and a town went mad with grief*. Every cop knows that the simplest stories are usually the correct ones.

I zip up my bag. Carry it out to my car.

I won't be telling anyone about Harper Fenn's tattoos. The ones she did herself, in the shape of marks that churned the air in the ruined party house and terrified me like no perp with a gun or a knife ever has.

I'll be trying to forget her smile as I set her free.

109

Harper

The first thing I did with my magic was kill a boy.

The second thing I did with my magic was hide it.

It was six years ago. Our parents had been drinking, and their dinner party was loud on the terrace below. Upstairs in the spare room, Bea and I lay side by side in sleeping bags, the movie on pause while Dan was gone. I was bored of her chatter about how San Diego was *so much more exciting* than Sanctuary, so I told her I needed the bathroom and went to prod Izzy awake.

But my friend wasn't in bed. She was standing in the middle of her room and Dan was all over her. She'd gone limp in his arms, like a rabbit that's tight in something's jaws.

'Hiya, Harper,' Dan said.

He slipped his hand from under Izzy's nightgown. Her eyes were rolling wildly above his other hand, clamped over her mouth.

'Nothing to see here,' he said, tipping his head. 'Bathroom's along the hall that way.'

Which was when my magic came in.

All my childhood, I couldn't wait to be a witch. To be strong and powerful like my mom and her gramma. So many times Mom and I had 'the talk' about what Determination felt like

441

– the wonder of seeing your gift light up your whole body. Of finally connecting with your ability.

She was right. It was the most amazing moment of my life. You couldn't see it, of course. No burst of light – that only happens during the rite. Which was just as well, as even our boozed-up parents would have noticed a magical supernova shining out of Izzy's bedroom window.

There was no light. But there was *power*. So much of it.

Enough to blast Dan away from Izzy and send him out the window.

Iz and I were still reeling when the first scream came from below. She started over to look out, but I grabbed her arm and held her back. If the adults knew we were there when he fell, the questions would begin.

Why? And *How?*

Izzy wouldn't want to answer the first one, and I didn't want to answer the second.

So we huddled against the wall, under the swinging pane, and listened. Listened as Abigail screamed and sobbed, and Michael Whitman ran through the medical checks for a response from Dan, then ran through them again, his voice more desperate.

Bea burst into the room.

'What's going on?'

'Shh!' I put a finger to my lips, then reached to pull her down. 'The three of us were eavesdropping on our moms, only we couldn't hear properly. Dan wanted to open the window so we could hear better, but the catch was stuck. He shoved it with his shoulder and it swung open and he fell.'

Bea's eyes went wide. She huddled against me too, and we all listened.

'He's dead,' Bea said in a breathless voice. I could imagine her telling the story at school the next day: *He fell. He died. I saw it.*

442

And then I heard my mom's voice, strong and clear. I've never been prouder of her than I was at that moment.

'There's something – something I could try. But . . .'

Abigail fell on her, begged her.

'Do it,' Izzy's mom said.

'Whatever you need us to do, we will,' Bea's mom said.

'But he's *dead*,' Bea hissed.

'Shut up,' Izzy moaned. 'Shut up, *shut up*.'

Izzy curled into a ball and pretended it wasn't happening. But Bea and I went up on our knees and peeped out the window as my mom and her coven brought Dan back from the dead.

Bea looked sick at each step of the rite. The blade and the blood. She put her hands over her ears as Mom whispered things that sounded like the worst words in the world, and crooned something that could have been the purest love song. She screwed up her eyes as black mist poured out of Dan's mouth, as it gradually turned white, then golden.

I didn't take my eyes off it all for a single second. I don't think I even blinked.

When we heard Dan cough, then moan, Izzy turned her head and threw up on the carpet.

'But he was dead,' Bea insisted. 'Witches can't bring people back from the dead. It's *illegal*.' Her voice had that breathless thrill again. 'Your mom could go to prison.'

Which was when I first felt afraid.

'Izzy's right, Bea,' I told her. 'Shut up. Besides, your mom was part of it too.'

'She's not magical. It's different for witches.'

It was when a cop came calling that I realized I had to do something. Sure, our parents made up a story. *Dan slipped on the stairs getting cookies*, Pierre told us when he came to check we were all okay. *If anyone asks, you tell them that.*

But I searched on the internet the next day, using the

443

computer in the public library so no one could trace it to our home. It was even worse than Bea had said. Any witch raising someone from the dead would never again be allowed to use their magic.

And any witch who killed by magic was locked away for life.

I made Izzy swear never to tell a soul what really happened. But I was still scared – and the fear got worse every day. I couldn't sleep. Instead, I'd lie there imagining the cops coming for us, Mom and I being stripped of our magic and sent to jail. I was afraid of the magic within me, but I was even more afraid to lose it. I stopped talking about anything magical. I know Mom noticed that.

It took about two weeks to make my plan. No one other than Izzy knew my power had come in. I needed to hide it. You can't kill a boy with magic if you don't have it. And witches don't always have witch kids. It'd happened with my mom's mom.

But *how* do you hide magic? I couldn't ask my mother. So I went to the best authority I knew – our family's Starcross grimoire. I already knew how to craft a rite. How to navigate a chart, choose the best objects and blend ingredients. So I drew on Starcross, and on everything I'd learned from watching Mom, to devise a ritual of concealment.

To make it as powerful as possible, I decided to use one of the Old Signs. Yes, I knew the sigils were dangerous and not something that any modern witch should turn to. But I was twelve years old, and I was desperate.

On the night itself, I worked through the rite I had devised. After several hours, it was time for the final step. I prepared the razor blade with a sevenfold purification before I cut the sigil for *Obscurity* into my stomach. The pain was awful, but even worse was the horror of seeing my own hand slash a bloody seam in my skin. Biting my lip, I thought of the times I'd watched Mom cut herself to make an offering – how much she'd given the night she brought Dan back. Great acts require a great price to seal them.

By the time I'd finished, my whole body was burning from the inside out, as if my blood had turned to fire in my veins. I was terrified that instead of hiding my magic, I had somehow purged it out of me. I cleaned myself, wound bandages round my middle and crept home, shaking with terror and pain.

It was on the iron bridge over the Accontic channel that I saw it. A car must have hit it – a huge gray and white seagull that flopped and screeched, one wing mangled. I hardly knew what I was doing when I crouched down and put my fingers to its neck. A moment later, I felt the power flow through me and the bird jerked beneath my touch.

I could have tried to heal it, I suppose. But I wanted to know if my ability was still there, so I intuitively used it as I had that first time. The gull's soft feathered head, with its heavy beak, fell limply away from my hand. Its wing ceased flapping. My magic had killed it.

And I was glad.

When Mom performed my Determination a few months later, I was fearful she'd discover my ability despite the sigil now scarred into my flesh. Maybe she'd even be able to tell what I had used it for – because she was my mom, after all, and every child thinks their parents have supernatural powers of detection, witch or no.

I hid my body from her as I changed into the white ritual robe. (At home, she now only ever saw me in a T-shirt or vest, and took it for the natural shyness of a girl becoming a woman.) And when Mom performed my Determination, we saw – nothing. She was distraught, convinced I was giftless, and it was all I could do to stop myself telling her the truth. But by that time, I'd come to love the fact that my magic was my secret.

Starcross became my teacher. Instead of in a dark workroom,

I practiced my craft in the open air. I discovered Green Point and got to know the folks there, who never looked at me with pity as the witch's giftless daughter. On my sixteenth birthday, Jonny Maloney gave me my first tattoo. And as I watched him etch my skin, I realized that instead of a blade, I could use a needle.

A magical design only possesses magical properties if made by a witch. And I was a witch.

Jonny's first design was a butterfly on my thigh. Then I asked him for coiling vines across my midriff to cover my scar. I'd told him it was from when I'd self-harmed as a child after a traumatic event, which in a way it was. And once the vines were complete, I started adding my own, small fruit: Starcross's Old Signs.

I marked myself with *Ruin*. With *Command*. With *Undoing*.

With each one, I felt my magic pulse within me. I felt – *I feel* – as powerful as a walking bomb. Yet I went to school, goofed off in Green Point, or curled up on the couch with Mom for movies and ice cream, and no one knew a thing.

Why did I get involved with Dan, knowing what he was really like? I've asked myself that. I figure it was unfinished business from that night all those years before. He was the other person involved in the best moment of my life. Sometimes, when we fucked, I'd reach up to feel the pulse hammering in his neck and remember the broken seagull on the bridge, and his own smashed body on the terrace below the window.

But the thrill wore off pretty quickly. He had a power all of his own – his good looks and popularity – but unlike us witches, he abused it. I knew he was fooling around with other girls, and when I heard that at some dumb party I'd skipped, he'd finally given Bea the attention she'd been craving for years, I broke things off.

I should have known his pride wouldn't stand for it, but I

always imagined I'd be able to defend myself. When no one knows you have magic, it's easy to use a little now and then without anyone noticing. I couldn't have guessed he'd drug me first. It made me too confused and uncoordinated to use my ability.

I still hadn't figured out the best way of paying Dan back — should I use my craft, or simply report his crime? — when Izzy settled the matter by pushing him over the balustrade at the party. The fall killed him. I didn't lie to the cop about that. But I called upon *Ruin* and burned the villa.

Dan wasn't getting a *second* second chance.

I know Jake Bolt caught me on camera, but I wasn't worried. I never learned the regular, precise ways of witchcraft — the gestures and the sticks. No one watching me work magic can say for sure that's what it is.

'Thanks for waiting, ma'am' the heavyset doorman says, interrupting my recollections. He waves me forward.

It's a warm night here in Atlantic City, just four hours' drive south of Sanctuary but a world away from its fancy suburbs. I've been queuing at the casino entrance for quarter of an hour.

'Routine screening,' he says. 'Though from the look of you, it's your age I'm worried about, not magic. You over twenty-one, ma'am? Got ID?'

'Of course,' I say, holding up mom's driver's license and laying a light *Command* upon him. 'You can see right here that I'm twenty-two.'

'Crystal clear, thank you. Please step over to my colleague. And enjoy your night here at the Silver Dollar.'

Witches are banned from casinos — indeed, from any form of gambling — as we might bend the odds unfairly in our favor. And obediently, we stay away. Stiff jail terms for even stepping through a door are an effective deterrent.

The doorman's colleague is an elderly Mexican lady – a witch – whose job is to check patrons for any magical artifacts or enchantments that might enhance their luck. From the look of her, she's paid peppercorns. Her wrists are scrawny, the skin shiny and smooth over large-knuckled hands that reach for mine.

Witches like my mother are the lucky ones, born into a recognized tradition with an ancestry as 'respectable' as that of any Mayflower New Englander. And even she only made enough money to give us a normal life. This country is full of magical practitioners forced to eke out a living in the margins.

The witch drops my hand almost immediately, baring her few teeth in a wide smile. A career in black-market magic rarely comes with health insurance.

'All clear, *nenita*. But watch yourself in there.'

'Don't you worry,' I tell her. 'I can look after myself.'

Mom will be sleeping, back in our cheap hotel room. She's already worrying about money, and how we'll live. I'll win here tonight, but not so big that the managers will get suspicious.

And if Mom suspects, I'll finally tell her. I'm done with keeping my secret.

Because despite the centuries since Salem, despite the Moot and laws and 'human rights', we're still feared and hated. Still policed and persecuted. And we go along with it. Accept it.

Why should we? I'm done with that, too.

I am the girl who hid her scars. Who hid her pain. Who hid her magic.

But not any more.

448

A Note on the Magical System

The magical system described in *Sanctuary* is fictional, not contemporary Wicca or paganism. It draws on varied historical sources. Sarah Fenn's familiar, Aira, is named after one of the Enochian angels from the Renaissance magical system of John Dee and Edward Kelley.

The Western European-derived Old Work practiced by Sarah Fenn represents only one strand of the many magical traditions existing in the contemporary United States of this novel. 'Magic' as depicted in *Sanctuary* is never to be equated with any real cultural, spiritual or religious practice.

Credits

V.V. James and Gollancz would like to thank everyone at Orion who worked on the publication of *Sanctuary* in the UK.

Editorial
Rachel Winterbottom
Brendan Durkin

Copy editor
Jane Selley

Proof reader
Jade Craddock

Audio
Paul Stark
Amber Bates

Contracts
Anne Goddard
Paul Bulos
Jake Alderson

Design
Lucie Stericker
Joanna Ridley
Nick May

Editorial Management
Charlie Panayiotou
Jane Hughes
Alice Davis

Finance
Jennifer Muchan
Jasdip Nandra
Afeera Ahmed
Elizabeth Beaumont
Sue Baker

Marketing
Cait Davies